Murder in Fernandina

Murder in Fernandina

By
Amelia Clinch

(Pen name of the Nassau County Writers and Poets Society)

Lead Writer
David Tuttle

Contributing Writers

Nita Bridges	Don Parker
Jim Coe	Dale Pedrick
Cara Curtin	Joani Selement
Jan McCaffrey	Denny Smith

George Furnival

————•■•————

Editors: Joani Selement and Emily Carmain
Graphics and layout: Jan H. Johannes

Technical Advisors:
"Chip" Hammond, Chief, Fernandina Beach Police Department
and Jim Coe, Fernandina Beach Police Department.

Library of Congress Control Number: 2004111772

Tuttle, David 1941 -
Murder in Fernandina

ISBN 0-9677419-3-9

Published by Lexington Ventures, Inc.
107 Centre Street
Fernandina Beach, Florida 32034

Printed in the United States of America by
Fidlar Doubleday, Inc.
6255 Technology Avenue
Kalamazoo, MI 49009

Cover: The grand old Fairbanks House is now an elegant bed-and-breakfast inn at Fernandina Beach. This late 19th-century image is used, with the permission of the owners, to capture the ambience of the Fernandina Beach Historic District. The house, however, has no connection with any of the events portrayed in this purely fictional story. Any similarities between this novel and actual people or events, is strictly coincidental. Cover design by Thomas R. Johannes.

Foreword

This project began after the success of "group co-writing," a play that was the idea of one Joani Selement. The Widow Rapunzel, written by members of the Nassau County Writers and Poets, was staged before five sell-out houses and was a boost to all the writers' egos.

I suggested that we co-write a book, perhaps a murder mystery. We had heard several stories about a buried treasure on Amelia Island. All seemed plausible and at the same time had a bit of mystery added. Thus the book Murder In Fernandina was born.

I was asked to submit an outline to the group of writers who wished to be involved. After the first reading of the 23-page outline, we selected where the chapter breaks would be. Then we selected characters we wished to create biographies about and chapters we would write.

We met again and gave copies of the bios to other writers and refined the story. When the chapters began arriving, I placed them in order and within five months had the first draft of Murder In Fernandina. Very little smoothing had to be done between chapters that were written by different authors. We asked for technical advice from the Fernandina Beach Police Department's Lt. Jim Coe. He went over the investigative procedures used in cases like ours. Later in the process we also asked Fernandina Beach Police Chief "Chip" Hammond to read and advise.

Copies were distributed to the authors requesting them to note any glaring errors and suggested changes. After many hours of work and eight months of reading, editing and rewriting, we had something resembling a murder mystery. The technical advisors suggested some changes where we added other cases for the detective to work on. We distributed these assignments and added them in sequence throughout the work. Now we were into the third year of work on the book.

Joani Selement graciously agreed to give the book an editor's eye. I now believe in editors. The reworking of the flow of the book was great and with the changes she suggested, it was really coming together. This edited version was passed around and it was agreed that we now needed someone not connected with the project to read the book and offer further suggestions.

The writers found Emily Carmain, a local editor, to do this task. She and I worked (Emily edited, revised and made suggestions and we both did the typing) on the book for nearly eight months, ultimately "punching it up" so it really reads well. It was now in the form that will be published, with the only changes found in punctuation and spelling.

A rabbit gestation is 30 days, human gestation is nine months, elephant's gestation is two years and our book gestation was four years. We started in March 2000, and it's now March 2004 as we celebrate having given birth to this novel.

The story begins in the year 2000. The fictional setting for Robert LaFontaine's house is now a quaint and quiet Bed and Breakfast, which appears on the cover.

I give thanks to all the contributing authors and editors.

David Tuttle
Fernandina Beach, Florida
March 2004

CHAPTER 1

Wilson crouched beside the body. The overpowering hot stench seared through the mask he wore. A black bodybag was at his side, ready to receive the remnants of a human. He again looked around the body, splayed out, almost in a swimmer's pose. The left arm was raised above the head and the right arm twisted back at the side. Wilson's rubber over-boots made a "schmuck" sound in the mud beside the canal when he moved to roll the body over with his latex-gloved hands.

He stared at the face. No matter how many times he'd seen bodies in this state of decomposition, it never got easier. In Miami, Florida, bodies weren't always discovered the same week they died. He leaned closer, looking at the gaping hole of the mouth. It moved.

"Wilson!" it screamed.

Bolting upright in bed, Wilson's heart pounded in his chest. He felt cold as a trickle of sweat rolled off his hair and down his back. The same dream had jolted him awake too many times in recent weeks, leaving him edgy and tired. He looked over at the side of the bed where Grace should have been. Dim light from the streetlamp filtered into the room, revealing a chill emptiness. Crumpled sheets, an extra pillow. No wife next to him any more. Breast cancer had seen to that, last summer.

I've got to get out of here. I'll make that call in the morning.

The red numbers on the alarm clock read 4:45. Groaning, he got up slowly, and then went to check on his two daughters. They slept better lately, but they, too, had occasional nightmares. In the kitchen, he put a cup of yesterday's coffee in the microwave.

Looking into the darkness, sipping the coffee, he thought, *The Lieutenant in Charge of Investigations Division in Fernandina Beach sounds better all the time.* He rubbed his sleepy eyes. *And with Mom's stroke, I need to be nearby.*

Later that morning, in his office, he made the phone call to Police Chief John Cabe of the Fernandina Beach Police Department. It was settled now. Two weeks from today, he'd be out of here.

Wilson leaned back in his chair, looked around, and wondered how much he was going to miss the Homicide Investigations Division of the Miami Police Department. He knew he wouldn't miss the decomposing bodies, mothers crying about how good their fifteen-year-old sons were — even though "dear Junior" had just murdered someone — or late-night calls to a dark alley containing several bodies blown away in turf wars. He was tired of the death threats and bogus police brutality charges.

From the interview with Chief Cabe, he had learned the big cases in Fernandina Beach would involve petty larceny or the occasional domestic violence call, although drug-related crimes were now starting to creep into the picture. Nothing like the Miami scene, though.

"We're moving from being a shrimping and pulpwood products mill town to a resort community, where families come for relaxing vacations," Cabe had said. "People like to live here, to raise their children here. Haven't had a killin' in six years; even then the boyfriend called for us to come get him."

The Chief had an easygoing manner that was probably reflected in the department. That suited Wilson just fine.

He'd be moving from the southern tip of Florida to a small coastal town as far northward as you could go and still be in the state. A pretty, peaceful island on the Atlantic Ocean, just below the Georgia state line, called Amelia Island.

Four hundred miles from Miami. But it might as well be in another world.

CHAPTER 2

Wilson's new life was about to begin; it was a warm, cloudless Saturday in April, and he was only a few miles from the next phase in his life. The ten-hour drive up I-95 was nearly over as he stopped at the light in the little village of Yulee on Highway A1A. The road was also known as the "Buccaneer Trail," if he remembered correctly. smiling at the name, he thought the kids would probably like hearing the old pirate tales that clung tenaciously to this part of Florida.

In the back seat, seven-year-old Prissy stirred while four-year-old Lisa slept on.

"Where are we, Daddy?" Prissy asked.

"Another fifteen miles and we'll be there, honey. Let Lisa sleep a little more."

"Okay," she whispered. Prissy reminded him of Grace, so sweet and open to his suggestions. The only time Grace had ever stood up to him was about a year before the diagnosis of cancer shook their world.

Lying in bed on one hot summer night, she'd told him she was worried about him. "I married a man with Paul Newman eyes and a smile to match, not the man you are becoming now. You are changing into someone I don't know. And it's not good."

She never mentioned it again, but it had started him thinking and realizing the job was getting in the way of his more important family life.

After that was when his mother had the stroke. And then came his wife's death. Three life-altering experiences had slammed him into this shift of his life's direction.

The Yulee traffic light turned green and the noisy log truck next to him started moving, as a dark gray Mercedes spun through the yield sign at the right from U.S. Highway 17 onto A1A. The slow acceleration of Wilson's aging Volvo was not a problem for the fast Mercedes. But shortly he was doing the sixty miles an hour to keep up, when the pulpwood truck roared past, then slowed for a car in front of it. Right behind the truck was a black Camaro. Wilson had noticed the car weaving in and out of traffic while gaining on him. His irritation level rose, seeing the erratic driving.

The Camaro, with its forward progress blocked, cruised beside him and Wilson caught sight of blond hair whipping in the wind. On the passenger side, a sunglassed woman's face was turned toward him, a few feet away. She puckered and air-kissed him. With little room to spare, the Camaro sped up and whipped in front of Wilson's car, speeding past the truck that still hogged the left lane. The mop-haired driver urged the Camaro ahead, shifting lanes all the way out of sight. Wilson couldn't tell if the driver was male or female.

Ahead, he saw the sleek gray Mercedes, stationary in the emergency lane of the small span across Lofton Creek, a tree-shaded ribbon of water. He pulled in behind the car to help the silver-haired man standing beside the trunk. Two more log-carrying trucks rocked the Volvo as they sped by. Wilson cautioned Prissy to lock the doors when he got out and to stay in the car.

"Looks like you need a little help," he shouted over the traffic noise.

"Thanks, son. Appreciate it. Damn flat tire." The two men stood eye to eye, and Wilson noticed immediately the expensive suit the driver wore. He'd seen equally expensive clothes on some of his Miami crime victims - and sometimes on perpetrators. "We're trying to decide whether to call Triple A or change it ourselves."

Wilson asked for the keys and removed the car jack and tire iron. When he was squatting by the tire, he heard the passenger door close. Squinting against the sun, he saw a disheveled man in a stained plaid shirt and dirt-splotched khaki pants — a startling contrast to the driver.

The passenger limped slightly to the trunk and one-handed the spare tire to the ground. "I'd a changed the tire, Bobby," he said in a gravelly voice.

"I know, Jack, but it's almost done," replied the other man.

The driver introduced himself, "Name's Robert LaFontaine."

Wilson nodded and smiled up at him briefly. "And this is Jack Laffon." Again Wilson nodded.

"I'm just moving to Fernandina from Miami. Wilson's my name." Through the ensuing small talk, he learned LaFontaine had a small shrimp boat fleet, and they learned Wilson was on his way to begin a career with the local police department.

"Do you know Chief Cabe?" he asked, as he finished tightening the lug nuts.

"Sometimes for more years than I'd want to recall," LaFontaine said. Both he and his passenger laughed at the comment.

"There you go; I'll leave the hubcap off. You'll be getting it fixed soon, right?"

"On my way there, now," said the driver.

He offered Wilson some money, which he refused, shaking his head and smiling. "Maybe you can help me someday when my tired Volvo gives out."

LaFontaine laughed. "Everyone in Fernandina knows how to get in touch with me. If you need me, just ask around. Thanks again." He held out a callused hand and Wilson felt the strong grip in the handshake. "Come on, Jack."

The Mercedes and the "tired Volvo" merged into traffic and headed for Fernandina Beach, just a few miles ahead.

"Who were those men, Daddy?" Prissy asked.

"They had a flat tire and I helped change it." He looked back at her in the mirror. He saw Lisa wake up and gaze sleepily around.

She brushed aside a wisp of blonde hair and tapped her father on the head. "Yes, Baby, what is it?"

"I gotta tinkle."

CHAPTER 3

Within five minutes, they had crossed the high bridge to the island, and Wilson had shown the girls the gorgeous view of the Amelia River, a silvery blue in the sunshine, and the wide green marshes. He negotiated the traffic of 8th Street to Atlantic Avenue. When he turned north onto 17th, the girls perked up, vaguely remembering it wasn't far now.

As soon as he pulled into his mother's yard and honked the horn, the girls flew out of the car, squealing and laughing, into the arms of their waiting grandma. He heard, "...down the hall on the left," and the girls were out of sight behind the slamming screen door.

His mother gave him a welcoming hug. "I worried about you all day. Come on in. You can get the suitcases out later. You're late. Where've you been?"

"Giving the girls a look at the island," he said as they turned toward the house.

"You didn't! I'm the resident docent of the Historical Society around here."

He grinned down at his mother's astonished look.

"Okay, I bypassed the Historic District. But I did point out the Shave Bridge, the mills, railroad bridge, airport, and the sign to the ferry out A1A. And of course the fast-food lane — all the historic sites on 8th Street, coming onto the island," he teased.

Priscilla Wilson was quite knowledgeable about the town and its history. She'd led groups on tours through the downtown historic district for several years and was sure to show the girls the genuine historic sites once they were settled in.

"I had a hard time explaining that the old high school sign, 'Home of the Pirates,' out by Bailey Road didn't mean that Captain Hook and his pals were living here."

For now, he let his mother lead him into her neat white house on Broome Street. It would be home to him and his children for the next few days, and it looked very, very good to him. She always kept the house in shape; the new paint job glistened and the trim green lawn was maintained by a local lawn service. The house sat at the top of a little rise, sloping down in the front and back away from the house. Huge live oaks, draped with Spanish moss, shaded the yard in summer and kept out some of the northeast winds in winter. Bright red amaryllis framed the front of the home.

He filled his lungs with April ocean air, tasted salt, and felt the tension of the day's drive drain away.

"I got a call from the movers," his mother said as they climbed the few steps to the porch. He held the door for her. "They want to bring your things over tomorrow or start charging storage fees."

"I'll pay for storage a few days until I find a place to live."

"Use the garage for awhile. Just leave room for the car," she encouraged.

They went into the kitchen and she motioned him to sit down. He obeyed like old times. She poured milk for the girls and two glasses of iced tea for them and put a plate of gingersnaps in front of the girls. "Only two cookies for now. You don't want to ruin supper."

She moved about the kitchen getting things ready for supper, rattling off questions without waiting for answers. "When do you start work, Son? Chief Cabe called and said you can call him sometime Monday morning, no hurry. You girls want to help me? Make sure your hands are clean. Son, will you mind that nothing ever happens here? I'm so glad you left that horrible big city for our peace and quiet."

The girls raced to the sink to wash their hands, as their

grandmother rattled off items she needed from the fridge. Wilson sat watching them scrub vegetables, happy that a semblance of family life had already begun to emerge. *One worry down. She doesn't seem to feel we're intruding on her. She's always been so damned independent.* He leaned back in the chair and rubbed his aching eyes, the motion of the car still with him, and listened to his mother continue her criticism of Miami.

"Who knows what all goes on down there." She looked back at him. "Well, I guess you do. Anyway, you're here and it's a safe place. You can let your children play out in the yard in Fernandina Beach and not worry about some psychopath stealing them."

"I know, Mom. I know this place is a hundred times better than Miami. But trouble is everywhere; you can't insulate yourself. Anyway, up here I'll be able to spend more time with them. And how about you, Mom?"

"What do you mean?"

"You've been having a tough time since the stroke. I don't think us staying with you is such a good idea. We need to get someone in here for you. The girls and I need to get a house."

She paused, resting her paring knife on a carrot, and looked at him with tears in her eyes.

"I have to be careful when I move around, but I'm not an invalid. I'll be okay. Let's try it for a few days. I love having the girls here."

"I know, Mom. But I don't expect you to be a nursemaid to the girls. We want to make things easier for you. That's all."

"My life has changed so much since the stroke. I can't do a lot of things I once did. I have to drive slower, walk slower. Thank God my speech has returned to near normal."

"You'd really be lost without that." They laughed companionably. "Listen, we'll see how it goes for a few days, then talk again. Okay?"

"I feel better already with you here," she assured him.

Suddenly the girls glimpsed a calico cat through the kitchen window and raced outdoors. He took advantage of their absence to share a concern he had about his older daughter. He explained how, in Miami, he could do only so much with the girls. His job had been hard, physically, and demanded long hours. Even the infrequent evenings he spent with the children often found him asleep in his chair. Mrs. McCaffrey had been great, but her job was to run the house.

The girls needed nurturing by someone who deeply cared, and this move was as much for them as for him. He wanted Prissy to have her childhood. The fact was that she had begun to see herself as mistress of the house and wasn't too happy about leaving Miami.

"Mom, Prissy had some run-ins with the housekeeper, who almost quit twice. Watch out for her bossiness," he warned.

"Oh, I will, I will. But she's only seven, dear." She looked him straight in the eye, as if to say Prissy wasn't the first child she'd helped to raise.

After dinner, he went to look at the garage. Maybe it will hold it all, he thought. His mother took the girls for their baths while he unloaded the car. Later he sat on the couch, a daughter under each arm, and watched a favorite TV program with them. His mother said she didn't understand the humor of four cartoon characters yelling at one another for an hour, but she sat nearby, reading, just to stay close and enjoy their presence.

The program ended and Wilson looked at his watch. *Time for the girls to go to bed.* But first, he wanted to step outside for a few minutes, and the children followed him onto the porch. A warm puff of air floated in from the west, crossed the tranquil marsh and the river, rose up and over the lovely barrier island called Amelia. The sun set in a blaze of orange, glowing through the trees and streaking the sky with shades of tangerine and lavender, fading into deep cobalt.

Lisa still had a problem going to sleep at night. Wilson tucked the children into the big guestroom bed and offered to read them a bedtime story. Three retellings later, he wondered how Grace had handled the parenting mostly on her own. He gazed down at the sleepy girls and saw Grace's features on their faces. They were so dear to him. He kissed them and, with a hug, promised to leave on the nightlight.

"Daddy?" Lisa said.

"Yes, Punkin?"

"Do you think tomorrow night Grandma would read us a story?"

"I'm sure she'd like that." He turned off the bedside lamp and went down the stairs.

CHAPTER 4

W e don't have much of a facility right now; the City Fathers are fartin' around looking for a place to put up a new building... somewhere. We've been in this one since I came here, thirty years back - and even before that."

Chief Cabe was muscular and stronger than other men his age. He led Wilson down the hall and motioned to his left, "In there are the records. Millie keeps them, among other things. If you need something, she'll know where it is."

They walked a few steps farther. "Down here is duty officer's desk; duty rotates so it don't become a pain. This is Dianne Spears," Cabe motioned to the young woman sitting behind a desk. She looked up and smiled.

The Chief continued, "Dianne and Millie sort of run this place; we're just here to make sure they don't run away with it." He laughed at his own joke.

Dianne looked at the newcomer and gave a little shrug of the shoulders. "Nice to meet you. Chief Cabe, does he have a name?"

"Oh yeah, Wilson is the new Lieutenant in Charge of Investigations Division."

"Nice to have you around." Her smile was genuine.

Wilson nodded, "Thanks. It's good to be in a quiet place for a change." He paused to take in her casually styled hair, almost the color of dark copper, her curving lips, clear blue-green eyes, and neat appearance.

"I saw you at Mass yesterday with your mother and girls," she continued.

"Really? I was still in a daze, I'm afraid."

"That's understandable. Cute girls. Your mother brags on all of you."

"Well, you know how mothers are." He grinned, then noticed the Chief was looking anxious to get going. "See you around." *Man, there's a smart statement.*

Turning to leave Dianne's office, Cabe said to him, "Well, most of the detective work you get here will be to find out why some dog crapped in a neighbor's yard."

"Don't mind him." Dianne shook her head and went back to her keyboard.

"That there is my office and the door is always open. If you see it shut, don't come in. Next to it is the holding cell. As you can see, it ain't much. Most prisoners go to the county lockup and some are held for the Jacksonville people. If we get more than three at one time, we just put the quietest ones in patrol cars until they are transferred."

They turned left at the corner, and along the wall there was an opening with no door. It led to a tiny break room. A table and three non-matching chairs stood against the wall. Opposite the room were a small sink and a counter big enough to hold the coffeepot and essentials.

"If you're brave, you can have the coffee; Dianne makes it in the morning and actually it's not too bad. Special blend I get at a local coffee shop. Give a coupla bucks to Dianne, bring your own cup." Chief Cabe kept up the rapid-fire rundown of the station.

"Back there is the gunroom, and only me and the Assistant Chief have a key. Never needed to go in there except for certification for firearms training and cleaning the weapons. We'll issue your equipment later today; standard issue Glock, your vehicle and your Nextel direct connect. You familiar with those?"

"Yes, we had those in Miami. Great item."

"We'd like you to use the issued vehicle about all the time."

By now they were moving out the back into the parking lot. "In that building over there is property storage and the evidence room. If you go in there, watch out for the rat; we've been trying to kill him for nearly six months now and he's smarter than we are." Three patrol cars pulled into the lot. The men waved to the Chief and eyed Wilson.

Cabe motioned to the building that butted against the sidewalk and the evidence building. "We've put you fellows back here; no room up front. I think everyone is in there. You have three men under you. They were a little sore that they didn't get your job, but they'll get over it. They are dedicated and good men."

"Are their personnel files here or up front?" He followed Cabe up the steps, and realized for the first time that the Chief walked with a hint of a limp.

Cabe pushed the buttons on the combination lock, and the door opened, "They're up front. Here's your office on the left."

Wilson heard a voice talking on the telephone and a chair grate across the floor as someone got up. As they entered the ten-by-twelve-foot office, he noticed darker rectangular patches of paneling where pictures once hung. Cabe leaned out into the small hall. "Bobby, you, Evans and Wilbur, come in here."

The phone conversation ended and two men entered the room, made smaller by their presence. "This here is Wilson, the Lieutenant Charge of Investigations. Came to us from Miami. Bobby Troop and Charles Evans."

They shook his hand, welcomed him to the force and made small talk for a few minutes. Chief Cabe, looking around, asked, "Where's Wilbur?"

"Oh, he's out checking on that vehicle that was stolen last night. Said he'd be back by noon," Evans replied.

"When he gets back, introduce him to Wilson here. I've got a meeting I have to go to. I say have to because I don't want to. Wilson, if you need anything, see these guys or Dianne, they'll get it for you." He turned and left.

The three detectives stood looking at each other. Troop, not quite six feet tall, had close-cropped sandy-blond hair and a cheerful, almost boyish face, which belied his age. Wilson guessed him to be between 55 and 60 years old. Wilson noticed his little bit of excess weight that comes unwanted with the years.

Evans, on the other hand, had rugged features and stood a few inches taller than Wilson with the build of a NFL linebacker. The detective stood at ease, but his deep-set brown eyes studied the new man in charge. His dark brown skin showed only a few wrinkles, but the graying temples gave him a look of honest wisdom, well suited to a man in his mid-40s.

Wilson liked what he saw in both men.

"It's good to be here," he told them. "I'll get some things together for the office and I'll ask you later to get me up to speed on what's going on. I've found out that changing procedures doesn't accomplish anything except create animosity and generally screw things up. So, unless there are glaring errors in operations, things will remain just like they are."

Troop and Evans looked at each other, and Troop said, "No problem, we're pretty laid back. Most of the calls are burglary, generally drug related. The car theft is not new but kinda' rare. Domestic disturbances, things like that."

"Same as everywhere else," Wilson said with a wry smile. He moved toward the window. "I'd like to see some statistical figures on the drug scene. Who would have that?"

The other two again glanced at each other. "I guess Dianne would have that, or Millie," said Evans. "Understand you're up from Miami?"

"Yes, and glad to be away from it." He turned back to the detectives and sat down in the worn chair behind the desk, trying it on for size. "My mother lives here and needs someone to be around." He opened the top desk drawer. It was empty.

Evans spoke up, "It's strange how some people are driven. MacAllister was Lieutenant in Charge of Investigations here, then went to Miami to get into some 'real detective work' as he put it."

"MacAllister? Yes, I met him once...on a case a few weeks ago down there. Didn't get a chance to chat, but I knew he was new to our department, because of the color of his face."

"Color of his face?"

Wilson stopped going through the desk and looked up at the two men, "Green. It was a homicide in a high-crime poverty area. You know how it goes sometimes; payback, dismemberment, very messy; with limbs scattered about."

He stood and looked at his watch. "Let me get out of here and I'll be back in an hour. Nice to meet you guys; I look forward to working with you."

CHAPTER 5

The rest of Monday and all day Tuesday, Wilson was sure he'd made the right move. The girls were becoming more comfortable living with their grandmother and, true to the Chief's predictions, Wilson's workload was so routine he was able to keep the men assigned while he reviewed files and got to know his detectives better. Each conversation at the department was positive. Fernandina Beach was a slow-moving, law-abiding town. The young woman named Dianne had a particularly pretty smile, which she flashed frequently.

Then Wednesday at 7 a.m., Chief Cabe called, interrupting a conversation with Prissy concerning her school uniform.

"Homicide," was the Chief's first word. "One of our prominent citizens lives in a big house on Seventh Street. Come on, we're headin' over."

Wilson motioned for his mother to help with the explanation of school uniforms to Prissy, got the address and left immediately for the crime scene. He almost welcomed the call to action. This was his expertise, and he looked forward to earning his salary. Or showing off a bit? *Wrong, Wilson*, his inner voice continued, *no homicide is ever a simple matter, in Miami or Fernandina.*

As soon as he turned off Centre Street down Seventh, his investigative mind assimilated facts. Prominent? Right locale, his filing system told him. Big elegant homes, tall old trees, money. From two blocks away he spotted the patrol cars and yellow police tape stretched around a broad yard. The house behind the tape was one of the largest he had seen in town. The three-story brick mansion had an imposing front entrance beyond a boxwood-lined walk. The Italianate tower commanded a view of the street and appeared lit up for the occasion.

He parked and joined the Chief, who stood at the front walkway staring at the huge house. Beside him a patrolman guarded the tapeline from several gawkers. The officer was a hefty man, bulging inside his uniform. Wilson looked at the name tag. *MacCumber, got to remember that; I don't have many of the names yet.*

Wilson spoke first. "MacCumber, before we go in, what've you got? When the body was discovered, any weapons, anything that might help us?"

The patrolman kept his gaze on Chief Cabe, who appeared transfixed by the house. *How can I get this guy's attention? Is the Chief always going to be in charge?* He was about to speak more sternly when the Chief helped him out.

"It's Wilson who's taking over here, Mac. Tell him what you know," Cabe muttered.

"And what do we know, Mac?" Wilson's voice was clipped, his intention to take charge clear.

MacCumber kept his eyes on the Chief when he replied. "Last night or early this morning, timewise. Victim was found this morning by the housekeeper when she came in at six a.m. No murder weapon found yet, but it looks like a stabbing, with all the blood. The victim is the owner of the house, Robert LaFontaine. Don't know much else."

"LaFontaine? Drives a Mercedes?" Wilson snapped, startled to discover that he knew the man. The patrolman nodded, and the Chief moved toward the house.

MacCumber frowned. "Chief, don't go up there. Let this here new guy do the work."

"Is there a problem, Officer MacCumber?" Wilson looked steadily at the balding, pudgy officer.

MacCumber's expression softened, "No, sir. It's just that Chief Cabe and Mr. LaFontaine were close friends." The patrolman's words roused his boss, who looked past Wilson to MacCumber. The two said a lot with a glance.

Wilson stepped over the tape. "We'd better get started. Have you secured the area?"

"Yes, sir. Officer Sarah Grant is at the other yard entrance. Officer Frank is in the house."

"Why weren't we called sooner?" Wilson hurled the question at whoever was willing to answer; it was greeted with silence. Moving quickly up the steps, he whipped out a handkerchief and reached for the front door.

Inside, he paused. He wanted that first impression, the one that often told him what had happened and how. The body was lying face down. A pool of blood from some hidden wound was drying, containing itself where it had ceased to flow. The victim was dressed in khaki pants and a casual shirt, not out of the ordinary for most men in town. The upper torso and arched right arm were in the tiled entryway with the man's head facing to the right, left arm down at the side, and legs splayed into the doorway of what appeared to be the library.

The late Robert LaFontaine had struck the swimmer's pose of the gruesome corpse that had awakened Wilson all too often from his troubled sleep. The old nightmare vision flashed into his mind. He leaned his tall frame down close to the body, squinted at the dead face and sighed in relief. LaFontaine's eyes were open, even if cold and staring. No maggots. In a small town, at least the dead bodies get discovered sooner than in Miami.

Wilson took in the details necessary to piece together some facts. LaFontaine had apparently fallen immediately after he was wounded, and the right hand lay in a small pool of blood. In his dying moments, he seemed to have made marks on the tile with his own blood. Wilson studied them, trying to decipher their meaning. Nothing came to mind.

He stood up, walked down the other side of the body, and saw the familiar bulge of a thick wallet in the back pocket. The man's large Rolex was still in place on his left wrist, apparently ticking away. No stopped watch for a time clue.

He glanced back at the door and saw the Chief, his deep tan paled to the color of a death mask. The Chief backed toward the door, beads of perspiration across his forehead as if he'd walked through rain.

"You knew him, right?" Wilson asked.

"Yeah, we all knew Robert LaFontaine." Without another word, Cabe stumbled back onto the porch and into the clear morning air. Wilson followed as his boss sat on one of the porch chairs. Evans and Troop came up the walkway.

In his quiet voice Wilson gave orders to the two detectives and two other arriving officers. "You two look around the grounds and see if you can find a weapon, maybe a knife or something like that. Bobby, call the Florida Department of Law Enforcement and let them know we have what appears to be a murder victim. We'll need the full package for the investigation, you know, the duster and evidence techs. Did you bring your camera?" Evans nodded. "Take some pictures now before we get a crowd in there."

He turned back to Bobby. "Get to the neighbors, too. You know what to ask. Get Wilbur to help you when he gets here." The young detective strode down the walk followed by the tall Evans.

Wilson took his time going through the house. He needed to have a look around himself. Coming downstairs, he checked all the doors and windows. His footfalls made a "clop-clop" on the wooden front porch floor as he walked up to the Chief. "No signs of forced entry that I can see. You picked up on anything?"

"Just the fact that an old friend is lying in there." Cabe ground his teeth together. "Known him since boyhood. Watched him make money and waste it. This last wife of his..." he stopped short. As if to himself, the Chief said, "You'll find it all out for yourself." Wilson figured he would. Secrets didn't stay hidden long in a murder investigation. They walked inside.

He watched Evans take pictures of the body from many angles, and then back away to get more of the scene in the photos. When he looked outside, a crowd had gathered on the sidewalk and the lights from four police cars were flashing. Turning to a uniformed officer, he ordered, "Go get those lights off. We're not a damn circus. Try to get those gawkers out of here too."

The officer started out the door. "Wait — first ask them if anyone saw anything, either last night or this morning."

He turned back to see the Chief kneeling beside the body. His right foot was near the outstretched rigid hand and was covering some of the bloody marks on the floor. "Chief," Wilson spoke softly. When Cabe looked up, Wilson pointed to where his foot was smearing the bloodstains. Cabe moved his foot, smearing the marks more as he quickly sprang up.

"Son of a bitch... sorry. It's just a shock to me. Just a mess." With his head down, Cabe moved slowly back toward the porch.

Evans' flash kept going off as he continued taking pictures. The room was relatively quiet as the detectives set about unraveling the crime scene.

Bobby Troop came up and said, "Wilbur's working the neighborhood. I'll help inside." Wilson nodded.

These men do know something about investigative work, he thought. In silence the two detectives worked carefully in latex gloves around the late Mr. LaFontaine, though each averted his eyes as he was forced near the body. *Evans and Bobby may have seen it all before, but they still don't like it. Or is it something more? This is a small town; maybe he was a friend in some way I don't understand.*

He gave directions to his two men, indicating clues to look out for and things to note. He looked forward to the time when he'd have complete confidence in his detectives as a cohesive group of investigators. They were not far from it now, and he appreciated the detailed work they were doing.

"Chief, do you want someone to take you back to the station?" asked Wilson.

Cabe shook his head. "No, I think I'll go next door and talk to Miz Upton. We go back a ways. She's a little difficult at times." He tapped his temple. "She sometimes lives in the past." Wilson raised his eyebrows. "She might have seen something though. She's always seeing things and calls us out here. I see her out there by the tape. You handle the inside details." He sighed heavily, and Wilson walked with him to the top of the steps.

Cabe stepped off the porch and headed toward the house next door. Suddenly the screeching of brakes sounded from the street; a car door slammed. The sharp tapping of high heels on the walk told Wilson that a woman had left the car and on her way toward the house.

"Oh hell. Here's the wife." Cabe swore. Wilson joined him in the yard, saw the anger on his face and took the cue. They moved quickly to block her from coming into the house. MacCumber was behind her.

The woman's voice demanded. "What's going on here? Is this one of your silly drug busts?" She fixed her narrowed steel-blue eyes on the senior officer. "Well?"

The Chief met her stare. "I'm afraid we have some disturbing news for you, Darlin'. Robert's been killed, apparently murdered. We're waiting for some investigators from Jacksonville to get here to give us a hand." He inclined his head to the interior of the house where the body lay. Wilson noticed her face twitch when he called her "Darling."

Marlene LaFontaine swerved past the officers, still keeping her eyes on Cabe. He and Wilson followed her up the steps. Inside, she looked down at her husband; not a sound escaped her. Wilson watched the scene with a trained observer's eye, looking for signs of her reaction.

What a looker this woman was. Immaculate blonde hair, sleek and slightly curving under, the latest fashion, he supposed. It would be useless to attempt a guess at her age. *Is she a "trophy wife?"* he wondered. Her clothes suggested money and style, and her figure was one any man, trained or not, would be sure to take note of. Her face paled, the only sign of any emotion.

Still not a word, thought Wilson. *She's either a cool cucumber or a trained actress.*

Finally she turned away from her husband's body and with apparent composure, demanded, "Who did this? And why?" With her voice, sparks entered the atmosphere.

"That's what we're here to try to find out," the Chief said. "We're so sorry about this, Marlene"

She looked at Wilson for the first time, as if she'd just discovered an insect she didn't like. "Speaking of loss, has anything been taken?"

He shot a questioning look at the Chief, whose eyes were fixed on the widow of his friend. Without another word she flung herself past them and into the library which adjoined the front hall. The Chief didn't move, so Wilson followed her as she stepped over the body and entered the room

"Perhaps you could tell us if anything has been disturbed? It's your house." The Lieutenant spoke quietly, still intrigued by the woman's reaction. As he watched, she reached the huge desk in the bay window and stretched out one hand toward the top drawer.

"Please don't touch anything," he said. She stopped cold. "Fingerprints."

"Of course." She made a circle of the room with its shelves that lined the walls, floor to ceiling. Then she glanced back at Wilson.

"I don't spot anything out of order, but I won't know till I go through things more thoroughly." She walked back to the Chief, and again stepped over the prone body of her late husband. "Have you checked his wallet? Is it gone?"

Again Wilson felt electricity between them. Her tone suggested she might take over the investigation in the next minute.

"Calm yourself, Marlene. There's nothing missing that we can see. Robbery doesn't seem to be a motive. We haven't touched anything yet, waiting for the people from Jacksonville and the Medical Examiner." Cabe seemed to enjoy his role of authority, which Mrs. LaFontaine obviously hated. "Just for the record, may I ask where you've been the last twelve hours?"

"Don't try to infer anything, Cabe. Even you've got sense enough to know I'd rather be a rich wife than a stepmother battling with Robert's brat over the will."

"Are you sure there's going to be a battle?" Wilson decided to try for conciliation. "Are there siblings or relatives you should notify?"

The widow raised an eyebrow and riveted him with her look. "Yes, there's a son and a nephew and their assorted companions, who will no doubt be very interested in this news." She strode into the hall, headed for the stairs.

Chief Cabe's harsh tone was designed to get her attention.

"Where do you think you're going, Marlene? And just where've you been? This is a murder investigation, and everybody involved will be required to make a statement. You can make this easy or hard for yourself; it's up to you."

She halted halfway up the steps and turned back to him. Wilson could see fire in her eyes, and the Chief's clinched fists indicated he'd love to use them on this woman.

"Get this straight, Cabe, because I'm only going to say it one time. I've been in Jacksonville for the last three days helping a sick friend, and I just rolled back into town. I am not involved in this matter, as you choose to put it. Now I'm going upstairs to pack some fresh clothes, and then I'm getting out of here. I never felt safe in this house, even when Robert was around, and I'm surely not going to spend a night here alone." She glanced around at the busy men. "I assume your people will be out of here before tomorrow."

Cabe turned to a female officer. "Sarah, go up with her. Make sure she doesn't mess with anything but her things." The Chief's hands shook and his face burned red with anger as he turned his stare on the body. "She could at least have said she was sorry, the bitch."

"Shall I get someone to take her statement when she comes back down?" Wilson was more confused than ever at the Chief's reactions.

Cabe shifted his gaze up the steps. "I'll handle her; just stay out of the way and see to the other details."

Wilson turned back to the hall to see Bobby and Evans looking at him. Wilson shrugged and they went on with their tasks, both inside and out on the porch.

"No sign of forced entry, but any door could have been the way the murderer entered and left the house," Bobby said as he nodded toward the back door.

Wilson cleared his throat. "Let's check outside again. That last little shower might have helped us out. Is there anyone else in the house? I mean, who discovered the body?" He looked at Officer Frank, who had just come back in the house.

"I'm not sure, sir. I believe it was the housekeeper. I'll check. If no statement's been taken, should I take the statement or let one of you do it?" Wilson knew it was a genuine question and saw the eagerness in the eyes of the middle-aged officer.

"You interview her, and go slow. I'll leave it up to you," he told Frank, smiling.

Wilson led Bobby outside to make a closer examination of the site. The stone patio and paved drive left him frustrated. The lawn and garden showed no signs of litter, nothing out of place among the orderly flowers, graceful palms and well-groomed shrubs. Still, it was early in the investigation. Out in front, a car and van pulled up. Block letters on the van's side read "Investigations Unit." Good. Forensics and the Medical Examiner. He glanced inside where the Chief still stood at the foot of the stairs, determined to intercept anyone who tried to leave.

The new widow appeared with a small suitcase in her hand. It was the size of a make-up case. *My wife could never cram any clothes into anything that small,* Wilson thought.

Marlene LaFontaine had changed into dark blue linen slacks and white blouse with navy loafers. The buckle on her belt looked more expensive than anything his mother or Grace had ever owned. She carried a jacket over her other arm.

"You are not going anywhere, Marlene, until I get a statement out of you," growled the Chief, facing the determined woman.

"Oh, come now, John. I told you where I've been, and I'm too upset now to give you any kind of coherent statement. You sound like this is some sort of TV script we're all reading from. I'll get in touch with you later and make a statement. Right now I'm getting out of here."

Officer Grant reached for her handcuffs and looked at the Chief. Wilson almost smiled at the intuitive action of the officer. Chief Cabe gave a little jerk of the head and Grant relaxed.

"And just where are you going? I need a phone number where I can find you."

"Don't worry about it; I'm going to the condo at the Plantation, and I know my friends there wouldn't want to be involved in anything like this. I'll call you later." She marched straight ahead, sure that the Chief wouldn't try to stop her. Wilson knew about the Amelia Island Plantation, an exclusive gated community and resort on the south end of the island. It was home to the great, not so great and the wannabe's. Tennis stars, owners of professional sports teams, real estate moguls, and nameless affluent retirees made it their home. His mother told him it took its name from the 18th-century Harrison Plantation, which had once occupied the site – and which had been built on top of a Spanish mission, which itself had been built on top of an ancient Indian encampment. You could escape the rat race of the big city on Amelia Island, but you couldn't escape history. It was everywhere you turned.

When she reached the door, she turned back. "Robert had friends, you know, some who could oversee this investigation and make your life just a little unpleasant, if you know what I mean."

With the final word she stepped through the doorway and handed her keys to the nearest officer. "Would you please bring my red convertible out of the garage? I just must get away from the scene of all this horror." Her tone was soft and despairing, and the young man jumped to follow orders.

Ah, yes, the grieving widow. Wilson watched her walk toward the garage, ignoring a man standing in the doorway of a little lean-to nearby that was made into a greenhouse. Wilson saw the black man say something to Mrs. LaFontaine. When she did not respond, the man disappeared into the little enclosure.

CHAPTER 6

The Fernandina Beach Police Department was in an unusual stateof confusion the next morning. Wilson entered the main building's back door; he had learned quickly that it was the closest to the coffeepot. He went down the hall and made two rights to the mail slots. He heard the familiar clicking of computer keyboards from the office Dianne and Millie shared. He ducked in where they were working.

Dianne looked up and gave a smile, then went back to the keyboard. Millie waited for the slow printer to do its thing and noticed Wilson.

"Whatcha need, big boy?" She stood and reloaded the printer with paper.

Slightly caught off guard, he was still quick on the uptake, "I think I'm going to like you." He grinned at her. "Are there any messages?"

Millie removed a slip of paper off her desk and handed it to him. "Call the mover. He called late yesterday."

"Um-hum. I've got to start looking for a place."

She sat back down and started on the keyboard. "You can always move in with me."

Wilson did a double take and glanced at Dianne. She raised her eyebrows and cut her eyes in his direction with a glint of humor. "Millie, he has two daughters with him."

"Forget it, Jack," Millie shot back at him.

"Don't pay any attention to her. How are the girls, by the

way?" Dianne asked.

"Fine. Adapting well and have found friends. Thanks for asking. I've got to get back to the office." He nodded to Dianne and she returned to her typing. As he walked away he called out, "Millie, me and the terrors will be over later." He heard some unintelligible mumbling coming from their office.

The April morning was cool and a wave of anticipation came over him as he went into the "building out back." He didn't see the Chief's car in the parking lot. *In Miami, a single murder wouldn't faze us, but how often does a homicide appear on the crime board here? A statistic I'll check, later. Now, I'd better focus on setting a serious example. That Millie's going to be a trip. Dianne is something else.*

He placed the coffee cup on the desk, hung up his jacket on the coat hook and carefully sat in the squeaky chair. *This is about as steady as sitting on a basketball.* He didn't hear any noise from the other offices and looked at the status board on the wall across from his office door. The other three detectives were out on calls. He reviewed notes taken by Evans and Bobby at the murder scene. *No one sees anything, no one knows anything. Looks like we're going to have to dig.* He looked at his watch.

Nearly 9 o'clock and no sign of Chief Cabe yet. Apparently Cabe didn't take all this too seriously, or maybe he was used to "letting the boys do it." Never would work in Miami; turf wars. He frowned at the memory. *But this is Fernandina Beach, thank God, and I'm here to learn to do things the way they do them in Fernandina Beach.* The only sound inside was the chair responding to his shifting in the seat. Outside he could hear the telephone installer running new lines for the building.

His thoughts bounced around the murder scene, prioritizing tidbits and fitting them in a pattern. He was suddenly conscious of Evan's phone ringing insistently. The answering machine picked up and a woman's voice left a short message. His concentration broken, he stretched, and leaned back, making the chair complain again; then he finished the last dregs of cold coffee. His thoughts had turned to Dianne when he heard heavy footsteps on the wooden stairs. *Maybe that's Evans, I need to ask him a question.* Instead Chief Cabe burst into the office.

"I think I know who did this. Come on over to my office and let's talk."

He pushed his chair back gingerly and watched it lean to one side as he followed his superior out the door. *Why not talk here? Maybe Cabe wants to make some sort of point.* The Chief held his office door open for him, closing it noisily behind them.

"Have you found out anything?" Cabe's voice was calm, almost as if he knew he had the answer.

"I've got a call into FDLE to see what they've found. Our boys haven't found a murder weapon, but it looks to me like probably a large knife. The coagulation of the blood is, of course, important. Those bloody marks on the floor... I'm wondering what they could mean?"

"They're unimportant." The Chief casually dismissed the question. "But I think I know who did it. Spent all night wondering about it. I want to see my friend's murderer put away. Permanently. Robert had people who hated his guts, but only one I know who'd want to kill him. He's a local character, a guy with a reputation for meanness, been sneaking 'round LaFontaine for years, bad mouthin' him behind his back. Cajun Jack."

Taken aback by his boss's quick accusation, Wilson spoke cautiously. "Have you heard of this man threatening LaFontaine?" He let the question hang in the air.

Cabe chewed his lower lip, searching for the right words. "No, but I know of an old, festering sore between 'em. Cajun Jack's always.... hell, he's the one, I tell you, and I want you to prove it."

Wilson hedged. "Give me a description of him. Maybe we could pick him up for interrogation, say we're questioning all of LaFontaine's friends, or something like that."

"Good, good, just go on with your regular investigation, but concentrate on Cajun Jack. He's your man. You'll have a hard time finding the old pirate, but even with one gimpy leg, he can get away quicker'n you think, but everybody in town knows him. He's about five-foot-eight. He's on the grungy side, brownish hair, occasionally shaves and always has a cigarette goin'. Just don't let on I told you this. Don't let it get around the office, either, but once you see him, you'll know it's him."

"Got a ponytail in back?"

The Chief nodded.

Wilson got up, took the doorknob, then stopped, "Chief, do you remember my telling you about changing a tire on my way into Fernandina the other evening?" Cabe frowned, and Wilson stared him in the eye as he went on, "I don't understand. The man driving the car was LaFontaine; I remember the name. And the man with him sounds like it might be this Cajun Jack, game leg and all. His first name was Jack, anyway. I think you're jumping the gun a bit, Chief, but we'll pick him up."

Before the man could make another irrational charge, Wilson opened the door and walked out into the hallway.

"I'm going back to the crime scene, if anybody needs me," he announced to anyone who was listening. He had to get outside, out of the building, get some fresh air to his brain.

Twenty minutes later he was at the LaFontaine house, parked in the brick mansion's driveway. The yellow tape was still in place around the grounds. He had only quickly scanned this part of the yard the day before and had missed the Japanese yews that framed this end of the garden, which was obviously well tended. He walked through the shrubs, wondering what else he hadn't noticed, and came across the black man snipping away at a dogwood tree's low branches.

"Sorry," Wilson said as the older man was slow to stand. Time and twisted limbs slowed his efforts. He wore a body-length apron and an Atlanta Braves baseball cap covering salt-and-pepper hair. His medium brown skin looked like beautiful soft leather. He was obviously prepared for the day's sun.

He smiled at the gardener before asking his first question. "You know of the crime here yesterday?"

The man quickly lowered his eyes. "I know. Been with Mr. LaFontaine ever since I got out of...." he caught himself, followed by a deep breath, "You that new policeman from Miami, ain't ya?"

"I am. My name's Wilson." He held out a hand, "I'd like to ask you about Mr. LaFontaine, if you have a few minutes?"

"Yes, sir. Name's Roger Callahan." He motioned to a couple of iron chairs placed on either side of a matching table. "Guess you'll need to know about the help. You'd find out quick enough. When Mr. Robert got started in the shrimpin' business, he took me on to work on one of his boats. I was one of the few black men that worked on the boats. He paid me fairly. And I sure needed the job, because I'd just got out of a short stay in prison."

"What were you in for?"

"Fightin'."

"Time in prison for fighting?"

"I broke both his arms."

"Yep, that'd probably do it."

Callahan leaned over to shift one of the iron chairs, and Wilson noticed that his left arm looked stiff and hard to move. The gardener saw him glance at the damaged arm and said, "No, sir, this wasn't from the fight. I got hurt in an accident on the boat, oh, more than 20 years ago. Messed up my arm, pretty bad. I couldn't work for a while, so Mr. Robert said for me to take care of this yard, and here I am. We was a pair; he didn't know more about plants and gardening than I did. But he put it to me plain: 'Roger,' he says to me, 'I don't know any one-armed shrimpers. Don't know any gardeners, neither, with one or two arms. But it's a way to earn a livin', unless there's something else you'd rather be doin'.'"

He snorted. "I knew I was up the creek an' only one arm to paddle with, so I set about learnin' to be a gardener."

Callahan took off the cap and wiped his forehead with his sleeve. "But you want to know about Mr. Robert. I know he helped lots of folks, like me. Anything else you'll find out for yourself, I reckon. I don't know much."

"Were you here late yesterday?"

"Yes, sir. Didn't see nothing out of the ordinary."

They sat in silence for a few minutes, mentally measuring each other. Wilson asked, "Is gardening your main job here?"

Callahan gave a chuckle. "Main job, yes, sir. I run errands, ran errands, for Mr. Robert. And my wife, she's the housekeeper."

Wilson looked toward the house and saw a figure that had been watching them move away from the window. "Is she up to answering a few questions, you think?"

"She's takin' it pretty rough. Don't expect much." Callahan stood and picked up the clippers. He turned his back and returned to his slow, methodical dressing of the tree.

"I may have a few more questions later," Wilson said, wondering if the aging gardener really didn't know any more. Roger Callahan would be another little puzzle for the new man in town.

"Yes, Sir. I'll be here."

Wilson walked across the soft grass, noting the little paths among the flowers. *Somebody loves this spot. Is the gardener's loyalty complete?* Movement caught his eye at the house. A woman moved away from a first floor window facing the garden, head down and a towel in her hand. Must be the housekeeper. He'd read yesterday's interview with her. It was a little short and he wanted to talk to her.

He rapped softly on the glass pane of the side door. She came from the kitchen and stood at the door, her red-rimmed eyes questioning him. After he had shown his badge, she turned the key and opened the door, then went back to the kitchen.

Wilson went through the dining room to the tiled entryway, where a police officer was standing. The chalk outline of the victim was still on the floor. The bloodstain on the carpet had become a black blotch. Someone had cleaned the tile, but the dark outline of the pool remained. Wilson walked around the bloodstains and into the library. He asked the officer to get the housekeeper for him.

The officer returned. "She won't come in here. Not into the library or hall," he said, nodding toward the dining room, indicating the woman was in there.

Wilson joined the housekeeper where she sat at the dining room table. He kept his voice soft as he asked if she'd remembered anything more about the night of the murder.

The woman stared first at the tablecloth, then directly into his eyes. He saw distrust, dislike and a few other emotions he wasn't ready for.

"I still can't get over finding Mr. Robert like that. He was a kind man, why would any one want to hurt him in that way?" She looked back at the table and dabbed her eyes with the towel in her hand.

"I know this is hard for you, Mrs. Callahan."

"I'm Lillian, just plain Lillian." Sweat from working beaded on her dark skin.

"Miss Lillian. Do you know anyone who would want to harm Mr. LaFontaine? Any enemies you know of?"

"No, sir. He was good to me and my family. He'd help us out when things would get bad."

"How's that?"

"Everyone needs a little help, now and then."

"That's true."

"Never asked for any money back, either. My mama worked for his mama, then she worked for him when he was just startin' out. I just naturally went to work for him when my mama died. He helped bury her." She again wiped her eyes and stood. "You're the detective, you find out who did this to Mr. Robert." Wilson nodded, and she disappeared through the doorway.

He sat back and tapped the table with his fingertips. *Loyalty from the housekeeper and gardener, the last thing I'd expect in such large doses. Doing things here in Fernandina is different. I wonder. Well, back to the office and start again. It's not much use to continue here, at least not for now.*

He went back into the library, stooping and bending over, then standing on his tiptoes looking for something that would be out of place. He took his time. Finding nothing that caught his attention, he nodded to the patrolman at the front door and went back to his car. He had wondered about small towns and the tight-lipped reputation they have. He looked up to see the lace curtains from the house next door close as if someone was looking out them and let them go.

Yep, everyone knows something. Can't blame 'em too much. I wonder if they feel they're protecting their own. Damn, I hope not, this is a murder. Loyalty is good...to those who deserve it. He looked again at the LaFontaine house, noting its 19th-century architecture and all the frills about it.

He heard the laughter of schoolgirls passing on the street as he got into his unmarked car. He immediately thought of his daughters. *Oh, when will they stop picking at each other? Prissy is about to drive everyone crazy. I love those little girls, but they do have the tendency to really put me and Mom to the test.*

He started the car. *I'll have to take them to the beach and let them run their energy level down. Yeah, right!*

Lillian Callahan watched the detective drive off, retrieved her glass of iced tea from the kitchen, and headed out the door. Roger was sitting on the stool at his workbench.

"Whatja say to that policeman?" Lillian asked, putting the plastic tumbler down on the bench.

Roger let out a little laugh, "Nothing but the truth, the whole truth. He wanted to know about Mr. Robert and if I had any ideas who might want to hurt him..." he took a drink, then added, "or kill him."

"Listen, you don't get involved. If you get in this, they'll likely send you back to prison," she warned.

He put the tumbler down and stared at the condensation rolling down the sides. He looked at his wife. "I ain't involved in nothin'. I don't know anythin' about Mr. Robert getting' killed. Everythin' about it looks so strange."

"Well, you just tell as little as possible. Once you get in trouble, the man is always looking to put you back."

"This man is a little different." The gardener took another sip.

"They all the same." Lillian turned to go back in the house.

"Well, if I had to guess, I'd say da bitch did it."

She stopped short and spun around. "Don't you go cussin' in front of me. Now when we go to church on Sunday, you're going to be regretful of sinnin'. And don't tell anybody about what you think, you get us all in trouble." She fumed off toward the house, muttering to herself.

Callahan watched her go, shook his head and took a long drink of the sweet tea.

CHAPTER 7

Nobody looked up when Wilson entered his office. He checked the status board, leaned into Bobby's office, said a quick hello, and then went to his desk. He half closed his door and plopped into the creaky chair. *Wonder where they keep the WD-40?*

No sooner had he made notes on the morning interview with the Callahans than he heard a commotion in the hall. He looked up to see Marlene LaFontaine come gliding through the doorway, escorted by Dianne. Wilson stood and Dianne moved aside to let the new widow brush by.

Mrs. LaFontaine said, as if dismissing a servant, "We won't be needing your services, ah, Dianne, isn't it? I'm sure the detective has a tape recorder somewhere on that desk." She raised an eyebrow towards him.

"How can I help you, Mrs. LaFontaine?" He opened the top left drawer and saw that his tape recorder was in place.

"Help me?" The widow cast a withering look at him. "I'm here to help you." She glanced at the only other chair in the room, a dusty wooden ladderback. "I didn't realize you worked in such a dump. Don't you have a different chair in this office?"

He straightened and took a deep breath. "No, ma'am. This is it."

She pulled out several tissues out of her purse and mindfully dusted the front edge of the chair. "No housekeeping, either, I see." She wiggled the chair from side to side and finally sat down, apparently none too sure of its stability. "Sit, sit," she instructed. "You said yesterday morning you wanted a statement, so I'm here to give it."

Wilson eyed his own chair, as if it was any more substantial than the ladderback. He sat carefully, leaning his arms on his desk. "Did Chief Cabe call you?"

"No, but this is a convenient time for me. And I understand you are the new man for murders." She smiled as if expecting him to appreciate her tasteless little joke.

He looked over at Dianne, who had remained by the door. She gave a little shrug of her shoulders and twisted her mouth grimly. "Would you please come in and take Mrs. LaFontaine's statement?" he asked. She went to get a chair from Bobby's office.

"On no," Marlene groaned when Dianne was out of sight, "now what I say will be all over town before noon."

"I assure you, Mrs. LaFontaine, we work in complete confidentiality." He was determined to take control of the scene. He couldn't help noticing how the widow carefully crossed her legs and leaned back in the chair. She smiled as she saw his stare. *She knows she's an eyeful,* thought Wilson, *in her skin-tight black dress and all that makeup. Grace never needed all that.* A thought flashed in his mind back to when he would lie on their bed, watching her apply the few lotions and cosmetics she used. He recalled the pat-pat of her powder puff, followed by the light brush of cheek color. If Mrs. LaFontaine read his thoughts, she seemed to enjoy them. Her demeanor changed from hostile to inviting.

"I'm ready when you are." She spoke precisely, seeming to imply more than she should.

Women. He coughed slightly and attempted to hide his smile. "Yes, ma'am." Dianne returned, dragging a chair, making more noise than necessary. Wilson guessed that she hoped the noise irritated Marlene.

"Here, let me help you set up," he said, happy to delay the beginning of the interview. Mrs. LaFontaine watched with a bemused expression, eyes darting from Dianne to Wilson. Dianne now had a stenographer's pad at the ready.

"Detective? Is that what I should call you? I want to do this right. I don't want to come back." She brushed some invisible speck off her skirt.

"Lieutenant actually, but detective will do, Mrs. LaFontaine. I'll begin by pointing out we are recording what is said. When your statement is typed up, you will be given a chance to read it over and sign it."

Reaching across the desk to the pencil holder Prissy had made for him in school, he removed a pencil as his visitor said, "And correct it, if I so choose?"

He stopped in mid-reach, looked at her and tried to hide his irritation. "With all care we will go over the transcribed version, and I believe you will find it accurate."

The widow narrowed her eyes, and unexpectedly spoke before he could ask the first question. "I'm going to give you my version of events before you hear ten others." Wilson held up one finger. She stopped, a puzzled look on her face.

He started the tape recorder, recited date and time. "Interview with Marlene LaFontaine. Witness, Dianne Spears. April Twenty Fourth, Two Thousand. Time, Ten A.M." He leaned back in the chair and nodded to Marlene, who narrowed her eyes, clearly annoyed at being interrupted.

"My name is — I've seen this on TV — Marlene Meriweather Carlin LaFontaine, wife of Robert, so recently deceased. Yesterday, as a matter of fact."

With rapid-fire words, she went over useless information about her "romance" with LaFontaine and their subsequent marriage. Several times Wilson tried to lead her back to pertinent information. She finished, with a deep throaty chuckle as if reading his thoughts, "In other words, Detective, Robert knew what he was getting, and so did I; someone who could afford me."

She sat back in her chair and challenged Wilson for a response. When he remained silent, she continued, "Oh, I knew right from the first, people didn't approve of me. I'd taken in the most eligible man in town, and all the old biddies probably had their eye on him, and the younger women, too." She re-crossed her legs and eyed Wilson smugly. "I got the expense account — and Robert...well, let's just say he got what he wanted, too.

"That is, until lately. Recently, he seemed obsessed with something he wouldn't talk about. I heard snatches of phone conversations, and several times there was something about a map that seemed to be important, but I never caught any details. For the last few months, Robert went his way and I went mine, if you know what I mean."

"And yesterday, Mrs. LaFontaine?" Wilson jumped into the recital to redirect the questioning.

"I'm getting to that. A friend of mine had some little minor surgery last week, and I had stayed with her for several days."

"In Jacksonville, I believe you said yesterday?"

The startled look on her face told him he'd made a good point. "Oh yes, Jacksonville. Anyway, I wanted to stop by the house yesterday for extra things, and when I drove up, there were lights flashing and people all over everywhere."

"You can give Dianne the Jacksonville address."

"Is that necessary?"

"Yes, it is." He didn't flinch.

She turned to Dianne and mumbled an address that later Wilson located in the Ponte Vedra area, about 45 miles south of Amelia Island.

"Were you surprised by Mr. LaFontaine's death?" *At last, I got in a relevant question.*

"Yes, in a way. I was surprised you were there, but not completely surprised that someone had been after my husband. He'd been very restless, even mysterious, in his comings and goings. His phone conversations were guarded. I thought it all a little weird..." She paused. "Sinister might be a better word. By the way, how did they do it?"

"You say 'they,' Mrs. LaFontaine. You think more than one person was involved?"

"I asked you first. What happened to Robert?" Her response was quick.

Wilson sat back and twirled his pencil, thinking whether or not to answer the question or get up and smack her, which was his first thought. He wanted to wait long enough to let her know she wasn't going to bully him the way she did the Chief. He leaned forward.

"It appears Mr. LaFontaine was stabbed with an unknown sharp instrument. Do you keep many knives in the house, so that you'd know if one was...say, missing? And why did you say 'they?'"

She dismissed this with an indifferent shrug. "You'll have to ask the housekeeper that question. I'm hardly ever in the kitchen, and certainly don't know anything about the equipment. And Robert was a strong man. It would seem to take more than one person to kill him."

She stopped, waiting for a comment. When none came, she rose from her chair. "That's about all I can tell you. But do keep in touch, especially when you find out what this is all about."

He stood up, mindful of the peculiarities of his chair. "Just a minute, Mrs. LaFontaine. I'm sure the Chief will have other questions. For instance, where are you staying and what's the phone number?"

She gave him a suggestive leer. "No, you don't. I don't give out my telephone number to just anyone who wants it. I'm at the condo. Check with Chief Cabe. I'm sure he has it."

"But I'm not just anybody, Mrs. LaFontaine. I represent the police in a murder investigation." *My God, who does she think she is?*

"Don't worry, I'm not going to 'flee,' as you police say. And I'll call you people every day about this time." She stepped swiftly toward the door. "Got all that down, sweetie?" She waved a little finger in Dianne's direction.

"Oh, Mrs. LaFontaine, stop at Detective Jordan's office down the hall to your left and have him fingerprint you." Wilson added, "Please," but tried to put some acid in his tone.

"Wilbur's out picking up a suspect on last night's robbery,"

Evans shouted through his open door.

"Okay, see Detective Evans then, Mrs. LaFontaine. He'll be glad to help you."

"Fingerprints? Why?" She glared at him.

He shuffled papers on his desk. "It's standard procedure. Detective Evans will show you how it's done," he said with a firm look that closed the interview.

She flounced out, and Dianne quickly directed, "To the left, Marlene, not the right." He sensed Dianne's claws coming out. She closed the office door soundlessly, walked over to his desk, and whispered, "I'd love to snap off that little finger and stick it...."

"Why stop with just the one." He chuckled softly. "Now, now, she's a grieving widow. Let's be charitable."

In a few minutes they heard the widow's strident voice out in the hall. Wilson motioned for Dianne not to open the door. Marlene let out a stream of profanity as she left and the door's pneumatic piston wheezed shut.

Evans came into the office laughing. "She tried to slam the door and it bounced open and hit her in the butt."

"What have I gotten myself into?" Wilson asked in general. He watched Marlene LaFontaine through the window as she stomped to the red convertible.

So small towns handle murder a little differently from the big city way. Every suspect handled in a different way. Damn, I should have been more in control. Then he shrugged. *I'll bet I'm not the only male who ever had a hard time trying to handle that woman.*

CHAPTER 8

Friday morning, Wilson sat at his desk scanning the LaFontaine Next-Of-Kin list that Dianne had prepared for him. It had been waiting for him when he arrived. Tossing the list on the desk and leaning back, he found he was still sorting out the jumbled events of the morning. Prissy was "going to die" if her hair wasn't just perfect and toyed with her Eggos, not wanting any syrup to get on her new school uniform.

Lisa had her hairstyle suggestion rejected. This led to a four-year-old's idea of retaliation. "Comb it all down in front of your face," she had told her older sister, over a forbidden bowl of Fruit Loops.

"That's enough!" Grandmother interceded. She solved the dispute in a flash with a piece of red ribbon holding the shoulder-length blonde hair in a ponytail. "I've noticed a lot of the prettier girls wear ribbons holding their ponytails." Problem solved.

Wilson had escaped with a kiss for each of the girls and a tiny piece of toilet paper covering the shaving nick on his chin. Now in the office, the toilet paper long gone, he popped off his empty travel-mug's lid. *Umph!* He made his way to the coffeepot next door, only to see Dianne disappear around the corner.

"Thanks for the NOK list," he called after her.

She reappeared with a smile. He took a second to take her in. *Damn, why does she always have to look so great?*

"When did you have time to do it?"

"Sometime between midnight and 4 a.m.," she said with a

twinkle. There was an awkward pause, as if both wanted to say something. She saluted with her coffee cup and departed with, "Back to the grind."

He stood smiling at the empty hallway. *Grace was cheerful and light-hearted like that...and also good looking. Do I really want to start again? There would be so many complications. Lisa and Prissy are still off balance from Grace's death, and my mother's stroke has aged her rapidly. Not to mention, a new job in a new town and a new homicide to solve.*

He sighed and went back to the office and the list. His eyes skimmed the neatly typed paper until he reached the entry for Jacques Laffon, AKA "Cajun Jack." This was the passenger in LaFontaine's car the day he'd changed the old man's flat. Was he related to LaFontaine? Doesn't say here. He read the entry, trying to digest possible connections.

A small man, five foot eight, one hundred and thirty-five pounds, graying brown hair worn in a ponytail at the nape of his neck. According to Dianne's report, Jack Laffon and Robert LaFontaine had started out together as shrimpers back in the '60s. While LaFontaine concentrated on business, his pal had partied hearty. Robert would bail him out of scrapes — and sometimes jail — and lend him money when he lost it to cards or muggers.

Laffon had no street address, Wilson noted, but the address line read, "lives out by the Pogy Plant."

He picked up the phone and speed-dialed the front office. Millie's voice answered.

"Millie, where's the 'Pogy Plant' and what's a pogy?" He could hear Dianne's voice in the background.

"Come on over and I'll show you on the wall map."

"Okay." He paused. "How are you at keeping secrets?"

"The best," said Millie.

Keeping his voice low, he asked, "Does Dianne have a boyfriend or is she seeing someone steady?"

"Neither. And I don't either," she flirted with him.

"I'll keep that in mind, too," he shot back. "See you in a

minute."

Coffee mug in hand, he went into the administrative office. Dianne was there alone. "Where's Millie?" he asked.

"Down in Records. Let me show you where the Pogy Plant is." She moved to the wall map, and with a fingertip indicated a spot up at the northwest end of the island, at the edge of the blue area that indicated the wide Amelia River

"Back in the early and mid-1900s, pogy fishing was a big business here," she began.

"Jim Corbett's grandfather started the Nassau Fertilizer and Oil Company and had a big fleet of offshore fishing boats. They caught tons of small fish called menhaden; the locals called them 'pogies.' They weren't much good for eating, but the Pogy Plant pressed the fish for oil, then used the residue to produce feed and fertilizer.

"It was quite successful until the fish sort of ran out and expenses got too high. Now Jim uses the old site as the Amelia River Warehouse and Wharf."

He grinned at her. "Thanks. So, if I wanted to go to this pogy place, how would I get there?"

"How familiar are you with the area? Do I keep it simple or make assumptions?"

"Keep it simple."

She put a smooth shell-pink fingernail on the map. "We're here. Go over to Centre, east to the second light, that's Fourteenth, over here. Turn left onto Fourteenth." He nodded, understanding the directions. "You'll go up a little rise; that's McClure's Hill. Then go over the Bridge to Nowhere...."

"Bridge to Nowhere?"

"You'll see," she replied. "It crosses Egan's Creek; there're marinas on either side. Follow the road around the bend, past the back gate to Fort Clinch."

The mention of Fort Clinch, the Civil War-era fort – now a state park — that his mother had already suggested he should take the girls to visit, gave him a better sense of the general area Dianne was explaining. He nodded and took a sip of coffee.

Station house brew was famous for its foulness. He said, "This is actually quite good."

Dianne laughed and said, "The Chief considers himself a java aficionado. We pay a little extra into the coffee fund so we can buy the Special Blend from Amelia Island Coffee on Centre Street. Like it?"

"It's delicious. I might have to spend more time here instead of the field."

"Well, at ten bucks a month dues, you'll have to drink a lot of coffee."

Moments later, Wilson was turning onto Centre Street, which was still quiet at this hour. Most of the shops wouldn't open until ten. Brisk trade at the coffee shop caught his attention and reminded him he wanted to stop in soon.

The left onto Fourteenth took him up McClure's Hill, which sure wouldn't look much like a hill to anybody except Floridians used to the flattest of landscapes. A sign on the roadside announced this was the site of the "Battle of Amelia" in 1817. *Wonder what they were fighting about in 1817?* he thought, smiling to himself as he drove on up the narrow road and passed Bosque Bello, the serene, tree-shaded city cemetery. The holder of the Spanish land grant had donated the land, he remembered reading somewhere.

The sign for Old Town was next, the site of the original Fernandina, but little else nowadays. He'd like to look around here someday, too, in his spare time. Then he was crossing a scenic, curving bridge, with Tiger Point Marina to the left and Egan's Creek Marina on the right, and going around the bend past the fort's gate — until the road dead-ended at the old plant and the edge of the river. The bridge really had led to nowhere.

Nearing the quiet, almost deserted plant, he heard voices, so he continued on around, where several small businesses had set up shop in the outbuildings. He nodded to the workers as he parked near the main building. He saw more work sheds to the north, but didn't venture their way.

The woods grew almost up to the buildings' walls. *Wonder if that's where Mr. Laffon lives?* He saw no sign of a homestead. He'd come back when he was dressed for a tramp in the woods. His walk around didn't take long. He asked a few questions, but no one knew anything about Cajun Jack.

Heading back, he stopped at Tiger Point to ask if anyone knew where Cajun Jack bedded down. One of the men at Egan's Creek Marina waved vaguely toward the woods. "He's camped over in there for years, but I sure couldn't tell you where."

When he returned to the station, Dianne asked, "Find the plant okay?"

"Yeah, but no sign of Cajun Jack. I stopped at both marinas, but no one knew where to find him."

"He's wily. Put the word out; he'll find you," she suggested.

Then she invited him to lunch. "Sort of a 'welcome aboard' gesture, since the Chief wasn't exactly at his best the day you arrived."

He accepted, wisely refraining from asking if the Chief had a "best," and within moments they were walking down Second Street, enjoying the soft April sunshine.

Dianne began an informal walking tour: "The Hampton Inn and Suites has been open only a little while, and it's made downtown even busier." They stopped at Centre Street and she gestured to her left, toward the riverfront. "Brett's is great for lunch and dinner, but a little priccy for my budget right now — I'm saving for a new car."

Before he could offer to go dutch, she was already pointing out the next possibility: The Palace Saloon. They watched as a group of tourists read the menu board posted on the saloon's swinging doors, then went in.

"I've been here," said Wilson, recognizing the big ornate sign painted in the style of at least a century earlier. "We stepped in there for a drink while we were here visiting Mom a few years ago. It's pretty amazing inside, isn't it? Good to see it's still around."

"There was a big fire in 1999 that almost destroyed the place," she told him, "but the owners did a great job restoring it, right down to the murals. It's the oldest bar in Florida, you know. Used to be the watering hole for the Carnegies and their pals, who'd sail over in their yachts from Cumberland Island."

"We could eat there, if you like," he said.

"Or we could walk down a block or so to O'Kane's for potato soup," Dianne replied.

"Sounds good. Then stop at the coffee shop. I want a pound of their beans to take home." They strolled on down the south side of Centre.

Their seat at a tall table in the Irish pub's front room afforded them a view of the sidewalk scene outside as they ordered their meal. "From what I can see, this is a great little town," said Wilson, resting his elbows comfortably on the round table.

"I think it must have always been a great town," Dianne mused. "I've lived here all my life, but I still like finding out things about the place that I never knew before."

He cocked an eyebrow, and she grinned. "Okay, let me see if I can think of something besides local history to tell you about. I know.... I was at the MacArthur YMCA last night. You'll have to go try out that place when you get some time."

"Great. I've kept up my running, even with the move, but I need a place for weight training."

The waitress brought their soup: a round loaf of bread hollowed to hold creamy potato soup. "Hey, Amy, how's Eeyore?" said Dianne.

Amy laughed. "He's fine, but misses you since we moved from downtown."

"Meet Wilson, our newest Lieutenant."

"Hi, Mr. Wilson, how's the soup?" The red-haired waitress looked Irish enough to have been sent from Central Casting.

"Great. Who's Eeyore?"

"He's my basset hound, and he adores Dianne."

She and Dianne both laughed. "Yeah. Whenever he sees me, he cuts loose with that big basset bay of his."

Wilson studied Dianne's face and found it refreshing. His

instincts came to the surface; he felt he could trust her. He leaned back in the chair and slowly folded his napkin while looking at her. She dabbed the corners of her mouth with her napkin and looked at him.

"What?" she said.

"What, what?" He smiled, raising one eyebrow..

"You're looking at me funny."

"Oh, just assuring myself that I can talk freely."

"Shoot." She leaned forward on her elbows.

He looked around and began, "I'm used to working with a partner. Someone to bounce ideas off of. Besides you, that is," he grinned. I need a couple of suggestions on people I can trust to be discreet with stuff not ready for prime time. Tell me about my fellow detectives. You know them pretty well?"

She took a sip of her iced tea and looked at him thoughtfully before she started to talk. "Bobby Troop is a good ol' boy from over in Callahan, drives a pickup and is big on dogs, beer and wrestling. Was married once, don't know what happened there. He's loyal and follows orders. He thinks the Chief is the greatest. He's getting tired, though, and word is he'll be putting in papers in soon."

"I didn't realize he was that close to retirement."

"He's got a place on Lake Santa Fe, southwest of here, and wants to move there. When he didn't get the Lieutenant's position, he mentioned to Millie he'd be by in six months or so for the papers." She paused and nodded to customers that were leaving. "Actually, he said he was kinda glad he didn't get it. So, there's no hard feelings there."

Wilson nodded, and she continued, "You could trust Wilbur, too, but he's not as experienced. For some reason, the guy you replaced didn't care for Wilbur and put him on boring stuff. He's the quiet one on your staff - keeps his own counsel, as they say around here. It's difficult to get three words out of him at a time, but he doesn't miss a trick."

"What about Evans?"

"He's a good cop," she said. "One of the four black officers on the force now. Chief Cabe used to be as prejudiced as many old timers, but with time he's changing his behavior, if not his ideas. I think Charles Evans is largely responsible for the change. The Chief has learned to respect him.

"Evans was loaned to FDLE for a huge drug bust in Tallahassee a few years ago and was wounded in the fracas. Doesn't want to talk about it much. He could have been a good choice for head of the Division, and I'd guess that of the three men, he might resent your presence the most."

"I see," said Wilson. "I thought he was a little reserved, but he's been very professional in his attitude."

"Yes, he's a good guy. He knows how to honor a confidence and he has a good, analytical brain. You can count on him."

"Thanks. I just wanted to know if the..." he searched for the right word, "atmosphere I detected was right."

She laughed and said, "You can always talk to me, too."

"I'll keep that in mind, too. You ready to head back?"

With that, they stepped out into the dazzling sunlight, and began their walk back to the station, this time along the north side of the street. The aroma that spilled onto the sidewalk at the Amelia Island Coffee Shop smelled wonderful. Wilson spent several minutes choosing which blend to take home. Dianne spent the time trying to choose between chocolate and butter pecan ice cream cone for her dessert.

"Isn't ice cream and coffee an unusual combination to sell?" he asked, as they continued on their way.

"Not really. It used to be the Water Turkey, an ice cream shop. The ice cream was such a good seller, the owner kept the line when the coffee shop moved here from around the corner." She laughed. "You know you're an old timer around here when you describe things the way they used to be."

"What do you mean?"

"Well, for instance, I remember when Fernandina Beach Antiques and Collectibles used to be the Ace Hardware Store. Watson Electric is an old bowling alley; Fantastic Fudge used to be Hardee

Brothers Hardware, and Harbor Lights was one of the first Ford automobile repair garages in the state."

They walked to Front Street and its dock area, where he was glad to see there were a couple of shrimp boats still resting by a pier. The salty, fishy smell was strong in the air. Dianne made a vague gesture to her right. "We've always been a port, with shrimpers, cargo ships, even pirates pulling in."

"Yeah, mmm-hmm.... Mom's tried to get me to believe in those pirates," he said, grinning at her. "She seems to have fallen for those old legends."

Dianne smiled back. "Well, they're more than legends," she said. "At one point, Fernandina was a real pirates' lair. Luis Aury, for one. He was really a privateer, but most people call him a pirate. More romantic, I guess."

"So tell me a bit about this bad dude."

"Let's see. He landed on the island just days after the Battle of Amelia - McClure's Hill, remember?"

Wilson nodded, "Yeah, 1817, sometime." They stopped to watch the pelicans at Atlantic Seafood and the city boat ramp and dock.

"Right. Then a couple of months later, he declared himself supreme military and civil commander of the island. It didn't last long, though. He was overthrown, and gone by December."

They picked their way over the railroad tracks that crossed Ash Street, circling back to the police station. "Some say that pirate treasure is still buried on the island," Dianne said, looking up at him impishly. "And every once in a while, a rumor pops up that there's a map or two floating around that could lead someone to the booty."

"Marlene LaFontaine said her husband mentioned a map in some 'sinister' phone conversations. But then, she's kind of weird herself," he said, shrugging.

"Don't discount the possibility. Real or fake, it'll cause quite a stir."

CHAPTER 9

S omeone to see you, sir," the Desk Officer said, as Wilson and Dianne walked back into the station. Wilson turned to see a short, stocky young man slowly rising from the bench he'd been occupying. Wilson introduced himself. When the visitor didn't reciprocate, he added, "And you are?"

"William Carless — Bill. I heard you wanted to see me about my uncle's death."

"I'm sorry for your loss."

"Yeah, whatever." The man's brown eyes darted around the room, avoiding eye contact.

Wilson thanked Dianne for lunch and said to Carless, "Come back to my office."

When they were seated, he began the interview. "I understand you worked aboard Mr. LaFontaine's boat, the Miss Jane."

"Shoulda been mine."

"Oh?" Wilson's antennae went up.

"Yeah. The deal was, see, I'd work for him, learn the ropes, then be captain of my own boat. Worked for that old goat for ten years, since I was sixteen. Had every job you could imagine. Even cooked...once." He barked a humorless laugh, "That didn't last long. I'm a lousy cook." His smile displayed the gaps of missing teeth.

"How'd you get along with your uncle?"

"We had our differences." He shifted in his chair and stared at nothing.

Wilson waited, unwilling to interrupt. When Carless remained silent, he probed a little, "What were the differences about?"

"Well, me bein' captain an' all." The younger man ran his hands through his dirty black hair. "See, I told him, when I started out in 1990, that I'd be captain by the time I was 27." His expression turned mulish. "Birthday's in six months. But he kept sayin' I wasn't ready. 'Wasn't ready,' hell! I've been ready for two years. He was the one wasn't ready. Wouldn't give up. Kep' holdin' me back, ya know?"

Wilson gazed into angry dark eyes and wondered. Bill Carless moved to the edge of his seat, elbows on knees. His work-roughened hands opened and closed into fists with tension.

"Always holdin' me back. And then, when I heard about the treasure..." His face became vacant as his thoughts wandered off.

"What did he say about the treasure?" Wilson prompted. He didn't want to spook Carless, and now he was more interested in what the man had to say.

"Maybe there's nothing to it," the shrimper mumbled. "Just rumors, that's all."

"Yeah, I've heard some of the rumors, haven't put much stock in the stories either. Who told you about the treasure map?"

"That's what Uncle Robby said, just rumors." The mulish look was back. "But Cajun Jack said it ain't no rumor. There really is a map. An' a treasure." Now Wilson saw greed glittering in the narrowed eyes.

"But Uncle, he said...he said it wasn't no business of mine. Map or treasure, it was his business! Always holdin' me back, keepin' me from what's rightly mine!" He pounded a large fist on his knee.

"And now it's all gone. My uncle, the map, the treasure, even me bein' captain of the Miss Jane. That worthless George will get it all and he'll ruin everything. This time next year, all of Uncle Robby's hard work will be down the drain. Or snorted up somebody's nose." He slid a look at the Lieutenant to see if this broad hint had caught his attention. Wilson kept his poker face and let the silence grow.

"Now what?" Carless glared. "I've spilled my guts to the police. Do ya think I killed that old man?"

"Did you?"

"Hell, no! Uncle Robby was my only hope. He'da made me a captain, if not this year, then next. And I'd be set for life. Now..." He slumped back.

"Where were you Monday night, Mr. Carless?"

Carless looked at him, this time eye to eye, "You do think I killed him!"

"Just routine. I'll ask the same question of everyone." Wilson rocked in his chair.

Carless ran his hands through his hair again and sighed. "What time?"

"From six to midnight."

"Huh! You don't even know when he was killed yet?"

"Six to midnight, Mr. Carless."

"Finished on board Miss Jane around six, cleaned up, had some chow." He paused to think. "Monday, Monday...Oh yeah, went over to Sharky's Place for a brew." He gave a bitter laugh, "Had ten bucks in my pocket, bought ten dollars' worth'a fun."

"How'd you get to Sharky's?"

"Walked. Car's broke. Blew the engine last Saturday." He snorted in disgust. "It'll take more'n ten bucks to fix that, let me tell ya!"

"See anybody you knew?"

"Sure, I'm a regular. Bartender, Shorty. Pool hustler they call Stingray. An' One-eye — he's another shrimper on the Miss Annie. Coupla other guys, off other boats."

"When did you leave?"

"Ten-thirty, eleven, I guess."

"How'd you get back to the boat?

"How'd ya think? Shoeleather express."

"And about what time did you get back to the Miss Jane?"

Carless shrugged. "Dunno, 'bout eleven-thirty, midnight."

"Took you an hour to walk from Sharky's?"

"Nice night. I was tired and close to bein' drunk. Beer made me sleepy.' He shrugged.

Wilson rocked slightly back and forth in his beat-up chair for a minute, digesting the little information he'd gleaned from the nephew.

"OK, Mr. Carless," he brought the interview to a close with a small smile for his visitor's discomfort. "I'll probably want to talk to you again. And like they say in the movies, 'Don't leave town.'"

"Ha! On what? I ain't goin' nowhere. No money, no car, maybe no job. An' maybe no future."

After Carless left, Wilson wanted to see Wilbur, but the status board showed he was out. He stepped into the office across the hall, "Bobby, when Wilbur gets back, if I'm not here, have him check on Carless' story at Sharky's. I'll leave the information on his desk."

Bobby saluted with his pencil and went back to talking on the phone. Wilson turned back, "Oh yeah, I'm going out to George LaFontaine's for an interview. Be back later." Bobby nodded and continued his conversation.

CHAPTER 10

Wilson turned his unmarked car into Ladies Street, traveled the newly-graded road looking at house numbers, and realized he was going to get a tour of Old Town sooner than he'd expected. One house in particular caught his attention; it was shaped like a boat. He was easing past its prow when he saw a number and recognized this was his destination, George LaFontaine's house.

After jockeying the car into the oyster shell driveway, he took a moment to inspect the odd two-story dwelling. He could see two porthole windows in the bow; their red trim contrasted nicely with the white siding. He searched for a second or two before he found the brick porch and the front door, in what he knew sailors would call amidships. The white picket fence formed the boundary line, and its red gate completed the color scheme. He rang the bell several times, then heard a shout from inside.

The door jerked open and he faced a person he assumed was the lady of the house. "Mrs. LaFontaine?"

"Well, well, what have we here?" She leaned against the doorjamb. One shoulder was bare and she moved slightly so her multi-colored caftan slipped further off its creamy curve. Her pale green eyes surveyed him as she raised a half-full glass to her hot-pink lips. She pulled the disarrayed once-blonde hair to the side, away from her bare shoulder.

She musta combed that hair with a firecracker. Wilson sighed as he dug out his gold shield. He wasn't in the mood for a predatory female. This wasn't going to be easy. Judging from the slight glaze in her eyes, that tumbler didn't hold iced tea. "Lieutenant Wilson, Fernandina Beach Police. May I come in?"

"Screen's unlatched, Sugar." She turned to lead him inside. "Oh, my manners!" She whirled a trifle unsteadily, and offered her hand, "Rheba LaFontaine. George's wife. The Mrs. LaFontaine, now that dear ol' Mr. Robert has gone to his reward. You'll see I'm not the silicone Mrs. LaFontaine." She sniffed daintily at her obvious reference to Marlene.

Definitely not iced tea, he thought, keeping his expression bland. They shook hands. The blonde prolonged the contact a few seconds more than necessary, keeping eye contact.

"Is your husband here, Mrs. LaFontaine?"

She let go of his hand and turned back into the house. "George!" she screeched, "The police are here to see you!"

Wilson followed her as she tried to jiggle a seductive slow walk into a large room at the back of the house. *The stern of the house.* The sunlit room at the end of the dark hall produced a silhouetted Rheba LaFontaine. She stood about five-foot-five, he guessed.

The room spanned the width of the house, with the back wall mostly window. It afforded a view of a jungle-like garden; years of neglect had left it an over-grown jumble of plants struggling to survive. Overflowing bookshelves lined the left wall, while the right housed an entertainment center. The large television was tuned to CNN, the sound muted. A slight movement caught Wilson's attention, and he saw a man in the recliner.

"Well, the policeman finally got around to talking to me, just a couple days after my daddy died," came a mocking voice.

"Mr. LaFontaine?"

The man nodded. Wilson expected him to get up and offer his hand, but he did neither. "I'm sorry about your loss."

Wilson's glance at Rheba included her in his condolences. Her vague wave with her cigarette in hand encompassed the room. "Have a seat, anywhere."

He looked around helplessly. The detritus of bad housekeeping covered every flat surface, including all the chairs.

She noticed his hesitation. "Please excuse the mess, Lieutenant; we're just so distraught over Mr. Robert's demise."

"Shut up, Rheba."

She subsided into her own chair across from Wilson, the caftan slipping once more.

He moved a stack of newspapers from a nearby chair and studied LaFontaine's face. The eyes were the dominating feature; they were red-rimmed, and Wilson felt sure it wasn't from tears of sadness. The man's sandy hair had been combed, maybe yesterday, and the rumpled jeans and tee-shirt hung like yesterday's wash. Wilson couldn't guess about his height because of the crooked way he sprawled in the chair. His wiry frame looked like he'd worked with weights at one time, but now he just hefted beer cans. Wilson couldn't tell from the cans on the table next to him whether they were today's collection or further evidence of Rheba's housekeeping.

"I want to assure you, Mr. LaFontaine, that we are doing everything we can to apprehend your father's killer."

The response was a snort. LaFontaine lifted a can, and glared at his wife when he discovered it was empty. She flounced out of the room. "I appreciate all your pretty words, Detective, but that doesn't bring back my daddy." He stared at the silent television, then pierced his visitor with a gray-eyed glare.

"My father was a difficult man, Wilson. He was rough and tough, like the shrimpers who worked for him. And he was demanding. Demanding on himself and everybody around him." A fist softly pounded the recliner's arm. "His kid, his wife. Hell," he snorted again, "he worked my momma to death." He shifted in the chair. "He went straight from her funeral to that house. And started bringing all those bitches there. To the house my momma should'a been living in."

"We all know about your sainted momma." Rheba was back, with two Old Milwaukees and a strong whiff of newly applied cologne. She plunked one can on George's table, then waggled the second at Wilson. When he shook his head, she shrugged and placed it on her husband's table. Wilson noticed she'd replenished her own drink as well.

"How would you characterize your relationship with your father, Mr. LaFontaine?"

LaFontaine broke off musing about his mother and regarded the Lieutenant. "Fine. Just fine."

It was his wife's turn to snort. "Tell him, George, just how 'fine' it was." She had adjusted her caftan so it no longer slipped off her shoulder. She leaned forward to display a braless cleavage, and avidly watched for Wilson's reaction as she flicked cigarette ashes into a full ashtray.

He kept his expression blank, and turned back to the husband. "You worked for your father?"

"Off and on. When I'm not in school." He took another sip of beer.

"What are you studying?"

"Almost got my degree. In graphic design."

"Right, Georgie; and what are you going to do with that?"

"Shut up, Rheba."

He could tell that was an oft-repeated response. The woman took no offense. She winked at Wilson and offered another flash of cleavage while putting out her cigarette.

"What exactly did you do for your father?"

"I worked on those damn boats, like any other shrimper!" LaFontaine was showing a little outrage. "Hauling nets, swabbing decks, humping shrimp. While he sat in his pretty little office, wheelin' and dealin.'" He took another swig of beer. "I mean, I'm the boss's son; and I should've been groomed to take over, when he..." His tirade ran out of steam when he realized what he was about to say. There was a moment of silence, broken by the clink of ice as Rheba took another sip.

Wilson broke the pause. "And now? Do you inherit and take over?"

"I damn well better."

"Have you talked to any of the employees since your father's death?"

"Uh, no." LaFontaine looked away and Wilson knew that the idea had never entered the man's head. "I, uh, thought I'd give it a few days."

"When was the last time you saw your father?"

George's head whipped around and he glared at the Lieutenant. "Am I a suspect?" Suddenly Wilson recognized the mop-haired young man who had been driving the Camaro that zipped in and out of traffic the first day he arrived on the island. He made a mental note to check the tag number when he left.

Rheba rattled the ice in her now-empty glass. "Follow the money, George. That's what they say on all the cop shows. Right, Detective?" She lit another cigarette and slowly blew smoke in his direction.

"Shut up, Rheba."

Wilson almost joined him this time. He didn't want her to break the flow. He shrugged, "It's just routine."

"They say that on TV, too."

"Shut up, Rheba."

Amen, Wilson thought.

"We're asking everyone the same questions."

"I saw Daddy late Monday afternoon."

"What time?"

George shrugged. "Four-ish."

"At his office or the house? Somewhere else?"

"At the office. Won't go into that fancy house of his."

"What did you talk about?" No answer. He tried again. "Anything worth mentioning?"

George shook his head and reached for the beer Wilson had declined.

"Money. They argued about money," Rheba volunteered.- LaFontaine threw the empty beer can at her, but it was wide of the mark and clattered harmlessly to the floor. Wilson tensed, ready to intervene. He subsided in his chair when Rheba flashed him a wicked grin as she left the room. This time his eyes followed her out of the room before he looked at her husband.

"Is that right? You argued about money?"

The man picked up yet another empty can and began to crumple it in one strong hand. "Yeah," he admitted finally, "we talked about money, not argued." Wilson waited.

"Well, hell; I suppose it'll all come out, anyway. Daddy and I never saw eye-to-eye about money and what to do with it. I wanted to go back to school. I'm tired of being a deckhand. Want to get my degree and work like a gentleman instead of trawling for shrimp like a common seaman. But Daddy, he... he cut me off. Said there wasn't any more money for school. And the only way to get off the boats was to do what he wanted. I'd work my way into the office." He looked at Wilson, "Which is where I shoulda' been."

Rheba's cologne announced her return. She carried two more Old Milwaukees and a new drink for herself. She placed one beer next to George and bent slightly toward Wilson to offer him the second — along with another shot of her chest. "Sure you don't want some of this, Sugar?"

He looked her straight in the eye and used his frostiest smile to say no thank you. To both offers.

"So, Monday your father told you he wouldn't pay for school. Were you going to go back to work for him?"

"Told him I would, but he didn't like my price."

Rheba sat up with a jerk. Obviously she hadn't heard this part.

"What price was that?"

LaFontaine looked for a way to retrench, but there was none. "Shares," he sighed. "I wanted shares of the take."

"You mean profits from the business?"

"That, and other things." George now had Rheba's undivided attention as well as Wilson's. She put her glass down to concentrate on the exchange.

"What other things?" Wilson murmured.

"There's this map, see?" He waved an arm to stave off any ridicule, but nobody was laughing. "A map that shows where Aury buried some of his loot."

"Oh, Georgie." Rheba slumped back in her chair and reached for her drink. He shot her a venomous look.

"Aury?" Wilson stared at LaFontaine incredulously. "You aren't talking about that so-called privateer from nearly two hundred years ago?"

LaFontaine muttered, "It's true. Daddy had a map of some sort. He'd found it in some old papers. And I know he talked to Cajun Jack about it."

Cajun Jack. Wilson had to find that man soon.

LaFontaine noticed the skepticism. He drew himself up in the chair, "So I told him I'd come back to work, permanently, for a share of the treasure. And I wanted to be in on the hunt for it."

"What was your father's response?"

The son's face flushed. "He laughed. Laughed at me, and said I couldn't find my backside with a flashlight, much less a treasure." He drained the last of his beer. "And I got mad, as usual, and stormed out." He took a long breath. "And that was the last time I saw him."

Wilson thought the tremor in the man's voice was sincere, though he wasn't sure where the emotion lay; for the loss of the supposed treasure map or his father. A dark cloud had blocked the sunlight from the room. The room was lit by the kaleidoscope of colors from the TV's changing pictures, giving an eerie cast to LaFontaine's sharp features.

Wilson stood and said, "Again, I'm sorry. I'll let myself out."

Rheba led him to the front door. He didn't know the name of the cologne she wore, but God help the next woman who wore that scent around him.

"And you, Mrs. LaFontaine? When did you last see your father-in-law?" His disgust put too much edge to his voice, and she whirled to face him.

She pointed a scarlet nail at him. "Let me tell you, Mr. Detective, that old man was mean and manipulative." She stumbled over the word, but it didn't deter her. "He was a rich and powerful man, and

I knew better than to cross him. I stayed out of his way. And let me tell you, he certainly didn't seek me out!" Her nail beat a tattoo on his tie. "I hadn't seen dear ol' Robert in weeks, and was glad of it."

He was on the porch now, holding the screen door open. "I gather that the two of you will be around for a while. I'll probably need to talk to you again."

The "come back...anytime" from Rheba was more than he wanted to hear.

He backed the unmarked car out of the driveway. His mouth felt cottony after watching those two drink so much. Anything cold, he thought, would be most welcome.

While he drove slowly down Ladies Street to Estrada, he reviewed the conversation of the last hour. Old houses surrounded him along all the narrow streets, named by the Spanish in the original Fernandina. Then he noticed a large pink Victorian house on his left, which was probably the Posada San Carlos that his mother had told him about when describing Old Town to him one evening. He wondered if the pastel hue was its original color or if it had been painted for the Pippi Longstocking movie that he'd heard had been shot there.

Across from the lovely Posada San Carlos was a historical marker on the grassy, peaceful-looking parade ground of Fort San Carlos, built by the Spanish in the 1800s overlooking the wide river. His mother had said that he could see some of its foundation in the riverbed if he looked at low tide. He looked at his watch. No time now to play tourist.

Back at the station, he sat motionless and reread the interview report he'd just written. The quiet air conditioner broke the silence. He heard Evans' chair scrape across the floor as he ended a phone conversation. His footsteps sounded in the hall.

"You need anything else?" Charles Evans' tall frame filled the door.

"No.... wait, did Wilbur get back?"

"Yeah, and he's over at Sharky's Place's now. Bobby's gone for the day."

Wilson knitted his brow and mumbled an "Okay. See ya." Evans left as Wilson made penciled notes on the report. He looked at his watch. His mother would have dinner ready in another few minutes. He put the papers down and walked out, knowing he was going to have to find her some day help.

———————•●•———————

On the way home, he remembered that he had meant to call about joining the YMCA that Dianne had recommended. He had passed the building earlier that day but didn't have time to stop then. The Y was next door to an "Egmont Park," and something about that name sounded vaguely familiar.

That evening, at dinner, he mentioned it to his mother, who seemed to know the background of most things around here.

"Why, you ought to know that name," Priscilla Wilson said. "Haven't I ever told you about how the British claimed this island for awhile in the 1700s? Lord Egmont was the British nobleman who had a huge indigo plantation here."

"Indigo?" Wilson was finishing his crab cakes, one of his mother's specialties. "The stuff they used to make dye?"

"Yes, it was really valuable then. And you know Egan's Creek, that runs under the Bridge to Nowhere? It's named after Lord Egmont's overseer, Stephan Egan!"

"I knew Fernandina was old, but the 1700s?"

"Actually, that's late for this island. You'll have to come over to the Museum of History..."

"Yeah, in my spare time!"

"...to get the full story," she continued, ignoring his remark. "The Timucuan Indians lived here five or six thousand years ago. Then the French came, in the 1500s, followed by the Spanish - just about the same time they were founding St. Augustine. The Spanish set up missions all along the islands as far up as South Carolina."

He knew Mom was off on one of her favorite subjects, so he settled back with another glass of tea and let her talk. After all, he needed to get to know this place he was now calling home.

"Then the English came in for awhile, then the Spanish again, not to mention the 'Patriots,' and the 'Green Cross' crowd who took over one time, and the Mexican revolutionaries - well, anyway, that was the flag that old pirate Aury used when he was in charge. The Confederacy held Amelia for awhile, and of course, the United States. We've been under eight different flags over the last 500 years!"

"Ahhh," said Wilson, grinning as she finally got to that point, "I do believe I've heard you mention that's why it's known as the Isle of Eight Flags, right?"

His mother tapped him gently on his knuckles with a spoon and shook her head. "All right, so maybe you did hear a little of that before, but you know how much I enjoy talking about this. I do get lots of practice when I'm giving the tours. And you can't say many small towns have had such an interesting past..."

He chuckled. "Okay, you've got a point there. I was only kidding, Mom, you do make it interesting. Hey, I'm the one who asked you about the Egmont name."

"And that reminds me," said his mother as she stacked plates to take to the kitchen, "did you know this island has had four names? Napoyca was what the Indians called it — then came Isle de Mai, Santa Maria, and finally Amelia, after King George the Second's daughter."

"Well, there's no way I'll remember those," he told her with a wink. "I'm having a hard enough time getting the names of all the streets down, so far."

CHAPTER 11

S aturday morning, Wilson sat on a sloping granite boulder that rested in front of Main Beach's boardwalk. He had decided to get the girls out of the house for a while, allowing his mother time to regroup. He watched his daughters play in the shallows left by the low tide. They ran in circles among the pools, kicking the salty water at each other. They danced about and their squeals of laughter penetrated the air in competition with the cries of the Atlantic terns and seagulls.

The sun warmed his face and he closed his eyes to the clear blue skies while thinking of the coming interview with Mrs. Upton, neighbor of the late Robert LaFontaine. His mother had chided him for working on Saturday but relented when he promised it was only going to be for an hour or so.

Reluctantly he looked at his watch and called to Lisa and Prissy, "It's time to go." They groaned and pleaded, but he shouted back, "We'll come back again."

An hour later, his ring of the doorbell brought hurried footsteps from inside the beautiful old home on Seventh Street. The massive oak door with its beveled glass stood open. He looked through the screen door to see a large black woman coming from the back of the house, drying her hands on her white apron.

"You must be Lieutenant Wilson." Her slight smile was pleasant but not quite welcoming, as she opened the screen door. "Miz Cornelia is expecting you."

She led him through the wide vestibule into the front parlor dominated by a marble fireplace. A twelve-foot ceiling capped a room filled with family memorabilia and heavy Victorian furniture.

Cornelia Caulfield Upton was a small, bird-like woman whose cornflower blue eyes pierced him. Her thick hair, swept into a bun atop her small head, formed a silver frame for a face that he thought must have once been beautiful. With a gracious smile, she offered her hand and he took it gently. He was surprised by the strength he found there.

"Lieutenant Wilson. How nice of you to call for an appointment. And," her blue eyes glinted, "right on time."

She sank gracefully to the wine-red Victorian settee on one side of a rosewood table. An open hand gently waved her guest toward a straight-backed Hepplewhite chair across from her. A large oil painting of a distinguished gentleman in muttonchops hung above the mantle.

She inclined her head toward the painting, "Promptness, my dear father always said, is a virtue. Don't you agree?"

Before he could reply, she turned slightly to the maid who waited in the doorway; "Sully, you may bring our tea, now."

Wilson's jaws tightened a little. So far, he'd not been able to get a word out, and the two women had effectively herded him into this stunningly uncomfortable chair. This interview, like the last one, was going to be a real challenge.

"Mrs. Upton," he began, only to be interrupted by the aging Southern belle.

"Oh, do call me Miz Cornelia. Everyone else does. 'Mrs. Upton' makes you sound like such a stranger."

No, this was not going well. "Miz Cornelia. You know, of course, that Robert LaFontaine, was killed Monday night, and...."

"Wilson, Wilson..." she placed one delicate pink nail to her equally delicate pink lips. "Wilson is such a common name — oh, dear me, not common...but popular." She appeared flustered. "Are you of the Wilsons from Macon? You know, that is where I went to Wesleyan College."

Surprised that he was expected to produce his lineage when he hadn't been asked to show his badge, he managed to get out, "No, ma'am. I'm really..."

"Or perhaps you're related to the Broward County Wilsons."

Wilson opened his mouth to say something, anything, to get this interview on track.

She kept talking, "I went to a Wilson wedding once. It was a grand affair, but odd." She tipped her head to the side, like the small bird she resembled. "Because it was a Wilson marrying a Wilson, you see! I'm sure they were related somehow. Distantly, of course." She checked to see if he understood there had been no impropriety with the union, then continued, "How convenient that would be. You wouldn't have to change monograms on any of the linen!"

Her tinkling laugh signaled the return of Sully, laden with an elaborate silver tea service. He moved to help, but she shook her head and placed it on the table in front of the old lady. He noticed that Mrs. Upton's cup was already filled. The two women exchanged a look that he could not decipher. *Nope, this isn't going to be an easy one.*

"Cream, sugar, or lemon, Lieutenant?"

He sighed and requested one spoonful of sugar to be placed in the delicate Limoges cup.

"How is it?" she asked as he took a sip, testing it for temperature. His finger would not fit in the handle, and he knew she intended to make him feel like an oaf.

"Delicious, Mrs., uh Miz Cornelia."

She nodded in approval. "Good. I only bring out this tea service for state occasions. Great-Grandmother Caulfield buried it so those Damnyankees couldn't steal it. Oh, don't look so surprised, Lieutenant Wilson. Damnyankee is not a swear word. It's the only term for those scoundrels who ruined the South." She took another sip of her "tea."

Those shrewd blue eyes pierced him again. "I hope I haven't offended you, Lieutenant? You're not from a, shall we say, more northerly branch of Wilsons?"

"No, I..."

"Of course, I have met your dear mother on several occasions, but we've never had the opportunity to exchange more than a few pleasantries."

"No, ma'am; my family hails from Charleston. But what I really...."

"Charleston?"

He chose to ignore yet another attempt to derail this conversation, "What I want to talk to you about is Robert LaFontaine and his family."

His hostess sighed and permitted her shoulders to slump slightly. "I know. Such a nasty man. Such a nasty family." She made the adjective seem worse than it usually was.

"Nasty how?"

She held up a plate of elegant-looking teacakes. He shook his head and kept his eyes riveted on hers. Placing the cup daintily on its saucer, she said, "Nothing but poor white Southern trash, he was." She mouth-pinched disapproval. "Came from Louisiana or somewhere. Bought a boat, Lord only knows where the money came from. Started shrimping."

Now she fussed with the lace at her throat, and Wilson noticed her dress for the first time. It was a filmy, pale lavender print with lace edging the sleeves as well as the neckline. The pearls that graced her ears and neck were real. On her wrinkled left hand was a wedding set; the large diamond engagement ring sparkled in the afternoon sun. Her right hand wore a pearl cluster ring that matched her earrings and necklace.

Now that she was on Wilson's track, he leaned back a little and for the first time noticed the smell that an old house gives, comfortable old wood.

"He worked hard, that one, I'll give him credit for that," she continued. "Had a pretty little wife. She worked as hard as he did. Had two babies, she did, but they were stillborn. No wonder, all that heavy work." Her voice trailed off and Wilson wondered what memories had been dredged up by the mention of the LaFontaine stillborn babies.

"Then they had Georgie, and spoiled him rotten. He never amounted to much. Never will." She shook her head. "What a pity. It will all be gone in a year or two; you'll see."

A smile suddenly lit her face, and he saw her for the beauty she had been. "There's my good boy!"

Wilson swiveled in his chair to see the ugliest cat he'd encountered in years. Big, red, with only one eye. It arranged itself in a sunny spot at the center of the Oriental rug and regarded him with disdain.

"Come here, Ramblin', and let Momma give you a treat!" She broke off a piece of the teacake Wilson had declined. The overweight feline regarded the morsel thoughtfully before stalking over to accept it. "You old Ramblin' Wreck." As she stroked the cat's chin, its eye closed.

"Robert was nasty to Ramblin', too." She leaned down and lifted the big tom to her lap. He draped himself regally on his perch and accepted another bite of cake. "Ramblin' is a free spirit. Goes where he wants to, when he wants. He just loves Robert's back yard, don't you, Sugar? I think he meets his girlfriends over there."

The cat answered her with a throaty meow. "Ramblin' would go over there, making his rounds, and Robert would go wild. Said Ramblin' killed birds. Messed in his flower beds." She sniffed disapproval.

Then her laugh turned wicked. "I remember the day they delivered the sundial and put it in the garden. Robert was right proud of that old thing. Came from Italy or someplace. Ramblin' was fascinated with that sundial. Sat on it, under it, sniffed it. Probably piddled on it a time or two. Didn't you, you rascal!"

The rascal, Wilson saw, had fallen asleep. His large back end had oozed off Miz Cornelia's meager lap and onto the sofa. She repositioned him and his eye flickered open briefly.

"A couple of years ago, Ramblin' was sitting on the sundial when Robert shot him!"

"Shot the cat?" Wilson clanged his cup into the saucer and

winced. The cup and saucer probably cost more than he made in a week.

"Yes! Oh, what a day that was! I saw the whole thing from my bedroom window. I raised the sash and screamed at Robert like a fishwife. Ran downstairs, scooped up Ramblin', and we — Sully and I — rushed him to the veterinarian." She cradled the cat like a baby. "Thought we were going to lose him, but the doctor pulled him through. Couldn't save the eye, though."

She rocked the sleeping feline to and fro, regarding him fondly. "I never spoke to Robert again. Oh, he came over to apologize, said he and Marlene were having a fight and he just lost control for a few minutes. But I told him he was nasty, and I was taking him off my Christmas party list. Did, too."

"You say you saw Ramblin' on the sundial in Mr. LaFontaine's garden?"

Cornelia Upton hesitated before answering. For the first time that afternoon, she seemed a little unsure of herself. "Why, yes, I suppose I did say that."

"So you can see the garden from your bedroom window?"

She clenched her lips shut, but Wilson could see that she was trying not to giggle at the realization she had let the metaphorical cat out of the bag. "I suppose I can." Now she was looking vague, but he suspected that was just put on to fool him.

"Were you home Monday night, Miz Cornelia?"

"Yes, I was." She wouldn't look at him. She concentrated on the cat instead.

"Did you see anything out of the ordinary from the window?"

"No, nothing. Nothing at all." She paused, then continued in a rush; "I went to bed early. Slept the whole night through. I was tired." She looked off to her father's portrait.He knew she was holding something back. He was trying to figure out how to play hard ball with an old lady when the cat broke the spell. He jumped off his mistress's lap, gave Wilson a malevolent stare and stalked out of the room. Ramblin' and Sully passed each other at the doorway.

"Time for your nap now, Miz Cornelia."

"Yes, yes, I am a little tired, Sully."

He knew the interview, such as it was, was over. He thanked the seemingly exhausted woman for her time and hospitality and followed Sully to the front door.

"How long have you been with Miz Cornelia, Sully? May I call you Sully? 'Sully' what?"

"I been with her longer that you've been alive, Lieutenant." She opened the screen door and they stepped out onto the porch. "As for my name, Daddy was Jeremiah Sully, and he worked for Mr. Caulfield back when he first started. Mr. Caulfield called him jus' plain ol' 'Sully.' When I came to help young Miz Cornelia, she jus' called me Sully, too."

He thanked her and stepped off the porch into the warm April sun. He climbed in his car and headed home via the station, where he wanted to make some notes and check the duty schedule. As he pulled onto Centre Street, he shook his head. *What a couple of days. Jerked around by George and Rheba yesterday, and now dear, sweet, helpless Miz Cornelia.* That old lady knew something, and he bet it was important. Question was, could he get it out of her?

Cornelia Upton sat alertly on the sofa where he had left her. Nap, indeed! Sully'd heard she was in trouble and had come to rescue her. As usual. She'd tell that young Lieutenant what she knew, but not before she'd done a little sleuthing on her own. Ramblin's terrified yowl had made her sit right up in bed Monday night. She'd thought Robert was after him again and she'd raised the window to give him what-for, but she hadn't seen Robert. She'd leaned out farther and heard somebody's footsteps on the gravel pathway, then saw only the movement of a dark car moving slowly down Seventh Street. She'd give her favorite pair of gloves to know who was driving.

Sully came to clear away the tea things. "Do you want me to turn down the bed for your nap, Miz Cornelia?"

"You devil!" Cornelia touched her old friend and confidante

lightly on the arm. "Word gets out I'm taking naps, the whole town will think I'm doddering! Sully," she added in that special wheedle of hers, "are you still friendly with Mr. Robert's housekeeper, Lillian?"

"Yessum." Sully sighed. "I suppose you want me to talk to her."

"If you get a chance."

"Uh-huh. Like in the next fifteen minutes or so. Anything particular you want to know?"

"Everything!" They both laughed.

"And tell your nephew Nathan to find out who was driving down Seventh with his lights off around ten o'clock Monday night."

CHAPTER 12

Monday morning found Wilson thinking about the fun he and the girls had flying kites at the beach late Saturday afternoon. After his interview with Mrs. Upton, he had needed some more time to think. He found that pieces seem to fall into place when his mind was completely off the case. The squeals of the girls made him laugh. They had spent the afternoon at Main Beach with others doing family things. At last, reluctantly, they reeled in the kites, but only after a promise of returning soon.

Now, in the office to begin another workweek, he drank the last of his coffee and decided to go get a refill.

He was walking out of the out-building office when he heard his phone ring. The Chief wanted him.

"Come on in a minute and let's talk." The Chief sprang up to meet him and closed the door. He sat and busily shuffled papers on his desk. "You're new here. It's best if I keep tabs on things. Nothing personal; after all, I know everybody around here, where all the bodies are buried, so to speak. What's going on with the LaFontaine murder?"

"Not much yet. Still waiting on FDLE for some prelim reports."

Cabe rocked back and forth in his executive chair, eyeing him, measuring up his new big-city Division supervisor.

Wondering just how good I am, thought Wilson.

"Who've you interviewed?" the Chief said finally.

He took out his notebook and read off a list of names. "The widow LaFontaine. You have a copy of the interview, such as it was. I need to talk to her again. William Carless, a good suspect, not too bright. And the honorable Mrs. Upton, an interview as pleasant as Chinese water-torture. She uses tea."

Cabe gave a short laugh; leaned forward and placed his elbows on the heavy desk. "Well, Miz Upton is a trip." Wilson nodded. "Did she see anything?"

"No, she slept the whole night, and besides a lot of history, that's about all I got out of her. The nephew..."

The Chief interrupted, "...was at Sharky's Place."

"Right." Wilson looked up, questioning.

"He lives there when he's not at the boat. He has an apartment somewhere, on the beach, I think. You talked to the son yet?"

"That's another 'sort of.' He didn't know much and the wife wasn't any help either."

"Oh, yes, Rheba." Cabe tapped a pencil on the desk and looked off in the distance. "I don't think we can count on much from her. She's in outer space a lot of the time."

"George said he wanted to move up in the business, sooner than later, and mentioned something about a treasure or a map; he wasn't too talkative. Clammed up when I pressed him."

"Is that all?"

"Only that George seemed to think there really was a map. His father had told him any map didn't concern him."

"I'd forget about any treasure map. That old chestnut's been around forever. Just idle talk to attract more tourists. I still want you to check into that Cajun Jack, though. Don't arrest him; call me when you find him. He knows me, and I have a feeling he may have a lot to do with this. If you see him, don't let him out of your sight."

"Why him?"

Chief Cabe leaned back in his chair, "I've been lookin' over the evidence collected and I've got something that puts Jack at the scene."

"Oh?"

"Yeah, seems Cajun Jack's habit of chewing on a toothpick

put him there. I had Evans make an extra picture so's I could show you." Cabe removed an 8x10 black-and-white photo from his desk and tossed it across the desk. It was of a chewed toothpick, all right.

"How does this connect Jack Laffon to the murder? I've chewed a toothpick in my time."

"It's broken in the middle, just like Jack does it. He's been doing that since I've known him, 'bout a hundred years. Also, he and Robert have been seen together regular lately. Hell, you said you saw them together, didn't you?"

Wilson nodded.

"Rumor is...they had a fallin' out. Threats made, an' such. You need to find him and call me. He may be older than you, but he's strong as an ox and just as unpredictable."

Later that afternoon while driving home, he couldn't help wondering why the Chief wanted to keep so close to this case. He dismissed his concern as he pulled into the driveway and saw Prissy's bicycle in the way. He moved it so he could get to the garage in the back.

The house was unusually silent. A note on the kitchen table read, "Gone shopping with girls. Don't fill up with junk food. Home at 6." He smiled, after all these years, she was still telling him not to fill up on junk food. Potato chips, pretzels, beer, popcorn...fulfills the daily requirement for the four basic food groups.

He tossed his jacket and tie in his room and took the morning paper and a beer to the back porch. He didn't read much more than the headlines before he laid the paper aside. Squirrels were busy chasing each other around the yard and up the wind-bowed oak trees. A gentle sea breeze played through their leaves. Birds flitted from the trees to a feeder set up next to the birdbath. Wilson closed his eyes.

It feels good to have life make sense again. Grace, you would love it here. The girls are making it and I think they will be fine. Mom's doing okay but I'm going to have to get help in here soon. This case I'm on is crazy. Like a lot of the Miami cases, this one doesn't make much sense. Everybody involved has a secret and won't talk. God, I miss talking to you. I miss you.

The fresh air, tinged with warmth, blew his hair across his cheek. His hand was slow to rise and rub the long hair. *Grace, I have to get a haircut.* Wilson was nearly asleep, when a squirrel's chatter ballooned to a new pitch. He looked up to see a lone female squirrel being chased through the high limbs by four males. He smiled and felt good.

His mother's car turned into the driveway and stopped in front of the garage. She handed paper towels and napkins to the girls to carry in and motioned for him to come get the rest of the groceries. He kissed the girls on his way to the car.

Once they were in the house and putting things away, Priscilla announced she'd made plans for him for the evening. "I'm staying with the girls and you are having dinner with Shirley Deal and some of her friends. That's an order; you have to have a life, too."

Wilson grumbled under his breath but knew escape was hopeless.

"Mom, I really can't do this. I don't know those ladies too well, and anyway they are much older than I am."

"Listen. It's a chance to get to know some of the people around town. I think that pretty Dianne, the one that works with you down at the station, will be there."

He said he'd planned to spend the evening with the children, but her voice was firm. The girls finished storing the last of the groceries, went into the living room, and turned the TV up too loud.

He called out, "Your brains will turn to mush. Turn it down." He got no argument. The volume dropped by several decibels.

He resigned himself to his fate. "What time?" he asked his mother.

CHAPTER 13

Warm coral tints reflected off clouds as the sun rose over the ocean. The trill of birds and the scents of magnolias and jasmine mingled with the sea air to spread slowly across the sleepy island. At Main Beach, hungry gulls prowled, looking for food. Pelicans formed a long majestic line as they skimmed the breaking wave crests, riding the air currents.

A dozen blocks away, Wilson woke early and lay looking at the ceiling. He was living with three women but he still felt alone. He suddenly realized it was April 18. Tuesday. *Ugh.* He didn't want to go to La Fontaine's funeral.

He dressed in his only suit so he would blend with the crowd, and arrived an hour early to see who showed up and who didn't. He decided to wait until most people had arrived before he would move forward.

Majestic oak trees shaded Bosque Bello's cemetery plots where many of Fernandina's finest, and worst, people were buried. The ten a.m. service was to be simple, in keeping with LaFontaine's wishes. Wilson moved deep under the oaks hoping to find a spot where the sand gnats weren't quite so aggressive. Shortly, he gave up and retreated to his car.

Half an hour later, the hearse came slowly up the drive raising a little plume of lingering grayish-white dust. Dry conditions lately had caused even the grassiest places to yield somewhat to the ubiquitous sand of the island. Wilson watched as the men from the funeral home talked with the grounds workers and, with a lot of gesturing, apparently agreed on the agenda for the morning.

A vivid red cardinal landed on the lower limb of the tree in front of Wilson's car. He listened to the sharp "chip...chip." He remembered that was a call indicating territorial boundaries — or anyhow, that's what a stakeout partner in Miami had told him once. The bird's quick jumps and turns on the branch distracted Wilson until a small white sedan pulled up. The driver got out. The hearse blocked Wilson's view; he couldn't see what transpired, but shortly the man returned to his car. Wilson's eyes followed the unfamiliar vehicle as it circled to a lane leading out of the cemetery.

Two workers leaned against shovels while others laid out green Astroturf to cover the pile of dirt beside the grave. It was a ritual they had obviously performed many times, silently preparing a place for everlasting residence.

He thought back to his wife's funeral and the heartache that surrounded it. He'd gone to a grief counselor, a friend of Grace's, who had spoken bluntly with him. They'd spent many hours together, sometimes just sitting and talking about things that had nothing to do with Grace's life or death. She told him once that the sessions together had been as much for her as they'd been for him. He liked that kind of honesty.

Abruptly, the cardinal flew away, and Wilson recognized Dianne's car pulling in behind his own. He watched as she got out, then slid in on his passenger side.

"Hi." She had on a broad-brimmed hat, blue with a yellow band. It made her look glamorous, though he was certain that wasn't her intention.

"Hey." He took off his sunglasses, and she turned and smiled.

"Been here long?"

"About twenty minutes. It's always interesting to see who shows up at a funeral like this."

"In books, the killer always comes to the funeral to make sure the victim gets in the ground."

"Well, maybe the killer will be here. There're plenty of suspects to go around." Wilson put his sunglasses back on and powered down the windows. .

"That little breeze feels good," said Dianne, as she looked through the little purse she brought with her, found a small compact and checked her makeup. He watched her.

"You know, it's funny." He gave a little chuckle.

"What is?"

"Women go to great lengths to look just right and men throw on a shirt and tie and let the chips fall where they may." He could smell her delicate floral perfume.

"Women do this so other women won't talk behind their backs," she explained, laughing.

He watched her sitting next to him and felt pleased that she was at ease with him. Her dark navy blue suit was just right for the occasion. Her pale skin was smooth with just a touch of blush on her cheeks. "You look lovely," he blurted out before he could catch himself. She smiled.

"Thanks. Oh, here come the first cars."

Three luxury cars pulled past them and stopped. Wilson watched, tapping on the steering wheel with his fingertips and humming an unrecognizable tune. "I don't know any of these people. But I suspect I won't see many people I know."

"Those first two cars held members of the City Commission and the last car is the State Representative."

"I thought LaFontaine asked for a simple service. Politicians. They never miss a chance to glad-hand." He looked at his watch, and two more cars pulled up, "They're a half an hour early. Was the victim big in the political circles?"

"He was at a lot of rallies for local politicians. They courted him because they needed his money to help finance their campaigns. The last arrivals over there are two of the County Commissioners and their wives." She pointed out a group making the hand-shaking circuit with the other early arrivals. They watched in silence for a time.

Finally he opened the door and got out. "I'm going to head on over. I feel a need to snoop."

"Can I do anything?"

He looked over the crowd, then leaned down. "Keep your eyes and ears open." Smiling at her, he shut his door and sauntered toward the gathering people. He found a spot under a large oak tree several yards away from the main group. People were talking in hushed voices; no one took the empty seats under the green graveside canopy. He watched Dianne get out of the car and walk up to a small knot of people. She stopped several times to shake hands with fellow mourners, then joined Wilson. The breeze had increased and the sand gnats had ceased their pestering for now.

"See anything yet?" she whispered.

"No, probably won't. Everyone will be extra careful so's not to attract attention; that's the cat-and-mouse part."

More cars arrived. The funeral directors gave directions for parking along the narrow lane. Wilson noted that just about everyone knew one another and belonged to LaFontaine's generation, except for a few younger men accompanied by strikingly beautiful women. There were also a few older men with much younger women.

"Is the secretary here?" He kept his voice low.

"Yes, that lady over there, Mable Whitcomb." She nodded toward a tiny, neatly dressed woman standing off to one side, talking to a taller woman. "She's been with him for about eighteen years. His first wife did most of the office work, and when she died, he hired Mable."

"Okay, that's her. Bobby interviewed her at the office the day of the murder."

Wilson looked at the woman, whose face was tear streaked. She kept her slight frame rigid. He had an idea that she'd run the office in a very efficient manner. He looked around for the family and took a quick glance at his watch. *9:45. Where, oh where, can they be? This could rival a circus in town.*

Dianne touched his elbow, and she nodded toward the lane. A noisy Camaro pulled into an empty spot.

It was George and Rheba LaFontaine. George had on a dark suit and sunglasses. Rheba walked a few feet behind him. Wilson

slowly shook his head at the sight. The tight yellow skirt came just
to her knees and clashed with the deep cerise of her sheer blouse.
The pair moved towards the canopy. Heads turned and followed
them to where they took their seats. The breeze tossed Rheba's hair
about. She made no move to remove the strands from her face.

I wonder if she is really here today, thought Wilson.

His attention was diverted by a pickup truck pulling in. William
Carless got out, and the pickup continued on around a corner to
park. The driver, apparently not being up for the occasion, stayed
with the truck. Carless went over to stand behind George and Rheba.
LaFontaine didn't acknowledge his cousin but Wilson could see
Rheba turn, give a big smile and say a few words to Carless. His
hair lay flat against his head, glistening in the morning sun. His
outdated double-breasted suit had all buttons fastened. Even though
it was slightly cool, sweat was beginning to roll down the side of his
face. Trying to disguise his discomfort, he gestured towards George
and smeared the sweat with his coat sleeve.

Wilson checked the crowd again. *Cars are still lined up and
no sign of the Widow LaFontaine.* More business leaders made the
rounds of the groups standing around. The sun glinted off a gold
cross on the lapel of the preacher, standing with his hands behind
his back at the mobile podium. The man checked his watch
repeatedly, each time reclasping his hands behind him. Wilson
wondered if the preacher had other important things to do.

Then he checked his own watch for time: 9:50. He estimated
at least a hundred people were standing in the morning sun.
Mockingbirds' calls echoed among the tree branches.

In the last invasion of mourners, Wilson had missed the arrival
of Chief Cabe, who stood next to the State Representative, talking
in low tones. After a few minutes, the Chief moved over where he
could see the seats under the green canopy. He faced Wilson but
gave no indication he saw his chief detective or Dianne. Wilson's
position allowed him to easily see the people he was interested in.

His peripheral vision picked up movement at the cemetery gates.
A red Jaguar convertible eased up the lane at a walking pace. *This*

has got to be out of an Alfred Hitchcock movie. The driver, dressed
in black, sat erect in the seat. The car stopped and everyone turned
to watch. The Widow LaFontaine opened the driver's door and
made an exit that would have brought Hollywood reviewers to their
feet.

A long, shapely leg came out first. Then she stood up slowly.
A black veil accompanied the wide-brimmed black hat. The veil's
edge hung just above the neckline of her low-cut dress, which was
sleeveless but had a delicate black lace overlay flowing down to her
wrists. The hem ended just above the knees, while the lace fell
almost to the ground. The sun penetrated her veil just enough to
glitter off her diamond earrings; they matched the necklace that
positioned itself in her ample cleavage. It had nowhere else to go.

Dianne grabbed Wilson's arm. He suppressed a smile and
whispered, "Be nice." She bit her lower lip. There were murmurs
and whispers in the crowd.

The widow moved in an undulating rhythm, reminding Wilson
of a snake slithering toward its prey, not in a hurry to spook the
target. People gave way quickly, whether out of fear or respect.
She looked neither right nor left but took the seat at the end away
from her stepson and his wife. When Marlene sat, she gave a slight
nod; the preacher closed his open mouth and stepped up to the
podium.

The words barely entered Wilson's mind; he didn't want to
hear them. They were always the same, and he was there to watch
the crowd. He looked at any movement in the crowd, including
people scratching or waving off an errant mosquito. During a
sentimental recalling of La Fontaine's life by the preacher, he saw
William Carless put his hand on Rheba's shoulder, on the side away
from her husband. George didn't move. Rheba covered William's
hand with her's, and Wilson checked the look on the Chief's face.
He was giving Carless an ugly stare. Carless either didn't notice
the stare or didn't care. *Seems Rheba has lots of friends.*

Dianne nudged him again and nodded toward the line of parked
cars. Roger Callahan, with his arm around Lillian, stood beneath

one of the giant oaks that graced the cemetery. They were dressed in their best clothes.

The ceremony ended. People paid their respects to Marlene, who played the grieving widow to the hilt. Rheba took a few steps away to be alone with her cigarette. The quiet chatter dwindled as people left. Carless glared his way past the Chief, joined Rheba and lit his own cigarette. Cabe's stare followed him, only to be broken by a tall man in a light green suit. Their eyes met, and Wilson wasn't sure if he saw Cabe's head give a little nod. The man looked toward George and Rheba, then left.

When the Chief glanced around the thinning crowd, Wilson knew by the flexing jaw muscles that the man was under an unknown pressure. Wilson's penchant for remembering faces rose to the surface; he knew the man in the green suit, but couldn't dredge up from where. The man was out of place for the memory to click in.

Before long, Mrs. LaFontaine moved through the crowd and made her way to the red Jaguar. Sunglasses in place, she glanced at Wilson. He watched her drive around the arc of the lane toward the street. His view was blocked temporarily, but the hat and veil were gone when she zoomed past the entrance, her blonde hair flying carefree in the breeze.

He watched people leave; Rheba and William Carless exchanged waves. George went straight to the car and waited for Rheba. *I'd love to be a fly in that car on the ride home.*

Dianne took off, saying she would see him later. Roger and Lillian stayed until everyone had left, except Wilson himself. They moved toward the men shoveling the pile of sand into the grave. Wilson got out of his car and went over to them, hearing the clipped "chush" noise of the shovels digging in the sand pile. By the grave, Roger removed his brimmed hat.

"Where to now?" Wilson spoke softly.

Trails of tears streamed down Lillian's soft brown cheeks. It was only the second time today that Wilson had detected sadness from anyone. She held a small white handkerchief in one hand and clutched a worn Bible to her breast with the other. She nodded to him, and Roger looked at him with red rimmed eyes.

"Oh, we gonna stay on until Miz LaFontaine either sells the house or gets rid of us. Mr. Robert was smart enough to set aside a little bank account for the runnin' of the place. Miz Lillian has the checkbook Mr. Robert gave her. It's some sort of 'rangement he made with the bank a long time ago. A little money comes in for our pay and groceries for his house each month."

Lillian dabbed her eyes and shook her head, "He never once asked to see the statement or the checkbook."

"You will miss him, won't you?"

"Yes, sir, that we will." Roger gently led Lillian toward their old car.

"Can I drop by and see you later?"

Roger half turned and nodded, and Wilson drove back to the station, wondering about these scenes he witnessed. *Who the hell had cared enough about LaFontaine to wish him dead, much less murder him?*

CHAPTER 14

*I*t is sad to think even here on this beautiful little island there is *reason for murder,* thought Wilson. Yet, here he was walking the murder scene again.

Roger Callahan didn't add anything new, except he had genuinely liked the dead man and that his work as Robert LaFontaine's gardener had been completely satisfying.

"Yes, sir, Mr. Robert was good to a lot of people." He leaned over, pulling an errant weed with his good arm. "Damn weeds, never can get them all."

Wilson smiled. It was the care given to the small details that made life flow smoothly. "I wish I could spend a little more time working in the yard. Most all I seem to do is cutting the grass and raking leaves."

"Yes, sir, it takes time. People don't have time anymore. They hire these boys to come and cut the yard each week, an' they only care about getting' in there, cuttin' the grass and gettin' out to the next yard." He saw another weed and bent over to pluck it, then led Wilson over the soft cushion of grass to an azalea bush, alive with blazing red flowers.

"You know this azalea is something," Roger mused. "It is so full of life when it blooms. Color everywhere, and if it had a sweet smell it wouldn't be able to stand itself." He laughed softly. He eyed the flowers and cupped one in his hand, "Yes, sir, some things are full of life and others just smell." He moved on toward the house, looked at the sky and said, "It's going to be a pretty day, I believe."

"I think you're right." *This isn't getting my investigation anywhere*, thought Wilson, realizing he was beginning to relax in this attractive setting. "The grounds are beautiful, Roger, almost like a park."

"Yes, Sir, I take care of it. I try sometimes to come up with a new variety of plant...orchids actually. Would be nice to have your name attached to something after you're gone. Yes, sir."

"That would be a legacy. Mind if we go in the house?" He asked out of courtesy. He had official access.

"Oh, I don't know. I generally don't go in 'cept for lunch, or when it rains. Anyways, I got to do a little watering over there." Roger pointed out some gardenias.

"That's okay. Is Miz Lillian in?"

"Yes, sir. The only time she missed work is when she had those babies." Wilson raised his eyebrows, questioning his meaning. "All still-born. God got them early," Roger explained, and he moved toward the thirsty gardenias. Wilson watched his measured steps, realizing that this gardener was a person he would love to talk to sometime when the subject wasn't murder.

"Miz Lillian?" Wilson called out through the screen door.

"Come on in!" Her voice came from the kitchen.

He looked back a second to where Roger was watering the gardenias and noticed movement of sheer curtains on the second story of the Upton house. *She never misses a beat. She knows more than she lets on. I've got to learn what she knows, somehow.*

He opened the screen door and entered the back hallway. Off to the right was the kitchen, and to the left, the dining area.

"May I look around a bit more?"

"Yes, sir. Just don't ask me to go with you."

"Yes, ma'am. I'll close the doors to the library." Wilson used his thumbnail to split the seal between the two doors and entered. He spent some time in the room, opening windows to dispel the coppery smell of death, examining all the furnishings and knickknacks. Interesting, but no clue as yet to who killed LaFontaine or why.

The desk was old, massive and ornate. Its top was littered with papers, pens, and memorabilia. The drawers were stuffed with files and office supplies. He'd have someone collect everything and go over it later.

Wilson reopened the double pocket door and stepped into the foyer. He stared across the marble-tiled vestibule to the room where Robert LaFontaine had been killed, trying to picture the moment of the attack. He looked up to see the enormous antique chandelier hanging from a cypress beam 16 feet above him. The lead crystal prisms split light into rainbows even in this darkened area. The candleholders, now electrified, were tall cylinders and penetrated into the tunnels formed by the prisms. Wilson noticed the four mounted deer heads near the ceiling, one on each high wall, almost invisible in the available light.

"Mister Robert got that fancy light when he went to Italy." Lillian appeared in the door from the back hall to the dining room. "He seemed to like those foreign things."

Wilson turned to see her disappear toward the kitchen. Her voice came back, "I'll get you a cup of coffee. I ain't serving it; you got to come back here to get it."

"Thank you, Miz Lillian. I'll be there in a minute." His gaze traveled back to the library and the spot where LaFontaine had lain. The bloodstain was still on the expensive Persian rug, but the stains had been removed from the entryway floor. *Got to be Italian marble.* He wanted to take it all in when there was no one to disturb him.

He played the scenario several times in his mind, then went into the library and looked at the bookshelves. The native cypress paneling glowed with a high polish.

Here we have a man who harbors a secret, shared maybe with one other person. He appreciates fine antiques, art...and women. He's got money and can afford all of them. What was the motive...not robbery, nothing taken...jealousy? I don't think so, could it be control of the business or the treasure map?

He read the titles of the books.

LaFontaine liked the classics all right. The shelves were filled with first editions of many complete works. *There must be a fortune in books here.* He looked closer at the wide, smooth shelves. Dust had settled on the wood, and Wilson wiped a little away with his finger. He called for the housekeeper. She came as far as the dining room door.

"Yes, sir?"

"When did you last dust these shelves? Since Mr. LaFontaine..."

"No, sir. I always dust in there at least once a week. Haven't been in there since the tragedy though and don't plan on goin' in anytime soon, either." She stood tall with hands folded in front of her.

"Yes, ma'am. So, how long before the tragedy did you dust?"

"About four days. Dust gathers in there pretty quick. Mr. Robert liked to have the windows open sometimes and he said he wanted it kept clean because some of those books are valuable."

"Thank you, Miz Lillian." Wilson started looking at the dust on the shelves. He went to the windows, opened the drawn curtains, then returned to the far end of the bookshelves. *Everything is in place and nothing's taken.* He looked along the shelves with the light reflecting off the dusty surfaces. He saw where his finger had cleaned off the offending motes. Shelf after shelf showed a smooth thin layer of dust. Wilson sat in a chair and removed his shoes. The chair he unwittingly selected was a 200-year-old Hepplewhite. He stood on the velvet cushion to look along the top shelves.

Down at the end of the line he noticed a difference in the dust. He pulled the chair to the spot and stood on the chair again to look at the titles. *All by Poe. Goes from here along to there.* He moved close to the shelf and looked at the dust.

There was one spot where a book had been removed and replaced, taking some of the dust with it. He read the title of the thin little book: *The Gold Bug.* He stretched to look at its top, no treasure map sticking out.

Wilson removed the slim volume and thumbed through the pages with care, noting there were no papers hidden among them. *Wonder why that book.*

He stepped down, wiped his footprints off the seat and returned the chair to its original position. He heard Lillian clear her throat and saw her standing in the previous pose, "Your coffee is getting cold, Sir."

"I am coming in right now, Miz Lillian." She returned to the kitchen.

The light coming in the dining room windows reflected off the marbled entryway floor. The shifting light revealed marks on the floor that made Wilson stop and look closer before going into the kitchen. He squatted, leaned one way and then the other, propping himself up with an extended arm, stretching to look at the marble and its marks.

He glanced up to see Lillian at the other doorway. She shook her head and disappeared. He heard her muttering "looks like a monkey dancing." He stood and flipped several wall switches until the chandelier came on. He looked up for a moment, then turned them all off.

Again he called to Lillian and again she appeared at the hall door. Pointing to the foyer tiles, he asked, "What are those marks on the tile, Miz Lillian? Do you know where they came from?"

"Oh, those? A while ago Roger brought in a ladder to change the light bulbs in the chandelier. Scratched the marble something awful. I worked to get them out but it was no use. We have to get someone that works with stone to fix it. I thought Mr. Robert would explode, but just as calm as you please, he said 'Don't worry about it,' and let it go at that. I'm surprised you can see them. I had them almost invisible."

"That hallway's kinda' dark, isn't it?" He sipped on the coffee.

"Mr. Robert had that wallpaper special made, and I kept sayin' it should have been brighter but he insisted it was just what he wanted and for me to never cover it up."

"All those lines and squiggles. Doesn't look like much of a design."

"I told him it looked like kids played with ink markers and couldn't stop. But he liked it an' it's his...it was his house."

"What about that mirror? It looks ancient." Wilson waved the coffee cup toward the hallway.

"Don't spill the coffee in here; come back to the kitchen. You spill that coffee in there, you have to mop it up."

He followed the housekeeper into the kitchen. "What do you know about the mirror?"

"He said it belonged to his great-grandmother. Looks like it too. Can't hardly see yourself in it."

Wilson wasn't getting the kind of information he needed. He tried another tack. "Has Mrs. LaFontaine been back to the house since the tragedy?"

"Only to pack up and leave."

"Did she say where she was going?"

"She didn't say 'boo.' Just got her things and left." Lillian turned away to open the refrigerator.

"Was she alone?" He took another sip of the lukewarm coffee, a little too sweet to his liking, and waited while Lillian sorted through the contents of the refrigerator.

"The day after it happened, that lady police officer went with her upstairs, along with that gentleman."

"Gentleman?"

"Yeah, some young buck she's picked up." She maneuvered a whole chicken onto the cutting board and selected a meat cleaver from the knife rack at the back of the counter.

"Ever see him before?"

"No. He carried two suitcases out to the car."

"What did he look like?"

"Tall, reddish hair, sort of good looking. Didn't say a word." With one swift motion she chopped the chicken in half.

Wilson left her to her cooking and walked to the back porch. Roger sat in the small greenhouse beyond, hunched over the bench, potting an orchid. *I wonder who gets this place in the will.* He waved to Roger on his way out and noticed that the living room curtain twitched at the Upton house.

CHAPTER 15

Driving down Centre Street toward the station, Wilson had an idea at the same time as he saw Marlene LaFontaine disappear into Waas Drug Store. He pulled into the parking place next to hers and waited. When he saw her at the register, he stepped out of the car, hoping to appear as though he'd just arrived.

As she came out he spoke, "Mrs. LaFontaine, how are you?" He couldn't help but notice the change in her clothes. Black was out and white was in. An embroidered silk blouse topped off matching pants that were a little too tight.

She looked at him and frowned slightly, trying to figure out who he was. When she recognized him, her demeanor changed. "Oh yes, Detective Williams, isn't it?"

"Lieutenant Wilson, Ma'am. I wonder if there is anything we at the department can do for you?"

"Just find out who murdered my husband." She reached for the door handle of the bright red Jag.

"Can I ask just a few questions? There are only a few details that we lack so far and it would help."

"You mean conduct an interrogation here in the middle of town?"

"Not an interrogation. Like you, we want to find out who did this."

She stalked to the front of the car where he stood. A ruddy-complexioned young man came out and brushed by Wilson, saying, "Everything all right, 'Lene?"

"Yes. Be with you in a sec."

The young man eased himself into the passenger seat of her car. She slipped on the expensive Foster Grants. "Well?" The honey blonde hair fell in a wave across the right side of her face.

"Who is Robert's lawyer?" He took off his sunglasses and stared into her shaded eyes, his irritation with her now under control.

"Howard Jacobson." came the short answer.

"Have you been back to the house?" He knew the answer but wanted to know what she would say.

"Yes, to get a few things. I plan to move out completely once you people let me back in. I didn't realize it would take so long and, of course, there are loose ends to get tied up. Stuff to get rid of and the like, you know. I'd like to get a place down on the south end of the island. The condo is a bit small for entertaining." She looked at her passenger and smiled. "I like it here on Amelia Island. Now if you will excuse me, we...I have a lot of things to do." She stood at the driver's door waiting for a response.

"You are most gracious. Thank you for your time. Have a nice day." He hoped she'd choke on that about as much it choked him to say it. He returned to his own car as she sped off.

———————•■•———————

Later that afternoon, Wilson entered a beautiful old house just off Centre Street.

"I'm Lieutenant Wilson; I called Mr. Jacobson about an hour ago." He handed his card to the secretary.

"Yes, sir." Using her desk phone, she announced Wilson to LaFontaine's attorney and pointed him toward the tall double oak doors at the other end of the spacious suite.

Inside the private office a nattily dressed man in his early sixties rose from behind a massive mahogany desk and held out his hand. Wilson noted the original paintings on one wall, the pictures of a wife and children on the desk, and several expensively framed diplomas on the wall.

"Lieutenant Wilson, glad to meet you. Any headway on the

investigation? Nasty thing that happened. Robert LaFontaine was a dear friend."

"Not much new. We're still tracking down information. I need to ask a few questions, if you have time."

"Listen, Robert was a down-to-earth guy who made a few bucks and a few enemies along the way, but he also helped many people that were down on their luck at the time and no one knows anything about. He always wanted to stay out of the limelight."

"How long did you know him?"

Jacobson leaned back in the soft leather of his chair, "Oh, twenty- five or more years, I guess. Advised him on some legal matters when he first got the boats."

"Do you know a man named Jack Laffon?"

"My, yes. Who doesn't know Cajun Jack? He's a cagey guy, but he doesn't bother anyone. Is he tied up in this?"

Not waiting for an answer, he continued, "He and Robert were kids together I think. Robert kinda liked ol' Jack. They would be seen together sometimes. Odd, really. Cajun Jack, penniless, and Robert, he had more money than anyone in town and yet the two were friends." Jacobson looked up at the ceiling.

"I understand you drew up Mr. LaFontaine's will."

"Sure did. I filed it with probate; it'll be read in about a week or so, when the State gets back with me. You see, his assets were over $650,000 and the State would appreciate its share. You work your ass off so they can take the pennies off a dead man's eyes." Jacobson tone was acid. "Nice arrangement." Jacobson took a folder out of a side drawer and placed it on the desk.

I'd like to get a look at that file. "I have a minor problem and you may be able to help me."

"What's that, Son?"

"I am looking for a motive, and it seems a lot of people real close to Mr. LaFontaine may have a reason to rejoice at his death. The will may hold a clue as to who would benefit the most." Wilson paused. Jacobson continued to look at the ceiling. "We could get a court order to see the will, but I don't want to chase off any suspects, if you know what I mean."

"Um-hmm, I see." Jacobson steepled his fingertips together thoughtfully and looked inside the folder. "Robert was a generous man, I can tell you that. Even to those who don't deserve it.

"Well, Wilson, I can't let you see the will without a court order, of course. Unethical and all that." He stood and pushed the folder gently toward the Lieutenant. "I have to see my secretary for a minute. Would you excuse me?"

"Yes, sir." He watched the attorney leave the room then reached over and opened the file. "Last Will and Testament of Robert T. LaFontaine." He scanned it quickly, looking to see who got what. No one person benefited hugely from LaFontaine's death. The widow got the bank account; the son got the business; the nephew got a boat of his own; the gardener and housekeeper got the house and Robert's Mercedes plus the money in the household account. *The grieving widow will be pissed about that.*

When he heard the door handle shake, he quickly returned the will to the file. He sat down and folded his hands as Jacobson came in, looked at the folder, and remained standing. "Is there anything else I can help you with, Lieutenant? I do have to get over to the courthouse." He placed the file back into the drawer.

"No, Mr. Jacobson, thank you. If I need anything else, I'll be in touch." He took the offered hand and left.

The secretary cooed a "good-bye" at the tall Lieutenant as he left. Somehow the businesswomen on this island are a lot friendlier than the ones in Miami. He waved, feeling his ears redden at her sexy voice.

CHAPTER 16

How's our newest sleuth doing?" Dianne greeted him at the station. He stopped by her desk. "Nothing new. I did run into the Widow LaFontaine a while ago. She doesn't seem to be in deep mourning."

"That marriage never was a fairytale romance." Dianne laughed, then grew sober. "She never gave a flip about her vows while Mr. Robert was alive, so I guess it matters even less what people think about her now."

She clicked the "save" icon on her computer, and Wilson asked, "So who's the guy I saw her with? He's about half her age."

She shrugged. "Dunno. Just her latest honeybunch, I guess."

He cocked an eyebrow at her choice of words, and she blushed. "Well," she blustered, "'Honeybunch' is a lot more polite than how we usually refer to her latest… um...."

"Honeybunch?"

"Exactly!" And they both shared the laugh. He laughed a lot when he was with Dianne. He looked at his watch and realized he needed to get home. Mom had plans for him tonight. Bidding her a hasty good-bye, he headed for the door.

"See you later," she called after him.

He waved without turning around. "Later." *As in tomorrow*, he thought.

Mom was in high dudgeon, at her fluttery worst, when she met him at the door. "And not a moment too soon!" she exclaimed while he kissed her powdery cheek. "Your dinner's all ready. Just zap it in the microwave. Everybody'll be here by eight."

"Mom."

"That gives you enough time to shower—"

"Mom...."

"—And change into something spiffy."

"Mom!"

He put his arms around her to hold her in one place. "Spiffy? I haven't heard that word in years."

She blushed. "I'm OK, just a little excited, that's all. Go eat. I promise to dither a little more quietly."

The Mesdames Fitzsimmons were the first to arrive, on a cloud of lace and lavender. *Two old maids*, Wilson though. Turned out they were widows of twins, killed together in a mill accident years ago. Mrs. John was tall and bony; Mrs. Jacob was small and bony. *Were there any chubby old ladies in this town?*

Next came Ralph and Flora Stephano, approximately the same vintage as the widows. The unkind thought crossed his mind that this party was going to look more like the recreation room at a nursing home than anything else. Good. Old people got tired early. They'd leave and he would have an hour or two to himself before turning in.

"These are my friends from St Michael's," his mother explained.

He knew the lovely old Catholic Church on Broome Street was a central part of his mother's life. He could recall snatches of its history, but he thought he'd like to explore the grounds of St. Michael's again when he had some free time. Maybe he and Dianne would take a stroll over there some afternoon after work. *Damn! Put work out of your mind and make nice to your mother's friends.* Several more guests arrived over the next half-hour; he was introduced to each one and dutifully made small talk.

He was chatting with a horse-faced woman about the reestablishment of the parochial school, when his mother interrupted. "Son, I want you to meet a dear lady from church."

He turned, expecting to meet yet another elderly parishioner, when he saw a smiling Dianne standing there.

"We've met, Mom."

"Oh? I suppose you have, working at the same tiny place." Mrs. Wilson's speculative glance flitted between the two. *Oh, no you don't, Mom; I'm not ready yet. Although the evening has improved considerably.*

He had introduced his daughters to each person who arrived. They were beautiful, and Prissy liked her assumed position and took to the role. However, when Dianne arrived it was a little different. Wilson called the girls over to him.

"Dianne, you remember my two sweethearts? Prissy and Lisa."

"Yes, I do. How are you tonight?"

Lisa took Dianne's offered hand with a wide smile. Prissy took the hand but didn't smile; she mumbled a "hello" and just stared. Wilson took note of this and quickly offered Dianne a cup of his mother's punch. As they walked away, Prissy whispered something to Lisa.

His prediction about the older guests proved to be true. They were gone by ten, leaving only Dianne behind. Wilson had tucked the girls in around nine o'clock.

"I'm tired, too," his mother announced. "I think I'll go up; you young people can have a quiet chat." She slowly climbed the stairs and they called a "goodnight" to her.

"I've got to fix up the downstairs bedroom for her, and soon."

Dianne covered the awkward moment by gathering a few party dishes. "Kitchen?"

"Back this way." He followed her trim figure with his own load of plates and glasses.

"The girls are adorable," she said as she got the hot water going.

"I apologize for Prissy's attitude. She's not like that normally."

"I didn't notice anything wrong. She's, what, seven?"

"Yup."

"She's right on schedule, then," she laughed.

"Thank God I have a few years before she morphs into a teenager."

Back in the living room, Dianne located her purse and the shawl she'd worn over her light cotton dress. Its sky blue color was perfect for her coloring, he realized.

"Do you really have to go? It's early yet."

When she hesitated, he continued, "I could fix us a nightcap and we could sit on the porch."

She chose the swing and Wilson sat in the nearby wicker chair, so he could see her. The streetlight provided just enough illumination so he could watch the expressions flit across her face.

"Are you up for giving me another history lesson?"

She laughed and sipped her drink. "Don't make it too hard; it's been a long day."

"Two people tonight — one of the Widows Fitzsimmons and somebody else — mentioned the Fernandez Reserve. Sounds familiar, but I can't place it."

"Thanks; that *is* an easy one," she told him with a smile. "That's what we call the little graveyard behind St Michael's."

He cocked his head, unable to visualize a cemetery behind the church. "I know Bosque Bello..."

"No, that's not what I'm talking about. Although they are related, in a way. I mean that wrought-iron enclosure behind the church, facing Fifth Street."

"Oh, yeah. Wondered what that was."

"Maybe because you're always late and have to race to make it before Mass starts?"

He pretended to give her a glare and she smiled before continuing her story. "It's known as the Fernandez Reserve because that's where Don Domingo Fernandez and some of his family members are buried."

"Wasn't he the guy with the charter from the king of Spain?"

She nodded. "One of the last Spanish land grants in America. He named the town after King Ferdinand, who'd given him the grant. In fact, Old Town Fernandina was the last Spanish town platted in North America. 1812, which seems awfully late, but there it is.

"Don Domingo's plantation — Yellow Bluff — was up around

where St. Michael's is today. As a matter of fact, he donated the land that the church sits on. And donated the land for Bosque Bello."

"That's why he's buried on church grounds?"

"And his granddaughter. I love her name: Leonilla Villalonga." She sighed. "I'd love to name a daughter Leonilla."

"She'd murder you in your bed."

They both chuckled, and Dianne slowly rocked the swing. Her face moved in and out of the light, making her seem more ephemeral.

"And does Leonilla have a claim to fame?"

"She sold Senator David Yulee what's now downtown Fernandina-"

"An oxymoron, if ever I heard one."

"Well, yes, after downtown Miami; but don't knock small-town life." When he merely grunted, she went on. "Sold it to him for ten dollars an acre so he could put the starting point for his new railroad there – the railroad he built from here to Cedar Key. Land between here and Old Town was too marshy for the roadbed."

"And Leonilla's buried on the site with her grandpa."

"Yes. And she donated the marble for the altar in the convent chapel."

"How'd you get so up on local history?"

"At one time, I dated a guy — he moved away years ago," she hastened to assure him, "who was a docent at the museum. I helped him with his homework, and got hooked."

"Now, a question about more recent history." His hand brushed at a mosquito.

She groaned. "I'm parched from all the talking, already!"

"More Bailey's?"

"Good heavens, no! Is there any more coffee?" They both settled down with thick earthenware mugs of his mother's strong brew.

"Recent history, you said? All right, I'll try."

"Tell me about the Widow LaFontaine."

She laughed and leaned over to slap his knee. "That's not history; that's gossip!" She took a sip of her coffee. "My second favorite hobby."

Even in the poor light, he could tell her eyes were twinkling. "Marlene came to town ten years ago as Mrs. Edward Carlin. He was some functionary at the mill and believed his own PR. Those two deserved each other. Had to have his 'n' her mirrors, so they wouldn't fight over who went first."

"What happened to him?"

"Divorce. Marlene liked younger men on the side even then, and Carlin finally got fed up, especially when she took up with his assistant. Mind you, he was no prize, either."

"What happened to him?"

"Married some local gal I never heard of and left town."

"Was Meriweather Marlene's maiden name?"

"Nah. That was from a teenage marriage. An auto accident took care of that one."

"So how'd she hook up with LaFontaine? He was a pretty high roller."

"Chamber of Commerce party."

"Say what?"

"That's right. After Mr. Robert graduated from shrimp boat captain to fleet owner, he decided to upgrade his image. Joined the Chamber and went to their networking evenings every month. Marlene was there. She wasn't a member, but could always wrangle an invite and come as somebody's guest, or not. They don't have bouncers at the door, you know. Just walk in like you were somebody."

She paused, then added softly; "She was always very good at that."

Wilson's antennae went up. *Something there.*

Her laugh was embarrassed. "I sound a little catty because she took a boyfriend away from me." She waved her hands in dismissal; "Oh, he wasn't the great love of my life. It just rankled that she could do it. And he wasn't even her main man; she had her sights on Mr. Robert by then, so my guy was just a little recreation on the side."

"What happened to him?"

"Oh, he's around." Dianne shrugged. "Has a fat wife and two screaming kids." Her chuckle was slightly wicked. "Funny, I used to call him 'Studly' because that's how he thought of himself. Looks a little dazed sometimes now, like he doesn't know what happened to him."

No competition from Studly. Wait! Where'd that come from?

"So," she resumed, "Marlene chased Robert LaFontaine until she let him catch her. Their wedding was the talk of the town. Know how they talk about diversity these days? Marlene and Robert invented the concept. Shrimpers, lawyers, mill workers, Plantation people, Chamber, you name it... all attended the thing.

"The bride's dress was a beautiful snow-white concoction she bought up North somewhere. Scandalized everyone!" She giggled. "The reception was at the house, in the garden. Food and drink like you wouldn't believe. Two bands: a string quartet and Zydeco."

They were both silent as they pondered that musical combination. "I can tell it was the social event of the year. Did you go?"

"Of course!" Her lips twitched. "Just walked in like I was somebody!" But then she turned pensive. "But things were different when they came back from a month in Europe."

"Where he bought the sundial."

"How'd you know that?"

He shrugged. "Somebody told me."

"Umm. They had a new garden designed around the sundial, with Roger's input, of course." She seemed to have finished her story of the LaFontaines.

Wilson looked at her, and then realized the sudden lapse in conversation. "You know, back when Grace and I were in Miami, we would come up here and spend time with the folks, but we never got a chance to do much else. Is there anything resembling a night life here?"

"How'd you like to go to a play?" she asked.

"A play. Like at school?"

"No, Fernandina Little Theater is putting on a play written by some local writers. It's a comedy — it's called *The Widow Rapunzel*. From what I've heard it's sold out except for the Friday night performance."

"Sounds like fun. It's been a long time since I've been to a play...other than school plays with the girls."

"Great. I'll take care of the reservations." Dianne looked at her watch and jumped off of the swing. "My, goodness! It's almost midnight! I'll oversleep for sure!" She grabbed her shawl, keys and purse. "I had a lovely time — tell your mama I said I'll call her tomorrow!"

And she was gone.

Later Wilson thought of "Studly" just before he drifted off. He fell asleep with a smile on his face.

CHAPTER 17

Wilson found himself humming as he showered and shaved Wednesday morning. The day dawned bright and clear, a perfect April morning. He could hear Prissy and Lisa as they got ready for school. From the sound of it, they were getting along better; no fights over the bathroom, no whining from Lisa to caused her older sister to snap at her. Perhaps the girls were beginning to recover from Grace's death. The priest in Miami had counseled him that each person heals in his own way, in his own time.

He heard his mother call the girls to breakfast and felt even better. Her stroke had frightened them, her most of all. He had been dismayed to see how fragile she'd acted and how tentative she'd been about attempting the simplest tasks. He had initially thought that the girls might be too much for her, but she had risen to the occasion. Once again, she was in control of her life and her house. Prissy and Lisa had surprised him by how naturally they helped Mom when her weakened left side gave her problems.

So he'd relaxed a little. And that made the three women he loved the most relax a little, too. *Amazing*, he thought, *how time passes and things get better without your noticing.* He washed the lather off of his face and stuck his tongue out at the mug in the mirror. It was also amazing how enlightening shaving could be.

Downstairs, he found his daughters scarfing down eggs and bacon at the same scarred table where he'd eaten his own before-school breakfasts. His mother sat in the same chair she had for the last fifty years, and saluted him with her glass of juice. He kissed all three and poured coffee into his travel mug. His mother only raised her eyebrows; he'd finally convinced her, he thought that he was all grown up and didn't have to eat breakfast if he didn't want to.

"I'll call you later today, Mom, and let you know when I'll be home."

"If I'm not here, just leave a message on the machine."

He grinned as he backed the car out of the drive. He'd brought the answering machine with him, and his mother had been adamantly opposed to its installation. "New-fangled thing; I'll never get the hang of it!" She'd complained. "Besides, where else would I be but here?" Her fears after the stroke had practically made her house bound. Now it was "Leave a message on the machine." *Lots of amazing things this morning.*

Back at the breakfast table Prissy pushed the last of her breakfast around the plate. "Grandma, why does Daddy have to see that Dianne woman?"

Priscilla stopped rinsing off the plate in her hand, "He doesn't *have* to see anyone, sweetheart. He likes her. Don't you?"

"She's okay, but she's not my Mama."

"Honey, no one will ever be your Mama." She looked at her two granddaughters, who were watching her for something else. "Your Daddy loved your Mama and will never stop loving her. God needed your Mama up in heaven to help Him."

Lisa's blonde hair hung at her cheeks, and she brushed it away. "Does that mean Daddy will never find us another Mama?"

"Your Daddy might someday find another woman to love... and may marry her, but he will be sure that you two like her too."

"I like Miss Dianne." Lisa offered, then finished the glass of milk.

"Well, I don't. I think she wants to marry Daddy. I saw the way she looks at him."

Her grandmother stifled a laugh, "And how's that?"

"Well, first of all, she put her arm through his when they went to sit down."

"He was being a gentleman. Offering her his arm to her seat. That's what a gentleman does."

"And then she laughed at his jokes. That's dumb. Nobody understood them. And besides she was looking at him the whole time she was here."

"Well, Prissy, I don't know what to say. She is awfully nice and I think she likes you two. Finish up, it's time for school." She shooed them upstairs to complete the "getting-ready-for-school process."

———————•■•————————

At the station, Wilson smiled as Dianne gave him a cheerful good-morning wave. *Another amazing thing this morning; I'm actually looking at another woman.*

She raised her eyebrows at him. "What are you grinning at?"

"I am surrounded by beautiful women."

She snorted. "And one Chief of Police who wants to see you. Forthwith."

Forthwith. The man had watched too many cop shows on TV.

A few blocks away, Dwayne Peters, a 30-ish drifter who occasionally "worked" as an informant for the local police, sat upright on the spread-out cardboard box. This is where he had spent the night, or at least he sort of remembered it was. Good ole Dwayne was just bright enough to know that he wasn't the sharpest knife in the drawer, but he knew that he had one sonofabitch headache. *Man*, his head hurt; hurt so bad he couldn't see straight. Everything was fuzzy. He was trying hard to remember what happened the previous night to cause such a headache.

Of course, the beer he'd had didn't do nothing for his vision, or his balance, for that matter, he thought. That "Coondog Arliss" had fed him beers like they was celebrating something. And then got mad when he'd said he'd had enough. Turned ugly, he did, and called him a wimp because he couldn't keep up. And smacked him hard upside the head. Probably why his head hurt so much, he thought.

He had to get something for this head before it plumb killed him. He lurched out of the alley and spied bright light. He usually tried to avoid the police, but this was an emergency. Police were supposed to help you, right? Mebbe they'd give him some aspirin.

The desk officer's eyes grew big behind the bulletproof glass as Dwayne tried to come through the front door. It took him three tries, but he finally made it.

Officer Patricia Campbell wasn't all that happy with her desk detail, but her broken ankle severely limited her usefulness out in the field. Now she was trapped behind a service window of bulletproof glass and was charged with handling whatever came through the front door. If she ever ID'd the kid she'd been chasing the night of her accident, he was dead meat. She'd vaulted the chain link fence right behind him, but had landed wrong. She could still hear the pop her ankle had made; tears came to her eyes with remembered pain.

She never took her eyes off Dwayne and his battle with the door as she hit the internal speed dial. "I do not have an emergency up here, but I would like some backup."

Wilson took several steps down the hall and stood just outside the little cubicle where Patricia sat. Evans had heard the call and shortly was standing behind Wilson.

Dwayne swayed and blinked on the other side of the window.

"Man, you got any aspirin? I got me the mother of all headaches!"

"What's with the board?" Wilson asked.

Dwayne blinked, and only then seemed to realize that he was holding a three-foot length of lumber against the back of his head. He flexed his fingers as he turned around, as if he thought he could see behind himself. Wilson, Patricia and Evans shared a look.

"Don' know, man." He slowly rotated again, and the three of Fernandina's Finest could see blood running down the back of his neck.

"Jesus Christ! Campbell, call the EMTs!" Evans barked.

Patricia dialed as the two men went through the door and slowly approached Dwayne with his board. Wilson couldn't pull up a chair for him to sit on because they were bolted around the perimeter of the lobby. "Can you sit on the floor for us?"

"No, man, these are my best jeans! Don' want to sit on no dirty floor in 'em!"

They eyed the man's torn and filthy jeans. He looked like he'd been rolling in a garbage-filled alley, which, in fact, he had.

"It's all right," Evans assured him. "We just scrubbed it."

Dwayne groaned and gratefully sank to the lobby floor. The two men loomed over him and bent to get a better look. Wilson heard Evans suck in air and quickly looked over the head of the smelly Dwayne. Evans pointed to the large nail head flush with the board; its point was obviously embedded in the man's head.

Wilson stepped up to Patricia's window and asked for a blank Incident Report.

He was down on one knee getting Dwayne's particulars when two EMTs came barreling through the door. Evans quickly explained about their impaled visitor. The paramedics were only mildly startled, and after a quick assessment, helped Dwayne and his unusual headgear into the ambulance.

Wilson and Evans watched them pull out, then turned to Patricia; she buzzed them through to the offices. "Thanks, guys. Another morning in paradise."

As they went different directions in the hallway, Wilson said to Evans, "I'll be there in a few minutes, Chief Cabe wants to see me." Evans just waved a hand and disappeared around the corner.

The door to Cabe's office stood open, and Wilson rapped his knuckles on its frosted glass. Cabe was on the telephone, so he pointed to one the chairs in front of his desk. Wilson sat in front of the massive oak desk and entertained himself by looking around. The desk's surface was cluttered with the detritus of a busy man — papers, file folders, pencils and pens. A misshapen pencil cup, obviously made by young hands, held still more pens. The brass nameplate held center stage; it was impressive in its dimensions and workmanship.

The three "I Love Me" walls were filled with plaques and photographs commemorating thirty years in law enforcement. He couldn't tell from this distance, but he imagined there were governors and mayors, city commission members and law enforcement officials, all looking happy to have their pictures taken with the man on the telephone.

"OK, Phil, let me know how it turns out." The Chief hung up and grimaced. "Police chief buddy of mine downstate. Prostate trouble, tests tomorrow." Both men let a tick go by as they contemplated that frightening prospect. "Reason I wanted to see you is that I want to know if anything new has developed on the LaFontaine case."

Wilson gave him a quick update, but there wasn't much new, especially since they'd had this conversation the morning before. And the morning before that.

"That sounds great; just what I'd do." The Chief paused. "But I wanted you to know that I put out a pickup order for Cajun Jack this morning."

"Isn't that a little premature?"

The Chief bristled. "Cajun Jack and Robert LaFontaine had a rocky relationship for years. And Jack is certainly capable of murder, has a ferocious temper he has trouble controlling."

"That may be, sir…" *The "sir" always helps when you argued with your boss.* "But I haven't even seen the lab reports. They're due in some time today. I'd like to see what they have to say –"

Cabe stood up. This meeting was over. "They'll say that Cajun Jack — or somebody with his capabilities — stabbed LaFontaine. Entry wound will have come from someone his height, delivered by someone with his strength."

Wilson could only stare at the man. He was saved from responding to the edict by the telephone. The Chief reached for it with one hand and signaled his dismissal with the other.

The reports from both the ME and forensics were on his desk. But his coffee was cold, and he wanted a minute to process his most recent run-in with his boss. *Has coming to Fernandina been a mistake?* The man's attitude was puzzling, and not a little frightening. To label a man a murderer without evidence was in itself criminal.

Fresh coffee in hand, he leaned back in his chair. Cre-EEE-eak. *Damn. I forgot to bring in the WD40. Again.*

The autopsy report was straightforward, but didn't really tell him anything new. Male, Caucasian, well-nourished, no visible tattoos or scars. Except for the wound, of course, which had been caused by a sharp instrument that had penetrated eight inches into the deceased's right abdomen, going from the bottom right to upper left, just nicking the right ventricle. Death occurred within approximately two to three minutes after the assault. The time of death was late in the evening, probably before midnight.

The knife, or whatever it was, had been two inches wide and had rough edges. Did the ME mean serrated? He'd have to ask. Actual cause of death was exsanguination: LaFontaine had bled to death all over his expensive library rug. Stomach contents were of interest only to indicate that the man had dined and imbibed well in the hours before his death.

The forensics report was no more enlightening. No stray fingerprints were found. They'd printed LaFontaine, his housekeeper, gardener and his widow. Wilson chuckled over that one. Judging from the little contact he'd had with Marlene LaFontaine, Evans — who'd printed her — should have received combat pay. George LaFontaine and William Carless were supposed to come in for prints. No bloody footprints, no foreign soil tracked in. Just sand, like every other house on the island.

He sighed and flipped the report closed. He leaned back in his chair. *Damn that squeak!* It was obvious that this case, unlike others he'd worked, would not be solved by forensics. Not that he doubted the techs, but he'd like to have another look at the library.

———————•■•———————

Lillian Callahan answered the doorbell promptly, wiping her hands on a dishtowel.

"I'm sorry to bother you again, Miz Lillian, but I want to look at a few things."

She unlatched the screen so he could enter. "That's OK, Lieutenant. You just find out who did this terrible thing to Mr. Robert."

They stopped by the closed library door, which still had the police seal on it. "How are you holding up, Miz Lillian?"

"Just fine." She looked away, blinking rapidly.

"How long did you work for Mr. LaFontaine?"

"Over twenty-five years."

"You were practically one of the family, then."

"They *were* my family, 'least he was." She took a breath to compose herself. "If you'll excuse me, I'll be working in the kitchen." She turned on her heel and left him standing in the hall.

He broke the seal on the double doors, then shut them behind him. He pulled out his notebook and compared the room today to the sketch he'd made eight days ago. As far as he could tell, everything was the same as it had been on the morning of the murder, with the exception of the body. That was one hellacious stain on the rug. He knew very little about Persian carpets, except they were expensive. *One this size must have cost the earth. Musta sold a hell of a lot of shrimp to pay for this baby.*

Movement in the garden caught his eye; the gardener was at work, planting impatiens in the bed around the sundial. Maybe he'd be easier to pump than the housekeeper would. He quickly closed the windows and resealed the door.

"Mr. Callahan!" He hailed the kneeling man. Roger looked every bit of his 60 years this morning. The wiry man slowly rose from the edge of the bed, the knees of his gray work trousers damp from the morning dew. They shook hands and Wilson noted sad eyes surrounded by the wrinkles inevitably caused by outdoor work.

"How are you holding up, Mr. Callahan? I know this is a hard time for you."

"You can call me Roger. There is, there *was* only one 'Mister' in this house."

"Roger, then."

"And, to answer your question, I'm not doin' worth a damn."
He looked blindly around the garden. "None of us is."

Wilson nodded his understanding. He'd known Grace since
the second grade, and by the time she died, he'd loved her for twenty-
five years. He gestured toward the impatiens. "Your work must give
you some comfort."

The old gardener shrugged. "Money already spent before he
died." This time his glance around the garden was more critical.
"'Sides, Miz LaFontaine will want the grounds kept up, whether
she keeps the place or sells it."

Wilson detected a little job insecurity mixed with bitterness.
He began a leisurely stroll down one path, and the gardener followed.
"Tell me about all this. Did you lay the brick for this walk?"

"Aye, that I did. An' dug ever' mother-lovin' bed, planted almost
every plant, shrub, and flower." Now pride sounded in the man's
voice; he stood a little straighter, moved a little easier. As they
walked, Callahan named each planting and told its history. "Ya see,
this garden's like a scrapbook, a memory book. Instead of buyin'
touristy stuff, Mr. Robert'd buy something for the garden. That
way, ya see, he could look at something out here and remember
where he'd bought it."

They had come almost full circle to the filigreed table and chairs,
which boasted a fresh coat of white paint, ready for spring. "Now,
take this table and chairs, fer instance. Mr. Robert, he was in
Jacksonville for some meeting or t'other, an' they was fixin' to tear
down one of the old hotels down there, ya know?" Wilson nodded,
and the man continued.

"He called me right then and there to come get this set. Don't
know how much he paid for it, if anything, but he said that presidents
and kings had stayed at that hotel, mebbe sat in these very chairs. A
piece of history, this is." The story ended, he lapsed into somber
silence.

It was broken by the arrival of Lillian, bearing a tray of iced
tea and cookies. "It's a little early for your break, Roger, but I thought

you and the Lieutenant would enjoy something cool."

"Thank you, Lillian, that was right thoughtful of ya. And ya brought my favorite cookies, too. Winn-Dixie bakery?" He winked at Wilson and both men were not disappointed at her reaction.

"Winn-Dixie, my foot! I slaved over a hot cookie sheet to make these!" She flounced off in mock indignation.

"Seems like a nice woman." Wilson reached for a warm chocolate chip cookie.

The gardener could only nod; he'd crammed two cookies in his mouth, and was munching away. A slug of iced tea allowed him to answer: "Mighty nice. Her 'n' me been a team makin' Mr. Robert comfortable for years." He paused. "A lifetime. Three lifetimes, really: hers, mine, an' Mr. Robert's, God rest him."

"I tried to get her to open up to me, but she wouldn't have any of it."

"No, sir, she wouldn't. She was here when I came. Turned out she'd been done so wrong by so many men that she'd given up on us." He looked Wilson in the eye. "An' that's all I'm gonna say about it. Lillian wants you to know more, she'll tell you."

"Fair enough. What about you? What are you going to tell me?"

A shrug. "Not much to tell."

"Were you here the day Mr. LaFontaine was killed?"

"For all the good it did. I'll tell you God's own truth, Lieutenant; I didn't see nor hear nor smell anything else unusual that afternoon. Ol' Cajun Jack came wanderin' up the road as Miz Lillian and I left to go home." His shoulders slumped. "Useless. I felt useless right after *this* happened." He thumped his left arm. "But 'twern't nothin' compared to how I feel now."

Wilson took a big drink of the sweet tea. "Did Cajun Jack see you?"

"Oh, I don't know. He comes and goes. Don't say much but waves to me."

"So he was here in the late afternoon?"

"Yes, Sir, I guess he was. Like I said, we was leavin' to go home and he was on the side street there." Roger pointed to the arched opening in the arbor.

Wilson knew there was nothing he could say to help the man, so he quietly thanked him for his time and left him sipping tea and blinking tears.

———————•■•———————

The office was at a quiet hum when he returned, so he figured there'd been no developments in the search for Cajun Jack. Dianne's shake of the head confirmed it as he passed her door on his way to his back building office.

"I've had a great idea; come back to my office when you get a chance."

He quickly outlined his plan when she showed up a few minutes later. She jumped at the chance to interview the housekeeper. "I've known Miz Lillian for years, just to speak to, of course. Besides," she added with a twinkle in her eye, "it'll give me a chance to work on my interview technique."

They quickly drew up a list of questions for Dianne to use before Wilson drove her to the LaFontaine house. "Stop at Dottie B's along the way," Dianne directed.

He parked in front of the florist's, and quizzed her with a raised eyebrow. "I know Miz Lillian dearly loves roses. Maybe it'll cheer her up, as well as break the ice a little." She soon emerged with one perfect pink rose in a bud vase, complemented by baby's breath and a ribbon the exact shade of the flower.

"We make a great team," Wilson announced as he stopped in front of the LaFontaine house. "My police expertise and your womanly touch."

The punch on the arm was not unexpected. "I'll walk back, thank you. I might stop for lunch along the way."

Lillian Callahan's face lost its frown when she saw Dianne and her floral offering at the door. "Dianne Spears, how thoughtful you are! Come in, come in!"

Dianne followed her into the cool house. They went to the

kitchen, where lunch preparations were underway. "Have you eaten? I was just fixing something for me and Roger. There's plenty, I assure you."

She readily accepted the invitation. Miz Lillian was well known for her good cooking.

"It's nothing fancy, just chicken salad and iced tea. Everyone's been dropping off food, at least two baked chickens, so far. So I thought I'd use one for us now."

Dianne looked around the cheerful yellow kitchen while Lillian took Roger's lunch out to the garden. Robert had taken good care of his housekeeper: top-of-the-line appliances; spacious counters, lots of cupboards. Lillian could — and did — fix simple lunches for three or a gourmet dinner for twenty in this kitchen.

They ate in silence for a few moments before Dianne could bear to interject death into the cheery room. She eased into it by asking how long Lillian had been a part of the household.

"Oh, Lord, child, before you were born!" Her eyes saw into the past. "When Mama died, Mr. Robert just flat-out adopted us. He gave me this job and paid me more than I was worth. My mama worked for his mama and then for him, an' when Mama died he was kind to us. I jus' came to work for him like it was natural." She chuckled, "A *nickel* would have been more than I was worth in those days. I didn't know much about running a house, but I learned real fast.

"And that money supported my family until they could support themselves. Helped the boys, my brothers, with tuition, books, all that. Got them summer jobs, jobs after school."

Dianne suddenly realized that she was probably the first person who'd sat and listened to the older woman reminisce and grieve during these last, terrible days. She felt guilty at her motives for the conversation, but she was going to have to get used to it if she wanted to pursue police work.

When the housekeeper's voice finally wound down, she interjected another of the questions on her list, the one about Mrs. LaFontaine. It was soon apparent that Lillian had misunderstood who she meant. "Oh, she was a saint. She and Mr. Robert struggled so hard during those first years. When they began to have a little more money, I'd do day work at the old place. Then Mr. Robert bought this house, and I came on full time. Tragedy is they only lived in it for a while before she up and died. Worn out, I think." She refilled their iced teas before continuing.

"The second wife, well. Everyone snickered about her behind her back, poor thing. And I'm not sure she was bright enough to catch on. I don't know what they said about Mr. Robert," she mused, "Men don't talk about that in front of us women. At least, they didn't in my day."

"This is a beautiful house." Dianne took a sip of tea and looked around.

"Yes, Mr. Robert loved this place. Always liked to show it off to his friends; he didn't have a lot of visitors but he was proud of this place."

"Did Cajun Jack come by much?"

Lillian's eyes narrowed, "They say he did it. I hope they catch him if he did."

"But did he come by much?"

"Like I said, Mr. Robert didn't receive visitors too much. But about five or six months ago Police Chief Cabe started comin' by kinda' regular, and they'd go into the library and close the doors."

"Did you ever hear what they talked about?"

Lillian sat upright. She gave a quick glare at Dianne, who saw her mistake. "Sorry."

"Mr. Robert's business was his and none of mine. Only once did I hear a raised voice."

"I didn't mean to infer that you listened on purpose. When was it you heard the raised voice?"

"About three weeks ago when the Chief went in there for a long visit. And I don't know anymore about it."

"Did Cajun Jack come by more often lately?"

"He came by once in a while. Mostly for a handout from Mr. Robert. But in the past two months he came a little more often.

They'd go in the library and talk." Lillian sat back again and pressed the blue apron in her lap.

"Did they ever argue...that you may have overheard?" She finished her glass of iced tea.

"No ma'am, in fact they laughed a lot."

A bright red cardinal came up to the bird feeder, and they both watched as it sang a few notes and pecked among the seeds.

"You don't recall anyone coming the day before..." Dianne's voice trailed off.

"In the morning, Police Chief Cabe, and then as I left in the early evening, Cajun Jack was comin' by. We left before he did; no one else that I can remember."

She lapsed into silence, and Dianne gently prodded her. "And the third Mrs. LaFontaine?"

Lillian rose abruptly from the table and gathered the sandwich plates. She clattered them into the sink, returning with a plate of bakery pastries someone had dropped off. "That one!" She sighed and lowered herself into her chair again. "Treated me and Roger like nothing more than the hired help!" That made her smile; "Which we are, of course, but still a little more than that, I should think!"

Dianne nodded, and the housekeeper continued. "Very demanding. And nothing, and I do mean *nothing,* was done right and never a please or a thank you. I remember one time, she had some of her snooty friends over, and one of them dropped an entire plate of food on the big Kerman rug in the dining room. Mr. Robert brought that thing back from his trip to Persia, you know.

Dianne smiled, just as if she knew what a Kerman was. She'd have to sneak a peek on her way out.

"Anyway, Mrs. LaFontaine says, 'Oh, never mind, the *girl* will clean it up!'" She was obviously still scandalized by the woman's choice of words.

"Is Mrs. LaFontaine here now?"

"Of course not! She's in her condo on the Plantation that she badgered poor Mr. Robert into buying!"

"Is anyone staying with her?"

The housekeeper snorted. "One of my friends calls her Madonna because she always has somebody hanging around. Some of 'em stay at the condo, and then she 'visits' them."

"Has she been back since that Wednesday morning?"

"She's come by a couple of times, has a temper tantrum because she can't get into the library, and leaves. It's almost like there's something in there that she wants."

"I've heard Mr. Robert had a treasure map," Dianne started. This was a crucial question on their list, and she had to tread lightly. Wilson had warned her that everyone got nervous whenever a map was mentioned. "Do you think that's what she's after?"

She was shocked at the fear she saw immediately in the other woman's eyes. "No! I mean, that's ridic..." Lillian stopped short, "Everyone's always talking about..." She rose abruptly from the table.

Dianne's glass was empty, and she'd been planning to ask for another refill to prolong the interview. But Lillian gathered up both of their empties and took them to the sink.

"Thank you for the rose, Dianne; that was thoughtful of you." Dianne let herself be escorted from the kitchen and the house. *Darn! She'd forgotten to check out the rug in the dining room.*

She barely made it to the ladies' room at the station. She was going to have to learn to *sip* during interviews. Her professor had never mentioned that particular interview technique.

Wilson was loitering in the hallway when she emerged. She led him back to his office and gave him an almost verbatim report. He had the bad grace to laugh when she shared her insights about consuming liquids during interviews.

"Since you've done so much to help, how about I treat you to dinner at the Down Under tonight?"

Before she could open her mouth to accept, he hastened to explain; "It's not really a date, but a reward for your extra duty, and the discomfort it caused you."

Drat! She thought.

"Do you know everyone in town?" Dianne had been greeted

by name at the restaurant, and they had been given a prime table.

"Only if they have something I can eat or drink." She laughed.

As he worked his way through the seafood platter that she'd recommended, he brought up the subject of treasure maps again. "Why does everyone get so nervous when this topic comes up?"

She shrugged as she forked shrimp into her mouth. "You have to understand that there have been a lot of stories about them on the island; they've been around for decades." She took a sip of white wine, and continued; "Some people took them seriously and almost drove themselves nuts trying to find pirate loot.

"One lady, about ten years ago I think, called the police in the middle of the night; thought she had a prowler. It was two slightly tipsy guys trying to dig up her back yard to find pirate gold." She let out a peal of laughter. "Turned out they'd been holding the map upside down!"

He started to laugh, but she held up her hand. "Wait, there's more. A couple of nights later, somebody else called us about prowlers; it was the same tipsy guys, only this time they had the map right-side up!"

Over coffee and a shared slice of key lime pie, she grew serious about the subject of pirate treasure and maps. "If you really want accurate information on all of the legends about pirate treasure, why don't you let me set you up with the island expert? He'll be able to answer any questions you might dream up on the subject."

"Sounds good. Who is he?"

Dianne thought for a minute. "You know, we've called him Cap'n Denny for such a long time, I'm not sure what his real name is. But I know how to find him. Would tomorrow afternoon be soon enough for you?"

"You make the arrangements, and I'll be there. How 'bout O'Kane's for a quick sip?"

CHAPTER 18

Wilson and Dianne left O'Kane's about 11 o'clock. The evening was pleasantly cool and he opened the car windows to let in the salt-tinged air. Cicadas screeched tunelessly. He eased the Volvo across Centre in the direction of Dianne's house, savoring the silence in the car after the bustle at O'Kane's. He liked rock music, the standards anyway, when they were done well, and the local trio was good. But it was nice to be alone now with his companion.

He glanced at her as he drove. The silence between them was comfortable and he was reluctant to break it. He admired this woman more and more, for instance, the way she interviewed Lillian Callahan that afternoon. She used words economically, but never without kindness. He liked that in a woman. He thought of his wife, Grace, less often now, less than right after she died, at any rate. *There's a surprise. Maybe I'm ready... getting ready anyway.*

Dianne's profile drew his eyes a second time. *I don't like sleeping alone, being alone, and raising the girls alone. Thank God my mother is helping, but she's not a wife.* He breathed deeply and looked west at the next road. His antennae twanged abruptly. He could see something he didn't like through the trees, something worrisome. He steered the Volvo to the side of the road.

"You in any hurry to get home?"

She shifted in the seat and turned to him. "What do you have in mind? A drive out to the beach to watch the moon rise?"

He matched her grin briefly, then sobered. "Just now, when we passed Seventh Street, I thought I saw a light at LaFontaine's house. Mind if we check it out?"

"Ever the detective, aren't you?"

He reached across the console and gripped her arm briefly, warmly, in a sort of wordless apology, then swung the Volvo around. He parked in the deep shadow of a nearby oak. The twisting giants were everywhere on the landward side of the island.

"I'll be right back," he murmured.

A flashlight beam jerked to and fro behind the sheer curtains of the wide front window. Wilson moved deliberately across the lawn and mounted the steps of LaFontaine's broad front porch. *I thought so. Nice peripheral vision, there, chum*, he commended himself. In retribution for that moment of self-satisfaction, a board creaked loudly beneath his weight and the flashlight went out.

He cursed gently. He leaned into the shadow of the house, tense and ready for action. *Someone should be making a hasty exit shortly.* A sudden movement from behind made him shift his weight to see who was there. Within a millisecond, he staggered, recovered, started to twist around as the glancing blow knocked him to the deck of the porch.

What the hell? He struggled to his feet. His assailant was gone, off the porch and into the garden in a crash and rustle of leaves. Someone screamed, shrill and indignant and shouted out, "Police! Police!" It was Mrs. Upton's voice.

"I *am* the police, Mrs. Upton, it's Lieutenant Wilson! Everything's okay. *And* thank you." He muttered the last words to himself. He heard the slam of a car door followed by Dianne's footsteps against the wooden porch steps.

Her hand trembled on his arm when she reached him. "Who was it? What happened? Are you all right?" Her fingers examined his face and head in the darkness. He stood, obedient as a retriever, stunned by the pain and surprise of the attack. After a moment she wiped her sticky fingers against her shirtsleeve, compressed a handkerchief against the wound and led him away from the house. Wilson covered her hand with his own, took the compress from her, and waited for his vision to clear.

"What happened?" She said again, studying him in the faint light of a distant antique streetlight. He covered what little there was to tell and asked her what she'd seen.

"You. Then a second shadow that came from the end of the porch, where it bends around the corner of the house, and then went through the hedge into Mrs. Upton's yard. You heard her scream, no doubt. I called for a zone car."

No sooner had she said the words than two zone cars pulled up, and uniformed officers crossed the lawn. Wilson asked them to see what had been disturbed inside and to secure the house. Meanwhile, he had some questions for Mrs. Upton. He asked the female officer, Sarah Grant, to accompany him. "Because of the lateness of the hour," he said, and invited Dianne along, too. "Unless you'd rather wait in the car?" He knew the answer to that one, though.

The Upton house was not so much a home as a maze of cat perches. The walls were lined with mahogany buffets cleared of the usual bric-a-brac. High, round tables stood ready at every window, strategically placed to catch the sun's rays, convenient for catnaps. Now, with midnight closing in, the rose chintz covered chairs in the parlor were filled with the curled-up sleeping bodies of cats.

"You ought to be looking after that wound, Mr. Wilson. Bleeding like it is," Mrs. Upton said, without offering aid. She picked up one of the slumbering cats, put herself in its place, and stroked it as it lay in her lap. Wilson and Dianne followed her example, but the policewoman remained standing, ostensibly to take notes, more likely to save her uniform from cat hairs.

"A couple of questions, then I'll have it looked at, Mrs. Upton." Wilson said without raising his voice, in deference to his aching head.

Mrs. Upton recounted her evening in great detail, what she'd had for dinner, how she'd stored the leftovers for the cats' meal the next day, the fact she'd watched television in the early evening, never napping, alert to any outside sounds, and how she'd gone to the kitchen to make a peach pie.

"Georgia peaches are good this time of year, you know. Big and juicy, they were, for this early in the year." She'd put the pie in the oven, heard a noise, and watched from the east window as the man went up onto the porch and crawled in through the window, right into the LaFontaine's living room. She smelled her pie, went back to the kitchen to check on it, and no sooner did she get back to the window than the man was hot-footing it through her hedge. Limping and hopping, he'd run off down the side yard. She'd screamed, plenty, and scared him off, too. She didn't want him coming into her house. Someone must have heard her, because she wasn't the one who called the police.

"You can check on that, young woman. Where the call came from and all," Mrs. Upton told the policewoman, who merely smiled.

Cat in hand, Wilson wandered into Mrs. Upton's kitchen, followed by the lady herself. Yet there was no lingering scent of peach pie. He touched the oven door. It was stone cold. The intruder had run by half an hour ago. "Hot-footed it through the hedge, limp and all, hmmm?" Wilson wondered aloud. Mrs. Upton nodded vigorously.

He strolled back to the front room to check the angle of view from the east window. He had to lean awkwardly across a square table with a tooled leather top in order to look out.

Mrs. Upton escorted the trio to the door. "He had a bad limp. Remember that. I want to help all I can, don't you know."

"Which leg was he favoring?" Wilson asked.

"Left...I, think. It was so dark. No, the right. Or was it the left?"

"If you remember for sure, Mrs. Upton, you let me know. Here's my card with my telephone number on it." She put the card under the Tiffany lamp. "Was there any chance that you were in your bedroom when you saw that man run through the yard?"

Mrs. Upton looked puzzled for a second, then surprised, "Maybe I was. It was yesterday I made that pie. Why, you're so clever, Lieutenant. It's so late at night. Sometimes things get a little jumbled," she said with a big smile.

Eventually her statement was clarified and read back to her, and they were out the door and on their way home. As they stepped off her porch, they heard two dead-bolts hit home. Dianne wanted to drive him home but he said he would be okay. They parked outside her house and she insisted he come in and let her tend to his injury.

Her hands were warm on his skin as she cleaned away the blood and applied a salve. She dabbed at little flecks of blood on his shirt.

"Oh well, there goes the shirt," he said.

"Nonsense. Your mama can get that out in a heartbeat and speaking of heartbeats, how about a nightcap? Mine could use some calming down."

"Sure," Wilson replied wearily. His own racing pulse had more to do with her soft touch cleansing his cut and the light cologne she wore.

"It's a Zinfandel; for medicinal purposes." She smiled, pouring the wine. They laughed over Mrs. Upton's ephemeral peach pie. Wilson admitted aloud that the Chief might be right about Cajun Jack. The man was small but strong. Maybe strong enough to deliver the eight-inch deep wound that killed LaFontaine. And he had a limp. If it was Cajun Jack poking around inside, perhaps there really was a treasure map waiting to be found.

After a moment of silence, Dianne asked, "How's the head?"

"It's okay, just a little sore. Had worse when I played soccer."

"Do you still play?" She took a sip of the cool wine.

"No. Finally had to give it up. Got really clobbered one year. My boss and my wife both laid down the law."

"Her name was Grace, wasn't it?"

"Yes, Grace Danielson. Met her in the second grade. Love at first sight. For me anyway," he laughed. "She was into unicorns and Barbie dolls, and couldn't be bothered." He knew they'd have this conversation sooner or later. Looked like it was going to be sooner. *Might as well finish it.*

"I backed off in junior high, after my old man told me she'd be more interested if I acted like I wasn't." Dianne grinned and nodded. "Took her to the freshman prom." Now he grinned. "Blew six months' savings on a dinner and limo." His eyes focused on that night long ago. "She was the most beautiful girl at the dance."

"No corsage?"

He laughed again, and she saw how handsome he could be when he relaxed. The tinge of gray at the temples added to his good looks. "Oh, yeah; she loved gardenias, and I gave her the biggest corsage I could find." He paused. "I put a blanket of them on her casket."

It got so quiet, they could hear the mantle clock ticking.

"We'd been married ten years when she found the lump, about three months after Lisa was born. And then everything went to hell. Doctors, chemo, radiation. They took the left breast off, and said they'd gotten it all." He stared at the wine in his glass. "Grace was devastated. Hell, what's a breast? I'd have taken her with no arms or legs." His eyes were haunted; Dianne was sorry she'd probed. He roused himself, and continued, "She got into Bosom Buddies, for breast cancer survivors."

Dianne nodded. A couple of her friends wore the organization's pink bows.

"She felt better then about herself. Went in for regular checkups like you're supposed to. It spread. They took off the other breast. More chemo. No good. It had metastasized, became inoperable."

He leaned back in his chair, consciously making himself relax. "We did all we could those last couple of months. Went places she'd always wanted to see, looked up old friends we'd lost track of. Even went to our high school reunion."

He was no longer in her living room; he was with Grace. "Finally, the day came when she said, 'it's time,' so she went into a hospice. They were wonderful. Worked on me as much as they worked on her. A week later, she died in my arms."

The mantle clock struck midnight and they both jumped. He downed the last of the wine.

"So, now I'm here. I moved out of Miami to get Prissy and

Lisa closer to their grandmother and me into a quieter job. With more regular hours." They both laughed softly at that.

He raised his hand and wiped the tear from Dianne's cheek. He whispered, "I have to go."

She followed him to the door. He stepped off the porch, headed toward the Volvo, then paused as he felt her eyes on him. He was drawn back by a small, tight frown between her eyes. "I'm fine. Really. The headache's gone. Almost. It wasn't a solid hit," he reassured her. He wrapped a comforting arm around her and gave her a quick hug, surprising them both. Raising her face to his, she brushed his lips with a kiss.

"Goodnight. Be careful," she whispered. She gave him a gentle push in the direction of the street.

This time he walked to the car without turning back, his thoughts shut down by the throbbing headache on the right side of his skull.

CHAPTER 19

The Chief called Wilson into his office early the next morning. "How's your head?" he asked.

"It could be worse. I guess word gets around fast in small towns. How'd you find out?"

Cabe looked pleased with himself. "Read last night's reports, soon as I got in. Mrs. Upton has an imagination that doesn't quit, huh? Don't lay too much stock in anything she tells you, Wilson. That's a good first lesson in island detecting."

The Chief waited a beat as if he expected his new Division leader to argue with him, then he plunged into the business at hand. He lifted a tall stack of files from his desk and held them out to Wilson.

"What's this?"

"Take 'em, look 'em over, and get back to me," the Chief ordered.

"And they are...?" He kept his hands in his pockets.

The Chief set the pile back on his desk. "Crime reports for the past twelve months. They'll give you a good introduction to the kinds of problems we run into here. Besides, Orlando PD wants some info on a man they have in custody, a pedophile who may have lived here. We need to check and see if we have anything on pedophiles in the area. Not much of interest to you, I expect, after Miami."

"And when am I supposed to do this?"

"I'm taking you off...."

"No, the hell, you're not. By God, Chief, I didn't move up here to be dismissed from my first case. Anyway, I'm making progress. Last night..."

"Last night you scared off a prowler, someone local who knew the place'd be empty and thought there might be a high end TV or camcorder in it for him. I have an APB out for Cajun Jack. He's our man. Your work's done. Finished. *Obierto*, as they say down in Miami. Evans is taking over the last of it." His voice graveled with scorn.

"Now take these damn files and give me some ammunition for my next budget fight. And fax the child molester info to Orlando; Dianne has their number." His muscles bulged tight against the fabric of his shirtsleeves as he thrust the pile at Wilson again.

This time Lieutenant Wilson took it and left the room without a word. He didn't intend to cut short his investigation but big-town politics had taught him one thing: when you're in a hole, stop digging.

———————— • ■ • ————————

Back at his desk, he finished out the morning by sorting through the files. He highlighted the entries for all missing files with a neon pink marker. According to the yellow Post-It stuck to the list, the missing files would be found on the new computer system, an on-going project.

He had two stacks, one for misdemeanors and one for felonies, not for any big logical reason but because the project was monotonous. He subdivided the misdemeanor files into slim and thick, again for no good reason, and flipped randomly through the thicker ones looking for God-knows-what. Moving the files around on his desk gave him time to think about how to continue investigating the murder without the Chief's getting wind of it.

Wilson's direct line rang. *This has to be a wrong number; I'm so new, no one knows I'm here.*

"Leon, 'zat you? Where you been, boy? I need you!"

"No, ma'am, I'm not Leon. This is the Fernandina Beach Police Department. Can I help you?"

There was a slight pause before the querulous "Where's Leon?" came back at him.

"He's no longer with us, ma'am." Wilson could hear the old woman's sniffles.

"Oh, Lawd! He's dead! Who's gonna help me now?"

"No, no! He's not dead, ma'am! He's just moved to Miami. *Way to go, jerk; you've just made an old lady cry.*

Dianne appeared in his doorway, and he rolled his eyes. She disappeared. *Chicken!*

"But Ah needs him! Bad! He tole me to call him whenever I had The Problem."

"I'm his replacement. So you can talk to me."

There was another pause while she digested his offer. "What's your name, boy?"

"I'm Lieutenant Wilson. What's your name?"

"Wilson your first name or your last?"

"My last. And yours is?"

"You related to the North Carolina Wilsons?"

What is it with these Wilsons in North Carolina? First, Mrs. Upton, now this one. "Yes, ma'am, but my family's from the Miami area. What's your name?"

"Miami! Full a' them Cuban Librarians!"

He snorted his coffee. His unidentified caller had just put a whole new slant on the political chant of *Cuba Libra!*

"Never mind about them now; my name's *Miss* Hattie Parks an' Ah lives on Tenth Street. Do you know where that is, boy?"

"Yes, Ma'am. And what's happening on Tenth Street that has you concerned this morning?"

"Aliens!"

Wilson removed the receiver from his ear and looked at it. He sighed and returned it to his ear.

"I been havin' terrible trouble with them aliens all winter, an' Leon was helpin' me. They settled down some, here lately, but they're at it again!"

"What are they doing, Miss Parks?"

"Throwin' trash and garbage all over my back yard! I works hard to keep this place up an' they're jus' *trashin'* it! You gotta come over here an' stop 'em!"

Aliens. Great. I'm in a strange town with a prominent murder victim, a bogus report the Chief has foisted off on me, and now space invaders. I should have been a shoe salesman.

Miss Parks gave him her address along with detailed directions. He promised to drop by shortly. He grabbed his jacket and headed out, going by Dianne's office first.

"Do you know a Miss Hattie Parks?"

Dianne's eyes lit up. "Aliens?"

Uh-oh.

"Miss Hattie Parks and her sister Mary live side by side on Tenth. They're sisters, never married. They both used to live in the family home — and Miss Mary still does. But she's so mean that Miss Hattie made her nieces and nephews buy her the house next door."

"How'd she manage that?"

"She called each one of them every time Miss Mary did something hateful to her. The kids finally bought the other house so they could have some peace."

His eyebrows rose. "No," he said.

Dianne laughed, "Yes, there're about ten of them, all told. One night Miss Mary put the toilet seat up when she went to bed. Miss Hattie washed her butt about 3 a.m. and called every one of them to report the latest outrage." Wilson chuckled, and she delivered the punch line: "It happened four nights in a row."

Miss Parks was standing on her porch as Wilson pulled to the curb. The house was a shotgun style, built around the turn of the century, and in excellent repair. It had been painted a blinding white a few months before, and the bright blue trim gave it a festive air.

"Miz Hattie?"

"Open that gate an' come in so Ah can show you what's happened this time!"

Wilson opened the blue gate and found himself on a newly

poured concrete walk that bisected the immaculate yard. The porch deck and steps had been painted to match the house trim and gate. The beds that bordered the white picket fence and the front porch were filled with spring bedding plants, blooming riotously and threatening to take over the new sidewalk. He stopped about halfway up.

"I'm Lieutenant Wilson. Let's see what your problem is."

"Hrumpf." She turned into the house, the screen door slapping behind her. He followed her through the house out to the screened-in porch at the back. Typical of the style, the house had no central hallway. He glanced around as he passed through the living room and kitchen; each was spotless, furnished with ancient furniture and appliances. He assumed the alcove off the living room was her bedroom, with a bath tucked in somewhere.

Miss Hattie was already standing in what had once been her pristine back yard. The yard was filled with flowering plants. The jarring note was four large trash bags, which had been tossed near the fence and had split on impact, and whose contents now decorated the beds of impatiens and roses. The more delicate plants had been crushed.

"See? Aliens! They come in the night when I'm asleep an' leave their trash!"

Wilson surveyed the mess, his earlier amusement with Miss Hattie's "aliens" forgotten. This was mean; it targeted something that the old woman obviously worked hard on and prized. "Yes, Miz Hattie, you have a problem. Have you been feuding with anyone?"

She was scandalized at the question. "No! I'm a gentle person! Ever' body loves me! That's why it's gotta be them aliens! Ah saw a program on TV!"

Wilson turned when he heard the back screen slap. Four of the largest black men he'd ever seen were headed his way.

"Aunt Hattie! You all right? Why's this white man standin' in the middle of your back yard?"

Wilson quickly introduced himself to the oldest of Miss Hattie's nephews.

"Where have you been?" She screeched. "Ah called your mama at seven an' it's almost noon! They could 'a had me in their space ship by now!"

Raymond, the oldest, exchanged a look with Wilson. "You know Momma. First we had to clean up, then she fixed us breakfast — "

"Take out the trash," Rashid offered.

"I had to go get her some stamps," added Reginald.

"And I had to go to Wal-Mart to get her prescription," Robbie finished.

Clearly the mother of the Four R's had not been impressed with the urgency of Miss Hattie's alien problem. Wilson retrieved his camera from the car, photographed the mess, and was filling out the incident report when a new voice interrupted his investigation.

"What's goin' on over there?" Six heads turned to the small woman on the other side of the fence that separated the two yards. Her white hair framed her face and her weathered nut-brown face was filled with curiosity.

"Just never you mind, Miss Busybody! Got back inside and leave us alone."

"Hey, boys! When y'all gonna come see *me*?"

"Hey, Aunt Mary. We'll be over in a little while." Raymond ignored the groans from his brothers.

Mary saw the trash in her sister's yard. "Hee, hee, hee! They got ya good this time! Them aliens done it again, huh?" Miss Hattie glared at her, her jaw jutting forward.

He left the Four R's to clean up and slowly drove back to the station.

Wilson entered the office, calling out, "Evans?"

A chair slammed back on its four legs and Charles Evans appeared at his door, "Yes, Sir?"

"What's with Miss Hattie?"

"Aliens, Wilson. Your everyday variety. We can't catch 'em." Evans offered to handle the filing of the report and he handed over his paperwork gratefully.

"Why me?" Wilson groaned and went into his office. He looked at the cold coffee in his cup while he sat down. He propped his feet on his desk and looked at the stack of folders again. He'd ask Dianne to keep him up-to-date on anything new that passed through her hands. *If anything, it's strange that the Chief isn't inclined to investigate further. What is it he isn't telling me? There is something new about the Chief's attitude, too. He was friendly at first, pumping me up to make the move up here, flying me up to Fernandina Beach to look around and then hiring me on the spot. Now he's got me on this crappy demographics project. I'd give a hundred bucks to know what's changed his mind. Like they say, he's got a mind like a steel trap, all right, clamped tight and rusted shut.*

He spent half an hour on the thick files, then he turned his attention to the stack of slimmer ones. He figured to give them a quick look-over and try to make a dent in the project before lunch. The third file of the bunch rewarded his optimism.

It belonged to George LaFontaine, Robert LaFontaine's son. The rap sheet inside covered a rash of recent specding tickets, a busted headlight a few months back and some other minor traffic violations, but no entries went back more than a year and there were none for drug violations. *Curious, there was a distinct scent of marijuana in the house when I interviewed George and his wife, Rheba. The folder itself is curious too. It bulges out of shape at the bottom, as if it once held a lot more papers.*

Picking up his Miami skyline mug, Wilson stretched and strolled over to the main building. He drew himself a cup of coffee and wound up at Millie's desk. The clerk cut short her phone conversation as soon as he walked up.

"Millie, is this all we have on George LaFontaine? Looks like his file's been cleaned out. Know anything about that?"

Millie worked her mouth but no words came out. She looked as if she was editing what she intended to say, and that wasn't the version Wilson wanted to hear.

"Okay, what do you know that you can say?" He pressed her.

The woman reached for her glasses, which she wore on a bola cord around her neck, and took the file from his hand. "Far as I can tell, you've got all we have. Looks the same as when I pulled it two days ago for the Chief. You got a problem with that?"

"Only that according to this file George LaFontaine has never been arrested, much less convicted on drug charges."

She shrugged. "You got that right. Talk is, he gets busted. But we never see the paperwork in here."

"And that's normal, is it? No cause for me to ask questions?" Wilson crooked an eyebrow at her, expecting at least a flicker of reaction from her. But she kept her face straight, then the phone rang, and she turned away to take the incoming call.

It was Wilson's turn to shrug his shoulders. He'd decided to stay in the office over lunch, leave early and take Prissy and Lisa on the evening bike ride he'd been promising them. The possibility that George might have killed his own father stiffened his resolve to stay friends with his own daughters. Murder did that to a man. That and the fact that he genuinely loved them. He'd take them on a ride through Fort Clinch, with Prissy on her new trail bike and Lisa riding tandem on his own.

When Dianne phoned and asked him to lunch, he surprised himself by saying, "I'm busy now. How about dinner tomorrow night at Slider's?"

"Fine. By the way, I got hold of Captain Denny and he can see you this afternoon at two o'clock. Stop by and get his address.'

"Great, I'll pick it up before I go."

Wilson put the files aside and removed the large envelope from his desk containing the crime scene photos Evans had taken. He spread them out on his desk and studied them once again, looking for something he'd missed. Homicide photos are always gruesome; there is never a good-looking murder. *I'm overlooking something.*

He propped his feet on the well-worn desk. He scanned the photos, one at a time. *Body from left side. Body from right side. Body from feet first. Body from head first. Library looking at body. Foyer looking at body. Entryway looking at body. Chief about to step on blood on floor. Man, what a screwed up look on his face. Chief stepping out of blood. Left hand of victim. Right hand of victim. Shoes of victim. Face of victim.* He tossed the photos on the desk and checked the time. He looked at the ceiling for a few minutes, then placed the envelope in the drawer.

The phone rang. He hesitated; it could be Miss Hattie again. "Investigations, Wilson."

"Investigations Wilson, are you sure about lunch?" Dianne's voice came across the phone.

"Ah...." He looked at his watch and reconsidered his earlier decision. "You made me an appointment with Captain Denny in an hour. It'll have to be quick."

"No problem. Meet me at my car."

Dianne was sitting in the car when he arrived. "Where we headed?"

"T-Ray's. Best burger in town."

"Haven't heard of it. Where is it?"

"At the Exxon station."

"Wait — we're eating lunch at a gas station?"

"You just wait and see. Remind me before we leave, I have to order the Chief a barbecue special. He heard me talk to Millie about going."

"To the gas station?"

"Yeah, he's crazy about their barbecue sandwiches."

"From the gas station?"

"You got it, buster." Wilson shook his head until the movement threatened to renew his headache. The food scene in Fernandina was a far cry from Miami's.

CHAPTER 20

After lunch, he found himself traveling the unpaved roads of Old Town, an area that was fast becoming as familiar to him as the downtown business district. He parked his car on Estrada Street, across from the Plaza San Carlos, looked at the vacant lot, and tried to envision Spanish soldiers marching on the parade ground in the hot Florida sun four hundred years ago. Had they really worn that metal armor he saw in all the paintings? The soldiers had his sympathy.

He turned toward his destination, a rose-colored Victorian home with all of the accouterments of its day: ivory gingerbread trim, a turret, and a white picket fence. It was built in the late 1800s, long after the Spanish had left, but still a venerable old lady. Diane had told him a little of its past. It'd been built for Captain James Bell, one of the first harbor pilots to come to Fernandina after the Civil War. A Captain Downes, who'd been born on a Cumberland Island plantation, bought it from Bell. Its official name was the Downes House, after its second owner. Its turret stood three stories high. He knew the view over the Amelia River would be spectacular. Maybe his host would offer a peek from its windows. *So I finally get to see Pippi Longstocking's house.*

He rang the bell and waited. Just before he rang again, he heard, "I'm coming! I'm coming!" Dianne had warned him that the Captain would be crotchety.

The door opened, and Wilson stood there, speechless. The man was every boy's dream of what a pirate should be. He was tall and lean, with wispy white hair that formed a halo about his lined face. *Einstein*, he thought. *Or maybe a dandelion.* One clear blue eye glared at him; a black patch covered the other.

"Don't just stand there staring at me, boy! Open the screen and come in!" Wilson looked for a hook at the end of the man's missing left hand.

The Captain led him back to the den. "I guess I shoulda asked, but I imagine you're the detective Miss Dianne called me about."

Before Wilson could reply, the Captain wheeled on him, "Unless you're a reporter?" He leaned closer. "You a reporter, boy?" The old man turned again and continued down the hall. "Nobody ever comes to see me 'cept reporters and preachers. Watch your step, now!"

Three steps down led to one of the most amazing rooms he had ever been in.

"Pour us some coffee, Wilson, and then I'll let ya sit down!"

Wilson interrupted his inspection of the room to pour coffee from the service on the battered dry sink the Captain had pointed to. "How do you like your coffee, Sir?"

"Like I like my wimmin; hot and dark. How 'bout you?"

"Light and sweet."

The two men regarded each other from across the room. Finally, the old man nodded. "You'll do. Bring me my coffee and you can look around."

The west wall was nothing but windows, overlooking the parade ground and river. Wilson's car was in the foreground, and he fought the urge to go out and move it so it would no longer mar the view of yesterday.

The other walls were filled with every kind of nautical memorabilia that Wilson could imagine; a collection of a lifetime, shelves of books, display cases, paintings, scrimshaw, and photographs. *And* treasure maps. He walked over to inspect the largest and most spectacular.

"Ain't real. It's a copy. The original's in a museum. It weren't real, neither, turned out. But it fooled everybody for decades."

Wilson turned and cocked an eyebrow. The old man cackled. "*I* debunked it!" He pointed proudly to himself. "Yessiree, them pompous windbags all thought they was so hot, but I, Dennis P. Woods the Third, Ph and D, took the wind right out of their sails." He took a noisy slurp of coffee. "Hated me for it." He set the sturdy mug down with a thump. "People hate you when you're right, but you already know that, don't you?"

"Yes, sir, I do." *A Ph.D.? In what?*

"Philosophy or History, Lieutenant, doesn't matter." *He reads minds, too?* "After I got this," he held up the stump of his arm, "and this," he pointed to the patch, "found out all I could do was think. And just so you don't drive yourself crazy wonderin' what happened, I donated those body parts to the great adventure called World War Two."

Wilson replenished both of their mugs and took a seat. He found himself in a wonderful leather chair and put his mug on the inlaid table next to it.

"Like the chair?" When Wilson smiled and nodded, his host explained. "New York City Public Library, when they threw it out a coupla decades ago. Since bein' nosy is a requirement for yer job, I imagine yer wondrin' how I got to be called 'Cap'n Denny.'"

"You bet."

"Simple enough." The old man stared out the bank of windows. "Always did like the water, bein' on it, in it, around it." He paused to glare at his guest. "Except for the time spent on that danged troop ship to Europe. Almost the worst experience of my life.

"Had me a little boat when I was about twelve. Thought it was the *Queen Mary*." He barked laughter. "Hell, that's what I named her, the *Queen Mary*. Called m'self Cap'n, an' made ever'body else call me that, too." He shrugged.

"Always had a boat, from twelve on. Some were bigger an' fancier than others, always named 'em after British royalty, fer some reason. Sounds downright regal to refer to my twenty footer as the Queen this or the Princess that. Natcherlly, I was the Cap'n." His grin was full of mischief, and Wilson knew that a younger version of the man sitting in front of him had been a force to reckon with. Probably still was.

"Enough of the palaver. Let's get down to business. Miss Dianne said you're interested in pirates and their maps. What do you want to know?"

"Everything."

"Hah! This is about the LaFontaine murder, isn't it?"

Wilson hesitated, saw the old man bristle, and told the truth, straight up. "Yes. Rumors of a treasure map keep cropping up."

"Found them yet?"

"Them?"

"Yep, I'll tell ya about 'em. Ain't found them, though?"

"No."

"You will, unless Cajun Jack's gotten his hands on 'em." A pause. "OK, here's the deal. I'm going to give you a quick course on the subject. I'm going to be combining about three lectures into one, so it may be a little disjointed at times." Gone was the folksy dialect; this was pure academician. He grinned; "But I'm an old geezer; I'm entitled to ramble and skip."

Wilson smiled at the man's false modesty. This "old geezer" was sharp as a tack. He took out his notebook and pen. He hoped he could take notes fast enough.

"Put that away, Lieutenant." He patted a compact tape recorder on the desk. "This tape will run sixty minutes. That's all the spit I've got, anyway." When he was satisfied that the machine was working properly, he began, and soon Wilson was a mesmerized little boy listening to a grandfather weaving tales.

"The first thing you have to understand is that pirates have worked this area since the 1500's, starting with Sir Francis Drake." He chuckled. "No one likes to think of Drake as a pirate, but that's what he was. If you could have talked to the folks in St. Augustine back then, they would have set you straight.

"Next we hear of William Kidd. Operated out of Fernandina for a while before they hanged him in seventeen-ought-one. The tale is he anchored off the beach and buried treasure, then killed the shore party to keep the location secret. Then he put out to sea, and threw most of the remaining crew overboard so they couldn't tell anyone about his treasure on Amelia. There have been a passel of diggers on what's now Fort Clinch, but no one ever found anything.

"Next we have Luis Aury, a Parisian gent who was a privateer in Napoleon's navy. Before that, he was mixed up with South American Revolutionaries and set up his own government on Galveston Island, off the Texas coast." He pointed to the map that Wilson had admired. "That's where that came from. Supposed to be one of Aury's, but I proved it wasn't. I'm still not welcome down there.

"But in the early 1800s — 1817, I think — Aury came to Amelia Island. Sailed up the river, pointed his 18-pounders at Fernandina's Old Town, that is, and declared martial law.

"Spent a couple of months here, dealing slaves. Trade had been outlawed by the States, but we weren't part of the country yet. President Monroe called Fernandina a 'festering fleshpot' and sent a gunboat to handle the situation. Aury surrendered and left with only his crew and provisions. No time to retrieve any booty.

"Aury moved on, ended up in Nicaragua. Thrown from his horse and died at thirty-three.

"But the man you should be most interested in is Jean LaFitte." The Captain had leaned back in his chair, eyes closed, during most of this lecture; now he thumped both feet on the floor and made sure he had Wilson's attention.

"This is where it gets complicated, so pay attention." He checked the recorder to see if he had plenty of tape. "Luis Aury and Jean LaFitte were contemporaries. They knew each other, and their men switched from one crew to another. Part of Aury's gang in Galveston had come over from LaFitte. And LaFitte replaced Aury at the Galveston Island enclave.

"LaFitte's name was actually Laffon. As a matter of fact, we have one of his descendants on the island, John Laffon. You probably know him better as Cajun Jack."

Wilson's mouth dropped open, and the Captain grinned. "That

got your attention, didn't it?" He clicked the recorder off. "Pour us some more coffee while I hit the head."

With both of them suitably refreshed, the Captain continued his story: "Now you have to go back to 1949, when Robert LaFontaine's mother died. She was a quiet, unpretentious woman, and Robert got several surprises going through her things. First, there were papers proving that her side of the family was descended from our old friend, Luis Aury. Guess he swashed and buckled his way into a boudoir or two during his stay here." Wilson returned the old man's leer.

"And then Robert found a treasure map, one supposedly drawn up by Aury so he could remember where he hid all of his gold, silver, and even jewelry — the hoard he didn't have time to retrieve when Monroe's gunboat crew escorted him off the island.

"Robert brought the map to me, asked me what I thought. I told him it was as good as any I'd seen, but what gave it a little more authenticity was that people had found two caches of plunder on land first owned by James Cashen — as in the Cashenwood neighborhood — then owned by Senator Yulee, and finally by Samuel Swann. First one was six thousand dollars in gold coins; the last one, in 1896, was coin amounting to thirty-nine thousand. At least, that's what the article in the *New York Herald* said. It's on file at the museum, if you want to check."

Wilson waved a hand in dismissal, so Cap'n D continued. "So when old Mrs. LaFontaine dies, Robert shows the map to me — and to John Laffon, Cajun Jack. Jack is astounded and produces his *own* version of the map, handed down through generations of *his* family!"

"The *very same* map?"

"Very, very close." Cap'n D sighed. "The two were going to get together and compare maps and family history." He looked out the windows to the parade ground. "Don't think it ever happened. And now Robert's been murdered, and Cajun Jack's disappeared."

"How'd the two families get the same map?"

"Aury needed money. LaFitte was in Charleston and took the

map as collateral for a loan. Nobody collected on anything." Captain Denny slapped his knee, "Hah, the loot's still here, boy."

He looked at Wilson with the one good eye. "Interview over."

"You saw the map and know where the treasure is, though?"

"Interview over. Hah. Didn't say I believed it!"

Wilson thanked Captain Denny and drove back to the station mulling over the new information. *Maybe the treasure map played a more important role in LaFontaine's murder than I gave it credit for.*

CHAPTER 21

Early the next morning, Wilson's direct line rang again and he gave it a glare. He really didn't have time for Miss Hattie today; trickling information had begun to make a little sense in the LaFontaine case.

"Aliens! They did it again last night! If y'all don't do something about this, I'm gonna get me a radar gun an' zap 'em good!"

Wilson had noticed the sign-out board indicated that everyone was out. He sighed and grabbed his coat. He muttered his destination to Dianne via the phone on his way out. She covered her mouth to stifle her giggle.

It was déjà vu all over again; the neat blue and white house, its manicured lawns and plantings, the smelly garbage bags spewing their innards all over the back yard. He took more pictures, wrote up another incident report.

The only thing different this time was Miss Hattie. Instead of the neat housedress she'd worn the first time, today she was dressed in a sweater and ancient blue jeans, with the big white rubber boots fishermen wear. Wilson could see the shovel and rake waiting to the side.

"Where are your nephews?"

"Working," Miss Hattie said glumly. "Their mama said they'd be here when they got off, but Ah cain't wait until no four or five o'clock. This stuff'll stink up the whole neighborhood."

Wilson noticed how quiet it was. "Where's Miss Mary?"

"Church trip. Gone all day." Miss Hattie sighed. "At least

I'll have peace and quiet instead of havin' to lissen to Miss Mouth."

Wilson talked to the shift supervisor and they agreed to patrol Miss Hattie's street more frequently for the next few days.

———————— • ■ • ————————

After an uninspiring day going over old files, Wilson looked forward to the evening out. He held Dianne's hand as they left the restaurant and drew in the night air, smelling the marsh as the west wind came across the expanse a few blocks away. They walked in silence to the car. He opened the door and a passing whiff of her perfume made him feel good.

He had this sense about him, which he had learned early in his youth from some unknown source. *Whenever you are with a woman, always treat her like a lady until she proves otherwise. When the "otherwise" occurs, just ease on out of her picture.* He knew that Dianne was a lady and he liked that. Grace was a lady in the Southern tradition, as was Dianne. He couldn't help noticing her legs as she slid into the seat, then she carefully slid her hand on the side of her skirt, covering the revealed thigh. He closed the door. *Don't be thinking those thoughts, ol' boy.*

They drove in silence, a silence that is between couples when thoughts are enough to capture the evening. Neither wanted to break the spell. The dinner had been perfect, the wine had been perfect, and Wilson wanted it to continue.

Dianne scooted closer to him, took his hand and said, "It's been a wonderful evening. Would I be too forward to say we drive down to Main Beach? The west wind won't be too cool."

"Sounds good to me." Wilson took Alachua Street to Eighth, then down to Atlantic where he made a left turn.

"You just broke the law, mister," Dianne said, using a mock-authoritative tone.

"What do you mean?"

"There are three signs at that intersection that indicate no left turn and you went ahead and did it."

"Guilty. I didn't see them." Wilson looked in the rearview

mirror as if expecting to see the signs.

"I know that they're there, because I got a ticket for turning left there about a year ago."

"No professional courtesy?" He asked as he turned off Atlantic and circled back to Seventh. He didn't wait for an answer. "I want to see the LaFontaine house again in the dark."

Giant oaks lined the small grassy strip between the sidewalk and street, blocking a good view of the house and causing shadows cast by the streetlight. Slowing a little, Wilson looked at the dark mansion. He didn't stop but kept moving to the corner and began to turn. Dianne turned her head quickly.

"That's Cajun Jack," she exclaimed.

"Where?"

"Back there in the shadows. His silhouette was by a tree at the sidewalk."

Quickly he stopped the car around the corner and turned himself around to look at the house. "What was he doing?" He turned off the dome light switch so it wouldn't come on when the door was opened.

"Just looking up at the house. Acted like he didn't see us."

"This time, please stay here and keep the door locked."

"Yes, sir. If you get conked on the head again, don't come running to me." She squeezed his arm, "Be careful."

He didn't answer but got out of the car quietly and moved in the shadows back to the corner. He could see the dark figure standing next to a huge oak; the glow of a cigarette brightened, followed in a few seconds by the cloud of white smoke being exhaled. Wilson walked down his side of the street, keeping an eye on the still figure across the street. A car was approaching in front of Wilson and he stopped behind a tree, hiding himself from the man across the street. He held his breath as the car passed, and then he slowly moved on.

The figure was still there. The street lamp cast sodium-gas yellow light, painting the whole scene in an eerie shade. He was now opposite the man who was unaware of his presence.

Wilson took a step back into the light so he could see the man better. The short figure stood with his weight on the left leg and the hip slung out to the side. *That would cause the limp.* The cigarette glowed brighter. Wilson took a look around him to get his bearings, trying to recall the layout of the street and environs. He took a step and the pop of an acorn sounded. *Damn oak trees.* He froze but it was too late.

The figure turned around to see what caused the noise, just as a huge dog in the yard behind a chain link fence broke into a ferocious snarling bark. Wilson jumped a couple of feet to the side looking for the dog, not realizing it was behind the fence he was next to. He quickly looked up and saw the figure on the run.

He called out, "Stop--police! I need to talk to you." and began his chase. *Smart move, Sherlock, he's running faster now.* He ran after the man and was surprised that even with the limping gait his quarry could move along the street with agility. By now all the neighborhood dogs joined in the chorus led by the monster that started it all. Wilson saw porch lights snap on as he gained ground on the other man. Both were running down the center of the street. A car loomed out of the darkness behind him and flashed its bright lights and honked the horn.

The man he thought was Cajun Jack disappeared around a car parked at the curb. Wilson stayed in the street. As the vehicle behind him sped by, the driver yelled out some obscenity and accelerated. This was enough distraction for him to lose sight of Cajun Jack for a split second. Wilson ran behind the same parked car and stopped, hoping for the sound of running footsteps. All he heard was the sound of his heart beating in his ears and the dogs barking. Then someone from a porch yelled to get away from the car or he would call police. More porch lights came on and several people were standing on porches.

Wilson took out his badge and held it up, all the while he was walking back to the car. "I'm the police. Go back in, it's all over," he lamely said. They just watched him until he turned the corner, and then several voices told the dogs to be quiet. The porch lights went off.

In the car, he sat looking ahead, then at Dianne, "That old man can run." They both laughed. He started the car, and as he drove off he said offhandedly, "He had a limp on the left side; the man that hit me also had a limp, but on which side?"

CHAPTER 22

Wilson, come on in, have a seat." The Chief nodded toward the chair in front of his desk. "Listen, about the other day. Guess I was a little gruff and it was one of those bad days, you know how it goes sometimes."

"Yes, sir." Wilson was still stinging over the incident.

"Lookie here," the Chief sat one cheek of his wide butt on the edge of his desk and folded his hands, "this is the closest thing you'll get to an apology. You have to get used to my ways, sometimes I mean it and sometimes I don't."

"Fair enough." Wilson still wasn't too warm toward Cabe. "Will there be anything else? I have to get on those files and see what I can dig up."

The Chief ignored the question. "Evans is a good man and he knows Cajun Jack. Jack helped him one time several years back, and Evans seems to be the only one that can handle him." He looked to Wilson for approval, but got none.

"Jack and me and ol' Robert go a long way back. Robert got where he was 'cause he worked his ass off and made something of his business. I got lucky and knew the right people at the right time and have been here for close to thirty years.

"That leaves Jack. He's done everything from moonshine to washing cars. He's not exactly book-smart but he's street-smart, if you know what I mean. He had to quit school early but we three kinda' hung together over the years until recently. I couldn't figure those two out. They had a falling out, and neither would talk to me or about their problem." The Chief got up and moved around to his chair.

"Any clue as to why they had this falling out?" Wilson's mind was taking it all in.

"You'll hear 'most anything, but I believe Jack wanted Robert to loan him some money so's he could get back to Louisiana and live with a cousin or something."

"That's not reason for murder, or do you think it may have been something else?"

"That we're not sure of, we'll know when we get him, but I do have something or rather someone for you to listen to." The Chief made a phone call and shortly there was a quiet knock on the door. "Come in."

In walked William Carless, the nephew. Wilson tried not to let his complete surprise show. Carless looked at him and mumbled a greeting as he took a chair. His clothes looked like the same ones he had on the other day, and now he had a noticeable limp.

"Wilson, it seems we have a witness."

"A witness?" Wilson sat up straighter.

"Not per se, but young William here saw, or it seems, heard something that could be important. I've already told Evans about it, but I wanted you to hear it too. Go ahead, Son."

"Well, the day Uncle Robert was killed, I was going to his house to talk again about me getting my own boat. The captain of *Miss Jane* is leaving and going out to the Texas coast. That means his job is open. I deserve it and was going to see Uncle Robert and do my best to get it." Carless paused.

"Go ahead, Son, tell him what you saw and heard."

Carless looked at the Chief, then at Wilson. "I was on the sidewalk in front of the house when I heard this loud arguing coming from Uncle Robert's house."

"Who was it and what did they say?" Wilson broke in.

"Give the boy a chance. Go ahead, William," the Chief whispered, keeping his eyes on Wilson.

"Cajun Jack and Uncle Robert. I couldn't tell exactly what

they were saying but I stopped and looked all around. That's when I saw that old lady next door out in the garden."

"Mrs. Upton?" Wilson looked into the man's frightened eyes. They were so dark that he couldn't distinguish where the pupils stopped and the irises began. This gave Carless a beady-eyed look; coupled with his sharp face, that gave Wilson the impression he was talking to a squirrel. *You poor ugly bastard. Why are you so scared?*

"I guess, I don't know her name. She saw me and then slowly walked around to the back of her house. That's when I started up the walk." Carless was nervously rubbing his hands together.

"Did you see Cajun Jack or just hear him?" Wilson asked. The Chief looked at him and then to Carless.

"I saw him. Just as I turned to go up the walk, Cajun Jack came out on the porch and turned back to Uncle Robert and said if he didn't get what he wanted, somebody would have to pay — and that he'd be back."

"Was there anyone else around?"

"I don't know. All I saw was that old lady."

"Is that it?" Wilson leaned back in the chair. "Did you hear what Cajun Jack was wanting?"

"No, sir, he just said if he didn't get what he wanted, he'd be back."

"What happened next?"

"He saw me and turned and almost ran out the yard through the back hole in the hedge."

"Did you go on up and see your uncle?"

"Yes, sir, we talked a little and he said he had another man in mind for captain, but he would give it a good think-over, and maybe I *was* ready." Carless paused and looked at his hands, then ran one of them through his thick oily hair. "It seems he always said that, but this time it almost sounded like it was my turn. I just kept hoping that this time was the time he really would think about it and let me have the boat." He looked up at Wilson. There was a long silence, broken only by the clock on the office wall.

Finally the Chief spoke in slow deliberate words. "So you see,

Wilson, when we find Cajun Jack, he'll crack. He never could lie very well. We got the arrest warrant for him. Evans is out at the pogy plant now and should have him back here by dinnertime. You did a lot of good detective work but, as you must know, sometimes you do get led down the wrong path."

"Yeah, maybe you're right." He hadn't told the Chief about the encounter the night before. Wilson looked at Carless who turned his palms up and shrugged his shoulders. Wilson had now been tossed a curve. Why wasn't he told this during his interview with Carless? He wasn't sure whom to pursue. He could almost guess what the next words out of the Chief's mouth were going to be.

"Wilson, how's that search thing coming along for Orlando? Don't worry about any more of this, I want you to enjoy yourself. We're really a likable little town." The words were like that of a father asking his son about homework.

Wilson was quiet for a second, still trying to take it all in. "Uh...still banging on it. In a day or two at the latest."

The Chief smiled and nodded toward Carless. "You can go now, son." He maintained his fatherly tone.

Carless was out the door in three steps. Wilson sat looking at the wall in front of him. They heard the heavy front door shut behind Carless. "Is there anything else, Wilson?"

He took a deep breath and stood. "No, sir, I guess that takes care of it."

Cabe held his hand out. "Sure it does."

Wilson felt the firm grip but noticed the Chief had a Band-Aid on his finger. "Oh! How'd you get that?"

Cabe put his hand in the middle of Wilson's back and urged him to the door. "Haven't you done enough sleuthing for today?" He laughed, "I nicked it working on the lawn mower, getting it ready. You know, getting it ready for summer. Damn thing wants to get infected, though. It'll be okay in a day or two."

Wilson sat back in his squeaky desk chair, wincing at forgetting the WD-40. The warming sun made him a little sleepy and he put both elbows on the desk. He rubbed his eyes, then put his face in his hands and closed his eyes. These late nights with Dianne were killing him. He was too old to hoot with the owls at night and fly with the eagles the next morning. He groaned out loud when his direct line rang. He took a sip of coffee on the second ring, looked at his watch when it rang the third time. *Too late for Miss Hattie.*

"Lieutenant, this is Officer Bruster. I'm at Miss Hattie Parks' place over on Tenth, and she's asking for you."

He sat bolt upright. Coffee sloshed all over his hand as he slammed the mug down. "She all right?"

"Yessir, she's fine. We may have to charge her with assault, but she's OK."

"You catch the aliens?"

Officer Bruster's reply was drowned by a series of unearthly screeches. "I'm on my way!" Wilson shouted into the receiver.

Dianne was returning from lunch when Wilson telephoned her. "Caught the aliens! Be back in awhile!"

Lights but no siren got him to Tenth in five minutes. Two cruisers with light bars flickering decorated the house. He could hear the screeching as he ran up the front walk. Just inside the screen door, he saw two burly patrolmen, each of whom was trying to control a small, infuriated black woman.

"QUIET!" Wilson bellowed. And, for a second, they were. "You!" he pointed to one patrolman: "Take Miss Mary into the kitchen."

He wheeled around; "And you! Sit!" Miss Hattie sat on her own sofa, arms folded in rebellion.

"Sister's the alien! Ah seen her! She…"

"Wait!" he ordered. He turned to Bruster. Then in a quiet tone, he said, "Tell me."

"I was sipping coffee down the block in the cruiser about 1:15. Saw activity in Miss Hattie's back yard, came on up to investigate."

"Why were you parked there in the first place?"

Bruster shrugged. "Supervisor said to keep an eye on Miss Hattie's. It was quiet, wanted to drink my coffee in peace."

"Go on."

"I pull the car in front, hear thumps and clanks. Let myself into the back by the side gate." He flicked a look at Miss Hattie. "Saw this tiny black woman dragging a big trash bag over to a flower bed." He shot another look at Miss Hattie, but she only glared at him. "From the back, I thought it was her, but when she ripped the bag open and started kicking sh...stuff all over, I figured it wasn't her. So I went up and grabbed the lady and said, 'Gotcha!'"

Wilson squelched a smile.

"Then she turned around and started hollering. That's when I realized I had ahold of Miss Mary."

The old woman on the couch opened her mouth, but closed it when Wilson jabbed a finger at her. "And then?"

"Miss Hattie must have heard her sister hollering, because she came flying out the back door, doing her own fair share of hollering."

"And then?"

"I called for backup." He looked a little shamefaced. "I can handle a bar fight or two shrimpers facing off, but two women? Uh-uh."

"Watson got here in about two seconds and took charge of Miss Mary. I took Miss Hattie. We brought 'em inside and they seemed to calm down. That's when I tried to call you."

Wilson's eyebrows rose in question.

"But when I let go of Miss Hattie, she lit into Miss Mary." He shook his head. "Kicking and biting and slapping. We got them separated, then I called you."

"Alien! My own baby sister!" Miss Hattie's mouth worked. "Always was a little strange. Nobody ever liked her. Liked me better."

Wilson's mouth twitched.

Miss Mary was sitting quietly at the kitchen table. She was nursing a cut lip and her eyes were rheumy from tears. Both she and Officer Watson were nursing large glasses of iced tea. Just as Wilson poured a glass for Miss Hattie, he heard the stomp of heavy boots and loud voices from the living room.

The Four R's had returned. Rashid and Bruster were eyeing

one another warily, but both men relaxed when Wilson entered. He nodded to the patrolman, handed Miss Hattie her iced tea, and shook hands with each of the R's.

"Neighbor called and said the police were here. What's goin' on?" Rashid picked up on the smile that was twitching at the corners of Wilson's mouth. A twinkle began to grow in the big man's eyes as he waited for a reply.

"We caught the alien." All four nephews broke into big smiles.

"That's the good news. The bad news is that the alien is Miss Mary." The brothers exchanged worried glances. "Officer Bruster here," he nodded at the Blue, "caught her decorating the back yard."

"You sayin' mah sister's an alien?"

The Four R's parted, not unlike the Red Sea. Their movement revealed their mother, who was just as small and feisty as her two embattled sisters.

By now Wilson was an old hand at dealing with the women of this family. "No, ma'am; I'm saying that Miss Mary has been trashing Miss Hattie's back yard."

"Where is she?"

Not sure which 'she' Momma was referring to, Wilson gestured to Miss Hattie on her couch; "Miss Mary's in the kitchen with Officer Watson."

Momma, whose real name was Mildred, Wilson was to find out later, headed for the one on the sofa. "What have you done to our baby sister?" she screamed.

Miss Hattie jumped up from the couch in full outrage. "Ah ain't done nothin'! It's her; it's always her. An' now ah know why: She's an alien! Ah seen her, and ah seen her dumpin' her alien trash all over my roses!"

Officer Watson appeared in the kitchen door before Mildred could respond. "Miss Mary'd like to go home now." When everyone turned to look at him, he shrugged. "She's tired, and her lip hurts."

"Why's her lip hurtin'?" Mildred demanded.

"It's hurtin' 'cause Ah pasted her one!" Miss Hattie explained. "An' I'm not sorry! Alien thang!" She glared at the assembled company, some of whom glared right back.

Officer Watson shuffled uncomfortably; "She's an old lady and she's right next door."

"Is she going to press charges for Miss Hattie's assault?" Wilson asked.

"Ain't agin' the law to hit an alien. Show me where it says so!"

Wilson held up his index finger and Miss Hattie subsided to the couch once more.

When Watson answered no, Wilson turned to Rashid. At his slight nod, Wilson turned back to the young officer. "Take her over there, make sure she's comfortable."

Mildred intervened; "I'll see to my sister, if you please." She turned to her sons: "Y'all clean up the yard." She quelled the assorted groans with a fierce glare, then rounded on her seated sister: "An' I'll deal with you later, Miss Alien Expert." She turned her glare to Wilson. "When there's no nice policeman to protect your sorry butt."

No, Toto, we're definitely not in Miami!

———————•■•———————

Prissy walked in from school and saw her grandmother sitting on the couch, eyes closed. "Grandma, are you asleep?"

"No, honey, just tired." Priscilla stirred and motioned toward the kitchen. "Go get something for a snack. Lisa will be home in a minute." She let her arm fall to the couch.

Prissy walked slowly away, all the while looking at her grandmother. Something was wrong with Grandma; she didn't look just right. "Grandma, should I call Daddy?"

"No, I'll be okay. Just want to rest my eyes for a few more minutes."

Prissy poured the milk and opened the plastic jar of cookies. She heard the school bus stop and Lisa's voice calling out to other kids. Quickly she went to the front door and motioned for Lisa to be quiet. They tiptoed past their grandmother into the kitchen. Prissy poured Lisa a glass of milk and they sat down facing each other.

"Lisa, do you like that Dianne person?"

"Yep." Lisa was more interested in licking the cookie filling than having a conversation.

"She's not mean or anything, but I don't want her to think she's going to be our mother. Do you see the way she looks at Daddy? I bet she's got her claws out to get him. Next time he and I talk, I better warn him. Daddy's so busy he probably doesn't notice things like that."

Lisa now had filling on the tip of her nose. "I like her. She'd be a pretty mommy."

"Listen, no one will ever take Mommy's place. You heard Daddy and Grandma both say that. That means you and I have to take care of Daddy. Are you with me?"

"Sure." The unconcerned Lisa broke open another cookie to lick the filling, only to have the cookie crumble in her hands.

Prissy's face took on a disgusted look. "Get a broom and clean it up."

"You're not the boss. I'll clean it up when I get through."

"Clean what up?" They both turned to see Grandma standing in the doorway.

"Prissy wants me to clean up the cookie and I want to wait until I get finished and she's not the boss and she hates Miss Dianne."

"Prissy?"

"I don't hate her." She shot an irritated glare at Lisa. "I don't want her to marry Daddy. We have to take care of him."

Her grandmother slowly walked over to the table. "Who said they're getting married?"

"We women can tell what other women are after, and she's after Daddy."

Grandma raised her eyebrows. "Oh my, we'll have to be on the lookout for that."

"That's what I was trying to tell Lisa."

Lisa looked at her sister and said, "I like her." This was followed by the time honored sibling gesture: she screwed up her face and stuck her tongue out.

CHAPTER 23

Wilson took off a few minutes early. The boring job of getting the paperwork Chief Cabe wanted was putting him to sleep. The warming weather oozed in on him and he found his eyelids drooping. He called out to Bobby, whose office was directly across from his, "Where's Wilbur? I need to get him to search a name for me."

"He was here a minute ago; there's a candy wrapper on his desk. Should I call him?"

Rubbing his eyes, Wilson yawned a response, "No, I'll get him tomorrow. What are you on?"

From the other room came, "Fight on the beach, one pulled a knife. Perp is over at County; victim is in the hospital. I went over and got the victim's statement a little while ago. You still chasing Cajun Jack?"

"Apparently not anymore. I toyed with the idea, you know, sort of a sideline, but Evans has a handle on it. I'm outta here for today. See you in the morning." Wilson swung his coat over his shoulder, it was warm outside and he liked the air.

He went east on Beech Street to avoid traffic on Centre and so on to Atlantic. He was lost in thought trying to figure out what clues he may have missed about the LaFontaine murder when his car, almost by itself, turned around and went to Seventh Street. He slowed and turned down the side street and saw Roger on hands and knees pulling weeds from the newly sprouting beds.

He stopped, walked along the flagstone path to where Roger

knelt. "It's a good afternoon for that."

The gardener looked up, "Um-hm. How can I help you?"

"I don't know. I was just driving by saw you working here and wanted to stop. You take good care of the place."

"Um-hm."

"I wish I had time to do some gardening." Wilson looked around while Roger kept his head down and, using his gloved hands, pulled out the sandspurs sprouting among the mulch. Wilson moved toward the house a little, hands in his pockets. Roger watched him while digging with the short hand-spade, turning over the rich dirt, pulling weeds. Wilson stopped in front of a heavy wooden arbor and looked closely at the plant that climbed up it. Shoots were coming from all over it. "Is this bougainvillea?"

Roger stopped and looked up. "Yes, sir, it is."

"I didn't realize it grew this far north. We had several in our yard in Miami. They grew so much each year that I had to severely trim them back every two, three years. Doesn't the cold get them here?" He turned to the other man.

Roger stood and brushed off the dirt his knees. Not yet answering, he moved over next to Wilson. "When the weather gets cool, I erect a frame over it and when the freeze comes," gesturing with his hands, "I put plastic on the frame." Roger pointed to a hidden electrical outlet and added, "I put a light in there to keep the temperature up."

"They look healthy."

"It works." Roger was surely a man of few words. He gathered his tools and put them in the wheelbarrow.

Wilson saw a man who was used to heavy work, and it showed when Roger easily loaded the wheelbarrow and headed for a small shed. He followed, trying to figure a way to get a conversation going. He stopped a moment to look at the sundial, then moved to the gazebo.

Roger watched, wondering what this policeman wanted. He hung up the last of the tools in the small greenhouse and looked at Wilson sitting on the bench in the gazebo. His head was tilted back as if he was looking at something in the ceiling, but his eyes were closed. Roger pulled off the gloves, laid them on the short potting bench, and went toward the gazebo.

"You okay, sir?"

"Yes, fine, thank you," came a soft reply, "just a little sleepy."

"The way you had your head back I though you might be ill." Roger sat down opposite from Wilson.

"I'm waiting for the spirits."

"Well, Mr. Robert don't allow no spirits here. No, sir, no drinking of any kind."

"No, not that kind. In Miami I worked with an officer from someplace in the Caribbean. He would go to a crime scene and sit, close his eyes, and he swore that the spirits would come and talk to him and tell him who did it and how."

"Um-hm."

Wilson lowered his head, opened his eyes and focused on Roger, "You don't believe me?"

"Do you believe you?"

Wilson tried not to, but he broke out in laughter and Roger joined in. "Well, he was an excellent detective, too. Maybe that had a lot to do with it"

"Yes, sir, I guess it would."

"You like this work. It tells in how neat the place is." Wilson stretched both arms over the back of the seat.

He thought back to an earlier conversation he had with Callahan. "How long did you tell me that Mr. LaFontaine lived in this house?"

"Oh, he bought it for the first Missus, back in the 1970s. I came to work on the gardens not too long after that."

"Then Mr. Robert and the first Missus lived here?"

"Yes, sir. Before that, they had lived in a small house over near the ice plant."

"He must have liked you," Wilson said quietly.

"I guess so. We never had a cross word. I'm sure gonna' miss him." Then Roger spoke a little louder, "Oh, he had his ways about him, he weren't no saint, but he always treated me good. When he and the Missus went to Italy one year, he brought me and Lillian back a present. Can you imagine that, here he was in far off Italy and thought of us. He loved Italy for some reason. Went there every couple of years for a vacation."

"That was a nice gesture." Wilson stretched his legs out.

"Yes, sir, it was." They sat in silence, Roger remembering his old friend and Wilson trying to conjure up what Robert LaFontaine had been. They were stirred by the close of the screen door of the house, and both men looked to see Lillian coming with some iced tea.

"You men need something to drink, I suppose," she said as she handed the glasses out.

"Thank you, ma'am," Wilson said, taking the cold glass from her. "That's very kind of you." Callahan nodded in agreement.

"Roger, we need to stop at the store on the way home. You gonna' be much longer?"

He looked at Wilson, who gave a little shake of his head. "No, maybe a half hour."

"Miz Lillian, when you leave the house here," Wilson nodded toward the large home, "do you always lock the doors?"

"I do nowadays. Used to, no one locked the doors, but I always do now. Is that all?"

"Yes, ma'am."

Lillian left and they sat in silence once again, only hearing the screen door shut with a bang. "I hope I'm not being too nosy, but I thought she had a room here," Wilson remarked.

"Oh, she does. It's here for her to use. You see she had a stroke a few years ago and Mr. Robert fixed up a room for her to rest in whenever she wanted. He never fussed about her taking a lie-down. In fact, he used to make her stop in the heat of the summer during the afternoon and make her sit in there and watch TV. She hated that too." Roger laughed softly.

"I see you looked at the sundial."

"Yes, it's unusual. Kinda big for a small garden."

"Yes, Mr. Robert brought that back from Italy when he and the third Mrs. LaFontaine went there. Had it shipped all the way here. I put it over by the yew tree to accent the English garden look."

Wilson raised an eyebrow. "English garden look?"

"Yes, sir. It gets boring cuttin' grass and putterin' around so's I got books and read on gardens. The English garden took my liking. Me and Mr. Robert figured it all out."

Wilson stood up, went to the opening of the gazebo and then looked back to Roger. "Do you know of anyone who would want to hurt Mr. LaFontaine?"

"Look out in the garden and you'll see a lot of things. Those over there..." he pointed to a gathering of bushes loaded with white blooms, "those come from the family rubiaceae and originated in South Africa, you know them as gardenias. And these here like little bits of butter are calendula officinalis. They're named in honor of the Virgin Mary and decorated church altars in old Europe. And 'calendula' refers to the Latin meaning 'first day of the month' because they can bloom every month of the year if properly cared for. So the churches always had flowers. You call them marigolds."

Wilson was dumbstruck. He watched as Roger waved his arm and pointed around the garden. "See that, in the greenhouse? It's a staghorn fern, family polypodiaceae. Don't do nothin' but hang there. Ain't got no flowers and it's one of the biggest plants here." He moved out into the garden and walked over to the sundial. Wilson followed.

"Mr. Detective, the smallest and simplest are sometimes the prettiest and the biggest are not much good 'cept to just be there and hang around, kinda' like some of the people here. Now you asked if anyone wanted to hurt Mr. Robert. Yes, sir, lots of people. There's all kinds that make up this place. I came from the original African slaves on this island, your mama came here a few years ago, and everyone comes from someplace, I reckon." He gave a quiet laugh.

"But I don't know of anyone here who would actually kill Mr. Robert. You see, he was also kind to a lot of people, mostly those that was down on their luck for a while, 'cause he remembered where he came from. He didn't like the 'neweys.'"

With this, Roger moved past Wilson toward the house. Lillian stood in the doorway, sweater on and umbrella in hand. Roger stopped and turned back to him. "You married?"

"Once."

"See that woman in the doorway?" Wilson nodded. "Then you know I'm on my way. Oh, if your men move anything again, please have them put it back right. They messed with the sundial and put it together wrong." He walked on.

"What did they do? I hadn't heard of this."

Roger came back to the sundial and showed him.

"This is the gnomon, casts a shadow on the numbers and tells you what time it is." He picked up the long rod that was cradled in place by two small forked rods on the dial face. "This arrow has to point toward the sky, they had it pointing down at the ground." Roger showed him how he had found it.

"Sundials have to be just right or they won't tell time right. See those marks?" He pointed to an inner ring and outer ring lying flat with the cradle on the inner ring.

"Um-hmm." Wilson knew he was in for more lessons.

"I move this inner mark each month to an outer mark and that aligns the gnomon with the sun as it moves across the sky. If it ain't aligned right or somebody messes with it, it won't tell the right time."

Wilson watched him and said, "I'll tell them to be more mindful. Thank you for mentioning it."

"Yes, sir." The soft reply meant the end of the conversation. Lillian came out of the house, locked the door; she and Roger left Wilson standing in the garden. He compared his watch and the sundial. Both timepieces agreed.

CHAPTER 24

Wilson parked in the municipal lot across from the Crab Trap. Dianne sat at the small bar inside, chatting with a man who turned out to be the proprietor. "It's a pleasure to meet you, Lieutenant; let me know if I can ever help you," the man said with a friendly smile, and turned them over to his son, who was hosting that night.

Soon they were seated by the window, at a table made out of a thick wooden hatch cover. Wilson was intrigued by the large circular hole in the middle.

"That's to throw your shrimp peels and crab leg shells into." Dianne explained. He bent over and looked. Sure enough, there was a large trashcan under the table. He studied the menu, determined to order something that had to go "down the hatch."

"And this window seat allows me to watch when someone steals my car," he quipped.

"Somebody should call a cop!" She laughed. "But I think you're safe."

He saluted her with his Scotch and soda. He looked around the large room, decorated with a marine flair. The building was obviously old.

"OK, town historian, tell me about this building."

Her eyes glinted mischievously. "Would you believe that two brothers and their wives and twelve children lived on the second floor?" He sputtered his drink.

"Sixteen people? This is a big building, but..."

"The Seydel brothers came over from Germany and had this place built in the late 1800s. There were two shops here, a general store and a millinery shop. Families up top."

The waitress rattled off the day's specials, but Wilson had already determined that it was an oyster appetizer and crab legs for him; Dianne ordered grouper, a local favorite. If he could con his mother into altering their dining room table like this, it would make the nightly clean-up a lot easier.

In just a few minutes, their waitress appeared with a platter of Apalachicola oysters. Wilson took great delight in throwing the empty shells down the convenient hole.

After Dianne had made sure she got her fair share of oysters, she resumed her tale. "After the Seydels, it was used as offices for a steamship line, a newspaper, and then the Papermakers' Union. It became a restaurant in 1979, just in time for Shrimp Festival."

"Ah, yes, the Shrimp Festival. It's coming up soon, isn't it?"

He polished off his pre-dinner Scotch with his last oyster. He disposed of the shell and almost followed it with his glass.

"Careful!" She blocked his hand just in time. "Sherry, our waitress, told me once they are constantly losing glasses and cutlery that way. She's a niece of the proprietor, by the way."

"A real family enterprise," he observed. "I'm learning that's true for a lot of the local businesses."

"Right you are. Everyone knows, knows about, or is related to everyone else around here."

"You'd better be good."

"Or be prepared to be talked about, if you're not."

Wilson mulled that over while Sherry served the crab legs and grouper. She poured their dinner wine and departed.

"The Shrimp Festival?" he prompted.

"It's week after next – first weekend of May." She had the mischievous look again. Wilson was learning to dread that twinkle; it was usually at his expense.

"Have you got your Shrimp Festival assignment from the Chief yet?"

He discarded an empty crab leg. "Assignment? I'm a homicide dick!"

Dianne sipped the excellent Chardonnay that he'd ordered. She laughed; "Wrong-o! Everyone— and I do mean everyone —takes a watch or three during that weekend." The twinkle intensified. "Strictly in uniform."

Wilson's crabmeat dripped butter in the coleslaw. He hadn't been in uniform for years. "Uniform?" he croaked.

"Check it out tomorrow," she advised with a grin.

They polished off dinner; she checked to see that he hadn't chucked glasses or silverware down the hatch, along with his crab legs. Both passed on dessert. Then she led him up the steep stairs to inspect the Seydels' old living quarters. The apartments were long gone, replaced with a bar and a lounge area. They sat in front of the small fire in the original fireplace and listened to the guitarist sing sea chanteys. April nights, even in Fernandina, could still be cool.

Dianne had opted for coffee with a small snifter of Bailey's Irish Crème. Wilson savored his single malt. "There is one piece of business I'd like to discuss, if you don't mind." He'd hesitated to bring up work, concerned that she would be irritated at its injection into what had been a very enjoyable, social evening.

He needn't have worried. Her eyes grew a little brighter, and she leaned forward on the settee in front of the fire.

"I'm having a hard time figuring out what to make of the Chief. He doesn't talk much about himself or his career."

"He's more a watcher than a talker," she agreed. "I'm told that a long time ago he found himself a benefactor, someone who introduced him to the right people, got him cleaned up after his wild ways as a young guy, got him into the right church, all that sort of thing. The good old boys thought they had themselves a manageable Chief of Police and that's what they made him. Only he turned out to be far less manageable than they thought. He's made a lot of enemies, but they can't get at him. He knows too much. And they know he knows."

Wilson looked at her skeptically. "He's that bad?"

"Ask around," she insisted. "Ask why the city manager just upped and resigned one day, about twenty, twenty-five years ago. Or check out what happened when money was missing from a city account not long after that."

Wilson raised his eyebrows and shook his head. He decided this might not be the time or place to ask any more questions. "Seems like I've got a lot to learn. Okay, enough police talk for one evening. I'm enjoying this place too much to think about anything that heavy."

Dianne was just as glad to relax and forget office politics. She changed the subject to places she liked to spend vacations and cities abroad she hoped to see one day. They were both smiling as they strolled out into the spring evening.

As he helped her into the car, he saw a small piece of paper under the wiper on his side. He scanned the note by the dim light in the lot. The city needed to work on that, too.

"Anything important?"

"Nothing that can't wait." They both knew he was lying. They were silent as he drove through the heart of the city. He walked her to her front door on Sixteenth Street and waited until she unlocked it. She knew he was preoccupied by the note and didn't take offense at his perfunctory goodnight kiss.

———————•—•—•———————

Wilson checked the Glock in his holster and then drove out to the old Pogy Plant. The unsigned note hadn't specified a meeting time, simply said to come when he finished dinner. This was his second trip to the quasi-abandoned factory, and at night it was damn spooky. He loosened the Glock and powered down all the windows a couple of inches so he could hear. He moved the gun from holster to lap, his hand wrapped around the butt. He had no idea what he was getting into. This isolated meeting with no backup was bad police work.

Thirty minutes later he had heard no more than the lap of the river, some frogs, and the distant noises of Smurfit-Stone's paper plant. Yet thanks to his Army Ranger training from some thirteen years ago, he didn't even flinch when he heard the twig snap.

Using the rearview mirror, he watched the limping figure approach the car from the rear on the driver's side. Wilson got out and the man stopped in the shadows. He could see the guy's belt buckle, but it wasn't distinctive, so he'd never be able to ID the guy that way.

"Lissen, cop," the man began. Wilson had to strain to hear him. "Tell ya a story." A pause while the man pulled on a cigarette. "Robert LaFontaine, John Laffon and John Cabe all went to high school together in St. Mary Parish, Morgan City, Louisiana. Best budzos for life, they swore. Ha!" The man spat his opinion on the dry grass.

"They'd all worked on family boats growin' up, thought they'd grow old there. But then, the fishin', she weren't so good. So the boys got itchy feet." Pause, puff.

"John Cabe joined the Army an' rose in the MP's before he quit that. Laffon came here to Fernandina. Robert LaFontaine's family sent him off to school somewhere in Alabama."

"I didn't know Cabe was in the Army," Wilson said, hoping to nudge the nearly one-sided conversation back toward where his interest lay.

"*Mais oui*. Then when he got out, he went straight back to Morgan City. But the farmin' was nearly gone an' the shrimp fleet was gettin' smaller and smaller. What used to be third- and fourth-generation fishin' businesses was now gone to sharcholders in boats owned by city folk. We'd all seen how government regulations and taxes was causin' the farmers and shrimpers grief.

"Yet that LaFontaine family, ole Bobby's people, was able to get on when everbody else failed. How was dat?" There was a pause. "Cabe knew the answer: Money. Old money. Family'd been in the business and knew the markets and had the contacts to get good prices." The speaker took a last drag from his cigarette, hacked the phlegmy cough of a heavy smoker, and ground the butt under his boot.

Wilson could smell the man — not just stale cigarettes, but the aroma of the rarely-washed. *Maybe the wind will shift soon.* He stood stone still, afraid any movement would distract the man or spook him into disappearing. "Go on," he said.

"Next, Johnny up an' left Morgan City to come to Fernandina. Lot of people did, for the shrimpin'. He took a security job here at the paper mill, because of his bein' an MP in the Army. Only the first week, he got tore up in a fight in a parking lot near the beach. That bugger cut him up real bad. Couldn't work, couldn't hardly make it to the head by hisself. Him and Laffon was sharin' quarters like, and Laffon played nursey 'til Cabe could do for himself."

"So that injury gave the Chief his limp?"

The lighter flared, and Wilson watched the hand rise when the man took a hit off the new cigarette. He held his breath, waiting for the man to disappear.

"*Vraiment.* Don't mention it, though, unless you want him to whup your ass, limp or not."

Wilson nodded. *Good advice. I'll take it. Whoever this man is, he's no outsider. He's got to be Cajun Jack. Laffon himself. LaFontaine's dead, and this sure as hell ain't Cabe.*

He could make out none of the man's facial features, not even the shape of his head or whether he wore a hat.

The voice continued.

"An' don't never call him Shrimp, lessen you want to be *morte*. That wound lost Cabe his job. Kept him from workin' for months. Made him real mean. No money, no way of earning any, not legal like, *n'est ce pas*?"

The breeze was turning cool, but Wilson was so wired he barely noticed it as he stood tensely listening.

"One night we're drinkin' at the Palace Saloon, and a bunch of tourists is givin' Francine trouble. In comes our Sergeant Poulon of the police with that Kel-light he uses for a nightstick. Suddenly one Northern tourist is droppin' to the floor like a sacka taters, showin' just the littlest trickle of blood startin' down 'tween his eyes. The tourist had made the mistake of putting his finger in Poulon's chest.

Me and Johnny never seen Poulon's arm move."

The man took a bottle from his hip pocket, shifted a little, spit and unscrewed the lid to take a big pull from it. He looked at Wilson for a couple of seconds before holding out the bottle to him.

"No, thanks."

"Well, you could hear the faucet drippin' behind the bar, it got so quiet. Sgt. Poulon says, 'Do we have a problem here?' He is one huge man. You know Poulon? His uniform must be a 3X and he still has a hard time keepin' his chest and arms inside his shirt. Not no body-builder type, just a healthy Southern boy who never missed a meal.

"About this time, another tourist starts to stammer somethin' about lousy service, and Poulon interrupts him to say, 'Yessir, we do got trouble. Y'all got one pissed-off officer of the law here an' if you don't haul your Yankee asses out of my city by the time I reach the end of this bar, y'all be playing kissy face with the floor of this here saloon.' Then he nods at Francine and started down the bar, greetin' people like he was up for election. Behind him, them Yankee boys gathered their buddy up and dragged him out the swingin' doors."

Wilson joined the man's quiet laughter at the image. "So what's Poulon's part in Cabe's story?"

"We knew him from back in Morgan City, but didn't recognize him. We was all kids together back there. When Sgt. Poulon gets to Johnny Cabe, he points his Kel-light at him like he was pointin' a finger, tryin' to put a name with the face. 'I know you,' he says, 'but I can't remember your name.' Then it's old home week for the two of 'em. That sealed it for Johnny. With Poulon in the police department, lookin' out for him, he got a sponsorship to the Academy, got hired by the city, and began his long career as one of Fernandina's Finest.

"Next, Bobby — who was callin' hisself Robert by then — came over here from Morgan City with his ol' man's money and started a shrimpin' business. Did right well from the get-go. Johnny never had a lotta friends. He was jealous of Bobby LaFontaine, though he played at bein' buddy-buddy with him, once Bobby moved here and Cabe saw he could be useful down the line. Cabe needed cash and got his share, too, lookin' the other way. Had his eye on Tallahassee by then."

Cajun Jack – if it was indeed he — took another long pull from the bottle. To Wilson's relief, he didn't offer to share.

"Cabe was lookin for financial backing, huh? So LaFontaine was the Chief's backer?" Wilson asked.

The man just looked at him and said, "Who's dead?"

"Doesn't make sense to me." Wilson hoped to get more. "I hear LaFontaine's death may be tied to a treasure map. Any ideas on that?"

"My own *maman* gave that map to me 'fore she died. She had it in her family and hid it in Old Town, way back in the '20s, before she ever went to Morgan City. Maman didn't want nothin' doin' with it. She up and hid it all those years, until on her deathbed she told me where it was, buried in the backyard of the folks she worked for here. I dug it up and gave it to Mr. Robert for safekeepin' years ago. I checked on it now and then, to see it was still safe."

Wilson held his breath, "And now?"

The other man hacked hard and spat. "That's what I been thinkin' on this past week."

"Have you been to LaFontaine's house since he died?"

"Too many damn cats! An' that ole biddy, lives beside him, is too nosy. I get anywhere near that house and her and her damn cats screech to the heavens. All of them cats hated Bobby. Used that fancy-ass garden of his for a latrine. Useta drive him wild!" A phlegmy laugh ended in a coughing fit. He lit yet another cigarette.

Wilson wasn't sure the cats fit into the homicide investigation, but gossip had its uses. "What did the cats think of the latest Mrs. LaFontaine?"

The man bit. "A few weeks ago, the Third – that's what everybody calls her, among other things —the Third, she's in her fancy silk nightie and bathrobe, has Miz Lillian deliver her café, in a fancy pot and china cup and saucer on a silver tray, no less. Miz

Lillian puts the tray on the little table in front of the winderseat, like usual. She notices something, but don't say nothin.' Hee, hee, hee!" The man could barely contain himself.

"An' then, the Third, she sits down to have her café looking out the winder, only.... only..." Now he slapped his thigh to punctuate the coming punch line. "Only the damn cat has lined the windersill with dead birds and mice!"

Wilson joined in the laugh at Marlene's comeuppance and they were still chuckling when a car turned down Fourteenth Street. He watched it cross the bridge at Egan's Creek and, still looking at the car said with assurance, "You are Cajun Jack, aren't you?"

Silence. He turned to find he was alone. *It had to be Cajun Jack, though I may never know for sure.*

The car backed into the short drive at the back gate of Fort Clinch and killed its lights and engine. Wilson stayed where he was, and watched to see if Cajun Jack reappeared. Both Cajun Jack and the Chief had a limp. Which one jumped him the other night? He waited another ten minutes but nothing happened.

I should check that car out, but what the hell. It was midnight, he was long off duty, and he was bone tired. *Probably neckers after all, although the car did look familiar.* He finally started his own car to life and drove past the other darkened vehicle.

A short time later, he lay in bed looking at the dark ceiling. His thoughts bounced between Dianne and this case. Finally he got up and went to the kitchen to sit at the table, staring into the darkness illuminated only by a night-light. Once he heard a car drive past, accelerate past the stop sign and honk its horn.

Damn! That car at the pogy plant was Evans' car. What in the hell was he doing there...unless he was sent to tail me? I'll have to tuck that little bit of information away for now. The Chief wants Cajun Jack pretty bad to go this far, which brings up more questions.

Does the Chief know about the map, and if so, is he afraid Cajun Jack will get it before him? And what about all the loving family? They have a hint of a map. Well, this will have to wait until tomorrow.

Wilson climbed the stairs and checked on the girls on the way back to bed. He slept for the rest of the night.

CHAPTER 25

Wilson turned over in the bed and shielded his face. The sun made the blinds an eye-watering white. He'd been aroused by the combination of the blazing light and a nearly silent "shusshing" sound: Lisa sneaking up on him in her bunny slippers. The bed jiggled a little. Wilson opened one eye. Lisa was sitting at the foot of the bed, watching him.

"Are you asleep?" she asked.

"I was. Now the BEAR is going to get you!" He quickly moved and grabbed his giggling daughter and made growling sounds as he pretended to bite her. Giggles filled the room as they tussled on the bed.

Shouts of "Stop...stop!" mixed with Lisa's giggles. Shortly she was sitting on his chest, saying "Bad bear" and tapping him on the head.

Then Prissy was beside the bed, her hands on her hips, shaking her head. "You two are just like kids."

"I'm sorry, baby. Did we wake you? Come here." He held out a hand.

"I'm not a baby."

"I know you're not, and you know what?"

"What?"

In one quick move he pulled her onto the bed. "The bear is going to get you now!" This rough-housing brought shouts of laughter from both girls. They jumped on him and rolled on the bed, tickling him in return. They didn't stop until they heard a throat being cleared in the doorway.

Grandma was standing there in her housecoat. She shook her head, smiling, and warned them, "Breakfast in fifteen minutes."

She headed downstairs and Wilson turned his attention back to the children. He asked Prissy about school and Lisa about her pre-K class. They shrugged and said it was okay. Prissy asked, "Daddy, can we talk?"

He looked at her serious face. He imagined that Grace had looked like this when she was the same age. Her golden hair fell loosely past her shoulders. He put his hand gently on her head, "Honey, we can talk anytime you want."

"Can we talk too, Daddy?" Lisa asked.

"Of course, punkin.' What's on your mind, baby...uh, Prissy?"

"Well, it's about Miss Dianne. We don't want you to get too friendly with her."

"Oh? We're not getting too friendly. We just went out to dinner a few times."

"Well, that's how it starts." She poked a finger at his chest. "First dinner, then she'll want to hold your hand.... and you know what *that* leads to."

Wilson knew where Prissy was headed with this one, but he didn't want to go there. "Well, let's see. Let's say we go to dinner again or she comes over here for dinner. What should I do?"

"Well, first of all, we think you should not go out and be alone with her."

Lisa decided to add her own remark. "Prissy says Miss Dianne has her claws out for you."

Prissy gave her a nudge, furrowed her brow and tried a new tack, "Daddy, I've seen how Miss Dianne looks at you. You're sort of good looking and we think she likes you too much." She again pointed her finger at him, with an intent look in her eyes. "I know how women think, Daddy, and you need to watch out for her. Besides if you marry her, she'd get bossy."

Wilson struggled to keep a straight face; it helped knowing that Prissy was totally serious in this. She wanted to be the center of his attention. "Bossy?"

"Yes. We don't want her to be our mother."

Wilson looked toward Lisa, who dropped her head and whispered, "I like her."

"I'll tell you what." He took both girls in his arms. He knew they needed mothering, and soon, whether they knew it yet or not. "When I find a woman I want to marry, I'll tell you before I make any decision. We'll talk about it all together. Until then, Miss Dianne and I will just be friends. Okay?"

"Okay," Lisa said with a relieved grin.

"Just be careful, Daddy." Prissy's admonition came with a hug.

"Anything else?"

"I would like to be called Priscilla. Prissy is for a very little girl."

"I will try to remember that — *and* I'll watch out for the lady tiger. I promise. Thank you for coming and talking to me. I loved your mother more than any woman in the world. *And* I will always have a part of her with me as long as I have you two monkeys around." He started to tickle them again, but Prissy held back.

She said, "Daddy, aren't you a little too old for this?" and walked out of the room.

Lisa yelled, "I'm not!" and jumped on Wilson's back.

———————•■•———————

First thing on Monday, after the morning brief and a quick refill of coffee, Wilson punched in the number for the Duval County Medical Examiner and asked for John Hershey. The perky voice on the other end said, "Sure thing, Sugar; my name's Janice. I'm always here, so you just tell me what you want and I'll help ya, ya bein' new, and all. Oh, and welcome to the area!" She put him on hold while he tried to recall the last time he'd been called "Sugar."

"Morning, Wilson. What's up?"

"I'd like you to meet me at the LaFontaine house today, anytime you can fit it in." He'd been warned about the ME's penchant for whistling '50s rock, so he wasn't surprised to hear the opening bars of "Love Me Tender" while he checked his appointment book. Nobody had told him the whistling would be off key.

"How 'bout two o'clock?"

He agreed and broke the connection. That would give him time to catch up on paperwork before breaking for lunch.

———————— • ■ • ————————

Later Wilson pulled his department vehicle into the LaFontaine driveway while John Hershey exited his own official car at the curb on Seventh Street.

"Good afternoon, gentlemen! Here to do a little more investigating?"

Both men turned to greet Mrs. Upton, who was decked out for gardening: faded, baggy dress, work gloves, and a large, floppy hat to protect her wrinkled face from the sun.

"If you're looking for Miz LaFontaine, she's moved out," Mrs. Upton volunteered.

"Are you sure?" Wilson said before he could stop himself.

She drew herself up to her full height. "As sure as these old eyes can see. Watched her from my second floor window yesterday. She and some young man — young enough to be her son, if you ask me — carried bags and boxes out to their two cars."

"Did she say where she was going?"

Mrs. Upton looked quite pleased with herself. "I just happened to wander down here to check this flower bed before they left." *I'll bet*, Wilson thought. "She was a little coy about the whole thing, but I managed to get a little information."

The lady was enjoying her inside information, and Wilson willingly played her straight man. "And just what 'little information' did you get?"

"Well, she and that young fellow — never did introduce us, like a civilized person would — they were moving her into a condo at the Plantation."

"I'll check which condo she's in later," Wilson said quietly

aside to John. Wilson had met folks like Mrs. Upton over his years
of police work; they want to help and be in on the investigation.

"After you left the other day, I recalled something that happened
the night Robert got murdered."

He wondered if this was going to be another pie-baking tale.
"What happened, Miz Cornelia?"

She lowered her voice, "Well, it was late and my precious
Ramblin' let out a howl." John looked at Wilson.

"The cat," whispered Wilson. The ME nodded.

"I opened the window to see what was going on when I saw a
car driving down Seventh Street."

He closed his eyes and sighed, "I wish I had known this earlier,
Miz Cornelia. Did you recognize it?"

"No, it was going into the shadows and behind that tree," she
replied, pointing a gloved finger at an ancient live oak near the street.

Wilson looked at her bedroom window and to the oak. *She
could have seen something. Line of sight is about right.* "Did you
notice the car's color or if any of the tail lights were out, anything
that might be of help?" His voice almost pleaded.

Miss Cornelia looked away for a moment. "Only that it was a
dark car. I don't know about the tail lights being burned out; the car
didn't have any lights on at all. Just drove off in the dark. I had
asked Sully to see if she could find out anything, but she couldn't. I
hope it's a help. I hate to think there's a murderer roaming these
streets."

"Me too, Miz Cornelia. You've been a help. Thank you." His
nod was received with a big smile.

She went back to puttering in the flowerbed while Wilson and
John Hershey made their way to the LaFontaine front porch.
"Wonder who's the widow's boyfriend?" the ME mused.

"Dunno. We'll ask."

CHAPTER 26

L illian Callahan answered the door. Although Wilson could
see that she was still grieving over LaFontaine's death, her
smile was less strained. But she was no friendlier than she
had been on Thursday.

"Good morning, Miz Lillian. This is John Hershey. He's in
from Jacksonville, helping me."

She nodded coolly. He explained they needed to look around,
to see if they had missed anything earlier. The housekeeper moved
aside and they entered the majestic foyer. She disappeared into the
back portion of the house as Wilson led John Hershey slowly through
the front rooms. "What I want us to do, you especially since you're
familiar with the wound technically, is to see if we can spot anything
that might have been the murder weapon." Hershey stood in the
middle of the library and looked around.

"Not a knife; too sharp. Those fireplace implements are too
dull. Tell me again what happened."

"According to the housekeeper, Robert LaFontaine spent the
evening in. She served him dinner in the dining room –"

"Pork with applesauce, rice, and cabbage. White wine."

"Yes." *Stomach contents from the autopsy.*

"After dinner, he went to the library, where Miz Lillian brought
him a carafe of coffee."

"Black. And a lot of brandy."

It was disconcerting to have the ME specify the gruesome
details, but the Lieutenant pressed on. "She left him alone in the

library, did the dishes, and went to her room at the other end of the house until she and the gardener left around six p.m."

"Any evidence that someone called on Mr. LaFontaine that night?" John asked.

"The few friends were in the habit of dropping in if they saw the library light on. He watched the ME's face. "The Chief is looking for a man named Cajun Jack. You ever hear of him?"

"Only that he's quite a colorful character about town."

"No extra brandy snifter in the library. I don't picture Cajun Jack as a brandy drinker, anyway." The ME nodded. "I had Miz Lillian check the dishes in the dishwasher. Nothing there except what she and LaFontaine used."

"What if somebody'd come into the kitchen to wash out a glass and put it away?"

"Good point. We'll ask."

Hershey stuck his hands in his pockets to avoid leaving fingerprints. He circled the room, letting his eyes make the search. His lips whistled a soft, off-key version of "Hey, Jude."

Watching patiently, Wilson idly fingered the Brussels lace tablecloth covering the antique cherry table. Hershey stopped in the dining room, looked out into the garden area, then back to the vestibule and library beyond.

"Want an educated guess?"

"An oxymoron? Sure." Wilson pulled a chair back and sat down.

"The victim came in the front door, or was already in the library, his safe place so to speak. The murderer came behind him, weapon in hand. The victim turned to the right, not fully but slightly, his right shoulder pointing toward the murderer. In one movement the weapon came from below up into the soft stomach, just under the right center rib cage to the heart. The murderer was right handed."

"You certain?"

"A lefty could do it, but I'd guess right handed." Hershey continued his off-key whistling and looked at the books in the library.

After hearing all the Beatles he could stand, Wilson led the way to the garden. *Mr. Robert might be dead, but the impatiens Roger Callahan planted that day are thriving.* Wilson told John about his earlier visit.

The two men walked up and down the brick paths, not so much looking for a weapon as giving themselves time to digest what they had seen. They ended up at the same white table and chairs Wilson and Roger had occupied on that earlier visit. Miz Lillian appeared with a tray, looking friendlier now that they were outside the mansion.

"Now I know you're ready for tea! You've spent almost an hour walkin' and talkin', so rest a spell before you go on." She turned to leave. "Just leave everything on the table; Roger will bring it in for me later."

"Before you go, Miz Lillian, I have a question." She waited. "I should have asked you this earlier," he apologized. "If Mr. Robert had had a visitor, and that visitor had washed out his glass or cup and put it away…."

"Assuming he knew where to put it," the ME interjected.

"Would you hear anything?"

"Oh, my, yes! These old pipes groan and knock something fierce when you turn the hot water on." She smiled. "But I don't think any of the men who come here even know where the kitchen is or would think to clean up after themselves! Besides, I left before anyone else came, I told you that." She left, shaking her head over the idea of one of Mr. Robert's visitors doing dishes.

As Wilson raised the glass of tea to his mouth, his eyes caught movement next door. Mrs. Upton was spying on them from her second-floor window. If his mama hadn't brought him up right, he would have waved to let her know he saw her watching them. He stretched a little, enjoying the warm sunshine. He slowly reviewed the murder, trying different scenarios of what could have happened that night. *LaFontaine was standing so that the murderer hit him on his right side. The weapon was taken away with him or her. LaFontaine may or may not have tried to write something on the floor. And, of course, no one saw anything. What am I missing? Everyone connected seems to have a motive and opportunity. Age old crap.*

He closed his eyes for a moment, opened them and took a drink of the tea. Lowering his glass, his eyes fell on the sundial.

"Shit!" He jumped from his seat.

Hershey sputtered tea. "What? What? What's the matter?"

"The sundial! The sundial!" He pointed excitedly to his discovery as the ME joined him. "The sundial's the weapon!" Hershey regarded the sundial with a perplexed look.

"What'd he do, pick up the whole thing and use the sharp point to stab LaFontaine? That sucker's got to weigh more than a hundred pounds, Wilson."

Wilson whipped out a clean handkerchief and removed the gnomon from its resting place. "Not the whole dial, just this doohickey! The— the gnomon!" He rotated the stylus to show its somewhat dulled point.

"Hot damn! It's a good possibility." The pathologist crowed, "Get it tested, pronto."

———————•━•———————

Wilson drove back to the station in high excitement, forcing himself to concentrate on the five-block trip. He arranged for FDLE forensics to examine the gnomon, telling them it was urgent. The clerk's laconic response of "they're all urgent" did little to dampen his spirits.

He went searching for Dianne, to tell her about his hot new lead. The look on her face stopped him in his tracks. "The Chief wants to see you, forthwith."

"Forthwith, again?" He mumbled on his way.

"Come in. Close th' door."

This was not good. He was not invited to sit; that was worse.

"Wilson, I know that you've only been here a short time, but..."

And that butt's about as big as yours, Chief.

"...We have certain ways of doing things here, and to borrow from an old bumper sticker, 'We don't care how you do it in Miami.' Maybe in the big city you're allowed to go off on your own." Cabe nailed him with his dark blue eyes. "Are you?"

"No, sir." Proper protocol was expected here.

"Or maybe you're a rogue."

"No, sir."

"Won't stand for no hot-shot detective goin' off on his own investigation. This is *my* police department, unnerstand?"

"Yes, sir."

"And since it is my police department, and you're one of my officers, you'll do things my way. Clear?"

"Very."

"Huh. Cajun Jack murdered Robert LaFontaine for God knows what reason. Meanwhile, this case is solved." He tapped his desk to emphasize the point. "All we have to do is pick him up. I have assigned Evans to do that. I told you that three days ago. Remember? Everybody in town is on my ass about this murder, the Mayor and *News-Leader* included. I got grilled at the damn gas station yesterday!" His voice was getting louder.

"Yes, sir." Wilson recalled that Evans had not mentioned the case to him in those three days so Wilson could bring him up to speed, nor had he apprehended Cajun Jack during those same three days.

The Chief moved from behind his desk. "And do you also remember that I assigned you to compile stats on pedophiles for the Orlando PD?"

At Wilson's nod, the Chief's voice grew deadly. "How ya' comin' on that, boy?"

"About half way through." *Thanks to Dianne's help.*

"Then let's get to the other half." He turned his back on Wilson, a move designed to show him that he felt no threat from his newest detective.

Wilson left the office with all the dignity he could muster, not that it mattered. The Chief kept his back to him. Wilson made a point of leaving the door open, to avoid slamming it behind him. *Not a good time to shatter the glass, but a pleasant thought.*

He walked back to his office across the driveway. Things didn't feel right in this case yet, but they would, eventually; he'd see to that. And if the Chief was right about Cajun Jack, well, bully for him. He pulled the thick murder book from its place on the shelf, and he flipped back and forth through its pages. It contained the lab reports, crime scene photographs and interview notes of the LaFontaine homicide. Rheba La Fountain's interview caught his eye, and he paused. *Crazy lady. Drunk lady.* He turned to the section that contained background checks. Rheba had had a few brushes with the law, all strictly local. *Possession, no intent. D&D.* He snorted; *no surprise there.*

He took the crime scene photographs out and studied them once again with a slow and deliberate eye. After an hour of study he returned them to the folder.

"Son of a bitch!" The door to the office banged against the wall so hard that it sent a resonant echo down the small hall. Evans stormed into Wilson's office and looked around. He stood with his hands on his hips, then threw them in the air in exasperation and began to pace. Wilson sat back and watched, as Evans spun back into the hallway, where he could be heard stomping his 235-pound bulk in the hall. Evans was usually very easy going; but anyone would be a fool to make the 6-foot-5-inch officer this angry. Finally, Evans reentered Wilson's office.

"Would you like to talk?" Wilson asked, motioning to a chair.

"Man," Evans threw himself into the chair. "I can't believe it!"

"What happened?"

"Chief Cabe just went ballistic."

"About?"

"Cajun Jack. He said I should have him by now and he went on and on. I have *never* seen the Chief like this. We were having a normal conversation about the drug arrests yesterday, and suddenly he asks why I haven't picked up Cajun Jack."

"What did you say?"

Evans looked at the open office door and spoke quietly, "I said I thought it should have been your case to finish and I was fitting it in with what else I had to do." He rubbed his hands together. "That's when he exploded. It was like lighting a firecracker. Boom! He went off on me. Telling me when he gives me an order he wants it carried out *now*. Face went from red to purple. He must've gone on for ten minutes. I know Dianne and Millie heard it." Evans looked at his shoes.

"Has he calmed down any?"

"Hell, no! He yelled at me to get out, go find Jack and get him back here. I got out and as I closed the door, he threw something against the wall behind me. If that son of a bitch hit me, I'd be in custody by now." Evans managed a smile.

"Yeah, we can't go beating up on the Police Chief, even if he may deserve it." Wilson sat up and placed his hands on the desk. "I know how you feel. He got my ass earlier. He really is agitated about this LaFontaine thing. I've been doing a little side work on this. What I've learned, I put in the file.

"Let's go at it this way," he went on. "Tell the Chief you have good solid contacts out there; and that you are calling in favors to find Jack. This will buy you some time. Call him in about an hour and tell him that you're working on the street people. He's smart enough to know it will take several days for the word to get out. Tell him you're sweetening the pot for them to give up Cajun Jack's whereabouts."

"You'll work with me, of course?"

Wilson smiled, "Do you want to share the glory?"

Evans looked at the floor. "The stall will work for 24 hours, maybe. With both of us looking for Cajun Jack, we'll get him in a few days."

"Or he'll get in touch with us first. Why don't you go on home, Evans? It's close to time anyway. Just don't take it with you, your family doesn't need that."

CHAPTER 27

After Evans left, Wilson leaned back in his chair, mentally damning the squeak, and read the information Evans and Troop had given him. The building was quiet now; everyone else in the outbuilding had left for the day. He tossed the folder on the desk and yawned. He looked at his watch: *Damn, 6:15. I've got to get home.* He'd go by the main building and let them know he was leaving.

Sarah sat at the night duty desk typing information into the new data terminal. An afternoon rain had tapered off and was drizzling its last drops, just enough to get him wet when he went to the car. Wilson was putting his arm through the sleeve of his raincoat when the phone rang and Sarah lifted her hand to Wilson, signaling him to wait. He could tell from her side of the conversation that it was a disturbance of some nature. She finished and looked up to Wilson.

"I really don't like desk duty," she complained.

"I never did either. You need something?"

"Oh yeah, on her way out Dianne said she would be ready to go to the Fernandina Little Theater tonight at 7. And...." Sarah hesitated, then handed him a note with barely decipherable information on it. "I am out of officers right now. Would you be a sweetie and take care of this?"

"Where are the zone cars?"

"I'll get Brad to come as soon as he can; he called and said he'd be about 15 minutes more," she smiled and tried to add something positive. "If you drive slowly, he may beat you there."

Wilson looked at his watch, *Damn no supper again*. He rolled his eyes. "I'm really not into this type of thing. Where is this Sharky's Place?"

"Honest, when Brad calls, I'll have him come over with a blue light. The place is over on the beach. The guy you're after is Shorty Livingstone."

She gave him directions to Sharky's, the bar and pool hall that he remembered William Carless mentioning.

He dropped his hand and looked at her. "If you know this guy, you go and I'll mind the store."

"I got him the last time. He does this once a month or so. Just don't rile him."

"Why's that?"

"He's a little temperamental about his height."

"I really think you should go."

Sarah pointed to the door. "Go."

"Be sure Brad gets there. I'll be his back-up." On his way out, he moaned, "I haven't done this in years."

He heard Sarah call after him, "I owe ya on this one."

The door shut behind him and he muttered, "Yeah, yeah."

The uneventful drive to Sharky's over by the beach took all of seven minutes. The light inside was so dim, he could barely make out a semi-circle of men near the back. He looked at the frightened girl behind the bar. Surreptitiously she pointed to the group of men, but stayed behind the bar. Several of those in the semi-circle turned to see who had come in. He could hear some trash talk coming from the circle, as well as from someone in its middle.

"Put that cue down, you little runt, and I'll show you what I mean!"

"Screw you!"

Wilson spoke up, "What's the problem? Back up, fellas."

Three of the biggest men he'd ever seen turned to him and eyed him with fire in their eyes. "And just who in the hell are you?" asked the biggest guy.

Wilson flipped his badge at them and they moved back, giving him a view of a midget standing in the circle's center. He held a broken pool cue like a baseball bat, ready to strike at anyone within range.

"Shorty Livingstone, I presume?"

"Screw you, too! You by yourself?"

"Not for long, pal. Put the cue down and let's go outside." He turned to one of the men, "What happened?"

"The little turd here said I cheated on a shot."

Wilson met his beady eyes. "Did you?"

"No, it was a clean shot. Ask anyone." There were a few nods and words of agreement.

Wilson turned his attention back to Shorty Livingstone. "Okay, let's go."

"I ain't goin'. That asshole cheated me outta ten bucks."

Why in the hell do I get these guys? "I don't want to use the cuffs, Mr. Livingstone. I just want us to go outside so we can talk about this." He looked at the barmaid. "Did he hit anybody?"

She shook her head.

"Let's go. I don't want to tell you again. If you don't come along, it's the cuffs and a ride." Wilson wanted to defuse this and send Shorty on his way.

The little ruffian smiled, "You ain't putting cuffs on me. Where's Sarah? I was hopin' she'd be here."

"That's it." Wilson moved quickly. The group of men parted to make way for him. Shorty swung the large end of the cue as Wilson advanced, its "whoosh" barely missing him. He sidestepped before Shorty could get a backswing going, then grabbed and jerked the stick away. He heard mumbling behind him and checked to see he wasn't about to be ambushed, then moved the midget to the wall.

"Let's go, tough guy. Against the wall and spread 'em."

In a flash Shorty lunged at Wilson and caught him in the groin with a quick upper cut.

"You little shit." Wilson sank to one knee. There was a flash of light and he remembered the first time he'd had a violent rearrangement of his privates in a high school football game – while the love of his life watched from the stands. He'd caught two things at once; a pass thrown too high and an opponent's helmet too low. The next thing he remembered was the coach asking him his name, like his name was important. What was important was for someone to take his testicles from his ass and put them back where they belonged. He had that same feeling now as he forced himself upright to grab the back of Shorty's shirt as he hustled toward the door.

He dragged Shorty back to the corner, his arms flailing.

"Settle down or else," he muttered.

"Or else what? You'll turn me over your knee? That's what they all say. Do ya get your jollies doing that?"

Wilson put his hand in the middle of the man's back, pressed hard, and reached for his handcuffs. That was all Shorty needed. He twisted to the left and was free, swung a hand out and caught Wilson in the knee, sending a pain shooting up his leg. He fell to the floor with Shorty firmly in his grasp. "You're beginning to piss me off," Wilson growled.

Shorty kicked at his shins. Wilson heard chuckling behind him and pushed hard between Shorty's shoulders – and finally one cuff clicked home.

"You ain't puttin' cuffs on me," Shorty grunted against Wilson's weight.

Holding the cuffed wrist, Wilson swung the feisty miscreant's free hand down hard to meet it. Shorty's arm was too short to reach the other cuff to fit. "Son-of-a-bitch," Wilson yelled.

Now the whole place erupted in laughter. Everyone but him knew what Shorty Livingstone had meant when he said he wasn't going to be cuffed. The little man wiggled like a fish on a hook.

"You relax or you'll kiss the floor," Wilson told him.

"You're breaking my friggin' arm, dummy. Relax, yourself!"

Looking around at the assembly, Wilson relaxed his grip a little. Shorty broke free, lunged at Wilson, and bit him, high up on the inside thigh.

"You little bastard!"

They both fell to the floor, rolling in beer and cigarette butts. Shouts of "Thigh bite! Thigh bite!" came from around the room.

Shorty's arm and legs windmilled like he was in a swimming meet, catching Wilson's shins and stomach. In a flash Wilson was off balance. Shorty was on top of him, fists swinging at his chest. Wilson rolled over on top of him and punched him to slow him down. Pain shot through his hand and up his arm. *Musta broke a knuckle or two.* Shorty looked up at him through an eye that was rapidly swelling shut.

"Damn, that hurt," the man said. Wilson nodded and felt the ferocious mass of midget relax.

"I've had enough fun, too."

"Let's go, Captain Prick." He grinned up at Wilson.

The crowd gave a roar and applauded, toasting the battle. Wilson didn't hear the uniform officer come into the bar, but he saw the group of onlookers part as Brad approached. Wilson looked up.

"Well, here comes the cavalry. Let me have your cuffs." Brad handed the cuffs over and Wilson quickly linked the two pairs together to cuff his man. They both lifted Shorty to a standing position. Wilson examined his puffed-up knuckles.

Brad looked at him and then to Shorty. "Shorty, you've done it this time. This is going to cost you big time. Maybe a year." Brad held on to the brawler's shirt and took him outside.

"Put him in my car. Fortunately, I have the issued vehicle tonight. We'll have to go by the hospital and see what the damages are. You can follow us over." Wilson looked around the floor to see if he'd dropped anything during the struggle. Satisfied, he limped out to his car to a chorus of cheers from the bar. He heard the crack of a rack of billiard balls being broken as the door closed.

Brad put Shorty in back of Wilson's car and then walked around to the driver's side, "You look bad. Where did he get you? Thigh bite?"

"Yeah, how did you know?"

"It's his trademark." He walked away.

Wilson looked back at Shorty, whose one eye was now

completely shut, but as he gazed at his captor through the other bloodshot eye, he grinned. Wilson felt safe from him now that the steel mesh screen separated them. He hadn't wanted it, but Chief Cabe had said he was a police officer first and an investigator second. "This ain't the big city." Tonight Wilson knew that was true, though this fracas just about qualified as a "big city fight."

On their way to the hospital Wilson called Dianne on his cell to tell her he wouldn't make it tonight, but that he'd call later. Shorty stirred in the back seat.

"Dianne's your girl?" he asked

"Shut up."

"She's a pretty woman. Banged her yet?"

"Shut up."

"Don't get nasty. Just a simple question." Shorty slumped back.

At the hospital the doctor came out to the car and looked into the back seat. "Hi, Shorty; at it again, I see."

"Damn, does everybody know him?" asked Wilson.

"He's in here every couple of months. Always in scrapes of one sort or another." The doctor checked Shorty and asked a few questions, then said, "He looks fine this time. Watch him, he's tricky. You come back for an x-ray when you get rid of him. Looks like a couple of busted knuckles."

"Yep. Feels like it too." Wilson got in his car gingerly, a throbbing pain in his hand.

He started the car, and the doctor leaned over and said, "Get the thigh bite?"

Wilson glared at him, put the car in gear and left the hospital.

A few blocks along, he looked in the rearview mirror. Shorty was sitting farther back in the seat. He stopped at the light at 14th Street and took a better look. Shorty held the cuffs up and jangled them.

"What the hell?" Wilson blurted out.

"Don't get your bowels in an uproar. These things never fit. My hands slip right out of 'em."

"You sit there and don't move. Hear me?"

"Yes, Sir." Shorty said with a military snap. The car went across 14th Street on toward Eighth Street for the left turn to town. They hadn't traveled two blocks when Shorty shouted, "Damn, you've done it now. I ought to kick your ass. Pull over and I'll do it right here and now!"

A startled Wilson looked in the rearview mirror and saw his prisoner moving about in the back seat.

"I said don't move around. We'll be there in a few minutes. What's your problem?"

"You broke my teeth." Shorty opened his mouth and spat out a broken bottom denture. In the dim lights Wilson could see his lower lip had receded, making his jaw protrude to a point.

The lip flapped as Shorty was spouting obscenities toward Wilson.

"You'll pay for this, asshole. I'm going to sue the city for this. You just wait. Damn, damn, damn."

"Sit back and shut up." He was tired of all this and his groin was beginning to ache again.

"Shut up? Shut up? I'll show you shut up."

Wilson made the turn onto Eighth and sped up, hoping to get this ornery midget out of his care. He ignored the stream of obscenities coming from the back seat and stopped at the station's back door. Brad was there waiting for him. Wilson lowered his front window and ordered, "Take your weapon out."

"What?"

"Take your weapon out and if this little jerk runs, shoot him."

Both Brad and Shorty looked stunned. Brad removed the Glock from his holster and moved to cover Wilson.

"Okay, game's over," Shorty said. "I'm not ready to die. I'll be good." He slid off the seat and stood there with his hands up. "You just ain't got no sense of humor, do ya?" He looked up at Wilson.

"Let's go." He marched the prisoner through the back door, with Brad in tow, weapon in hand.

Shorty knew just where to go. Sarah popped her head around the corner at the noise they made coming down the hall.

"Hi ya,' Tits." Shorty waved to her.

Wilson popped him in the back of the head, "Shut up. Get in that room," motioning to the small holding cell.

"What's wrong with you? She got 'em and they're fine."

"Garbage mouth." Wilson shut the door and walked to the front desk. He turned to Brad as they walked and gave him a brief description of what happened and asked him to fill out the report. He stopped at the desk. Sarah was already getting out the forms.

"Sorry about the Tasmanian Devil. He gets too many beers in him and gets six feet tall. Thigh bite?"

"Yes, what is this? Does everyone know his M.O.?"

"Yeah, he gets this way when the jobs run out and he gets to drinking too much." Sarah penned a couple of lines for him to sign.

"Sorry about his mouth when we walked in," said Wilson.

"Oh, that's okay. I had to bust him a couple of months ago and he got real mouthy." Wilson tried to imagine Sarah, all five-foot-seven of her, wrestling with Shorty on the floor of the bar. He smiled and shook his head.

"How'd the wrestling match go?" He grinned. "Thigh bite?" He looked at her.

"He missed by four inches."

He laughed and thanked heaven Shorty didn't go for the kill on him. He looked at Sarah and raised his eyebrow. "Four inches, huh? I guess the crowd cheered?"

"They always do." He grimaced and turned to go. She continued, "By the way, he'll file police brutality charges. And did he say you broke his teeth?"

He nodded.

"Okay, we'll put that in the report too; he always gets them broken. I don't think they ever get fixed. See ya."

He limped down the hall, the sound of his uneven footsteps echoing down its length. His groin throbbed and he couldn't wait to get into a hot shower. Sarah called after him. He glanced back.

She was standing in the hall, silhouetted by the fluorescent lights, "Left upper cut?"

He didn't say a thing and walked out to his car.

CHAPTER 28

W ilson, I thought you were a smart cop. I told you to leave the LaFontaine case alone. As soon as Evans gets that sorry Cajun Jack in here..." the Chief opened his hands, palms up, "it's over. Get it?"

"Yes, Sir, but..."

"No buts. Leave it to Evans."

"Yes, Sir." He turned to go, wondering why the Chief was refusing to answer a few questions about LaFontaine and the "grieving" widow.

"Uh, Chief, sorry to interrupt, but we might have a *situation* here." The desk officer knew she was going to get killed, but bravery was part of the oath she'd taken. "About twenty minutes ago, 911 got a call from a near hysterical female about a missing dog."

Chief Cabe stopped in mid-tirade. "Dog! You interrupted me to tell me that *Poopsie* is missing?"

"...and then a couple a minutes later, this man calls 911 about the dog."

"Tell 'em to call Animal Control."

"...and now, a Mr. Wadsworth-Langford is on line one, wantin' ta know why we're not doin' the speedy response thing."

Chief Cabe shut his mouth against the abuse he was about to heap upon the hapless officer. Paul Wadsworth-Langford was a very rich and powerful man. He'd brought his money down from Bridgeport, Connecticut, and had somehow managed to transfer some of his clout as well. And Paul was *almost* convinced to use both to further Cabe's political ambitions. Cabe picked up the phone.

"Paul, my officer tells me you have a problem; what can I do to help?"

Wilson could practically see oil oozing from the receiver. *Hope I don't get splashed with any of that.*

"Problem? It's a fuckin' disaster!" the voice on the other end screamed. "Patton's Pride the Sixth is a champion bull terrier, she's in heat, and she's loose! I need some fuckin' help here! We're talkin' a thousand dollars a pup, and if she has mongrels outta this, I'm gonna let 'em shit in your bed!" Paul Wadsworth-Langford had a thin patina of civilization, but in moments of dire stress, his rougher days of running crews at his road construction business in Bridgeport popped out.

"I'll send two of my best men out right away. You at home?"

"Of course I'm at home! Where'd ya think I am, onna freakin' moon?"

The Chief looked at the dead receiver a beat before slamming it home. "You!" He pointed a finger at Wilson, "Take Wilbur with you and haul ass to the Amelia Island Plantation! Paul Wadsworth-Langford at, at ... *shit!*" He fumbled at his Rolodex; "10227 Longpoint Drive. See the man!"

Yep, got splashed by it, big time, Wilson thought as he went to find the elusive Wilbur. The only thing he found was a candy wrapper and a note on Wilbur's desk saying he'd gone to check out a lead on a B&E. A black-and-white pulled into the parking lot. He raced outside and said to the policeman in it, "Come with me."

Officer Jordan followed Wilson wordlessly out to his car. They sped to the Plantation, about eight miles south. It was only the second time Wilson had used his siren and dash bubble since he got to the island, and he enjoyed the thrill. *If the taxpayers knew they were diving into ditches for a lost dog call, there'd be a revolution.*

Their high-speed run ended at the resort community's entrance gate. It was their misfortune that Art was on gate duty that day. He'd gotten this job through luck and the Good Ol' Boy network back when the Plantation was in its infancy, and he loved it. He especially loved devising new and subtle ways to aggravate outsiders whom he considered riff-raff trying to enter this inner sanctum of the wealthy. Art had disliked cops almost as much as he hated riff-raff, since he failed to make it to the Police Academy.

"What seems to be the problem, Officer?"

"It's Lieutenant! Open the gate! We're responding to a 911!"

"Are you sure, Officer? This is a pretty quiet community; I can't imagine anyone here needin' not one, but two policemen, and out of your jurisdiction; this is the county."

"Open the gate! Now! Or I'll bust through it!"

Art wanted to explain the consequences of damaging company property. Just as he leaned out his booth's window to better annoy the men in the car, his telephone rang. He glanced over and saw it was an internal call. He held up a finger to halt Wilson's yelling. "Excuse me. Gotta get this."

He left Wilson pounding his fist on the steering wheel. But Art's attitude changed and he almost, but not quite, snapped to attention when Paul Wadsworth-Langford began barking orders in his right ear. After several "yessirs," he replaced the receiver; Wadsworth-Langford had long since hung up.

The guard took his own sweet time moving back to the window. "That was Mr. Wadsworth-Langford saying I should be expecting a policeman soon. That would be you fellows?"

Wilson limited himself to a nod.

"Well, then!" Art smiled. "You should'a told me right off who you was gonna see."

"Open the gate. Now!"

"Sure thing!" He fumbled with switches, finally flicked one switch again, and the arm slammed up, then quickly down.

"Sorry, Officer, does that some times. Say, I never told ya where to go!" The double meaning was his masterpiece.

"What is your name?" *It's amazing how well I can talk through clenched teeth.*

"Brandywine, Art Brandywine, Officer." Their first names were the same, but the last name belonged to another guard. Art

Moseley would gladly sabotage Brandywine's job for a little fun with a cop.

"I have the address already, Mr. Brandywine, so if you'll just open the gate, we'll tell Mr. Wadsworth-Langford how helpful you were. *Thank God I'm a trained hostage negotiator; too bad I'm the hostage.*

"My pleasure, Officer; we're here to serve." He finally flipped the right switch, and the arm rose. If Wilson hadn't peeled rubber to pass through, the arm would have hit the trunk on its way down. Yet another example of Art Moseley's malicious servitude.

"Art Brandywine, Jordan, write that down," he told the young zone officer, "That SOB is *dead*." It would take the real Art Brandywine a lot of sweat and a lot of talking to convince the Chief of Security that he had not been on duty that particular morning.

The car's speed was limited by the winding roads, lushly landscaped with azaleas, saw palmettos, Indian hawthorn bushes and native trees. The pavement wound around majestic oaks in the middle of the roadway. *Just as well; Brandywine's probably alerted Patrol to pull me over if I speed.*

The Wadsworth-Langford house was magnificent. Glass, stone, and wood combined to blend with the landscape and to afford a panoramic view. There was no need to ring the bell; the master of the house flung the front door open just as the two men stepped onto the porch. The man stood in the doorway with fists on hips. Wilson saw that he was in his late 50s or early 60s, and had an Elmer Fudd fringe of almost pure white hair. His face, which now went all the way to his nape, was a furious red. "It's about goddam time you two showed up! I've got $15,000 worth of lost dog out there, and no one seems to give a flying..."

"Paul, bring them into the study, please."

"Huh!" he grunted, and his slight paunch jiggled. He stomped into the house. Wilson and Jordan exchanged a glance and followed him inside.

Deborah Wadsworth-Langford was far calmer than her husband and considerably more attractive. She, too, was nearing 60, but

Wilson knew she had once been a real beauty. The rose colored loveseat she now occupied added a subtle glow to her skin.

He quickly introduced himself and Jordan; both men moved their sport coats so she could see the shields on their belts.

Her eyes flicked over them. "I'm Deborah Wadsworth-Langford and this," she indicated the flushed man at the French doors, "is my husband, Paul." When Wilson nodded, she continued, "It's very warm today; may I offer you something cool to drink?"

"For Godsake, Deborah, this isn't a social call!"

Wilson knew there'd be no refreshments served. The woman raised an eyebrow, indicated the chairs where they should sit, and began; "Patton's Pride the Sixth is a champion bull terrier. She is solid white except for a black patch over her left eye. She is 21 inches high at the shoulder and weighs 54 pounds. Her kennel name is Patty, which is what she'll respond to when you find her." An inelegant snort from the French doors interrupted her recitation, which Jordan had been transcribing in his notebook.

"And she's in heat, coming into it, anyway. We were loading her into the van to get a shot from the vet to stop the estrus, when she suddenly took off."

"Oh, Debbie! It's all my fault!" Wilson twisted around at this outburst. It hadn't come from the husband but from a wispy young man sitting out of Wilson's line of sight.

"This is Nigel Spense, Patty's handler. He flew down to take her up to Bridgeport for the Bridgeport Cluster."

Spense leapt out of his chair to pace and wring his hands. "*All* my fault! Patty's so well behaved, I never have her on a leash, except in the ring of course, and she loves to ride. She saw the van and made a beeline for it. And then this damn bird dive-bombed me and I ducked to avoid its talons."

"Oh, for Godsake! It wasn't a condor, you ass! That damn mockingbird's been dive-bombing everybody this spring! She's got her nest in that tree!" Paul's scathing outburst almost reduced the young man to tears.

"I know; you warned me, but it was so *sudden*!" He brought

out a linen handkerchief to dab his nose; its border was the same shade of light blue as his shirt. "And when I ducked, Patty raced past the van and into the brush!" He threw himself into his chair and buried his face in the handkerchief. For a moment, the only sound in the room was his groaning.

"So, what are ya gonna do now?" Paul addressed the officers.

Wilson was at a loss. Was he expected to beat the bushes for the dog? He hadn't a clue. "First, let me call the head of your security force so we can coordinate."

"Already done that. Harvey's deploying his men while you stand around with your thumb up your..."

"Why don't you get Harvey's name and number for the Lieutenant?" Wilson appreciated Mrs. Wadsworth-Langford's habit of interrupting her husband. *Beauty and the beast*, he thought.

"While he's doing that, may I use your telephone?" He wanted to call the Chief and get guidance on this one. Did Cabe want to tie up manpower to look for this VIP dog? As he walked to the phone, he bristled when he heard Paul grumble, "Can't find a dog or a murderer."

———————— •■• ————————

One road away in a backyard that stretched to the marsh and overlooked the Amelia River, Patton's Pride the Sixth shivered her sturdy white body in ecstasy. *FREE! Good heavens, I'm free! What to do first? The possibilities are endless!*

The undergrowth rustled and she jumped at the sudden movement, then sneezed from the disturbed dusty ground cover. *Stop that! I'm descended from the famous general's William, named after the Conqueror only the sixth of that line considered worthy of the title of Patton's Pride. I'm a big deal.*

Suddenly the underbrush exploded and a fat gray squirrel scurried up the nearest pine tree, chattering his displeasure. *Tree rat! That's what Pater Paul calls them.*

Patton's Pride felt wonderful after routing the squirrel. *What next? So much to do, so little time.* A flash of white in the distance caught her attention. She hoped it wasn't that white poodle that lived in back of her house. *What a wimp. And only pet quality. I've been to Westminster.* She looked at the wimpy poodle trapped in his master's house and drank her fill at the poodle's water dish. She leveled her most imperious glare upon him; he sat down and whined.

Patty resumed her explorations, but not before she left a calling card on the patio. *Explain that to the family, peasant!* She left him howling and disappeared once again into the woods.

———•─•─•———

Wilson's call to Cabe had been unrewarding. His boss told him three things: coordinate with Plantation Security; find the damn dog; and schmooze the Wadsworth-Langfords so they'd be happy with the FBPD.

He'd made another call to Dianne to give her a heads-up that this assignment would probably interfere with their after-work plans.

"Great White Hunter on safari on the south end of the island!" he'd growled at her. They hung up chuckling at his plight, but not before she'd promised to let his mom and the girls know what was going on. When he hung up, he thought, *Thank goodness they're all getting along well now; maybe Prissy has gotten over acting so hostile.*

"Did you hear a dog bark?" He asked the Chief of Security when he returned from calling in.

"There are dogs all over the Plantation; more dogs than kids back in here," Harvey Swails answered. They walked outside to concoct a plan. Tall and lean, Swails told Wilson he had landed this job after retiring as a Navy warrant officer from the nearby submarine base. He worked hard and worked his force hard, but he sometimes found the demands and the peccadilloes of the wealthy to be exasperating. Hard to run a tight ship when there were so many exceptions to the rules. He'd had to call in off-duty people to mount this hunt for a mutt. He thought that anyone would pay that much for a four-legger showed just how screwed up the country is. Now he and Wilson stood, with hands on hips in the lush grass of the hyphenated name's back yard.

"So tell me, Chief, how is this drill set up? I know this is out of our jurisdiction, but it seems that we're here as a favor to someone." Wilson was hoping Swails would take over.

Swails looked at him for a second, "I understand. Politics is kinda funny." He pointed toward the wooded lot. "I have two men deployed there, where Patton's Pride was last seen; that's Dog One." He swung around. "Dog Two's two men are in the wooded lot on the other side of the house. Both of these lots are owned by the Wadsworth-Langfords, so there's no problem with tramping all over 'em." Wilson knew that the term "men" was used generically; half of Dog Two was a diminutive woman.

"I got my last two folks deployed across the road; Dog Three." Swails turned to watch a security vehicle drive by slowly. "Regular patrol. I have 20 people patrolling 24/7, and each shift will be briefed about the dog."

He leaned closer and just above a whisper said, "We get about one of these a month, but usually not this *serious.*"

Wilson understood. "Sounds good to me. You seem to have all the bases covered."

Deborah Wadsworth-Langford, meanwhile, had busied herself arranging a *command post* for Wilson and Swails. She had had the cook fill two large thermos jugs with iced tea; Cook's husband had put up the small marquee tent in the shade beside the house. Deborah called to Wilson and Swails as several folding chairs were added to the arrangement.

"Is this a convenient spot for you? I can have it moved, if it isn't."

Wilson was usually left to swelter in the sun or find his own shelter from the rain. "This is wonderful; we certainly appreciate it."

Swails had already chugged one glass of tea and was launched on his second. He smiled and saluted his hostess with the plastic glass. Swails turned to Wilson. "She is one of the nicest ladies here.

Generally her husband is too, but he's wound tight about this dog."

"People get attached to their pets," said Wilson.

"She gives the security force a little something at Christmas each year. A woman of real class."

Wilson murmured agreement and then followed Deborah to the house. He watched as she sent the hand-wringing Nigel back to his guest suite to twitch and whimper in private. He was an excellent handler, she told Wilson, but useless out of the ring.

She headed for her study, indicating Wilson should follow her. She wanted to call her neighbors up and down the road to ask them to be on the lookout for Patty. She passed the open door to her husband's study. He was speaking quietly into the telephone to one of his golf buddies. She explained that Paul rarely used rough language, except when he was really upset, and apologized for his earlier tirade.

"He's been badly shaken over Patty's disappearance, mostly because he feels a certain amount of affection for her; she *is* a sweet dog. And partly because Patty represents a lot of money. Maybe a big reason he's upset is Patty legally belongs to my mother. The flight Patty and Nigel were expected to be on will leave for Bridgeport in a few hours. I'll have to call Mom soon if we don't find Patty."

Her study was expensively and tastefully appointed, like the woman herself. She sat at a small writing desk in the pale green room and indicated a paisley wing chair for Wilson's comfort.

Cook brought in tea and a small plate of finger sandwiches. The two women smiled at each other, and the servant patted her employer's shoulder on her way out. Obviously, they had shared many a laugh.

Cook's name was the same as her profession, Deborah explained. "With a name like that, what else was I gonna do?" She called her husband Cookie, even though he didn't know the difference between beef Wellington and a bombe. He served as chauffeur, handyman, helped the gardener with heavy work. They lived over the four-car garage, their modest Toyota nestled beside the Mercedes and the Jaguar.

Deborah took a sip of tea and sighed again. What was she going to tell Mother? She looked at the desk clock. She then attempted to explain how important it was for Patty to be located and on the plane to Bridgeport.

"You see, Lieutenant Wilson, he won Mother's unyielding censure over an unfortunate business with the Shah of Iran. In his last days at the helm, Paul's father met a Persian prince who arranged for Paul to travel to Tehran to advise the Persians on how that mountain metropolis could better manage its annual snowfall. One of his snow removal slash construction businesses is in Ohio.

"Mother assumed that Paul would be presented at Court. She conducted research on proper attire and etiquette. A very nervous Paul was sent off with two of his best men, scale models of several pieces of equipment, and, of course, his court attire. He returned from the trip with stars in his eyes and more stories than he could tell in a month. Mother hosted a large family dinner with Paul as the guest of honor. She was most interested to hear about his presentation at Court. What did the Shah say? Was the Queen there? Did the women all wear Paris originals?

"And Paul had not gone near a palace." Wilson helped himself to Mrs. Cook's sandwiches and nodded a show of interest.

She continued, "The Prince lived in a modest villa on the northern edge of town. Entertainment was a small business luncheon for minor functionaries from Tehran's public works department. The principal topic of conversation had been snow. From there they had traveled to the motor pool to look over the snow removal equipment; Paul broke out his scale models. He and his men spent two weeks talking about modifications, upgrades, and the purchase of new equipment. The suitcase containing his court clothes remained unopened. Mother, of course, was devastated," she said with a sigh.

"Too bad," Wilson sympathized and looked out the window, hoping for a quick rescue. Officer Jordan and Swails were having iced tea. *This is way more than I want to know about Paul W-L.* Deborah persevered, "Paul had saved the best story until the end.

The Persian word for snow tweaked his earthy sense of humor and he gleefully shared this new word with the rest of the family. The men who removed it were called *barf men*. Naturally, the younger set collapse with glee. But my mother gathered her cane and lace-edged handkerchief and exited the room without a word. Forever after, she's privately referred to Paul as *The Barf Man."*

Wilson stood, muttered condolences, and excused himself. He'd put in all the face time he could take for one day. Outside, he went over to Jordan, "These guys are good at what they are doing. No need for us to stay right now." Jordan nodded in assent.

Wilson wanted to get back and interview George and Rheba LaFontaine again. Something about those two didn't set right.

On the ride back toward the station, he thought about why Rheba had stuck around. *She could be betting that there is a treasure map and George will be able to find it, ergo the treasure. I don't think George by himself had the guts to do the murder... maybe Rheba pushed hard enough that it resulted in George doing it. His sullen attitude might be hiding a key to this. What hold does she have over George?*

CHAPTER 29

Wilson and Jordan grabbed two hamburgers at T-Ray's before returning to the office. Wilson briefed Chief Cabe about the situation at the Plantation; they agreed that the Security Chief should be able to handle both one lost dog and the Wadsworth-Langfords. Wilson told Cabe that he planned to finish up some phone calls and get back on the pedophile folders before he went home.

It took him only a few minutes more to realize he wasn't focusing. A lost dog and a file search? What the hell was he doing here? Why had he come to Fernandina Beach? He gave himself a meritorious half-hour off and left the office to head home. As he got into the car, his anger drained away like water down a sewer, leaving a lot of dirty residue. He didn't want to take the confrontation with the Chief home with him. *Mom and the girls deserve better.* He sat behind the steering wheel, keys in hand, unmoving. His mind drifted back a few months.

He had been working on the Gonzales case for months, and had begun to make progress. He'd turned up information that more than hinted the good Dr. Gonzales was a heavy hitter in the drug trade. Wilson's leads pointed him toward several prominent Miami officials. He began to dig deeper. This was why he'd become a cop in the first place. Nothing matched the thrill of fitting all the jigsaw pieces together.

Murder had become so commonplace in Miami that most homicides were barely reported by the media. Only the most heinous crimes, or those involving prominent people, got TV time or newspaper inches. Yet, he had one of the highest conviction rates in his department. Despite the backbreaking caseloads and being one of the youngest lieutenants on the force, it looked like he was on his way up. His master's degree in criminology from the University of Miami was just two years away. When Grace died, the zest went out of his life. He had become obsessive about the children's safety, calling Lisa's daycare center and Prissy's school often. Reliable baby sitters became harder and harder to find, especially when he worked long hours on a case, like the Gonzales murder. The case that convinced him to get out of Dodge.

He remembered feeling good the day he got called into the Captain's office. Captain Roland Iverson had been in charge of homicide for years. He was a short man with gray hair and rimless glasses that made him look scholarly. Wilson did not know him well, having so recently made Lieutenant. He took a seat across from the cluttered desk. Iverson wasted no time with preliminaries. "Wilson, I'm taking you off Gonzales."

He had sat stunned for a full minute, unbelieving. "But...but why?"

"I don't usually tolerate someone questioning my command decision; however, I will tell you that it has to do with the fact that you are a widower with two small children for whom you are justly concerned." Iverson tried to give his face a concerned look, but failed. "I understand you call often to check on them. This case requires complete attention." Wilson remembered that the Captain had the decency to look uncomfortable as he shifted in his chair, adjusted his glasses and looked out the window. "I don't like to do this, but I have the safety of all my men to think of."

Wilson didn't believe him, "This couldn't have anything to do with the fact I'm close to nailing down evidence to tie Councilman Doggett to Gonzales, could it?"

Iverson had started to rise but sat down quickly as his face turned a deep red. "I'll pretend I didn't hear that, Lieutenant. Don't question my decisions again. Now get back to your duties, before you say something that gets you in more trouble than you can handle."

He had made his decision right then and there to look for another job. The next week the murder of Dr. Gonzales was laid at the feet of a small-time hood; the man was indicted but never convicted. Lack of evidence.

"Christ, it's happening again," Wilson said aloud, pounding the steering wheel with his fist. Cabe had taken him off the case just as he'd developed the first bit of solid evidence in this murder — the gnomon as the likely weapon. He'd quite properly turned the piece of the sundial over to the Medical Examiner and FDLE. *Why should the Chief respond negatively to that? Who's he trying to cover up for? I've got to keep digging, without letting him know what I'm up to. Shit, that's no way to do police work. I should just quit. And do what? Police work is all I know, and damn, it's what I'm good at. Besides, the girls love it here, and Mom is recovering since we arrived.*

He pulled out of the parking lot and turned down Front to Centre toward home. Strolling along Centre Street was the unmistakable figure of Rheba LaFontaine. At the corner, she entered the Palace Saloon. *Here's my chance at Rheba. What the hell, I guess the Chief couldn't mind if I stopped in to have a beer.*

He turned on Second, found a parking place and walked back to the corner, passing three beautiful Harleys. The Palace was uncrowded at five o'clock. He took a seat near the end of the long ornate bar; Rheba was farther down, in a lively chat with a couple of leather-clad bikers. Dressed in scuffed boots and a leather vest over a red halter-top, she looked like a member of the group. Wilson ignored her, ordered a Lite and poured it into a frosted glass. He'd taken a couple of swallows when she moved closer, just as he'd known she would. She had a drink in hand.

"Well, well," she smiled as she slid onto the empty stool next to him, "Look who's here, my favorite handsome investigator, having a beer in public. How come you refused one at my house?"

"I was on duty then." He smiled at her.

"So you're not on duty now?"

"Since I don't wear a uniform, it's hard to tell, isn't it?"

She waved away his non-answer with her drink. "If you're off duty, would you mind a little company?" She crossed her legs and gazed at him seductively.

"Free country."

"That's not friendly. You're new in town. I bet you haven't made many friends yet, and I'm trying to make you feel at home. Good ol' Southern hospitality. So shall I leave you alone here, or do you want some nice conversation?" She pouted.

"What will we talk about?"

"That's better." She returned his smile. "How 'bout, 'do you come here often?' That's an old line, isn't it?"

"I guess it is. You wouldn't be flirting with me, Mrs. LaFontaine, now would you? By the way, where is your husband?"

"It's Rheba, sugar, and Georgie's back at the shack with his attention on that goddam TV set. Pro'lly getting his jollies over some babe on the tube. Hey!" She motioned with her glass to the bartender. "I guess you figured out by now that I'm not exactly a happily married woman. Oh, Georgie's all right in his way, exceptin' when he's all hopped up and hittin' on me. Also he's bone lazy. Been sittin' on his ass for years, waitin' for his old man to make him a boss, so's he can sit on his ass and get paid for it. Didn't happen."

The bartender brought her another drink, and she took a long sip. "When I first met George, he was a pretty good lookin' rich kid home from college. I wasn't bad lookin' myself, though not from the same social set as the LaFontaines. I had a job waitin' tables at Uncle Charlie's Pizza, which used to be back of this building till it burned." She paused and looked out the door. "Used to have some great jazz."

Wilson watched her reminisce, then she came back. "He asked me out after I got off, and we had a great time. His dad just about shit a brick when George knocked me up. Didn't approve of me, but he insisted we get married, when he found out that I wouldn't have no abortion. Hell, I knew a good thing when it fell into my lap. Then I lost the kid, but George stuck with me. I think he did it just to piss off the old man. Geez, here I am talkin' my fool head off, and you ain't said nothing. I understand you got a couple of kids."

"Yeah, two little girls."

"And your wife…?"

"She, ah, died just over a year ago."

"Oh. Sorry, I…."

That's okay. So does George inherit?"

"That would be nice, but I doubt it. The old man kept sayin' he'd cut him out of the will, but who knows."

"Does George get in a lot of trouble... with the police, I mean?" Wilson sipped his beer.

"Not too much anymore. His daddy'd take care of it. At least, most of the time." She slugged the vodka.

"Most of the time?"

Rheba laughed. "You *are* new in town, aren't you?"

"I'm learning. Takes a while. I need a good teacher too."

She leaned over and put a warm hand on his shoulder. She made sure her lips touched his ear as she whispered, "Sometimes, me and our wonderful Police Chief are more than just friends. I just *love* police officers." She kissed his ear and a laugh trickled out of her throat.

He felt his face flush. He was glad the place was dark. She sat back, waiting for a response to her invitation.

He saluted her with his glass and drank the rest of his beer. "Thanks, I'll keep that in mind...some cold winter night."

"Too bad things didn't go the way Cabe wanted. You coulda' been Police Chief Wilson."

"What was it Cabe wanted?" Noting her empty glass, he ordered another to keep her talking.

"He *wanted* to get elected Chief of the Port and all he surveyed or something like that." She tossed her head back and laughed. "Georgie's daddy, ol' LaFontaine himself, was going to bankroll him, but Daddy pulled out."

"Who told you this?" Wilson eased the fresh drink in her direction.

She leaned close again. "Ol' Big Butt hisself." She casually put a hand on Wilson's thigh. "So who do you think did it?"

"You." He nailed her with a dead-eye stare; she looked more than a little shocked. Then she started to giggle.

"You're right! I did it! But don't tell the cops." She giggled again, then stopped and stared at him. "Do you really think I did it?"

"Little Georgie gets the business, maybe, hmmm? Then you get to be whatever you want... or have whatever you need." He gave a wicked smile. "Where were you the night Daddy was murdered?"

Her expression grew vague. "Oh... out."

"Out?"

"Yes, here, there. You know. Out." She straightened up and lifted her chin.

"Oh, come now. Don't get mad. Just joking." He forced a smile, then asked, "What about this treasure map I keep hearing about?"

"Personally I think it's a crock of you-know-what. If there was a map, where's the treasure? After all these years and nobody's found any?"

Rheba took another big slug of the new drink, then went on, "But just between you and me, I think George believes there is a map, and he and his dad argued about it a lot. I think he dreams about it. That would solve all his problems, an' mine too. He'd dump me if he got a hold of that kind of money. So what the hell, have another beer. Jerry," she yelled at the bartender.

Wilson stood and dropped money on the bar. "Hey, Rheba, Thanks for the chat. I gotta go. Mama's got supper on the table."

Rheba had already headed back toward the bikers. Watching her look for fresh company, he felt a nudge of sympathy for the poor woman. *Mustn't do that. She could be a murderer.*

CHAPTER 30

Wilson sat at his desk in the early morning hours Wednesday, shuffling papers on various felons to bank up time to work on the LaFontaine case. The phone rang. Sarah was on the duty desk again.

"I'm sorry, Wilson." She apologized, "That Wadsworth-Langford guy called a few minutes ago. His dog hasn't come home yet and he asked specifically for you. Apparently he called Chief Cabe earlier and — "

"I know... okay." He paused, "I'll finish up here and head to the Plantation. Is there anyone on patrol who can go with me? I want to leave a uniform there after I settle things down."

"Let me see...um...no, sorry again."

"If Wadsworth-Langford calls back, tell him I've already left. I'll be a few minutes." He hung up the phone as the other detectives came in. They each spoke as they passed his door. Wilson looked out the window to see Chief Cabe's car pull into the parking lot and gave up hope of doing any skulking this morning.

At the Plantation entrance, Wilson flashed his badge to the security guard, who let him in without asking questions. *Better than yesterday, no dents in the car.*

Harvey Swails was looking as if he hadn't moved from the day before. He was sitting with a cup of coffee next to him. "Did you get home last night?" Wilson asked.

"Absolutely. I left a little after you did. Just got back about half an hour ago." He looked toward the woods behind the house.

"Little darling hasn't shown up yet."

Wilson sat down and Cook appeared with a cup of coffee. She handed it to him and asked, "Have you caught the man that killed poor Mr. LaFontaine?"

He looked up at her, "No, Ma'am. We're close and are after a suspect."

In a near whisper she asked, "Who you looking for?"

"Oh, just a person."

"A woman, I bet; Maybe that no-count wife?"

"I can't say, Cook. Chief Cabe wants this kept quiet." In an effort to give her some secret satisfaction, he whispered as he handed her his card, "If you hear anything that might help me... just call this number."

She stuffed the card in her sweater pocket and walked back to the house with a brisk self-important stride. He sat back and looked at Swails. They both smiled and Swails said, "She's a sweetheart, isn't she."

"Yes, indeed. Anything new? I really have something else I need to get to."

"A few people called to complain about dogs barking in the night, more than usual. So I guess she's still out there." The Security Chief was more pleasant company than Wilson had expected. It turned out Swails was a bit of a history buff about the island, just as Dianne was. In his case, it was the site now occupied by the Plantation that interested him most.

Wilson loosened his tie. All in all, it wasn't a bad way to spend a sultry spring morning. It was April 25 and already it was clear that the temperature would hit the high 80s by afternoon. Chatter from Harvey's radio, now plugged into a base unit, offered background noise. He could hear the various search teams talking with each other; they'd found nothing so far.

Wilson asked a couple of leading questions, and sat back to listen. *Might as well continue my education.* Swails, who seemed glad to find an appreciative audience, started by telling him about the Franciscan priests, who had set up a whole string of missions along the East Coast in the late 1500s. One that had been on Amelia Island was the Santa Maria Mission. "At first it was located near the Plaza in Old Town, but at some point, they moved it down here, probably in the late 1600s. We lost it — and found it again in 1985, in a really surprising discovery.. Surprisingly, it wasn't just some mud hovel, but a stockade with a church, barracks, and a convent. Surrounded by a nine-foot wall. And a moat."

Later, Swails explained, people from another tribe moved down from Mission Catalina when they abandoned St Catherine's Island in Georgia to escape the British. Things muddled along until the 1700s when the governor of Carolina, a Brit, burned Santa Maria on his way to St Augustine. After that, said Swails, "Florida's flora and fauna took over, and the whole shebang disappeared."

Wilson wondered if this tale was part of the stories his mother told visitors at the Museum of History. "So then what..." he began.

"Dog One to Dog Base; I see her!" Both Wilson and Swails jerked to attention.

"Dog One, copy." Swails looked at him, grinning. "Maybe we'll be home for dinner!"

"Dog One. In pursuit." Wilson heard the guard's raspy breath; the voice had a familiar sound to it. A few moments of silence, then "Dog One, Base, I lost — Oh! There she is!"

"Go, Dog One!" One of the other teams was the cheering section. "Haul it, Reginald!"

"Cut the chatter!" Swails ran a taut ship. Wilson approved.

Someone keyed a mike, but all they could hear was gasping. "Sorry, Chief; it's a white poodle."

"Roger. Resume patrol. See me at the end of your shift."
"Yessir."

"I been after Reggie to get in shape," Swails chuckled, "Now I've got the ammo to force that Pillsbury Doughboy to cut back on the barbecue and longnecks he's been carryin' around."

"Do you have four men on the force here named Raymond, Rashid, Reginald, and Robbie?"

"Yeah, four brothers. You know them?"

Wilson laughed, "In a roundabout way. I was working with their aunt on a little problem."

"The aliens, I bet. Heard you got 'em." They both laughed.

"Yeah, I hope it's settled. The boys' mama is, I think, going to settle the feud."

"Those brothers are good men. Smart, and work hard."

They settled back, with the sound of birds in the background. "So the mission disappeared…" Wilson prompted.

"Yeah. Then, in the 1790s there was this man, Samuel Harrison. He'd been a Loyalist during the Revolution, so he moved his family to Spanish Florida. Safer for 'em, you know?"

Wilson nodded, and the Security Chief continued: "Got a land grant for 700 acres on the south end of the island, where he proceeded to plant sea island cotton. Harrisons were on that land until the 1960s." Wilson raised his eyebrows, surprised. "It's a fact. Look it up yourself at the museum."

I have *to get to that museum,* he reminded himself.

"Anyway," Swails continued, "Harrison built his house right near the site of the old mission, only nobody knew it, see? And the slaves had Franklintown, where they lived. Turns out, Franklintown was right near where our main entrance is, the gate you and Jordan came through yesterday."

Don't remind me

"When the Union troops came during the Civil War, the family burned everything to the ground so the Yankees wouldn't get it. They rebuilt after the war, same location, better house. The family finally sold it in the 1960s." Swails stood to fill a glass with iced tea from the big thermos Cook had provided.

"Dog Two, Base."

"Base, Dog Two."

"Chief, we're at the marsh. Now what?"

"Hold on." Wilson watched Swails think. "Dog Two, head south. Otherwise, you'll run into Dog One."

"Copy."

"This isn't going to be as easy as I thought." The Security

Chief paused. "It would be embarrassing to be outsmarted by a dog."

Wilson nodded in sympathy. He was here mostly for show; it was Swails' neck in the noose.

Suddenly Dog One was on the air. "Base, you aren't going to believe this, but I just watched that damned bulldog fly! She raced towards a mound of mulch, launched herself airborne ten feet away and landed in the middle — it exploded all around her like the proverbial stuff hitting the fan. She just rolled and snorted in the mess and then trotted off again, full tilt. Her white coat is one helluva mess of muck and leaves, in case anyone wants to know."

"But you have her in hand now, right, Dog One?" Swails asked, his patience wearing thin.

"No, Base. She went straight towards a swimming pool, landed with a big belly flop, and I thought she'd drown herself. But she dog-paddled to the steps and climbed out like she'd trained for it."

"So you let her walk on by? What are you doing out there, Dog One?"

"Well, Base, two little dogs came up on her and Patty snarled at them, so they headed off to the Jordan house and Patty musta seen the woman inside, waving her arms, 'cause she took off like a bullet through the brush, Mr. Swails."

Listening as Harvey Swails gave new instructions to his team, Wilson was surprised to discover he was rooting for the escapee! *Patty, 1; Security, zip.* He faked a cough to cover his laugh when he realized he was actually rooting for the underdog. Swails gave him a funny look, tilting his head, and Wilson held up his glass of tea, suggesting he'd swallowed it wrong. He stood. "Head call," he informed his companion, heading for the kitchen door.

Cook glanced up as he entered. "Anything yet?" she asked.

"Sighting near the Jordans'. Know where that is?"

She nodded. "Poor Patty. The Jordans have two yippy little dogs. Probably set up a terrible ruckus." Her weathered face looked sad and Wilson sidled up close to her.

"Whose side are you on, Mrs. Cook?"

"Just 'Cook.' I'm the help." She looked around before she whispered back. "Patty's."

"Me, too." He shared his pun about the underdog and Cook chuckled conspiratorially.

Deborah Wadsworth-Langford was in the kitchen when he returned from the bathroom. "I hear that Patty was seen at the Jordans.'"

"Yes, Ma'am. Their dogs made a fuss and Mrs. Jordan scared Patty off."

"Boy and Girl."

"Pardon?"

"That's their names: Boy and Girl. They wear pink and blue bows so Phyllis can tell them apart."

Cook snorted. "Mr. Paul calls 'em goodfernothin' hairballs."

"Well! They were good enough to tell us where Patty is!"

"Yessum."

When Deborah left the room, Cook muttered, "If I was Patty, I'd double back, or somethin.'"

"Or do a zig and a zag," Wilson agreed. He returned to Dog Base, where the radio chatter had died down. So far the time spent sitting around wasn't as boring as he feared, *Damn; now what?*

Chief Cabe's Cadillac pulled into the drive, a blue light flashing on the dash. The Caddie coasted to a stop. Cabe eased himself from behind the wheel. He nodded at Wilson, then shook hands with the Security Chief. "How's it goin'?"

"Had a sighting a few minutes ago; looks like she's headed south."

Cabe nodded sagely, and Wilson refrained from comment.

"Seen the Wadsworth-Langfords?"

Harvey shook his head no; Wilson reported his brief conversation with the lady of the house a few moments before. "Mrs. Cook's in the kitchen; if you go in, she'll tell them you're here."

"Mrs. Cook? Oh, you mean *Cook*. No need for the 'Mrs.,' Wilson; she's help." Cabe marched to the back door and entered without knocking.

Swails grimaced, "Is that why he calls you 'Wilson'? Because you're the help?"

Wilson shrugged and played with the toothpick from the sausages *Mrs.* Cook had slipped him. "That's my name."

Half an hour later, they watched Cabe's car pull out of the driveway. He had come out of the house in an expansive mood, smelling of expensive cigars and 12-year-old scotch, and had directed Wilson to stay all day, unless something broke.

The novelty of a quiet day in the April air had long since worn off. More to pass the time than from any great interest, Wilson recalled his companion to the history lecture. "Well, after the Harrisons left in the '60s, what happened next around here?"

The Security Chief hesitated; Wilson didn't know him well enough to read what his hesitation meant. Finally he grunted, "How about calling me by my first name? It's Harvey, you know." Wilson smiled and Harvey resumed the tale.

"At some point, Union Carbide got hold of the land. And at least twice, they thought seriously about strip mining it. Titanium."

"Strip mining? On this island? Are you serious?"

"Yeah. Don't know why they didn't go through with it."

Wilson looked around. He saw lush natural vegetation – a thick canopy of trees between where he sat and the beach a half-mile east. He also saw landscaped lawns, pricey homes, cars, pools, greenhouses, tennis courts, and golf courses. "I can't imagine."

"Yeah. Lucky us."

Wilson shot him a look, but saw no sarcasm. *Harvey really believes we are fortunate to have this enclave. On the other hand, I guess we could be looking at an empty, treeless expanse left by titanium mining.*

Harvey stood up and stretched, then bent to touch his toes. "Sitting too long. I'm usually all over the place, moving, instead of playing Dog Base." He flashed Wilson a big grin; they'd agreed hours ago that their current assignment was well below their expertise level.

"Okay, then, in the 1970s, a company out of Hilton Head bought

3,000 acres, with four miles of beach, for a cool $4.6 mill. Four years later, Amelia Island Plantation was official. Opening ceremonies on July 4, and every muckety-muck you ever heard of was here."

"Things went along fine here for several years, building roads and golf courses. Then, about 1985 or so, this one couple buys three acres along Harrison Creek. An architect designs their house and they start to clear the land to build.

"Only thing is, the backhoe digs up a stack of old bones." Harvey waggled his eyebrows, and Wilson noticed that they met in the middle. "They'd found the Mission Santa Maria. The Dorions — the couple who *thought* they were going to build there — went on to fund two or three archeological digs at the site.

"The archeologists at the Dorion Dig found about 150 graves, all Guale-Yamassee Indians. Must have been converted by the Franciscans. Found three walls of the church, too."

"Did the Dorions ever build their house?"

"Not right there. But anyway, when the Dorion Dig was done, the archeological crew carted everything off. The most important thing they found was a brass mission seal – the only one, or one of just a few, ever discovered in this hemisphere. Dr. Dorion turned over most of the items they found to the state of Florida, and some to the museum downtown, and some went to his old school — Williams College, I think. An' somebody arranged a Catholic ceremony and reburied the bones in Bosque Bello. Haven't found the graves yet, but I'm told they're there."

Harvey got up and walked a lap around their small Dog Base. It was obvious he was tired of staying in one place. "An' that's about it, as far as history goes. Now we just keep on keeping on. Keep the residents happy, help them when they need it." He looked over his shoulder to make sure they were alone. "Babysit one or two of them."

They spent the rest of the day swapping stories about work. As Wilson was heading to his car he told Swails, "Next time we get together, I'll tell you about the Miami pimp who tried to duck from a bullet fired by one of his girls."

———————•—•—

To Wilson's great relief, his babysitting duty ended very early the next morning with a call from Paul Wadsworth-Langford himself.

"No ransom note, no maiming, no dead dog." He spoke like a man whose death sentence had just been reprieved. "Actually, that sly old bitch had herself a time, rolling in something dead. Probably fed herself on field mice. Came home filthy and smelly. That lazy S.O.B. dog-handler had to get his hands dirty for a change." Paul related the details of Patty's return, on her own and in spite of the security team's efforts to run her to ground.

Wilson confirmed the details with Harvey later that day, when Swails called to invite him to be his guest at the next Rotary Club meeting. He assured Wilson there wasn't a better way to meet the town's up and comers.

Up and comers? Now there's an old-fashioned phrase to warm the heart. Thank you, Lord. For every bad guy in this town, there's two good ones inviting their friends to come on out and settle in. Harvey's gonna make a good friend.

Wilson's face wore a broad smile as he sat down at his computer keyboard to write up his report for the Chief on the satisfactory conclusion of the Patton's Pride case.

CHAPTER 31

At noon the Chief left for Jacksonville to attend a meeting. Wilson decided the afternoon would be a good time to put a little pressure on the ne'er-do-well LaFontaine son. Lately Wilson felt he was walking around with one hand tied behind his back.

He took the lunch his mother had packed for him and sat in the little break room with his much-used brown sack and coffee mug. He tasted the freshly brewed coffee when Dianne came in with her lunch. "Mind if I join you?" She smiled.

"Not at all." He stood and pulled a chair for her.

"This is the first time that's ever happened around here!" She sat and watched him seat himself.

"What?"

"Somebody actually showed some manners."

He blushed, feeling both embarrassed and pleased. "I guess my mama taught me well."

They ate in companionable silence for a few minutes, until she said, "Do you mind if I ask you a question?"

"Not at all, if it's not too personal."

"No, it's not personal. It's about work. Did the Chief really take you off the LaFontaine case?"

"I'm afraid so."

"But why? None of the other guys have the experience to handle a case like this."

"That, my friend, is a good question. I had just discovered the murder weapon and turned it over to the ME and FDLE. Standard procedure."

"I know; I typed your report. From what I've learned about police procedures, that was what you were supposed to do." She touched his arm.

"Apparently the Chief doesn't trust me enough yet to make that kind of a decision without running it by him first."

"Oh, but that's not…"

"Not fair? And no way to treat somebody you just hired to head up the Division? Precisely. You seem to know quite a bit about police procedures. How long have you worked here?"

"About five years. I started as a clerk typist, but a year ago I got promoted to 'secretary for everyone.' That doesn't mean much. Millie and I run the office together. Technically she's my boss, but she doesn't act like it. The Chief used to make her do all the menial jobs like make coffee and straighten up the reception area. Now I do."

"I guess you learn a lot about police procedures by working here."

"You sure do but…"

"But what?"

"Promise you won't laugh at me? I'm taking classes at the community college because I want to be a cop." She said this with enthusiasm and looking away she added, "I bet you think that's silly."

"Not at all. I can see you as detective material. Some of the best cops I knew in Miami were women."

She smiled widely. "I'm about halfway through my program, and I have applied for the Police Academy."

"That's how I got started, too. Took that introductory program at a community college; now I've got my B.S. and I'm working on my master's. How would you like to give me some help? Can you keep it to yourself?"

"Let me guess. You have no intention of staying away from this case, and you need somebody to cover for you? You can trust me." She smiled and then looked down at her coffee cup.

"I'm asking more than that. Could you get away for about an hour after we finish here?"

"Sure. Millie will cover for me. We do that for each other all the time. What do you have in mind?"

"I want to pay a visit to George LaFontaine this afternoon. I've been there once before and I ran into Rheba at the Palace Saloon last night." Dianne rolled her eyes and he smiled. "Actually, I saw her going in and I followed her, made it seem like an accidental meeting. Do you know her?"

"Everybody in town knows Rheba. We went to school together. She was a hot number. All the boys panted after her. We were bowled over when she married George, one of the town's most eligible bachelors at the time, a college boy from a well-off family. It's a pity what's become of the two of them."

"Last night she told me George and his dad argued a lot about the treasure map. You know about it?"

"Of course, I read the reports. I guess we'd all like it to be true. It's like winning the lottery, we hope that we'd be the one to find it."

"I'd like to talk to George about those arguments and find out what he knows about the map. Want to come along?"

"Great, let me clear it with Millie."

He watched her trim figure disappear out the door and once again found himself admiring her. *Beauty and brains, I could fall in love with a woman like this.*

———— •■• ————

Arriving in Old Town a short time later, he and Dianne found George – big surprise — sitting in front of the television with a can of beer in his hand. He was watching one of those programs that feature women and men in bizarre situations. Wilson and Dianne took a seat without being asked, and George continued to watch a tearful girl talking about her boyfriend sleeping with her sister. Wilson could see that once George had been a good looking guy and must have been thought of as quite a catch in a place like Fernandina.

Now he looked defeated, with a permanent scowl on his unshaved face. His dirty hair was pulled back into a ponytail, and he was dressed in tattered jeans and a tee shirt with "Shit Happens" printed on it. George waited for a commercial before he grumbled a hello.

"I'd appreciate it if you turned off the TV for a while, unless you'd rather go downtown so we can talk." Wilson's voice had some weight to it.

George reached over and killed the set. "You don't have to get huffy about it. So what do you want this time?"

"Just to talk a little more with you. Wife not home?" While he began his interrogation, Dianne stood and moved around the room quietly, touching this and that.

George took a slug of Old Milwaukee and waved the can around lazily. "Nope, haven't seen her since sometime yesterday."

"You don't seem too concerned. Does she do this often?"

"Stay out all night? Sometimes she's gone for days. No, I'm not concerned. Maybe I'll get lucky and she *won't* come home."

"Doesn't sound like much of a marriage."

"She thought I had a lot of dough, 'cause of my old man. She told him she was pregnant, knowing he'd insist I marry her."

"And she wasn't?"

LaFontaine drained the remaining beer, opened another and plopped his feet on the coffee table. "You don't see no kid running around here, do you?" He gestured with the can.

Wilson changed the subject. "Tell me, LaFontaine do you work?"

"Sure I work! Or I did until — you know...now I'm in mourning." His eyes were red and Wilson felt a belated twinge of sympathy.

"Of course. What are your plans for later? Do you inherit your father's estate?"

"I doubt it. He cut me out of his will. He said he was going to, but that damn shyster lawyer won't let me see the goddam will. Bet he left everything to that damn gold-digger he married."

"When did he tell you that he was cutting you out?"

He shrugged his shoulders. "Lots of times. Whenever we'd get into a row, which was ever' time I asked him for a raise or something."

"And Rheba knew about this?"

"About the will? We don't talk much anymore."

"So, she thinks you're coming into some money?"

"I don't know. Probably."

"Is she capable of murder?"

"Hopped up on coke, she's capable of anything."

Wilson looked up at Dianne. She motioned that she was going to the car. He nodded and waited for a long moment, then spoke, "One more thing, I understand you and your father quarreled about the treasure map."

George stared straight ahead, then glared at Wilson. "What treasure map? I never seen one. How could we fight about something that don't exist?"

"I heard that you and your dad have quarreled about it."

"If Rheba told you that, she's full of shit."

Just then the phone rang, but George made no move to answer it. "Aren't you going to answer it?" Wilson prompted.

"What for? It's probably for Rheba."

"Maybe it is Rheba."

"So?"

"Maybe it's the lawyer about the will."

George looked at the phone. "Okay, I'll answer the damn thing." He walked across the room and picked the receiver up with his right hand. "Wrong number." He fell back into his chair.

Wilson stood. "I'd better be going, and I'll let myself out."

George blinked as if surprised anyone was still in the room and switched on the TV sound to blare once again. Wilson heard him channel surfing as he left the man to his mourning.

As he slid into the car, Dianne was returning her cell phone to her purse.

"I thought for a minute he wasn't going to answer the phone," he said. "Now, tell me what you saw."

"He had a limp, definitely. Left leg. And he's right handed. He's drinking way too much —and question is, what is the underlying reason for it. How'd I do?"

"Great. Now do you remember that night we went to the LaFontaine house and somebody knocked me over?"

"Yes."

"You remember that Cornelia Upton said she saw somebody with a limp run across the yard?"

"Yes, but she didn't mention which leg was lame, did she?" Dianne looked away, trying to recall Mrs. Upton's exact words.

"Unfortunately, no. How about you? You were there; do you remember seeing which leg my assailant favored?"

She shook her head, "No, I was concentrating on you. But here I did get a look in the bedrooms, like you asked, while you were questioning George."

"Find anything interesting?"

"Certainly no signs of a map. You said you didn't expect me to. But no drug paraphernalia either. Not even any bags lying around."

He hid his disappointment with a smile. "Don't worry. You did all I asked. All anyone could do. And as a reward, how about having dinner with me tonight? Maybe at the house — you can spend a little time with me and the girls."

"I'd love that. You sure it's all right with…"

"Mom? She loves you, but I'll call and make sure it's okay. Pick you up about 6.30." He kissed her lightly on the cheek before he pulled the unmarked car away from George's drive.

That evening when he brought Dianne home, Priscilla greeted them at the door with a big smile lighting up her face, which was pink from the kitchen's heat. She wore a floral printed apron over her sky-blue dress. The smell of frying chicken permeated the air.

Dianne, dressed in dark green slacks and a light green sweater, gave her a hug and offered to help in the kitchen. Priscilla beamed at her, but declined.

Wilson took Dianne by the hand and led her to the comfortable living room where the children were lying on the floor, playing with their American Girl dolls. The home on Broome Street was a large ranch style house, built in the '60s, with a family room and four bedrooms. Wilson told Dianne how proud his dad had been when he acquired the house. He'd made a good buy. His mother could never afford to buy there now, with the way real estate prices had risen. Amelia Island had become one of the most desirable places to live in the northeast Florida area.

The girls jumped up as they entered the room and Lisa took Dianne's hand. Prissy, her lovely blonde hair pulled back behind her delicate ears, tried very hard to act more grown up. She stood and took a step forward, offering her hand. "Miss Dianne, it's good to see you."

Dianne relinquished Wilson's hand to take Prissy's in her own. "I'm happy to see you both again, Prissy and Lisa."

Prissy looked up at her father, who spoke up, "We're calling her Priscilla now. She's getting older."

"Priscilla, then." Dianne corrected herself with a smile.

"I'm named after Grandma, but everybody calls me Prissy, even the teacher at school."

Suddenly Lisa was holding her doll in front of Dianne, "This is Emily. And I'm named for Grandma too." She laughed.

"Oh?" Dianne looked puzzled.

Prissy frowned at Lisa. "She's named for our other Grandma. Her name is...ah...ah..." She looked to her father.

"Lisa Emily," he came to her rescue.

"Yes," Prissy said, "it's Lisa Emily." She spoke with pride. "She lives in Naples, which is in Florida."

"Two very pretty names for two very pretty girls," Dianne told them.

"I want to sit by Miss Dianne," Lisa said, quickly placing herself in the spot. Prissy sat across from them and gave a "watch out for her" look to her father.

During the meal Dianne asked Lisa, "How do you like school?"

"Oh, it's okay. We're learning numbers and the alpabet."

"Alphabet," Prissy corrected.

"I don't care." Lisa made a scrunched face at her sister.

"Let's not be mean when we have company," Wilson admonished.

"Reminds me of summer visits with cousins when I was young," said Dianne. "And, Priscilla, how is your school? You're going to Southside Elementary, aren't you?"

"Yes, Ma'am. It's fine."

Her grandmother added, "Priscilla has been asked to be in a play and one of her friends wants her to be in a junior cheerleading squad."

"That's great. You'll make a very pretty cheerleader. What's the name of the play?" Dianne was working to get a conversation going with the little girl.

"Something about flowers in a garden. I don't exactly remember." She was not rude but didn't show a lot of enthusiasm. Wilson gave her a stern look. He knew what she was doing and would attend to it later.

From then on through dessert, Lisa became the center of attention when she chattered about her dolls and the story she was having them act out. Dianne offered to help with the cleanup, but the girls' grandmother insisted they loved to help her.

Wilson picked up two cups of coffee and steered Dianne out onto the patio. She sat on the glider, in a soft light coming though the window. He sat in one of the matching chairs and put his coffee on the black wrought iron table between them.

She sighed contentedly, "Your girls are adorable."

"They seemed to have taken to you, too. I've never seen Lisa warm up so rapidly to someone." He hoped Prissy's coolness hadn't been noticed.

"It's nice that you can be here with your mom. You know, both of my parents are gone pretty much out of my life. After their divorce, Dad left for the West Coast. Mom remarried, and they live in Tampa. I don't see her very often. My older sister and her husband live in Jacksonville, and we get together fairly often. You're an only child, aren't you?"

"Yep. Changing the subject, we need to talk some about the case."

"You have a hard time taking time off, don't you? Luckily, so do I, so go ahead."

"It's hard, being new in the community and running into such an important case. The Chief confounds me."

"Yes, it must be hard, being used to a certain professionalism." Wilson raised an eyebrow.

"I mean, the rest of us have lived here for a long time. We know all these people. We have long-held opinions and prejudices toward them. You can look at them with fresh eyes."

"Maybe, but I need to get a handle on some of those opinions, and soon. So far Bobby, Wilbur and Evans are friendly enough, but still unhappy about my coming in as head of the department. Can't say that I blame them. They're competent, but they don't fully trust me yet. The Chief hasn't set much of an example there. What I need is somebody who will trust me enough to share their opinions with me."

"And you want to know if I'm that person? We went over this that evening at the Crab Trap."

"Reassure me, Dianne. You could be putting your job at risk if Cabe finds out you're helping me."

There was a long pause, and he couldn't see her expression in the dim light. Finally she spoke almost in a whisper. "Okay, you have me, but…"

"You have some reservations? I accept that; you're a sensible woman."

"Not exactly reservations. It's just that you are right about the job. I'd like to hang on to it. It's a stepping-stone for me. If the guys or Millie get wind of us working together, they would go right to the Chief, and I'd be out of here."

"So we'll have to meet like this, away from the office. That suits me fine." He leaned close and kissed her for a long moment. She returned the kiss. When they parted, he settled back in the chair and took a deep breath. He looked at her and whispered, "Thank you."

"For what?" she said quietly.

He looked at her in the soft light. "I don't know."

She took a sip of coffee and smiled. "Okay, where do we start?"

"I'm still confused by the Chief and why he's so touchy about this LaFontaine case. Maybe I need you to fill me in some more on his background and what he's really like," he said. There was a long silence. "If that's a touchy subject, we can skip it."

"No, that's okay, it's just that it is difficult for me. Talking honestly about John Cabe is like talking about a member of my family. My dad was a car mechanic and ran a shop in town for years. He'd fix the Chief's cars and they became fishing buddies."

"Funny, I don't see Cabe as a weekend fisherman."

"I think it was mostly to get away from his last wife, but be that as it may, the Chief has been good to me, especially after my parents' divorce. I was 15 when that happened. In many ways he's been a father figure to me since then. He gave me this job, and he supports my wanting to be a cop.

"Look, he's not very popular in town," she went on. "He is feared, because he is tough. Years ago he killed a couple of men in the line of duty and some citizens questioned his actions. As far as I know, he has no family and no close friends, but a lot of admirers, mostly because of his toughness on criminals.

"I think he has a mistress somewhere over in Yulee, but I don't know that for a fact. That's as much as I want to say about him." She fell silent but seemed to be struggling with something.

"Obviously, he's a different man with you. He's your friend."

"No, it's not that," she said abruptly. "Yes, I have divided loyalties here, but I want to help you solve this case. Maybe that's the policewoman in me. I'm no longer a teenager going to John Cabe for comfort. I love him, he's like family, but sometimes, I don't like him very much. He loves power, more power than his job offers."

"A Chief of Police has a lot of power, Dianne. What more is

he looking for?"

"He's been talking to some politically powerful people about running for Port of Fernandina Director. Robert LaFontaine was one of the powers-that-be. You probably don't know this, but LaFontaine, his creepy little friend, Cajun Jack, and Chief Cabe all came from the same town in Louisiana."

"Cajun Jack told me about that when I met him at the pogy plant one night. I agree with you; he is certainly a suspicious character, like a will-o'the-wisp, appearing and disappearing all the time. The Chief sees him as the prime suspect. Jack Laffon had the opportunity, going in and out of the LaFontaine house often, but I don't know about motive. According to him, LaFontaine more or less supported him. They go way back, as you said."

He went on, "You remember that night you saw him in the house? Cajun Jack says his mother gave him a treasure map, which he gave to LaFontaine for safekeeping. Maybe he was looking for it. Cajun Jack inferred once that it was in Jacksonville for safe keeping; but it may have been brought back here; I think it's tied with the murder, somehow." He stood up and stretched. "Let me get some more coffee?"

He was back in a few minutes, ready to consider other suspects. "When I talked with William Carless the other day, he went on about wanting to captain his own boat." Wilson put his hands behind his head and leaned back, giving her time to consider her answer.

She said, "He's got a rap sheet, mostly for being drunk and disorderly, it's possible he's so angry that he could kill his uncle. But his death has left him with no job."

"Unless he thought he'd inherit?" Wilson asked, prompting another consideration of William.

"That's a possibility, but I think it's remote. But that's true for George and Rheba, too, either one of them could be the killer. And then there is the widow, Marlene." He was seriously interested in Dianne's take on "Number Three" as Roger called her.

"She runs with a fast crowd down at the Plantation. Definitely not Robert's kind of people. There are a lot of rumors about her and other men."

"About the Plantation... what is with those people?"

Dianne held up a hand. "Wait a minute. I know you ran into one or two of *those people* in the dog chase, but did you know Millie lives there, too?"

"No!"

"Uh-huh. She's loaded... and, like Millie, 99 percent of *those people* are really nice."

"I'm sorry. I let a first impression get to me. The lady-of-the-house, Deborah Wadsworth-Langford, was as friendly as you'd want. But dealing with her husband was like stepping on a sandspur."

He drank the last of his cold coffee. "Back to Mrs. LaFontaine."

"She's in that one percent. You'll find her kind anywhere." Dianne grimaced.

"She *is* a piece of work. That first day, when LaFontaine was found murdered, sparks were flying all over the place between her and the Chief." He gave a short laugh, "He said he was going to check out her story. I wonder if he ever did. She had plenty of motivation if, and that's a big if, she's the primary heir."

He glanced at the illuminated dial of his watch. "Hey, look at the time. I had better get you home. I'll tell Mom we're going."

In a few minutes he accompanied Dianne onto her porch. "Thank you," she said sweetly, "for dinner and asking my opinion. That was nice, feeling trusted."

"Likewise." They leaned in toward each other, and he noticed he was having a little trouble breathing. The fragrance of her shampoo mingled with a nearby night-blooming jasmine. He touched her hair and ran the back of his hand across her cheek. Their lips met tentatively and then urgently, their tongues flickered against each other. He felt her breasts pressing against him. Suddenly he wanted her. He took in her tremulous smile, her eyes, auburn hair, her youth, and he was struck by guilt. *I have two girls to raise. And a mother who's going to be a burden, soon. I don't have the right to love anyone new. Not now. Maybe...*

"Would you like to come in?" she whispered.

"I'd best get home. Promised the girls a story before bedtime..." His voice trailed off.

She kissed him on the cheek and whispered a "goodnight," opened the door and disappeared inside. Wilson stumbled down the steps toward the car. He heard the deadbolt click into place and the porch light went out. *You damn fool.*

CHAPTER 32

Wilson sat at the breakfast table, trying not to let the previous night distract him. Lisa was telling him of the little brown robin she found in the back yard.

"...And, Daddy, it was so small, I wanted to keep it but Grandma said it would die, so I put it back. Grandma said its mommy would come back and help it. Is that true? Daddy?" She toyed with her cereal spoon. "Daddy, you aren't listening to me."

"Oh...yes I am, sweetie. Grandma is right. The mother bird will be back." He looked at his little daughter sitting next to him. She began again spooning up the multicolored cereal.

"How'd the date go, Daddy?" Prissy asked, giving him a sideways look.

"Fine, and none of your business. Thank you." He returned the sideways look.

Lisa started in, "Daddy's got a girlfriend. Daddy's got a girl friend."

He got up. "Okay, I'm out of here. I know when I'm out numbered."

After quick kisses goodbye, he drove toward the station without thinking of the case, for a change. *How am I going to handle it when I see Dianne this morning? I'll just be cool. And friendly, I'll ask how she is and maybe apologize for not going in. No, that won't work. I hope she isn't mad. Hell, I'll just wing it.*

He entered the building through the back door to look in his mailbox. He went out of his way to pass Dianne's office, but she

wasn't in. *Strange, she's always early.* He picked up messages out
of his slot, scanned some, throwing away most, and saw one from
Evans, about the LaFontaine case. Evans kept him abreast of the
case as a courtesy, and Wilson appreciated it. He slowly moved
toward the door, reading the note. Evans hadn't picked up Cajun
Jack on the trip out to the pogy plant. *Indeed, Cajun Jack is wily. I
have to thank Evans for holding off, as promised.*

Chief Cabe rounded the corner, coffee cup in hand. "Wilson, I
need to see you in my office in about ten minutes. Whatcha' got
goin'?"

Wilson met his eyes. "Finishing the information for Orlando
and getting it on the wire, first off. I haven't read any of last night's
reports yet. Maybe one or two that I might need to look into." The
Chief grunted and poured a little coffee in his cup, tasted it, then
filled the oversized mug, almost emptying the pot. Without another
word Cabe turned toward his office.

"Chief..." Wilson called out as he followed.

"Yeah?" Cabe stopped.

"How about lunch? My treat."

The Chief's eyes narrowed. "Thanks, but no. I'm meeting with
the City Manager to go over final preparations for Shrimp Festival
security. You going, Wilson?"

"To the Festival? Oh, yeah. Dianne invited me and we're taking
my girls to the parade and the pirates' invasion and to catch all the
action on Saturday too. Looking forward to my day off. How's the
finger coming along? You got a tetanus shot, of course?"

Cabe frowned. "No, I had one several years ago. It's coming
along okay." He sounded puzzled by Wilson's interest and clearly
put off balance by his probing. He turned expectantly at the sound
of a woman in high heels coming down the hall.

"You guys going to block the hallway all day?" Dianne had a
bright smile to greet them. Wilson moved aside. She looked great
today in a black skirt and pale pink blouse. Her auburn hair was up
in a twist and her trim body was a blend of lovely curves. She
passed with a cheery "Good morning," coffee cup in hand. Cabe

mumbled a greeting and moved on to his office.

"I'll catch you in a sec, Chief. I need to see Dianne," Wilson said and moved after her without waiting for Cabe's answer. When he caught up to her, she was pouring the last of the coffee into her cup.

"Damn, you look good today," he whispered. "You make me very sorry I didn't come in last night." She looked up and met his gaze steadily.

"I thought about it after you left. I should be the one to apologize. I was rushing it. Rushing us, I mean."

"You're wrong there. It's time. Past time." He shrugged his shoulders and fumbled for words. "The girls depend on me, maybe too much, now that their mother's gone. I try to warn them when I'm not going to be there. If I'm not going to be there to read the nightly bedtime story, that sort of thing."

Dianne stirred sugar into her coffee, listening closely to what he was saying. "I admire you, Wilson. Few men I know put their children first. Ever."

"I'm all they have now. It's as simple as that."

"You're sure that's it? I'm not missing a turn-down here?"

"I'm sure," he growled, unaccustomed to being grilled. At that, she winked at him over the rim of her coffee cup.

"In that case, I'll warn you next time, way ahead of time. I'm giving you one more chance."

"Next time, I'll make sure my girls are warned. Make no mistake about that," he said.

She kissed her index finger and put it to Wilson's lips. "I have to get to work." She moved past him, brushing his coat sleeve. Her perfume lingered as he watched her disappear.

"Dianne..." He heard her stop.

"Yes, dear?"

Wilson moved in close again and murmured, "Let me know when the Chief leaves this afternoon." Just then Millie turned the corner.

"You really know how to turn a woman on," Dianne responded

loudly, grinning as she opened her office door, leaving Wilson to grope for an explanation for Millie. He waved his hand ineffectually toward the secretary and moved toward Cabe's office. It was the easier alternative.

———————•—•——————

Shortly after 1:30 Dianne called him, "Chief Cabe just left. He should be gone about three hours."

"Thanks. By the way, I will get back at you."

"For what?"

"You really know how to turn on a woman." He mimicked her voice.

"Oh, that. I'll be watching out for you," she giggled and hung up the phone.

With Cabe out of the way, Wilson left for the docks to look for the *Miss Jane*. Parking was a hazard on Front Street due to road repairs. He parked in the lot near Brett's and walked north, stopping at several shrimpboats moored at the docks to ask questions and get directions. He found the *Miss Jane* was further toward the mill at the north end.

Just behind him, a train chugging toward the mill blared its whistle loud and long. He stopped to watch the blue and yellow locomotive pull a long line of open cars filled with pine logs and chips. The smell of fresh-cut pine permeated the air. The engineer stared at Wilson impassively as three exhausts put out carbon-black smoke and the railcars clickety-clacked along the worn rails that ran beside Front Street. The sound of raw power reverberated in Wilson's chest. In another hundred feet, he stood where the *Miss Jane* was berthed.

A deck hand stood to challenge him when he stepped aboard. Wilson flashed his badge and asked, "Where's Carless?"

The man pointed to the stern. Wilson saw someone with his back to him working on a net. "Mr. Carless, mind if we talk?"

Carless looked up at him. "Free country." He didn't stop his work.

"Just wondering if you'd tell me again what you saw and heard the night your uncle was killed."

"Nothing to add to what I told you in Chief Cabe's office. I don't reckon I can help."

Wilson watched the man cutting something from the shrimp nets. He leaned against the gunwale. "What are you doing?" He found himself genuinely interested.

Carless stopped, took the cigarette from his lips, flipped it past Wilson into the Amelia River. Wilson didn't flinch. Carless lit another, and asked, "You thinking of taking up shrimping?"

"No, just curious what you're doing; it looks like some black rope got scrambled up in the net."

The shrimper spread out the net and, using a short, sharp knife, pointed at the black rope. "This is called whiskers. We split 'em and tie 'em to the bottom of the nets to protect them when they're being drug across the bottom. It saves the nets. Only we had too many on there. They weigh down the nets when we haul in the catch. That puts a strain on the winch."

"Interesting. What size crew takes a boat out?"

Carless took a long drag from the cigarette he kept in the corner of his mouth. "Three, maybe four, if shrimp're running real good. Look, is there anything else? I don't know who killed Uncle Robert." He turned his back and slashed angrily at the black whiskers.

Wilson looked around. Pelicans patrolled the waterfront, swooping and gliding within inches of the water's glass-smooth surface. A yellow-topped pelican hoping for a free handout from the boats occupied every piling of the docks. .

The wind shifted and came from the east. The strong smell of old shrimp hit Wilson in the face. He wondered how much a two-week stay out in the ocean paid a deck hand, but he didn't ask.

"You know all the people that your uncle dealt with in the shrimping business," he said quietly. "Who had a motive for wanting him dead?"

Carless stood, tossed the clean net into a pile, and grabbed another one from the deck. "Like I said, there was a few people that didn't like him. Hell, I bet there are a few people that don't like you."

That caught Wilson off guard. "Sure. But they're in prison," he said, surprised into telling the truth.

"I'd go after that oversexed wife — or now it's the widow, isn't it? Yep, I'd try for that one."

"Really? Why?"

"I'd say she has the most to gain." The man's knife cut easily through the tough black nylon fibers.

"You had something to gain, I'd say." Wilson stared at him steadily.

"Oh yeah? Now he's dead, Georgie boy and the bitch inherit the wealth."

Wilson tried a different tack.

"Look at it this way. I get information you were seen leaving the LaFontaine house late at night when Uncle Robert wasn't home." Carless stopped work and raised his flushed face, glaring angrily. "Could it be that you and the lovely Mrs. have come up with a plan, thinking that young George is out of the picture as far as the will goes? Maybe you plan that she gets the money and you get the fleet, since she hates anything to do with the smelly business. And all you have to do is make sure that you both outlive old Uncle Robert, if you get my drift."

Carless ripped at the net's whiskers with the knife. "You are so screwed up. There ain't no truth in that and further more..." The knife slipped and gashed Carless' finger.

Quickly Wilson reached for his handkerchief and pressed it against the cut. "Son of a bitch." Carless shouted, tugging away from him. "Why don't you leave me alone? I don't know anything."

The mate appeared with a first-aid kit. Wilson stood back, holding the bloody handkerchief at his side. "I'll leave after you answer one more question." As the mate poured disinfectant on the cut, Carless didn't look up.

"What is it?"

"How'd you get that limp? Maybe jumping off a porch? It

wasn't there the first time we talked."

The mate smirked, showing gaps where upper teeth were missing, and pointed to the narrow steps that led to the dock, "His drunk ass stepped wrong off those steps over there — he gets that way sometimes." He went back to bandaging the cut.

Once the mate had a semblance of a bandage on his hand, Carless stood up and leaned against the rail across the boat from Wilson, he said, "I have ideas about who killed dear old Uncle Robert, but I didn't do it. Marlene has high hopes of being a member of the Amelia Island Beauty Queen Society. This just may be her ticket." He was waving the knifepoint at Wilson, then flicked his wrist, sending the knife into the deck beside his own feet. He sauntered over to Wilson.

The two men stood firm, like bookends, inches away from each other. Wilson could smell today's sweat and yesterday's catch on the shrimper. He spoke slowly and distinctly, "If you ever point even a finger at me again, I'll take it from you and shove it up your ass." He paused for a second, "Be seein' you 'round."

William Carless didn't blink, but took a step back and made a mock bow as Wilson stepped off the boat. Both crewmen watched Wilson disappear behind the buildings on Front Street. He put the bloody handkerchief in a plastic bag in the trunk of his car before he took off for the station.

CHAPTER 33

B ack at his desk, Wilson read the Post-It note and recognized Dianne's handwriting. "Call M.E." He picked up the phone and dialed. "You asked me to call you?"

"Can't you read?" she teased, "There's a period after the M. and the E. Call the Medical Examiner in Jacksonville."

"I know that."

"Uh-huh."

"I just wanted to talk to you." He leaned back in the chair, tapping the desk gently with the eraser end of a pencil.

"I'm really busy. Trying to get the schedule for the Shrimp Festival arranged. Be nice or you'll have to work it all three days."

"How about later?"

"Call me at home. Bye."

He pressed the switch-hook and dialed.

"Duval County Medical Examiner. This is Janice."

"Hi, Janice, this is Lieutenant Wilson from Fernandina Beach. Is John Hershey in?"

"Honey, he sure is. When are you going to come see me?"

"Call me anytime. I'll come sweep you off your feet, if you aren't careful."

"Please...do that. Wait and I'll get John."

A calm voice came over the line. "This is Hershey."

"Wilson, Fernandina Beach Police. I'm returning your call and also have another favor to ask."

"Who's first?"

"You."

John Hershey, Wilson's newfound friend, spoke in a deliberate professional voice. He told Wilson that the wound entry and subsequent tissue damage were consistent with the gnomon's physical structure. The traces of blood were the victim's.

"In other words, in my humble opinion you have the murder weapon. A report is being typed up and will be on its way to you tomorrow. What's up? Anything else I can do for you?"

"I have a blood sample I need checked. In case we find any more at the scene, which I doubt. The cleaning woman did a thorough scrubbing."

"That reminds me. We found a nick on the gnomon's shaft with a different blood type in that area."

"What?"

"Sorry, it's in the report but it slipped my mind. I sent it off to Tallahassee with the other samples, for DNA. It's not the victim's blood, or either of the workers at the house. Any help?"

"Maybe so. Hershey, can you keep the information held back for a few days? I need some time. And I'll bring the blood sample by tomorrow morning."

"You guys playing cat-and-mouse will get me fired yet." There was a pause. "Okay. I'll give you a week. After that, anyone calls, I have to come clean."

"Thanks, John, I owe you." He hung up the phone, leaned back in the chair. "Wilbur, are you in?" He called.

"He's not here," came a voice from Bobby's office. "He went to the State Attorney's office. Left about fifteen minutes ago. Can I help?"

"No, thanks, I'll catch him later."

He added sarcastically, "I have an appointment with a tea-witch." then mumbled, "Bless her nosy soul."

———————— • ■ • ————————

Ten minutes later, parked on Seventh Street, he buried his face in his hands. *Oh, God. There is no help for it; I have to see Mrs.*

Upton again. He really didn't have an afternoon to sip weak tea out of a tiny cup while trying to extract a crumb of information from her ramblings.

He turned the engine off; without the air conditioner running, the interior quickly heated up. Damned if he was going to bake in Mrs. Upton's driveway. He powered down all of the windows, got out of the car and shrugged into his lightweight sport coat, which was a little old and way too small for him. It felt like an Arctic-quality parka. *Stop fighting it.* He squared his shoulders and slapped a pleasant expression on his face.

Sully answered the door, and his smile turned sincere. He liked Sully; she was a no-nonsense woman.

"Lieutenant Wilson. Do come in. She's ready for you."

I'll just bet she is. Sully must have read his mind, "An' I hope you're ready for her," she said.

"I most certainly am; it's always a pleasure to visit with Miz Upton."

Sully led him from the foyer into the front parlor. She eyed him critically. Mischief lit up her huge brown eyes, "You better be ready; she's been somethin' else today!"

Cornelia Upton was once again enthroned on the settee. Today she wore pale blue, accessorized by a magnificent collection of lapis lazuli: earrings, beads and brooch. A large cabochon graced her right hand, which she extended as if she were the Queen. He pressed it gently and sat next to her to avoid the uncomfortable chair that had tortured him the last time.

"How nice of you to come again, Lieutenant Wilson. Still punctual, too; right on the dot!"

His smile was noncommittal as he started to ask the first question on his list, then stopped himself. Cornelia Upton believed in observing *all* of life's rituals. There would be no business until tea was served.

Sully appeared with the state tea set, which she placed on the rosewood table. Wilson once again endured Miz Cornelia's pouring ceremony. The Limoges cup was just as lovely as on his first encounter, and as terrifying to handle.

"I have been in a rememberin' mood, Lieutenant. Old people do that, you know."

She patted a large book that lay between them. It was covered in deep green brocade, and contrasted nicely with the red of the settee.

"That's a beautiful book, Miz Cornelia; a scrapbook?"

"Indeed it is. I have over fifty of these, cataloguing my life from the time I moved to Fernandina as a young bride." She fluttered her eyes at him. "I was only eighteen when my papa let me marry Mr. Upton. He brought me here and we lived with his parents in this very house until we could find one of our own. We moved back here when Red's parents passed on."

"Red?"

She opened the book to the exact page she wanted and showed him a color photograph of a large man with the reddest hair Wilson had ever seen.

"My husband. His name was Frederick, but everybody called him Red. And his hair was that color up until the day he died, God rest his soul. "

She flipped to another page of photos. "Here we are at Moore's Grocery over at the beach. We used to go dancing there, some Saturday nights."

"You went dancing in a grocery store?"

"Well, they called it a grocery, but it was so much more." She smiled. "Morris and Mabel Moore started it, then his son took it over in the late 1940s. In its heyday, there was the grocery —Ed, the son, was the butcher — and a dance hall and a bar, all under one roof. Took up that whole corner where Sandy Bottoms and Beachside Commons are now."

As he assumed an appropriately astonished expression, she continued, "Mr. Moore was quite the businessman. Before the grocery, he ran a barbershop in the Three Star Saloon, on Centre Street."

"The barbershop was in a saloon?"

Her laugh tinkled off the chandelier above them. "My heavens, no! William Marsten had built the old Three Star Saloon in 1877 and held court there for many years. He evidently enjoyed being a publican a little too much for his family's tastes, 'cause when he died, his daughter sold it, with the provision that 'spirits' would never be sold there again. And they haven't. It's been a barbershop, a jeweler's, a clothing store, and now I believe it's a gift shop. Still in the same pretty building."

"I've noticed the stars embedded in its façade." He paused to sip his tea. "What I really wanted to ask you about is the other night when we, er..."

"Oh, look! Here's a picture of me and Red at the Palace Saloon!"

Wilson wasn't surprised at her refusal to give up her reminiscing. "The Palace? Looks like it's always been a hot spot, eh?"

"Oh yes. And it almost burned down a few years ago. The day after Valentine's Day. We all made jokes about hot-blooded folks setting the house on fire!" He gave an appreciative chuckle.

"That old building has had a colorful history," she went on. "It all started with that Damnyankee, Josiah Prescott. He was part of the Army of the Occupation, and after the war, he came back with his family."

Wilson knew enough to realize that the Army of the Occupation meant the Union troops bivouacked at Fort Clinch and in the town during the Civil War.

"He constructed the building, set it up as his Cash Boot and Shoe Store." Gently she stroked a photo. "Then Louis Hirth bought it and spent years turning it into a watering hole for the wealthy gentlemen waiting to be ferried over to Cumberland Island.

"That oak bar you see there today cost him fourteen hundred dollars, but he got the murals cheap. After the fire, the new owners made it a point to reproduce them while repairing the inside."

Wilson had put his teacup down and was uneasily shifting in his seat, hoping she was almost done. She held out a hand to forestall his interruption. "The last thing I wanted to tell you about happened before my time, in 1918, when they passed the Volstead Act. Of course, everyone knew Prohibition would go into effect the next day, so on August 19th, they all flocked to the Palace for one last fling. The saloon had stocked up...had cases of beer and liquor stashed all over town. Special trains and buses were laid on, and thousands of people came from all over. That day, they took in sixty thousand dollars! And that was before you had to pay income tax!"

His mouth dropped open. *What a neat chunk of change.* He looked at the picture Miz Cornelia had been caressing all this time, taken long after Prohibition had been repealed. The saloon was obviously thriving. Two men stood on either side of a much younger Red and Cornelia Upton. One fellow he recognized, and he felt he should know the other.

"Isn't that Robert LaFontaine on the left?"

"Yes, it certainly is! We were all celebrating his birthday in… " — she gazed back in time to recapture the moment — "Let me see… 1960! It was Bobby's twenty-something birthday; Bobby and Red both worked the boats then, long before either one of them made captain or owned their own boats."

"Who's the other man?"

"Why, that's Jack Laffon! Cajun Jack, they call him. Don't tell me you've never met him."

"Just once or twice, very briefly." He studied Cajun Jack more closely and then roused himself. "Speaking of Cajun Jack, I wanted to talk to you about the other night."

Mrs. Upton's shoulders slumped and her face lost some of its animation. "I know you do. It's just that the present is so unpleasant. I like to escape to the past when I can."

He felt a surge of sympathy; his impatience with her prattle evaporated. He'd often revisited Grace in his memories himself, to make his own escapes.

"Believe me, Miz Cornelia, I understand. But I need to find out more about the other night." She nodded. "Did you notice the prowler's limp when he was running?"

"It was rather pronounced, wasn't it? Especially after he ran through my rose bushes!" She chuckled.

He shared her laugh, and then asked the crucial question: "Which leg did he limp on?" She set her cup in its saucer with a clang and rang the silver bell on the tray. Sully appeared before it stopped ringing, bearing a cup of dark liquid for her employer and a fresh pot of tea for Wilson. *Oh, goody*, he thought.

"Think for a moment; it's important, so don't guess if you're not sure."

She raised an eyebrow and took a healthy swallow of the liquid in her teacup. "I don't guess, young man! I'm seventy-seven and I'm through guessing in this life. I've thought a lot about that night, and I am positive: he limped with a bad left foot. I'm almost sure." She reached down to stroke the nearest cat and began to croon to it.

He wanted to ask if she was absolutely sure, but her dreamy glance stopped him. A limp on the left would eliminate William Carless, the nephew; he had a bad right foot. That left George LaFontaine and Cajun Jack, both of whom had bum left legs.

What would a prosecuting attorney do with Cornelia Upton as a witness? Would her moving about in time erase any efforts to get justice in the courts? He plunged ahead.

"Miss Cornelia, our department is very grateful for the information you have given us. I know you have talked to Detective Evans, but I need to again ask. Have you recalled anything more?"

She cocked her head sideways, reminding him of a little bird looking for a tidbit. "Like what?"

"I've heard that on the day Mr. LaFontaine was...taken, several people came to see him. Do you remember who they were? Maybe while you were tending those beautiful roses, you heard something?"

"Well, let's see." She closed her eyes and spoke pensively. "There were some people by that day. It was unusual, how they almost came in a line. Hmmm. There was a young man, and ol' stinky Cajun Jack, and Chief Cabe, and maybe one other man."

She opened her eyes and looked at Wilson. "Does that help any?"

"Yes, Ma'am. Do you remember who came first and so on?"

"Well, that was...what two weeks ago? Let me think." She leaned back a little and closed her eyes again. "In the morning, just after ten, I was having my second cup of hot tea at ten and Chief Cabe came by."

"Did you hear any loud talk?"

"Well, I *was* in the garden, not being nosy, of course. Robert had his windows open, so of course, I could hear some talk and occasionally it was a little loud."

"Do you know what it was about?"

"Well, if I heard anything, I wouldn't want to make sense of it. It seemed to be about money. The Chief said he was disappointed that Robert wouldn't help."

"What about the others? Did Cajun Jack and Mr. LaFontaine have loud words?"

"Yes, but they were laughing. I don't see why. They are of a *different class*, if you know what I mean."

"Yes, Ma'am. So they never sounded angry? No threats? It's important. What about when Cajun Jack left?"

"Lord, no. It was later in the day, just before sunset. I was out in the garden then too. I was watering the flowers. You know we're supposed to water in the evening when we're in a drought?" Wilson nodded. "Well, as Cajun Jack came out the door, I heard him say he needed something — I can't remember what it was — and he would be back if he couldn't get it."

"Did he sound threatening?"

"I wouldn't say so. They kind of laughed."

"When did the last man come to see Mr. LaFontaine?"

"Well, right then, it was. Cajun Jack was leaving and here comes this dirty looking young man. He gave me a mean look that sent me to the back of the yard. I waited back there until he was in Robert's house." She leaned a little closer as if to keep the cats from hearing the tale. "Then I came back around to finish watering the flowers."

Wilson smiled at her resolve to hear more. "How long did he stay? And did he have a limp?"

"A short time and no limp." She sounded regretful. "There was loud talk almost the whole while. I got a little afraid for Robert and was thinking of calling the police. But then the man left in a huff. You could tell he was mad."

"Anything else?"

"He waved to me, as I was finishing the watering, The poor boy had lost some fingers, in an accident I suppose."

"Missing fingers?"

"Yes, when he waved, it was like this." She held up a folded hand with the middle finger raised.

With an effort, he concealed his laugh with a cough. "Was that the last man to come to visit?"

"Oh, no. About nineish I heard young George. I was at my kitchen sink and Robert's porch light was on."

"Do you know when he left? Did they argue?"

"No, I don't know. I went to get the kitties ready for bed and then I went on to bed myself."

He had what he needed from her, finally. But he knew better than to bolt out the door. He gave her his most endearing smile, the one he'd used with great success on Grace, before she'd learned better. "I have to go soon, but I have time for one more story, Mrs. Upton, pick a photo and tell me something I haven't heard before!"

She quickly found yet another photograph of her beloved Red and her face lit up one more time. He listened patiently for twenty minutes while he heard how Cornelia and Red found a treasure map that turned out to be yet another fake. Just as the old woman began to flag, Sully appeared like magic and escorted him towards the door.

"How many cups of tea did you have, Lieutenant?"

"Four or five. I lost count."

She stopped and opened a door to a tiny powder room off the foyer. "I imagine you understand why some people call this the...necessary!"

"Sully, could I talk to you for a few minutes," —he looked at the neat powder room —"in a minute or two?"

Sully looked back to the parlor and then said, "I'll tidy up and we can talk on the front porch."

Shortly, he was on the porch, and the screen door opened. Sully appeared at his side, "Yes, Sir, what can I do for you?"

He sat on the top step and Sully took a large wooden rocking chair. "You've worked for Miz Cornelia many years."

"Yes, Sir. Going on over forty-something, I guess. Why?"

"Fair enough. Does she spend a lot of time thinking of the past? I mean, sometimes when we've talked, she seems to be referring to happenings from a long time ago."

"Oh, she has good memories of the past...and some that hurt her." Sully paused and they listened to wind blowing through the majestic oaks that lined the street. "About two years after Mr. Red died, she saw a notice in the Atlanta paper that a man she'd been in love with when she was a very young lady had died in a plane crash. I had always suspected that something was not right between her and Mr. Red. She carried a torch for a young man from Georgia Tech all those years, like a foolish girl. She's not crazy, Mr. Wilson, she's just lonely and when she says she sees something now, she's seen it."

There was a long moment of silence before he said, "It's not crazy to hold on to memories of someone that was once dear to you."

"Yes, Sir, but you have to move on. If you don't, you will go crazy."

He stood and looked at her peaceful face, wondering if she knew of his loss, and said softly, "I believe you're right, Miz Sully." He went down the steps, and at the sidewalk he heard the screen door close.

CHAPTER 34

Just before the close of business Thursday, Dianne ushered the Duval County Medical Examiner into Wilson's office. "Hi, Wilson, how's it going?" They shook hands.

"John, this is a surprise. You aren't up here to get the blood sample, are you?" He offered the visitor a seat.

"I found myself in the neighborhood. I needed to get out of the lab awhile, after working ten days straight," said Hershey. "It was slow this afternoon, so my wife and I took off. We have a small house on Seventeenth Street and come here often."

Wilson nodded and recovered the plastic bag from his bottom drawer, containing the handkerchief with William Carless' blood on it. "This is it." He tossed the bag on the desk. "It'll help with the investigation if you can get it back to me ASAP."

Hershey agreed to do his best, and asked if Wilson was making any headway on the case.

"I laid a couple of suspicions to rest this morning. You know how it is; with something like this you have to go with your hunches and let the intuition flow. Sometimes it's tough to get the time of day from these people."

"Know what you mean. Look, I hate to run but the wife is in the car..."

Wilson put his hands up. "Know where you're coming from." He walked Hershey to the front door. Returning down the hall, he called out to Evans, "Wilbur come back yet?"

Evan's voice echoed hollowly from the complex of small offices in the back, "No, he got hung up over at the County jail."

"Huh." Wilson muttered, then said louder, "I'll catch him later. I'm going next door."

Dianne was talking to Millie near the Records room. Wilson sprinted down the hall and followed them inside, "Okay, who's going to dinner with me?"

He looked at them both. Millie eyed him over her glasses, which had nearly fallen off her nose. She ran a hand through her graying hair, which was pulled back today, out of the way.

"You coming on to me, big boy?" she purred. Taking a step forward, she ended up nearly nose to nose with him.

"Your place or mine?" he shot back.

"Take Dianne outta here before you find yourself in real trouble." She swaggered, chin up and wearing a sassy smile. Wilson capitulated. Dianne had told him Millie ruled over three dogs at home, plus a hamster and a 50-gallon aquarium filled with expensive tropical fish. One lone detective would hardly daunt her. He turned serious.

"Millie, has anything new come in that I should know about on the LaFontaine case?"

"You're off the case, remember, Sport? But since you have a hard time remembering that, I'll tell you something that may interest you...."

"...and?"

"You didn't hear it from me." She looked at Dianne.

"I am out of here." Dianne closed the door soundlessly.

Millie whispered, "I know who's been cleaning out George LaFontaine's records." Wilson moved closer. "If anyone knows about this, me and you will be fish food."

He nodded.

She opened the "L" drawer, took out a familiar folder, and laid it on the desk. The tab read *George LaFontaine*. "You have already guessed by the shape of this thing that some files were removed." Again Wilson nodded, grimacing. "Well, it seems that whenever George gets into serious trouble, Chief Cabe comes in and pulls the whole file. Signs for it and everything. An hour later he brings it back, signs it in, files it and that's that."

"How long has this been going on?" He scanned the pages of the slim file.

"More than ten years, I suppose. That's when the first record appears. George was busted for DUI and did community service. After that I'm not sure how many times he was arrested. I got curious when my nephew made an offhand remark once about George getting caught in a drug bust involving all the hip stuff."

"When was this?"

"I suppose maybe about three years ago. But like I say, it's not in there." Millie paused. "Did you see it?"

"No, just traffic violations and one DUI."

"Well, I played wiser in front of the nephew because he thought that, since I worked here, I'd know about it."

"Did the Chief come and get the records then?"

"Three years ago? I can't say. I didn't pay any attention to it at the time. Kids were getting busted every weekend, so I didn't put any mental marker on it. George can be pretty wild and the guys complain about him sometimes. I wish they'd get him when Cabe is gone and take him over to County. The sheriff would love to get him."

"Why?"

"George stays pretty close to home now, but a few years back the sheriff's daughter had an abortion without his knowledge and complications set in."

"I see."

"She made it, though. The sheriff couldn't do much as the girl was 21. So George escaped once again. People like him screw up and still land on their feet." She shook her head. "I don't see how they do it."

"George went flying past me in his car when I first came here, before I officially reported for duty. He was lucky that day."

"Yep, see what I mean?"

"Um-hmm." Wilson hefted the folder. "This seems thinner

than the other day."

"I've been putting them into the computer, the 'Bastard From The Future.'"

"Saying you don't like computers?"

She returned the file to its huge wooden drawer. "The 'Bastard's' going to help, eventually but manually entering all this?" She waved a hand around the room. "It's taking a lot of time."

"And you're the only one who can enter the records into the computer?"

"For now, yes. Later you guys will be able to. The terminals will be installed the first of June. Classes are scheduled for June or July. We'll be tied into the whole world then."

"We had that in Miami. When it works, it works good, otherwise, flush it. What about deleting files?"

"Only me, Chief Cabe and the Assistant Chief can do that. Password protected. The password is in the safe in the Chief's office."

Wilson looked at the door and remarked in a low voice, "It will require a little blackmail, huh?"

She smiled and moved toward the door. He followed her out into the hall. "Thanks, Millie. You've been a help."

Cabe was coming down the hall, "Whatchy'all doing in Records?" he demanded.

Millie patted Wilson on the butt and called back, "Makin' out!" She went into her office. Cabe gave a snort and walked on by.

As Wilson passed Dianne's office, he stuck his head in, "I'll pick you up in a few minutes."

She nodded cheerfully and he went back to his office to look over his personal files on everyone involved in the investigation. *Will I ever know what's been kept out of the official files?* He'd finished the bogus report Chief Cabe had ordered for the Orlando PD, but kept it under wraps. It bought him time to work on this case.

CHAPTER 35

Wilson hung up the phone. He'd been talking with Evans, asking if FDLE had any news that would help them. He leaned back to the sounds of the squeaks and propped his feet up on the desk. He tried to put it all together. *It's like any puzzle, just a matter of fitting the right pieces in the right places....*

The phone rang, interrupting his concentration. He scowled and angrily snapped, "Hello" into the receiver.

It was the Medical Examiner. "Sorry, John, I was miles away. What about the blood sample? Any results yet?" He listened and took notes as Hershey read his findings.

"The blood sample shows signs of anemia. It also indicates the subject had a smoke of pot and a little cocaine within the past twenty-four hours, a slightly elevated alcohol level and his sugar is a little high. However, there was no definite match for the gnomon blood."

Wilson thanked him and hung up, scratching his head. *Damn, back to the drawing board, then again he did say it was not a definite match leaving open the possibility...hmm.* He made a notation in his personal LaFontaine murder files, and turned to a robbery report from the night before.

Later in the day, he ran into his boss at the coffeepot. Cabe nodded at him and said, "How's the Orlando report coming along?"

"It'll be ready tomorrow. Any updates on Cajun Jack's whereabouts?" Wilson poured himself a cup of coffee.

The Chief shrugged, "No, nothing. I'm not worried though.

He'll slip up and be caught. He's got nowhere to go. You hear anything?'

Wilson shook his head and headed back to his office, leaving the Chief staring out the window. The sun was long gone behind Atlantic Seafood's building and Amelia River was a dark gray, and still Wilson sat in his office, trying to make the Orlando report look as if he'd done a lot of work on it. The day shift had gone. The push-button combination lock clicked and there stood Dianne in his doorway.

"Hey, are you trying to impress someone with all these late hours? How about coming by my place for some supper?"

He smiled at her, "You're here kinda late yourself."

"Actually, I'm not really here. I went up to Centre Street earlier to buy a birthday gift and just got back. Now I'm in the mood to cook. Why don't you call the girls and tell them you'll be late? Remember, 'all work and no play.'"

When he agreed willingly, she blew him a kiss as she left.

He watched her out of his window and reluctantly returned to the task at hand. He switched on his old beat-up radio at low volume to drown out the cleaning people down the hall, laughing and joking. When the two workers entered his office, he indulged in some idle talk with them about the Jaguars and their chances of getting in the Super Bowl next season. The conversation went back and forth mentioning this player, then that one, and finally switched to the Shrimp Festival.

"Hey, Lieutenant, you're going, aren't you?" The tall young Jaguar fan was the more talkative of the two.

"I think so. My kids want to see what it's like."

"Well, you should go, once anyway. Children like the fireworks on Friday night." The man removed the plastic sack from the can and replaced it with a new one.

"Yes, sir, lots going on. My kid brother's in the high school band. They'll play sometime Saturday afternoon."

Wilson's thoughts flashed back to his high school days, playing trumpet at football games and on the long bus rides in the night, getting surreptitious kisses from "The Lizard." *That girl loved to lick a guy's tonsils; funny I don't remember her real name. That four months in the eleventh grade was the only time Grace and I didn't date.*

Bang! He was brought to the present by the dropping of a trashcan across the hall.

"High school band, huh?" Wilson asked.

"They always put on a good show."

The other cleaning person spoke up, "I'm clearing out of town myself. Too many people."

"We'll have to take it in." Wilson turned back to shuffling papers on his desk.

As the cleaners moved and banged on down the hall, he could hear the hum of the vacuum cleaners and the opening and closing of doors. They stayed in the building maybe half an hour. Finally, he heard them leave. *Thank the good Lord, some quiet.*

Suddenly it hit him! He jumped up and chased down the cleaning crew in the parking lot, "Wait!" They turned, surprised, and came to a dead stop.

"What's up, man?" the younger Jaguar fan inquired.

"Look, this may sound a little crazy, but I need to ask you some questions."

"Go ahead. Shoot!"

He asked, "Are you guys about through?"

"Yeah. Just got to toss these sacks into the dumpster and we're outta here."

"Would you hold on for a few minutes?" They looked at each other.

"I suppose." They answered in unison, without enthusiasm.

"It's really important." Wilson began to feel odd standing in the middle of the police parking lot delaying the cleaning crew. He took his Nextel and put a call in for Evans to come back to the station, then he turned the two men, he asked

"Is Brunell really that good?" That sounded foolish, even to Wilson's own ears.

"Huh? Of course he is. Is that what's so important?"

"No, I have to get some information that may be in one of the trash sacks." Evans' car finally pulled into the lot. "Would you know which sack came from which office in the main building?"

"Well, maybe…" the younger man said, looking puzzled.

Evans approached, "What's up, Wilson?"

"I need a witness and verification of evidence." He looked over at the Jaguars fan, "Can you remember anything about the trash from the secretaries' office today, or say, Chief Cabe's trash?" The two men stared at him, and the quiet one backed away.

The young man gave an easy smile. "Well, the secretaries' trash can had a bunch of dead flowers in it – guess they finally threw out an old bouquet from somebody. And the Chief's trash had a fried chicken box in it. I remember that."

"Anybody else have one?" The two men agreed that was the only one. Wilson asked Evans to get a plastic evidence bag from his trunk and follow him to the dumpster. Evans walked slowly to his car, shaking his head.

"Don't tell me this is how they did it in Miami."

Wilson was standing on one door of the dumpster, head inside.

"Only if it got us a killer," he called back. He tossed garbage and trash around, then pointed to the adjacent door and asked Evans to stand up on it.

"I really think you're crazy, man."

"I know." He dug and tossed until he came to the flowers, first, and then the telltale box appeared. He eased the trash sack out of the dumpster and placed it on the ground.

"What now?" Evans folded his arms. Wilson took the sack.

"Just got to find something, and I see it. Give me the evidence bag and hold a light here." Evans leaned over and had a glimpse of the item as Wilson slipped it into the small plastic evidence bag.

"Good. Just got to mark it here with the information as to where and when. There." After signing his own name, he handed the evidence bag to Evans. "Sign here, please. Thank you." He sealed the bag so that if it were to be opened, the broken seal could be detected.

"You can go now. You witnessed this action, didn't you?"

"Yes, Sir, and it looked goofy to me," the cleaning man said.

Then they threw three plastic sacks into the dumpster.

"Thanks a lot, guys. See you tomorrow."

Wilson led his fellow detective back toward the office building. Once the workers were out of earshot he told Evans, "Listen, I know the LaFontaine case is yours, but I think this evidence may have some bearing on the case. Just go along with me here, for a day or so more."

"What I know now is, you're implying somebody I respect had something to do with this."

"I'd like to prove he had *nothing* to do with this. But think of it from the other direction. All the close relatives have motives and not too many alibis that hold water. Did you know the Chief was running for office with the Port?"

"A rumor." Evans stared at Wilson.

"I was told LaFontaine planned to bankroll Cabe and then pulled out."

"Unsubstantiated. Who told you that?"

"Rheba."

Evans broke out into a deep laugh. "That woman. Do you know how reliable her information is?"

"So I've heard." He still hoped to get something positive going here. Evans backed up a step and put his hands up.

"Hey, man, this has gotta stop. Chief Cabe is a good cop. He's done a lot to get rid of drugs and dealers. There is never been any questions about him." Evans paused, eyed Wilson, then said, "Before now."

Wilson started to pace the ground, "Listen...." he groped for the right words. "Where were you the night LaFontaine was killed?"

"Home in bed with my wife. So what?"

"All the major players in LaFontaine's life have nebulous alibis."

"What?" Evans stood his ground.

"Carless was drunk; Widow Marlene in Jacksonville, or so her 'sick friend' says; George was home with Rheba, who can't remember too well; I don't think Cajun Jack can have the strength."

"Well, do what you want, but it's your butt in the sling, not mine, if this gets out." Evans started to walk to his car.

Wilson called after him. "We need to keep this quiet." Evans just waved and got in his car leaving Wilson standing in the middle of the parking lot holding the plastic bag. Big drops of rain began to fall as he walked over to his car.

He looked at his watch. He grimaced and shook his head. He was two hours late for dinner with Dianne, and he had forgotten to call home too. After closing the car door, he sat looking at the soft raindrops on the windshield. *Looks like another early evening for you, guy. Maybe you aren't as ready as you think to stay the night with that sweet woman. Not ready, hell. I love her. There, I said it. I'm just not sure I'm ready to tell her so.*

He looked down at the bag lying on the seat beside him. *Hell, I'm not sure of anything much. What am I doing anyhow — gathering evidence against my own Chief of Police? Fernandina pirates called it mutiny, and it's punishable by a long walk down a short, lonesome plank.* His hands shook with fatigue as he locked the evidence bag in the glove compartment.

CHAPTER 36

Early the next morning, Wilson was in Jacksonville at the Medical Examiner's office with the plastic bag. After the routine paperwork, he drove back to Fernandina Beach in continuing rain.

Evans was walking out the station door as he went in. Their eyes met, but Evans just kept going. Finding some papers stuffed in his mail slot, Wilson threw most of it in the wastebasket next to the coffeepot. He sought out Dianne's office, looking for a friendly face.

He apologized for not calling her about missing the previous evening's dinner engagement. Then he smiled and said, "Am I really ready for whatever's going on at this festival you're taking me to next weekend? The cleaning crew told me if I knew what's good for me, I'd leave town."

She looked at him and didn't say anything. He could tell she was still a little irritated about his standing her up for dinner. But in a minute, her demeanor softened a little. "Well, if you can imagine a hundred thousand people descending on our little town for one weekend, that is the Isle of Eight Flags Shrimp Festival. It gets larger every year."

She walked over to the city map on the wall and pointed out the downtown streets. "These are lined with arts and crafts and food booths with shrimp prepared every way possible. There's music and entertainment at the dock and that's where the pirate ship lands for the invasion. I know Lisa and Prissy will love the cool parade

Thursday and fireworks on Friday night, and the Blessing of the Fleet on Sunday is great too." She sat back down.

"I admit, lots of us tend to get a 'been there, seen that' attitude after awhile. However, I'm taking you and the girls to your first one, so you can make up your own mind about future festivals. Okay?" Her voice still had a little edge in it.

"I can hardly wait," he said on his way out the door. The words hung in the air, his voice raspier than he'd meant it to be. *What am I waiting for, exactly, the proverbial ton of bricks?*

He stepped around puddles in the parking lot, getting to his office, his thoughts bouncing between his growing feelings for Dianne and the barriers he faced in the LaFontaine case.

Later that morning, he sat in his car, absentmindedly watching the windshield wipers remove the last few spritzes of rain. What sounded like thunder was the big mill's chipper starting up, sending whole 70-foot pine logs through its stainless steel teeth in three seconds. One after the other, the logs were fed into the supply chutes on long, tough, rubber compound conveyor belts.

Oh well, no use sitting here. He stepped out onto the oyster shell path and made his way to the front door of George LaFontaine's boat-shaped house. Remembering there was no use pressing the doorbell, he knocked.

"Come on in. Door's open."

Little had changed since his last visit. George was in his easy chair, tilted way back, beer can in hand, with an empty potato chip bag on the floor. "The Price is Right" was on the TV. Wilson looked at his watch, 11:53 a.m. George seemed mesmerized by the game players.

"You idiot, you're way over on that stupid bid," he snarled at the TV, then looked up at Wilson. "What are you doing back, forget something?"

Wilson's eyes scanned the room. What at first he had thought was a bundle of clothes on the couch was in fact Rheba, curled up in a heap and out like a light. He sat on the arm of the couch, hands on his knees, and looked at George from a foot away.

"LaFontaine, let me put it to you this way." He began to play a long shot. "There are several things you need to know. One, I'm not one of your TV idiots." The man looked away from the program. "I know it was you at the your daddy's house looking for the treasure map the night I was attacked. I know it was you that hit me, too." He watched LaFontaine's eyes, waiting for him to blink.

George's composure didn't break. His gaze returned to the girls in the swimsuits displaying a lot of flesh. Finally he said, "You're way outta line. You're wrong, pal. I was nowhere around that night. If that's all you got to say" – he nodded toward the door — "there's the exit."

"I have a witness, and let me read back the record for you." He took out his pad, flipped it open and started to read. "A neighbor saw you in your car waiting until the gardener and housekeeper left for the night. Shortly after that, when it was dark, you entered the house and went to the library, using a flashlight. You were there about 15 minutes before I showed up and spoiled your search." He spoke deliberately, spelling it all out. "You heard me on the porch, turned off the light, and hit me from behind with the flashlight as I turned around. Shall I go on?"

"Your witness can't prove anything. I was here all night. Rheba can vouch for me. Anyway, so what? There's no way you can prove it and make it stick."

Wilson felt the couch jiggle as Rheba turned over. He walked over to the nearer porthole window and looked out. "But I have a couple of men on their way over *and* this search warrant for the flashlight with my blood on it." He pulled a folded piece of paper from his coat pocket and waved it in front of LaFontaine. "So turn off the damn TV and let's talk."

He let the silence grow until the young LaFontaine finally looked him in the face. Then he continued, "I've contacted the State Attorney's Office in Jacksonville about the penalties for anyone who has official police records altered, destroyed, or tampered with in any way. That penalty, they tell me, is $10,000 and five years in state prison."

Wilson saw George start breathing faster. *Got you sweating now, you little prick.* "And, LaFontaine, I like to think that the State Attorney's Office outweighs a local Police Chief's badge. We can talk about this here or I can get a court order to ransack the police station looking for missing records."

George dropped his eyes and started to shake. "Listen, Cabe has enough evidence on me to send me to prison for a long time."

"Drugs?"

He nodded.

"Using? Possession? Possession with intent to distribute?"

More nods.

"And it was you that hit me?"

An almost inaudible "Yes."

"Well, let's say we'll keep this on the back burner for now. But remember I can use it whenever I need." He opened up his coat to show the bulge of a tape recorder in his coat pocket, then made a show of switching it off before he proceeded with the questioning. "Okay, was it your idea to go after the map or did someone put you up to it?"

LaFontaine put his face in his hands, "Cabe forced me. He said he'd get rid of all the arrest records for good if I found it for him. I don't know if a map even exists."

"You didn't find it?"

"What the hell do you think?" He gave a scoffing laugh.

"Let me tell you just what I think." Wilson paused. "You've been using and dealing. The Chief sees a good opportunity to use a wedge against you. He lets your daddy know he's taking care of his little boy, and then Daddy gets tired of it and tells Cabe to arrest you and send you up for a few years. You need money, more than Daddy passes out." Wilson glanced at Rheba again. "She can't sell herself fast enough, and you just might have some high debts.

"The Chief needs money too. He gets wind of a treasure map but needs Daddy out of the way. He sells you on picking up a lot of the LaFontaine fortune; he'll look the other way one more time, you'll give him the treasure map and no love lost anywhere."

"I didn't kill him." LaFontaine had his head in his hands.

"I have a witness that will swear in court that you were seen at the house, late on the night your father was killed."

"I didn't do it, I swear."

"Who did?"

"Look for Cajun Jack. I went over to my dad's at 9 that night and Jack was coming out of the house."

Wilson's frowned. *Carless was there too about that time.* "Did you see Carless there?

George looked away, "Screw him. I didn't see the little fag."

"You said you saw Cajun Jack coming out of your father's house?"

George nodded.

"What did he do then?"

"Nothing, just ran out and through the hedge in the back."

"Ran straight from the house, through the garden to the back?"

"Yeah, man. Leave me alone."

"Did you go in then?"

"No, I drove around for about 15 minutes."

Wilson grabbed a wad of muddy-blonde hair and snatched the man's head up. "Listen to me. I think you killed your father and somebody is helping you keep it quiet. Maybe the Chief or maybe Cajun Jack or maybe… maybe both of them together."

The man started with a nervous laugh, "How about that little whore my dad was married to?"

"She's not out of it yet." He flipped his wrist and let go of the hair. George didn't move. Wilson leaned down and whispered. "I'll find out everything, and I'm beginning to find a lot of skeletons, sonny. Fifteen to twenty years is a long time for being an accessory."

He walked to the door and then looked back. Rheba was returning to life. She slid her feet to the floor, the loosely wrapped robe fell open to the waist. Her puffy eyes squinted at the light coming from the doorway. She said, "Hey, honey, come back and let's party some more." She slowly fell over on the couch and her eyes closed for another trip into outer space.

"How long has she been like that?"

"A day or two. She'll wake, pop a pill, then she's gone again."

"Yeah, that's the good life. And remember," Wilson tapped his tape recorder, "this conversation never took place."

Back at his car, he took the envelope containing the "search warrant" – an old phone bill — out of his pocket. He pulled a plastic Timex watch box "tape recorder" out of the other coat pocket. He looked at the watch box and smiled, *Lisa will like the Barbie Watch.* He looked around. *There are a lot of pretty houses up here, even if some of them badly need rebuilding. I just might get one for us.*

CHAPTER 37

H e stared at the boat-shaped house for a few more minutes, curious about who had thought of building it that way in the first place.   He started the car and drove slowly out of Old Town. *There is such history in these old houses. It's a shame care wasn't taken early on to preserve the ones whose foundations are hidden by these weeds.*

Back at the station, Detective Evans came to his door and dropped off the mail. Wilson looked up. "Where's Wilbur?"

"At the DMV in Yulee, getting his driver's license renewed."

"When he gets back, have him see me."

"Sure."

As Evans moved down the hall, Wilson turned his attention from the notes to the small stack of mail. A big manila envelope bore the return address, C. Smith - General Delivery, Fernandina Beach; it was dated a day earlier. He pressed the envelope against the desk, feeling for any bumps or telltale contours. He wasn't expecting a letter-bomb but his instincts always led him to do this, ever since a friend in the Miami Investigations Division had been blown away at his desk by a relative of someone he had put away for life. *Sure, it could happen here as well as anywhere in the country.* Finally he opened the envelope with the letter opener Prissy had given him.

A lone piece of tattered, yellowed paper slid out onto his desk. It was coming apart at the ancient creases, which ran in all directions. He was afraid to touch it, afraid it might actually fall apart. He leaned closer, studying the symbols and drawn lines. *It can't be. It's just a tourist myth. The "C. Smith" in the return address is a decoy by Cajun Jack. Has to be.*

The faded ink outlined an island with distinguishing landmarks. Wilson recognized the long, tapering shape of Amelia Island. References to a lake and fresh water were faintly visible. Cryptic marks covered the north end of the island. But there was no "X" to mark the spot for buried treasure. Wilson liked puzzles and the solution to this puzzle was likely to be a murder.

Heavy footsteps fell on the wooden steps leading to the office. Wilson recognized the step of the Chief. He quickly opened the desk's center drawer and slid the paper and envelope inside. Cabe stuck his head through the doorway. "You got the Jefferson file?"

"No, sorry. Bobby or Evans may have it." He noticed a new Band-Aid on the Chief's finger.

"Okay, I need to see Bobby anyway. By the way, the computer guys will be in later today to install your terminal." He left and Wilson heard him talking with Bobby about a drug bust he was investigating. Once he was sure the Chief had left the temporary building that housed the Investigations Division, he reopened the drawer, took out the yellowed paper and placed it on top of the desk. Holding a small envelope open to receive a sample of the paper, he snipped a corner off. He sealed the little envelope and placed it in his shirt pocket. Carefully he slid the remaining yellowed paper between two sheets of clean paper and stored the evidence away in a fresh, large manila envelope.

"Bobby," he called out as he headed out the door, "I'm off to the post office. I'll be back in ten." He didn't wait for an answer. At the post office he wrote his mother's address on the envelope. The clerk smiled, took his coins for the postage, and said it would be delivered in the next day's mail. Since the Chief was already leery of his new Lieutenant, Wilson wanted the map in a safe place in case his office was searched.

The next day, he took the sealed envelope with the little corner of the map to Byron Chance, chemist at one of the paper mills, and asked if he could analyze the paper for him.

He touched base with FDLE a couple of times in the next few days and checked with Evans for any new developments. Other than that, he spent sometime giving a deposition in the Livingstone vs. The State broken denture/police brutality case. Wilson's knuckles still had a tinge of yellow bruise showing. Occasionally he would be found with his feet propped up on his desk, looking over reports from several ongoing investigations.

He didn't learn anything new — until the Wednesday morning of Shrimp Festival week. In a day or two, the city would virtually shut down its normal lifestyle to become a mecca for jovial hordes of visiting seafood lovers and weekend partiers.

That morning, John Hershey of the ME's Office called.

"Hi, John, what's up?"

"It looks like you have a good lead now. The blood samples you gave me and the blood on the weapon have a DNA-match. Do you know where the second sample came from?"

"Yep, sure do. Is this positive enough to hold up in court?"

"Well, I'd say you have your killer. And DNA proof is getting more respect now; juries are smarter and accepting it."

"That's good to hear. Could you do something else for me, John? Could you keep this quiet for a day or two? I need time to set this up."

"Sorry, by law I have to let FDLE know; they're doing some work on it too."

"Okay, okay, you're right, I'll call my contact at FDLE direct. Thanks again, John."

A second call to FDLE rewarded him with the time he needed.

He leaned back in his chair, hands behind his head. *That young punk is right, that third wife of LaFontaine's could be into this whole scene, right in the middle. I wonder whether the Chief's tackled her yet.* He smiled at his own lewd thought. *Not literally, of course, but for questioning in this crazy case. It should be a simple who-done-it, in this nice, quiet little town, but it's not simple. Murder never is.*

Wilson felt the old chair give way beneath him suddenly, almost tipping him on the floor. The movement jerked him back from his musings and he returned to work. He pulled his casebook out of his pocket and flipped the pages for the phone number where Marlene LaFontaine could be reached. With Dianne's help, he'd wormed it out of the files. *This is a job for yours truly, Lieutenant.*

He closed his door. No need to invite curiosity. And no need to advertise that he still had a few leads to follow.

The first ring brought a quick throaty answer. "Marlene LaFontaine here," then an expectant silence. *Who the hell is she expecting?*

"Mrs. LaFontaine, this is Lieutenant Wilson. We haven't had an opportunity to chat since the funeral except that short conversation on the street. There are one or two points I'd like to clear up with you."

The tone of her voice changed at once. "Oh, it's you, is it? Nothing's changed as far as I'm concerned. My answers are going to be the same as they were the first time."

"But you haven't heard these questions. Without talking face to face, I can only say now that there is some conflict with what you have said and the interviews with other members of the family. Only you can give me the answers." He waited for a few seconds for her reply, but heard only silence. "I must see you, Mrs. LaFontaine, as soon as possible. It's quite urgent."

The muffled thump of someone covering the mouthpiece was the only sound on the line. Wilson figured Marlene was consulting someone else. Finally she came back on. "Oh, all right, I'll see you, but it will have to be brief, and I want a friend present."

"Only if that friend is your lawyer, Mrs. LaFontaine. This is strictly police business."

Another long pause. "Lieutenant, drive out to the Plantation and come to the main check-in office in the resort. I'll leave directions for you there." The phone went abruptly dead.

What kind of charade is this going to be? She'll leave instructions for me? Lady, I can find my way around the Plantation by now just fine. He gritted his teeth, reached for his coat. Was it the locale or the widow herself that seemed to dictate a dress code?

Suddenly he was interrupted by the crashing open of his door. "What's going on in here that you've got to shut yourself up?" The Chief's tone was angry.

"Chief, when you give me something to do, you've got to let me do it my way," was the best Wilson could come up with. Could the man read his mind?

Hands on hips, Cabe glared stonily. "You're up to something, Wilson, and I know it." He blocked the way out.

"I am, indeed, Chief. I'm assisting Evans." He stopped and stared right back at Cabe, whose ears turned a red to match his cheeks.

"Have you picked up Cajun Jack yet?"

"You told me that wasn't my job, that you had your own man on the search," Wilson challenged. The Chief's expression didn't change, but he turned to leave the room, pausing at the door.

"I'm watchin' you, Wilson. You help Evans, don't run the investigation. Understood?"

Wilson nodded. He knew when to back off, and the Chief had blinked first.

The drive out to the Parkway was as rapid as Wilson could legally make it. The mid-morning traffic was light, and ten minutes later he turned into the entrance to the Ritz-Carlton. He quickly circled in front of the hotel, then came back out onto the road, looking around to see if a familiar official car was following. *Ha! The city detective still knows how to make himself scarce.*

He drove on southward to A1A and maneuvered around the second traffic circle, to reach the Plantation's entrance. He parked in front of the main resort office, expecting Marlene to meet him there. There was no sign of her, so he went inside.

"Mrs. Robert LaFontaine, please." To make up for it, he used his best manners as he faced the bored clerk behind the front desk.

"Are you Detective Wilson?"

"Lieutenant Wilson." He corrected the young man. *Where in*

hell is Miss Marlene? Did she actually leave instructions for me? This really is a game to this lady.

The clerk handed him a resort envelope. "Mrs. LaFontaine left this for you."

"Thanks." Wilson ripped into it. *That damn woman.*

He read: "Come to the Ritz Tower. Take the elevator to the top floor and turn left. Someone will show you in."

He crumpled the paper in his fist and stuffed it into his pocket. No throwing it away, just in case the Chief still had someone on his tail.

"Thank you very much. This clears up everything." He saluted lightly and headed back to his car. *Well, at least the Chief will have to wonder what the hell is going on, just like I am.*

Circling the building to leave the parking lot, Wilson looked around. No significant car in sight. *Good, on with the chase.* He burned rubber as he took off up A1A toward the Parkway, but he immediately slowed down, ashamed of his quick temper over Marlene's bizarre instructions.

He had failed to notice the pale green coupe near the resort exit. If he had, he might have wondered what Dianne's old car was doing at the Plantation.

———————— •■• ————————

At the hotel tower, Wilson slipped into the Visitors lot, this time not caring who was there. He walked into the lobby and quickly punched Penthouse, covering the dial with his palm. *Let 'em guess where I got off, if anybody's around.*

It was a swift, silent ride to the top floor, Exiting, Wilson was met by a tall, distinguished looking man, who appeared to be dressed for a game of tennis. "Mr. Wilson?"

He nodded and was led to a massive door standing ajar. Inside, the tennis player closed the door quickly and stood with his back to it. "Mrs. LaFontaine is waiting for you on the terrace."

If this guy is the butler he's pretty casual for the job. Wilson looked around. Ahead the loggia, covered in Mexican tile, led to the dining area that opened to the terrace, and an unobstructed view of the Atlantic waves beyond. *Spectacular.   The beach, the ocean, and the filtered screens of the shades. This place is almost heaven.*

Wilson saw Marlene, wearing a plush white terry robe, sitting in the terrace lounge chair with her back to the room. "Just ahead, Lieutenant," his guide said in a smooth, cultured voice.

As if on cue, Marlene turned and beckoned them, "Good morning, Lieutenant. Have you met Boisfeuillet Ravenel?" She dragged out every syllable of the name. "Bo has agreed to represent me during our little talk. His law firm's in New Orleans, but that shouldn't matter, should it?"

Wilson shook Ravenel's hand and smiled broadly into the tanned face beneath the thatch of white hair. "Mr. Ravenel, I'm sure you know that our Florida laws are a bit different from the Napoleonic code you people use in Louisiana, and since you aren't familiar with all the details of the case, I much prefer to talk privately to Mrs. LaFontaine. You really don't need a lawyer for the few points I want to clear up, Ma'am. This should only take a few minutes. I suggest that Mr. Ravenel sit inside while we chat. If you feel threatened in any way, you can just wave him out." *Like an obedient dog.*

Ravenel nodded his assent and turned to Marlene, his brows raised. "That might be a good plan. I'll be just out of earshot, but very close by." Wilson was pleased that the man agreed so easily, knowing he could have refused.

He drew up a chair close to the table where the widow sat enjoying the view.

She smiled, almost demurely. Wilson realized she was acting for the elegant man who had taken up his position indoors in full view of the proceedings.

"Just exactly why did you think you needed a lawyer? Has anybody accused you of anything?"

"Oh no, Bo and his son are here for a vacation. We know you're working for Cabe and you'll go right back to him the minute you leave here…"

That's what you think, Marlene. "And what's with this chase you put me on?"

"It was Bo's idea." She smiled toward the living room with a little wave. "Bo said he's had a lot of experience with police techniques, and he suggested the details, to make sure you didn't set up a wire. He said it would be a lot harder to do if you didn't know where you were going."

Wilson almost challenged that he had a tape recorder, which he didn't, but let it go. "You don't waste time, do you?" His words caused her to look directly at him for the first time. "First I saw you with that 'younger man' and now Bo?"

"If you want straight answers, you'll have to be very nice, or I'll call in my friend." Again she smiled. Bo was reading the paper, so his response wasn't satisfactory. She frowned. "I think I'll ignore your implications, Lieutenant." She pulled one knee up and let the falling robe expose her tanned leg.

"I met Bo some time ago. He was intrigued by my French name, but quickly lost interest when he heard there was a *Mr.* LaFontaine. Fortunately, I discovered his sons use this apartment, and they were here when Robert died. They seem to have called their father, because he flew in right away. I was staying with a friend at the Plantation, and you know how the grapevine is at this end of the island. Bo found me and offered his help. And believe me, that's been very important in my … recovery."

"I'll just bet it has."

Movement inside the apartment caught his attention. The young man he had seen with Marlene at the drugstore walked into the room and spoke to Ravenel — who Wilson realized must be his father.

She spoke again, sharply. "And let me set the record straight, before you begin concocting any 'motives,' as you police like to say, I told you that Robert and I each enjoyed certain things about our marriage, position and friends being my part of the equation. Bo found me 'interesting' — but as a murder suspect, my appeal would slip to zilch to a straight shooter like Bo. He is here to be very sure no bad old policeman tries to accuse me wrongly."

"Does he know *all* the facts?"

"The fact is I had absolutely nothing to gain from my husband's death, as far as I knew at the time. It's only after the fact that my prospects have changed. I want to know who killed Robert as much as you do." She paused and frowned, then seemed to make up her mind as she covered the exposed leg with the robe. "And I think I can tell you who did kill him, though not entirely the why."

He sat back in his chair. "I'm listening." *This is beginning to sound like a Perry Mason story. Widow doesn't confess all, but knows all.*

"John Cabe has been coming to the house more and more often and always left in an ugly mood, if door slamming and loud voices mean anything. I was never a party to any of these rows, thank goodness. Whenever Cabe knew I was away, things got worse. Miss Silly, our next door snoop, could tell you that.

"I know he's hated Robert for years, been jealous of him," she raised her eyebrows, "in every way. And men kill for a lot of different reasons, as you no doubt know. So there's your killer. Just one little thing you have to do: prove it!"

She stood up quickly, breaking the mood. "You're the big-city detective, I hear. Surely you can solve a simple murder case, when you have all the facts laid out for you." She clenched her fists, and Ravenel stood and leaned out the door.

"Everything all right out here?"

"I've told my story, so Lieutenant Wilson was just leaving."

"You're absolutely right, Mrs. LaFontaine. You've been a bigger help than you can possibly know." He turned to the lawyer, who stood, slightly tense. "You'll be glad to know we have a few big city ways here, Sir, to go with our small town life style. Fernandina Beach's a great place to live, as I hope you'll find out."

He eased through the opening of the glass doors, ignoring the lawyer's offer to see him out, and headed to the front door.

CHAPTER 38

The following day Wilson stopped by the paper mill to visit Byron Chance's office. The walls of the chemist's office partially filtered out the noise from the mill operation.

"Lieutenant Wilson, the sample of paper you gave me is quite old and authentic. It seems to have been produced in France in the mid-18th century. At that time most paper was made from old rags and linen. Varying amounts of each produced the different grades of paper. The very best papers in earlier times were reserved for the well-to-do, who could afford them.

"After looking at your paper under the microscope, I saw it is not of the highest quality but it was good enough to stand up against time and some abuse. It's made of low-grade cotton fibers and some bits of decent linen." The chemist stopped to take a sip of pale beige coffee from a cup with the legend "No. 1 Dad" on the side.

He told Wilson that between 1789 to 1812, Fourdrinier, a Frenchman, worked on developing a papermaking machine, but the real working models of the Fourdrinier were made after 1812. "Newer papers turned yellow due to the sulfur that was added — something almost done away with now. Now papers have additives that make them white and pretty, usually kaolin clay or titanium oxide, something like that," said Chance.

"The ink is from the same era. Inks used to be made of black minerals, such as carbon, coal ground to a super-fine powder, and a suspension agent. That type of ink would not last too long, but inks that dyed paper would last longer. You know, vegetable dyes. There is the remote possibility that the ink was put on the paper after the time frame you are asking about. Also, there are forgeries, in ink and paper, with modern technology. I've been doing this for a number of years and am pretty good at it, but if you need definitive proof, you have to go to the University of North Carolina. I can give you a contact and they probably can give you the name of the man that made the paper."

"I am impressed," said Wilson, making some notes. "I really appreciate your checking into this so thoroughly."

"No problem."

"I emphasize again that this is part of a murder investigation and is not to go beyond these doors."

"Of course," said the chemist. "I've never been called to do anything like this and it's been interesting for me. This job can get to be routine and you've brought a quite extraordinary diversion. Is there anything I can add to what I've told you?"

"You feel certain that the paper is authentic 19th-century, as well as the ink?"

"Yes. And I'd love to see the rest of the page."

"When this is all over, I'll see that you do." He thanked Chance and left the plant.

Back at the office he found a note to call the Chief about the Orlando reports. He called to say it was under control and being typed "...as we speak." Cabe gave his usual gruff answer and hung up.

Wilson phoned Dianne. "How about dinner at Brett's tonight?"

"Sounds better than leftover spaghetti and the talking heads."

They relaxed happily on the porch at Brett's late that afternoon, sharing a crab-cake appetizer and watching sailboats gliding into the marina to tie up for the night. When their table inside was ready, they sat down and looked out the huge windows at the shrimpboats along the wharf. Out in the waterway, yachts and smaller boats rested at anchor, silhouetted romantically against the glowing rose and blue sunset sky.

By the time they finished dinner and strolled into the parking lot, he was in no mood for the note he found on his windshield. He read it and put the slip of paper in his pocket. "The plot thickens," Dianne teased.

"More anonymous love notes." He gave her a side glance.

"What did she say?"

"Can't say, but it looks good."

"Don't trust me, huh? It's more like a spy mystery."

They rode through town in silence, listening to quiet music on the radio. Dianne put her hand on his and suggested, "It's a lovely evening, let's go to Elizabeth Pointe Lodge and get some coffee and dessert."

He pulled the car into her driveway and said, "I'd really love to, but I have to go, early day tomorrow."

"It's the note, isn't it?" She didn't try to hide her disappointment.

"Yes. If our relationship is going further, you understand that sometimes my work will get in the way, it comes with the territory?"

She nodded, and said quietly "Do you want the relationship to go further?" Her eyes searched for an answer.

He leaned over and kissed her gently. The porch light softened the shadows. "You are such a beautiful lady. Everything about you appeals to me. Yes, you know I do want it to go further. And when it does, I want it to be the right way at the right time – for both of us."

She looked down and after a moment, gave a light laugh at herself. "You've got me as nervous as a sixteen-year-old on a hot date."

"Believe me, I want you, but this note might be the piece of the puzzle that solves the case."

"Will you come back?"

"Depends, but I doubt it. I want to, but it may not be tonight." They sat in silence for a few minutes, then he got out and opened the car door for her. He tried to lighten the mood as they walked up the sidewalk to her house. "You won't believe what Mom has done now. She made an appointment to have pictures made of the girls and me tomorrow, and I'm not really into posing. Although Lisa and Prissy will love it."

Dianne laughed. "Oh, I hate to have my picture taken. One of the worst photographs I ever had showed my face all screwed up and crooked. It looked like I was making an angry face at the camera."

Wilson stopped on the porch steps. "What? Wait a minute. Say that again."

"What? I don't like to have my picture taken?"

"No, your face appears screwed up. Yes, that's it."

"You've got a date with that wanton woman of the note, don't you?" she teased.

"You caught me." He stood beside her as she unlocked her front door. "I have to get FDLE out here."

He kissed her goodnight and turned to leave. "I know who the killer is."

CHAPTER 39

Two cars sat in the vacant Shell Station at Centre and Eighth Streets. The occupants talked to each other in low, even tones. A cyclist rode by, looked at the cars. Raindrops splattered on the pavement, making round circles of reflected light from the Hoyt House across the street. The drivers rolled up their windows part way.

"Do you have the directions?" Wilson asked.

"Yes, and this rain isn't going to make it any easier," came the reply from the other darkened car.

"Yeah, I know. Fog may be rolling in later. Thanks for coming out on such a crappy night, but I think we're about to wrap this up."

"It's strange why people do what they do." The driver's cigarette glowed brighter in the darkness as he took a drag. "What time is your appointment?"

"In about 20 minutes. Y'all can go on out. Got a raincoat?"

He could hear other voices from the car, one of them female. "No, but it's a light rain." The car pulled out onto Centre and headed east to Fourteenth Street, then disappeared into the darkness.

Wilson rolled his window against the quickening rain. He could smell the dust kicked up by the drops. A FBPD cruiser pulled up to the stoplight and the officer looked at his car. The light changed and the cruiser made a turn into the station. Wilson rolled down the window and showed his face to the officer. The cruiser didn't even stop, just moved on slowly, then stopped before turning onto Eighth Street. Wilson could see the officer talking on the radio. He quickly flipped over to the zone channel and heard the officer finish with a "10-4." The radio was silent and the officer drove north on Eighth Street.

Wilson used his handkerchief to wipe the raindrops from his forehead. *Those guys are good but I hope they don't screw this up.*

He looked at his watch again. The timing had to be right. He started the engine and drove to the police station. He ran in, flipping on the light and making noise to be sure he was seen at the station, if he was being tailed again. Back outside in just a moment, he got in the car and headed up to Atlantic Avenue. Several cars were out on the rain-slick streets, as were the ever-present pulpwood trucks. Most were headed out of town at this hour of the night.

Thoughts of Dianne came to him as he drove toward Old Town and the Spanish fort site. His feelings of guilt diminished, as he acknowledged that the effect she was having on him made him feel good. She made it clear she was interested and would let the relationship develop at his pace. His talk with the priest recently had helped put things in perspective. He wanted to be sure of himself and Dianne.

He made the turn on Fourteenth Street. *Damn, I want to do what's right but who's to say what is right in this case.* Once over McClure's Hill, Wilson's thoughts were interrupted by a car pulling out far behind him at a side street.

The drive north led to the turn off to Fort San Carlos. The FDLE officers' car was silhouetted in the darkness and Wilson parked ten feet away. Wilson counted six cars parked facing Amelia River. He looked around him to let his eyes became accustomed to the darkness. He lowered the window a little to catch sounds. The car that had followed him stopped in the shadows along a street that dead-ended at the Fort.

In a few of the dark vehicles facing the river, he could see two heads close together, or one head laid back against the headrest, and in one pickup truck, no heads showed. He thought of high school days when he and Grace would drive to "make-out-city," a dark hideaway near the city airport.

Before long his eyes became accustomed to the dim glow cast by the lone streetlight by the houses. The diminishing raindrops pattered on the windshield. A big beige Taurus suddenly drove up, its headlights illuminating the line of cars, and stopped next to the pickup truck. A door slammed and an angry father shouted curse words as he pulled a teen-ager from the parked truck. The girl, too, was yelling as she was trying to tuck in her blouse. The father ordered his errant teen into his car, and anger spilled over when the man spun the tires, throwing dirt over the area. *He's probably lost his daughter for good now.* A gangly boy got out of the truck and looked after the receding taillights of the Taurus. Occupants of other cars surfaced to see what the ruckus was about and laughter could be heard. Several car horns honked as the deserted young lover started his car and drove off.

Just then, Wilson saw a shadowy figure moving along the fence line that bordered the park.

He removed his Glock from its holster and his eyes followed the form. Once at the edge of the river embankment, the dark figure moved toward Wilson's car, parked only a few feet from the fence. *I bet I'm the only one that sees him, except for FDLE guys.* He hit the switch breaking the connection to the dome light and got out. The rain had stopped and the night spat out little gusts of wind along Amelia River.

"Have you put cuffs on him yet?" The gravelly voice was just a whisper.

"No, maybe soon. We're going to need you to testify, of course." The musty scent of Cajun Jack washed over him – the aroma of old clothes and a long time since a bath.

Wilson looked up at him, "You know you are the prime suspect?"

"Yeah, that's the street talk. Why haven't you arrested me?"

"I just might have to, if I don't break this soon."

The man lit a cigarette. "You should have enough on him." Cajun Jack leaned against the right front fender and Wilson leaned against the left one, both looking out to the gently moving water beyond.

"Oh, we need a few more things." He hoped to get Jack to open up just a little more. "Like, how do you know for a fact that he killed LaFontaine? You said you didn't see it."

"Like I said, de' was two maps. Mine was a copy of the original that Bobby owned. Of the three of us, Bobby had made it out of the bilge and into society, of course with the help of his daddy's money." Jack lit a second cigarette and blew the smoke out slowly, the wind carrying it toward the river.

Wilson turned up the windbreaker's collar against the advancing sea fog. The night breeze carried the fog westward, quickly blotting out the lights of the mill across the river in St. Mary's, Georgia. The fog muffled the din from the other mill a few blocks away from them in Fernandina. Wilson liked the fog; the thick blanket wrapped him around, like a cocoon or a return to the security of the womb. A safe place. Nothing could hurt you now. The navigation lights out in the river were now lost in the mist. He felt a drop of cold water trickle off his hair and down his neck, causing a chill. The surreal scene on the riverfront gave him a sudden surge of excitement.

He looked over his shoulder to where the car had parked in the shadow of the trees. It wasn't there. He hadn't heard it start up and move. It must have happened when the irate father caused the commotion.

"Look, Jack, we need some definite proof. Why was LaFontaine killed? You say it's not because of the map. There are many questions we need to have answered before we can move. You just can't make an arrest like that without some real hard evidence."

The end of Jack's cigarette glowed and he asked, "Do you still have da map?"

"Yes, I brought it here, as you asked." He took the folded paper from his shirt pocket and handed it to Cajun Jack. For an unknown reason Jack raised it to his nose and sniffed it.

"You know, Bobby and I were going to dig the treasure up soon. Now...."

Laffon broke into a hacking cough. "I know what would happen if our old chum got this map from me or the one that Bobby's hid.

He'd deny he ever had it. Like something Edgar Allen Poe would write, he'd dig it up in the middle of a dark and foggy night. Do you ever read...say, Poe? I like good books. They can teach you a lot." Cajun Jack gave a laugh and said, "Yes sir, never turn your back on anybody, if he's looking for a big gain."

Wilson heard a car start and pull out. He watched the fog-blurred taillights disappear. A chill ran down his neck as he saw a black silhouette approaching. Wilson put his hand on the Glock and lifted it slightly. Cajun Jack saw the move, and, map still in hand, he turned toward the figure limping toward them. It stopped a bit too far away to be fully recognized.

"Well, well, look what we have here," said a grating voice.

"Chief? What are you doing here?" Wilson tried to sound surprised.

"Helping you arrest this murderer, of course." Cabe moved closer and Wilson saw he had his .38 Special revolver out. "Wilson, you move slowly to the back of the car."

Cajun Jack gave a crackling laugh, "You old son-of-a-bitch, you did it. Well, Shrimp, how did you do it?"

Wilson moved away in the direction of the gray car where FDLE officers waited. "That's far enough, Wilson. I've waited a long time for this arrest, Jack." Laffon edged away from the right fender and came around toward Wilson.

"Chief, I'll put the cuffs on him." Wilson holstered his Glock and got his handcuffs. Cajun Jack raised his hands and moved toward him.

The sharp crack of the .38 Special exploded in the darkness. Girls screamed in the nearby cars. Wilson froze as the gun's blast reverberated across the waterfront. He turned toward Laffon, their eyes meeting. Cajun Jack's face had a puzzled look as the dark red spot spread on his dirty shirt. He fell back and tumbled down the embankment. The tattered map fluttered up and a gust lifted it, sending it farther out until the yellowed sheet of paper floated to the water below.

The echo of the shot ricocheted from the island over the wide river and then rolled across the marsh to be hushed by the fog. Looking back at the Chief, Wilson saw the glint of the revolver pointed at him. Cars all over the grassy Plaza started up and sped away from the scene.

The Chief walked over and looked down the embankment at the body lying at the water's edge. Laffon's feet were toward them, and his head was toward the river. "He was going for you, that's the way I see it." the Chief said.

As three figures came running up, he shouted, "Hold it there."

"Chief, they're FDLE people. Lower your gun." Wilson yelled.

"What the hell are they doing here?"

"They're here at my request." He slowly walked over to Cabe and firmly grabbed the gun, holding it so the hammer could not move. He looked directly into the Chief's eyes. "It's over."

"You don't know what you're getting your ass into, boy," Cabe growled. "Let go and I'll forget this. Paperwork will take care of it."

"Not this time. I know everything now." The Chief gave a quick tug on the pistol but Wilson's grip was strong. The FDLE people had their weapons drawn.

"I own this town and my influence runs deep."

"So does resentment."

They stood motionless, and finally Cabe seemed to sag, releasing the revolver.

The woman officer from FDLE put handcuffs on him and led him to their car. In the distance came the wail of sirens. Wilson grabbed a flashlight and walked over to the edge of the bluff. Slipping as he went, he moved down to the sprawled body of Cajun Jack. The brickwork, possibly a relic of the old fort, showed at low tide. Jack's face was leaning against a wet brick, and the flashlight beam showed blood trickling from the corner of his mouth. Through the shriek of the nearing sirens, Wilson could hear tiny waves lapping against the old bricks. The unshaven face looked up at him with unmoving eyes that seemed to still have a questioning expression.

Wilson felt for a pulse. There was none. *Clean heart shot, he died instantly.*

He stood and climbed back to his car and his radio. "Carl, send out...." Flashing lights of the rescue vehicle and the police cruiser came through the fog. "Never mind, they're here."

CHAPTER 40

Dianne rose up on her right elbow and looked at him. The sheet slid off her shoulder. She leaned closer, snuggling against him as she laid her hand gently on his stomach. She felt the warmth of his body. He lay looking up at the ceiling, one arm crooked up over his head.

"Does it bother you? I mean, being the first time since…" she murmured.

"No," he looked at her with a smile "It's time to move on." He held her close and she laid her head on his chest. "I wondered how it would be to make love or even if I would again after Grace died. Those thoughts came much later but nonetheless they were there."

After a quiet minute, she said, "Thank you."

"For what?"

"For letting me be the one." She lifted her head and looked at him. The flowery smell of her hair delighted him, and he kissed her neck, then looked at her face and felt happiness flood over him.

Later, Dianne emerged from the shower, one towel turban-wrapped around her hair, another around her body.

"What are you looking at, stranger?" she said with a grin.

Wilson grinned and said, "A lovely woman in a lovely body." She slipped into a robe. He looked at the bed; sheets wrinkled and in disarray, one pillow on the floor and the other askew. The blanket was tossed aside on a cedar chest.

Dianne watched him. "You aren't sorry, are you?"

"No, not at all. I just don't quite know how to act now." He gestured with his hands, "Getting up and going home."

"You have a few minutes, let's go the kitchen and I'll get some coffee for us." She went past him and into the kitchen. He followed and sat at the table. "You don't owe me anything nor do I expect anything." She sat next to him and held his hand.

"I know that."

"Hey, let's be honest. My last time was four years ago, with my fiancé, and I found out a few weeks later that he was making the rounds before we got married. Needless to say, that was the last time together for us."

"Honesty? Okay." Looking into her eyes he said, "I think I'm falling in love with you."

"Is that such a bad thing?"

She was smiling, and he laughed as he admitted, "No, it's wonderful. I just don't want to rush you simply because we're both lonely."

"Nor do I. Just for the record, Lieutenant Wilson, the feelings are becoming mutual. We'll take it slow and one day at a time." She kissed him and got up to pour the coffee. "By the way..."

"Yes?"

"How did you finally figure it was the Chief?"

"Same old questions an investigator asks — why, why, why, and who can fit those whys?"

"But I don't know how it fit together."

"Now you're taking courses... think about it. The Chief wanted to run for office. His backing by LaFontaine was pulled out from under him. That was the catalyst; an argument ensued in LaFontaine's garden. Cabe lost it and grabbed the first thing he saw, which was the gnomon from the sundial. He followed LaFontaine into the house, and then LaFontaine heard him and turned, only to have the arrow end thrust into his stomach."

"But the gnomon was still on the sundial."

"Yes, he washed it and put it back, thinking it had been cleaned of all blood. Roger Callahan found it upside down the next day, and he blamed it on the cops, who he thought had disturbed it."

"There was a sharp burr on the gnomon, where Chief Cabe cut himself and left a bloodstain. Even though he had cleaned it, FDLE came up with two DNA samples on the gnomon — LaFontaine's and the Chief's."

"But how did you know it was the Chief's?"

"The age-old sport of 'dumpster diving.' Cabe said he had a slight infection on his finger and kept changing the Band-Aid. I found a Band-Aid that I knew the Chief had taken off – it was in the trash from his office. FDLE did a quick type match, then DNA confirmation, and it was the same as on the gnomon."

Wilson sipped his coffee. "But not until the Chief and Cajun Jack were face to face did I know for sure Cabe had killed LaFontaine."

"You mean, when he shot Cajun Jack?"

"No," he said, "it was before that. You see, when LaFontaine was stabbed, he had written something on the floor with his blood – or so it looked when we found his body. We'd studied the marks from every angle and no one could figure it out. But last night I found out."

Wilson took his pen and drew some cryptic figures on a napkin. "When I took you home last night, you said you had a picture that showed your face screwed up. I've been racking my brain about the photos taken of the murder scene. I saw two photos that happened to have the Chief in them.

"In the first photo, he is about to step on the bloody marks on the floor put there by LaFontaine. The Chief said he accidentally stepped on those marks, but in the picture, he's looking directly at the marks. His face is screwed up with fear, looking as though he had made out what the message was and wanted it erased. He stepped on it, making it look like an accident. The second photo is of him moving away afterward, with a different look on his face. By chance, Evans got those shots."

He moved the napkin so Dianne could see clearly the marks he was drawing on the napkin.

"Last night, I figured it out when Cajun Jack called Cabe by the nickname they had as youngsters — 'Shrimp.' See here, finish closing the 'p' and move these other scrawled letters a little. LaFontaine knew his killer and told us; but only LaFontaine and Cajun Jack knew who 'Shrimp' was. The Chief had to get rid of Jack. If anyone else had deciphered it, the word 'shrimp' refers to the business and doesn't make sense. Cabe probably planted the broken toothpick, figuring Cajun Jack was likely to be there that night anyway."

"Well, well, ain't you somebody."

Wilson winked at her, "Ain't I."

"But Mrs. Upton said she didn't hear a thing."

"She went to bed early, around 9 p.m., she said. LaFontaine was murdered about 10:45. Her cat yowling woke her up around 11 o'clock or so. She saw a car moving down the street with its lights out, could have been anyone."

Dianne smiled at him. "So, what's all the excitement about the so-called treasure map?"

"Believe it or not, it really existed. At least, for Cajun Jack and Robert LaFontaine it did. Jack sent me his copy, and I had a corner of it analyzed at the mill. It was genuine, or at least the paper and ink were. He said LaFontaine had the original, but one was a copy made almost two hundred years ago as collateral for Luis Aury, the pirate. Cajun Jack's map is somewhere in the Amelia River, it blew out of his hand when he was shot and floated away in the river."

"Where's LaFontaine's map?"

"That's the BIG question. According to Jack, Robert kept a copy hidden in the house — but where no one would be able to find it, not easily, at least." Wilson stood up to leave. "According to Jack, LaFontaine's real map is somewhere else."

"Did Cajun Jack tell you where LaFontaine put it?" Dianne put her arm through Wilson's.

"He said LaFontaine was true to the Aury heritage. LaFontaine wrote cryptic directions to the spot where the map is located. And according to Cajun Jack, they actually had found where the treasure was buried. They had taken a long iron rod, shoved it in the ground and it hit something solid about seven feet down."

"Oh, that could have been anything, like coquina or old brick from the Spanish days."

"Not where he said the treasure is."

"All right — but where are the directions hidden now?" Dianne persisted.

"Well, all I know is what Cajun Jack told me."

"And….?"

"He said, "'Read *The Gold Bug* by Edgar Allen Poe.'"

———————— • ● • ————————

"I don't know why you have to bring that ladder in here. It already made marks on the floor."   Lillian Callahan was beginning to get a little testy about "people traipsin' in an' out, dirtying my floors."

Wilson carried a large plastic tablecloth in and Dianne helped him spread it on the floor so the ladder wouldn't scrape the Italian tile. Lillian gave it one look, though not of approval, and went back to the kitchen.   They looked up at the deer heads mounted on the high wall in the entryway. Roger stood outside with the ladder at the ready.

"Miz Lillian said Roger had changed some light bulbs and she had removed most of the marks, but the day after the murder, I noticed fresh marks on the floor." Wilson moved around the small space. "LaFontaine wanted to get up there for some reason, and I think it was to hide the map."

"I don't see what could hold the map. The deer heads?"

"No, I don't think so," he said.

"You said *The Gold Bug* was a clue." Dianne stood in one spot, gazing up intently.

"Yes, I read it again and didn't see anything in it, or at least it didn't register."

"Well, I have the answer," she announced.

"What?" He quickly stepped to her side and looked up.

She raised her left hand, the one sporting the beautiful diamond Wilson had given her that morning, and pointed. The diamond's sparkle competed with the chandelier overhead. "In *The Gold Bug,* the treasure was found by putting the bug on a string and running it through the eye of the skull. Right?"

"Go on."

"Put a weighted string over a deer antler and see where it falls."

They stood staring at the antlers, which stood out from the walls over most of the room. "Let's stand under different antlers and see where they line up. Might work."

"I had an idea it would be here, but that's more clever than I suspected. Good work, Detective Spears."

She grinned at him and slowly they made their way about the room.

"Here it is," she whispered.

Wilson was beside her in two steps. He looked up. "It just might be." Of all the antlers that reached out above the huge chandelier in the entryway, there was one that curved out so that the point was near the center.

"I brought this." Dianne handed him a string with a small fishing sinker attached. He motioned for Roger and the ladder.

Wilson climbed it and stretched to reach where a spike branched off the main antler. He took the weighted string and looped it over so that it hung from the V-shaped start of the spike. The sinker slowly fell to the chandelier. "Clink." It hit the top of a light bulb.

Wilson reached down to the artificial "candlestick" and Dianne handed him the flashlight. He studied the candlestick before he rocked it back and forth. Suddenly it popped off the holder, and he looked down inside the hollow tube.

"That was a good idea about bringing the weighted string." he called down. He glanced over to see Lillian standing in the doorway watching, hands on hips. Putting a finger into the tube, he pulled a piece of paper that was loosely wrapped around the electrical wire feeding the light bulb. He silently read the words on it, and then, handed it to Dianne. Roger and Lillian moved in closer, as Dianne read the typed message aloud:

"There are two authentic maps of the Aury treasure. Jack Laffon is in possession of one, and I, the other. We have made a pact to never divulge the whereabouts of the treasure. I don't need the money, and Jack is taken care of by myself, his needs are few. When either of us dies, the other may come forth with the map. If we both die and neither has come forth, the mystery remains. I know Jack has buried his map and he knows the hiding place of my original map. I buried it within a safe container and not on these grounds. I also made a copy. You found this message by using skill and cunning. You can find the copy by using the same. Reflect on it."

Her voice trailed off and they all stood in the hallway looking at each other.

"Well, I'll be damned," Roger whispered.

Lillian elbowed him. "Don't swear in front of me."

Dianne looked from them to the ancient, mottled mirror in the entryway opposite the pocket doors to the library. The silver was almost gone from the back. "He'd never hide it in a mirror. That's too obvious." She stared at the fuzzy image of the four of them standing there in the ornate entryway.

"Well, I've had enough treasure hunting for awhile." Wilson walked out to the porch and collapsed into a wicker rocking chair.

"Miz Lillian, Roger, y'all enjoy your new home. Mr. Robert thought a great deal of both of you." Dianne hugged them both and went out onto the porch. "You ready, Wimpy?"

"Hey, that's not fair. I'm... I just...."

"Yeah...yeah." She led the way to the car.

"I think Evans will make a good Chief," she said, glancing back at him.

"Yep, I believe so." Wilson caught up with her and put his arm around her shoulders

Roger returned the ladder to the shed and then stepped out to the little glass enclosure to check on his orchids.

———————•—▪—•———————

Inside the house, a little gray-and-black spider crawled to the middle of the library's pocket door opening. It paused and looked around. Then it crept over to exactly six inches from the edge of the opening and lowered itself down the fine filament of silk. It hovered at five feet eleven inches from the floor and silently viewed its surroundings.

Dangling there, the spider was quite innocently looking at the reflection in the mirror of a curious, large, subtly shaded map that was part of the hallway's intricate wallpaper design.

"Smack!!" The sudden sound was Lillian slapping two paper towels together to kill the tiny creature. "I hate spiders."

And off went Miz Lillian into the kitchen to dispose of the last witness to the real treasure map.